明远通识文库

通川至海，立一识大

主 编：张 秦

副主编：李 娜 李 莉 孟 炜 游 航

（排名以姓氏笔画为序）

文本内外

莎 士 比 亚
经 典 解 读

一

四川大学出版社

SICHUAN UNIVERSITY PRESS

通识教育的"川大方案"

◎ 李言荣

大学之道，学以成人。作为大学精神的重要体现，以培养"全人"为目标的通识教育是对马克思所讲的"人的自由而全面的发展"的积极回应。自19世纪初被正式提出以来，通识教育便以对人类历史、现实及未来的宏大视野和深切关怀，在现代教育体系中发挥着无可替代的作用。

如今，全球正经历新一轮大发展大变革大调整，通识教育自然而然被赋予了更多使命。放眼世界，面对社会分工的日益细碎、专业壁垒的日益高筑，通识教育能否成为砸破学院之"墙"的有力工具？面对经济社会飞速发展中的常与变、全球化背景下的危与机，通识教育能否成为对抗利己主义，挣脱偏见、迷信和教条主义束缚的有力武器？面对大数据算法用"知识碎片"织就的"信息茧房"、人工智能向人类智能发起的重重挑战，通识教育能否成为人类叩开真理之门、确证自我价值的有效法宝？凝望中国，我们正前所未有地靠近世界舞台中心，前所未有地接近实现中华民族伟大复兴，通识教育又该如何助力教育强国建设，培养出一批批堪当民族复兴重任的时代新人？

这些问题都需要通识教育做出新的回答。为此，我们必须立足当下、面向未来，立足中国、面向世界，重新描绘通识教育的蓝图，给出具有针对性、系统性、操作性和前瞻性的方案。

一般而言，通识教育是超越各学科专业教育，针对人的共性、公民

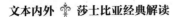

的共性、技能的共性和文化的共性的知识和能力的教育，是对社会中不同人群的共同认识和价值观的培养。时代新人要成为面向未来的优秀公民和创新人才，就必须具有健全的人格，具有人文情怀和科学精神，具有独立生活、独立思考和独立研究的能力，具有社会责任感和使命担当，具有足以胜任未来挑战的全球竞争力。针对这"五个具有"的能力培养，理应贯穿通识教育始终。基于此，我认为新时代的通识教育应该面向五个维度展开。

第一，厚植家国情怀，强化使命担当。如何培养人是教育的根本问题。时代新人要肩负起中华民族伟大复兴的历史重任，首先要胸怀祖国，情系人民，在伟大民族精神和优秀传统文化的熏陶中潜深情感、超拔意志、丰博趣味、豁朗胸襟，从而汇聚起实现中华民族伟大复兴的磅礴力量。因此，新时代的通识教育必须聚焦立德树人这一根本任务，为学生点亮领航人生之灯，使学生深入领悟人类文明和中华优秀传统文化的精髓，增强民族认同与文化自信。

第二，打好人生底色，奠基全面发展。高品质的通识教育可转化为学生的思维能力、思想格局和精神境界，进而转化为学生直面飞速发展的世界、应对变幻莫测的未来的本领。因此，无论学生将来会读到何种学位、从事何种工作，通识教育都应该聚焦"三观"培养和视野拓展，为学生搭稳登高望远之梯，使学生有机会多了解人类文明史，多探究人与自然的关系，这样才有可能培养出德才兼备、软硬实力兼具的人，培养出既有思维深度又不乏视野广度的人，培养出开放阳光又坚韧不拔的人。

第三，提倡独立思考，激发创新能力。当前中国正面临"两个大局"（中华民族伟大复兴的战略全局和世界百年未有之大变局），经济、社会等各领域的高质量发展都有赖于科技创新的支撑、引领、推动。而通识教育的力量正在于激活学生的创新基因，使学生提出有益的质疑与

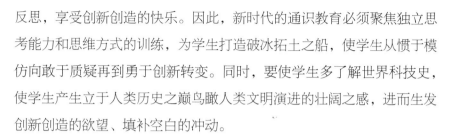
反思，享受创新创造的快乐。因此，新时代的通识教育必须聚焦独立思考能力和思维方式的训练，为学生打造破冰拓土之船，使学生从惯于模仿向敢于质疑再到勇于创新转变。同时，要使学生多了解世界科技史，使学生产生立于人类历史之巅鸟瞰人类文明演进的壮阔之感，进而生发创新创造的欲望、填补空白的冲动。

第四，打破学科局限，鼓励跨界融合。当今科学领域的专业划分越来越细，既碎片化了人们的创新思想和创造能力，又稀释了科技资源，既不利于创新人才的培养，也不利于"从0到1"的重大原始创新成果的产生。而通识教育就是要跨越学科界限，实现不同学科间的互联互通，凝聚起高于各学科专业知识的科技共识、文化共识和人性共识，直抵事物内在本质。这对于在未来多学科交叉融通解决大问题非常重要。因此，新时代的通识教育应该聚焦学科交叉融合，为学生架起游弋穿梭之桥，引导学生更多地以"他山之石"攻"本山之玉"。其中，信息技术素养的培养是基础中的基础。

第五，构建全球视野，培育世界公民。未来，中国人将越来越频繁地走到世界舞台中央去展示甚至引领。他们既应该怀抱对本国历史的温情与敬意，深刻领悟中华优秀传统文化的精髓，同时又必须站在更高的位置打量世界，洞悉自身在人类文明和世界格局中的地位和价值。因此，新时代的通识教育必须聚焦全球视野的构建和全球胜任力的培养，为学生铺就通往国际舞台之路，使学生真正了解世界、不孤陋寡闻，真正了解中国、不妄自菲薄，真正了解人类、不孤芳自赏；不仅关注自我、关注社会、关注国家，还关注世界、关注人类　关注未来。

我相信，以上五方面齐头并进，就能呈现出通识教育的理想图景。但从现实情况来看，我们目前所实施的通识教育还不能充分满足当下及未来对人才的需求，也不足以支撑起民族复兴的重任。其问题主要体现在两个方面：

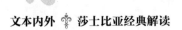

其一，问题导向不突出，主要表现为当前的通识教育课程体系大多是按预设的知识结构来补充和完善的，其实质仍然是以院系为基础、以学科专业为中心的知识教育，而非以问题为导向、以提高学生综合素养及解决复杂问题能力为目标的通识教育。换言之，这种通识教育课程体系仅对完善学生知识结构有一定帮助，而对完善学生能力结构和人格结构效果有限。这一问题归根结底是未能彻底回归教育本质。

其二，未来导向不明显，主要表现为没有充分考虑未来全球发展及我国建设社会主义现代化强国对人才的需求，难以培养出在未来具有国际竞争力的人才。其症结之一是对学生独立思考和深度思考能力的培养不够，尤其未能有效激活学生问问题，问好问题，层层剥离后问出有挑战性、有想象力的问题的能力。其症结之二是对学生引领全国乃至引领世界能力的培养不够。这一问题归根结底是未能完全顺应时代潮流。

时代是"出卷人"，我们都是"答卷人"。自百余年前四川省城高等学堂（四川大学前身之一）首任校长胡峻提出"仰副国家，造就通才"的办学宗旨以来，四川大学便始终以集思想之大成、育国家之栋梁、开学术之先河、促科技之进步、引社会之方向为己任，探索通识成人的大道，为国家民族输送人才。

正如社会所期望，川大英才应该是文科生才华横溢、仪表堂堂，医科生医术精湛、医者仁心，理科生学术深厚、术业专攻，工科生技术过硬、行业引领。但在我看来，川大的育人之道向来不只在于专精，更在于博通，因此从川大走出的大成之才不应仅是各专业领域的精英，而更应是真正"完整的、大写的人"。简而言之，川大英才除了精熟专业技能，还应该有川大人所共有的川大气质、川大味道、川大烙印。

关于这一点，或许可以做一不太恰当的类比。到过四川的人，大多对四川泡菜赞不绝口。事实上，一坛泡菜的风味，不仅取决于食材，更取决于泡菜水的配方以及发酵的工艺和环境。以之类比，四川大学的通识教育正是要提供一坛既富含"复合维生素"又富含"丰富乳酸菌"的"泡菜水",让浸润其中的川大学子有一股独特的"川大味道"。

为了配制这样一坛"泡菜水",四川大学近年来紧紧围绕立德树人根本任务,充分发挥文理工医多学科优势,聚焦"厚通识、宽视野、多交叉",制定实施了通识教育的"川大方案"。具体而言,就是坚持问题导向和未来导向,以"培育家国情怀、涵养人文底蕴、弘扬科学精神、促进融合创新"为目标,以"世界科技史"和"人类文明史"为四川大学通识教育体系的两大动脉,以"人类演进与社会文明""科学进步与技术革命"和"中华文化(文史哲艺)"为三大先导课程,按"人文与艺术""自然与科技""生命与健康""信息与交叉""责任与视野"五大模块打造100门通识"金课",并邀请院士、杰出教授等名师大家担任课程模块首席专家,在实现知识传授和能力培养的同时,突出价值引领和品格塑造。

如今呈现在大家面前的这套"明远通识文库",即按照通识教育"川大方案"打造的通识读本,也是百门通识"金课"的智慧结晶。按计划,丛书共100部,分属于五大模块。

——"人文与艺术"模块,突出对世界及中华优秀文化的学习,鼓励读者以更加开放的心态学习和借鉴其他文明的优秀成果,了解人类文明演进的过程和现实世界,着力提升自身的人文修养、文化自信和责任担当。

——"自然与科技"模块,突出对全球重大科学发现、科技发展脉络的梳理,以帮助读者更全面、更深入地了解自身所在领域,学习科学方法,培养科学精神、科学思维以及创新引领的战略思维、深度思考和独立研究能力。

——"生命与健康"模块,突出对生命科学、医学、生命伦理等领域的学习探索,强化对大自然、对生命的尊重与敬畏,帮助读者保持身

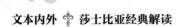

心健康、积极、阳光。

——"信息与交叉"模块，突出以"信息+"推动实现"万物互联"和"万物智能"的新场景，使读者形成更宽的专业知识面和多学科的学术视野，进而成为探索科学前沿、创造未来技术的创新人才。

——"责任与视野"模块，着重探讨全球化时代多文明共存背景下人类面临的若干共同议题，鼓励读者不仅要有参与、融入国际事务的能力和胆识，更要有影响和引领全球事务的国际竞争力和领导力。

百部通识读本既相对独立又有机融通，共同构成了四川大学通识教育体系的重要一翼。它们体系精巧、知识丰博，皆出自名师大家之手，是大家著小书的生动范例。它们坚持思想性、知识性、系统性、可读性与趣味性的统一，力求将各学科的基本常识、思维方法以及价值观念简明扼要地呈现给读者，引领读者攀上知识树的顶端，一览人类知识的全景，并竭力揭示各知识之间交汇贯通的路径，以便读者自如穿梭于知识树枝叶之间，兼收并蓄，掇菁撷华。

总之，通过这套书，我们不仅希望引领读者走进某一学科殿堂，更希望借此重申通识教育与终身学习的必要，并以具有强烈问题意识和未来意识的通识教育"川大方案"，使每位崇尚智识的读者都有机会获得心灵的满足，保持思想的活力，成就更开放通达的自我。

是为序。

（本文作于2023年1月，作者系中国工程院院士，时任四川大学校长）

前　言

　　所谓通识，即为博学多识，而后能通情达理，通权达变。古人以为唯有多识方可融会贯通，出神入化。在古希腊，亚里士多德提出了全面教育的概念，强调个体的全面发展，认为教育不仅仅是知识和技能的传授，还包括道德、品格、审美、体育等方面的培养。在中国，更是早有做学问应"博学之，审问之，慎思之，明辨之，笃行之"的论述，至于"大学之道，在明明德，在亲民，在止于至善"则赋予了教育更高的境界。

　　通识教育的本质在于打通知识边界，培养出德才兼备，能站在不同维度认知世界，创造和谐社会关系的未来公民。在这一过程中，经典阅读常被视为其核心组成部分，因为经典不仅承载着人类共有的核心价值，其存在本身更是跨越时空与边界的明证。在经典的殿堂里，语言不是简单的工具，而是一种艺术的表达。经由它们，我们得以见证科学的进步、文学的探索、历史的对话以及哲学的审视。

　　莎士比亚的作品正是这样的经典。其作品语言精巧，洞悉人性，既承袭古典文学之精华，又投射出关于现代问题的思考，具有独特的审美价值及文化书写意义。他的作品是文艺复兴时期人文思想的典范，是地

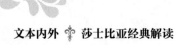

理大发现时代博物知识的集合，而在不断的阐释演绎与传播中，莎士比亚的作品更是跨越学科，融通文明，展现出非凡的创造力与生命力，也因此成为通识教育不可或缺的一部分。

莎士比亚的作品依据创作顺序可分为十四行诗、历史剧、喜剧、悲剧及传奇剧。本教材针对不同文类，逐一展开分析。教材第一部分对莎士比亚其人、其经典性以及经典阅读的方法进行了概述。第二至第六部分则分别聚焦十四行诗、历史剧、喜剧、悲剧及传奇剧，首先从诗学传统、文类定义、风格特色等方面切入，通过历史溯源，勾勒出整体图景；而后选取最经典的文本，辅以详尽的注释与经典译文，展开文本细读；最后再从莎士比亚与当代、莎士比亚与中国、莎士比亚与跨学科三个不同视角引导学生思考探索。通过文本内外的观照阅读，呈现出莎士比亚经典作品的丰富内涵。

作为核心通识课的配套教材，本教材在设计上遵循教育部关于高校教材建设的要求，具有以下特点：

第一，以教育质量为根本，坚持选材经典性。教材坚持原文阅读，剧本选自学界公认最权威的莎士比亚第一对开本（First Folio）。为方便读者进行比较研读，教材还同时提供了同一文本的不同中译本。所有译本均出自名家，包括朱生豪、梁宗岱、辜正坤等一众知名学者与翻译家。

第二，以学生发展为中心，追求教学交互性。教材以发展学生知识、能力、素养为目标，通过丰富多元的活动练习设计，在培养学生跨文化交际能力的同时，力求拓宽知识边界，启迪学生思维，为教师和学生创造力的发挥提供广阔的空间。

第三，以内容结构为核心，体现人文科学性。教材结构系统完整，覆盖莎士比亚作品的不同文类，以创作时间为序，将文本细读与人文思辨相结合，紧扣时代脉搏，探寻中西文明互鉴视域下的莎士比亚解读，

展现学科发展方向。

第四，以数字融合为支撑，呈现多模态特征。教材在书本内容体系之外，充分考虑线上线下融合学习的需求，以二维码形式提供数字学习资源，使教材兼具学术性与亲和力。

本教材第一、三部分由张秦老师编撰，李娜、孟炜、李莉、游航老师分别负责第二、四、五、六部分。教材的成形得益于四川大学核心通识课程建设项目，其间四川大学教务处、外国语学院领导、学校教学专家团队及同事们都给予了我们无私的指导和大力的支持。在此向他们致以最诚挚的谢意。

同时，教材能够付梓也离不开四川大学出版社编审、校对、排版老师们的辛苦付出，谢谢每一处的精益求精。

教材的编写始于课堂教学，而对莎士比亚的热爱与研究则更为久远。虽反复打磨，仍心存惶恐，因为面对说不尽的莎士比亚，始终难免挂一漏万，在此也恳请同仁及读者们批评指正，不胜感激。

编者

2023 年 9 月

目录
contents

Part One   Approaching Shakespeare

Unit 1 Who Is Shakespeare?

章节概述

　　威廉·莎士比亚（William Shakespeare）被誉为屹立于文学之巅的巨人。他是"语言甜美的诗人"[①]，是可与埃斯库罗斯（Aeschylus）比肩的戏剧大师。他为世人留下了约37部戏剧，154首十四行诗，2部长诗。在跨越百年的时间里，他吸引并影响着古往今来无数的读者。从这个意义上讲，莎士比亚不仅见证了历史，也创造了历史。

　　塞缪尔·约翰逊（Samuel Johnson）称莎士比亚为自然的诗人，他的戏剧是"生活的镜子"[②]。海涅（Heinrich Heine）则将他比作"精神上的太阳"[③]。在歌德（J. W. von Goethe）的眼中，莎士比亚更成为智慧的神灵，"从读到第一页起，一生便属于了他"[④]。他的作品被翻译成100多种语言，拥有4400多个译本，是除《圣经》以外，引用率最高，

[①] 弗朗西斯·米尔斯（Francis Meres）是最早给予莎士比亚肯定的评论家，他的盛赞奠定了莎士比亚文学地位的基础。原文为 "mellifluous and honey tongued Shakespeare"，参见 Shakespeare, William. *Venvs and Adonis*. London: The White Greyhound, 1593, p.ix。

[②] 原文为 "his drama is the mirror of life"，参见 Brady, Frank & W. K. Wimsatt, eds. *Samuel Johnson: Selected Poetry and Prose*. Los Angeles: University of California Press, 1977, p.303。

[③] Leland, C. G., trans. *The Works of Heinrich Heine*. London: William Heinemanne, 1891, p.256.

[④] Goethe, J. W. von. *Essays on Art and Literature*. Princeton: Princeton University Press, 1986, p.163.

影响力最大的作品。仅在马克思的著作中，引用或谈到莎士比亚就有三四百处之多。时至今日，他的诗歌仍在不同场合被吟诵，他的戏剧也在世界各个角落，通过剧场表演、戏曲、歌剧、电影、电视、动漫等不同方式，获得持续呈现和接受。在不断地被模仿、引用、指涉，甚至戏仿挪用中，莎士比亚滋养了整个西方文学。无怪乎，哈罗德·布鲁姆（Harold Bloom）会对他顶礼膜拜，将他置于"文学经典的中心"①。

然而，人尽皆知的莎士比亚却并非无人不晓。事实上，因为历史文献记录的缺失，人们对莎士比亚的了解极为有限。一张明信片的背面或足以记录下他的生平。莎士比亚由此幻化为世人的想象。正如英国著名作家安东尼·伯吉斯（Anthony Burgess）在传记《莎士比亚》卷首所写，每一个莎士比亚爱好者，都有"按自己的意思为莎士比亚画像的权利"②。

莎士比亚是谁？他无疑是天才，一如上帝梦见世界般梦见了戏剧；他也是平凡的小镇青年，怀揣梦想，孜孜以求。他是知识的撷取者，于生活中汲取养料；他也是知识的创造者，以文字构建世界。他家喻户晓，受人仰慕，但也曾遭人奚落嘲讽，甚至诋毁抨击。莎士比亚就是俗世的威尔③，是众多救赎者中的一个。透过他的作品以及他与同时代人的互动，我们或可遇见一个真实的莎士比亚。

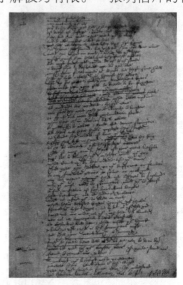

The Booke of Thomas More, a play originally written before 1601 and extensively revised by a series of playwrights between 1603 and 1604, is believed to contain the only surviving copy of William Shakespeare's handwriting, in a powerful speech by the play's hero. (Image credit: British Library)

① Bloom, Harold. *The Western Canon: The Books and School of the Ages*. New York: Harcourt Brace & Company, 1994, p.46.

② 安东尼·伯吉斯：《莎士比亚》，刘国云译，桂林：广西师范大学出版社，2015年，卷首页。

③ 斯蒂芬·格林布拉特（Stephen Greenblatt）在其所著的《莎士比亚新传》中将莎士比亚称为"俗世的威尔"（Will in the World）。

Selected Reading

What Manner of Man Was Shakespeare?
Stanley Wells[①]

How can we hope to know what Shakespeare was like? It's a question that characters in the plays ask about other characters. When a nobleman intrudes upon the revels in the Boar's Head Tavern (1 *Henry IV*, 2. 5.295), Sir John Falstaff asks 'What manner of man is he?'. In the same scene [lines 422−3] Prince Hal also asks Falstaff, who is standing in for King Henry, 'What manner of man, an it like your majesty?'.

Biographical studies of Shakespeare vary in the degree to which they attempt to dig below the surface to interpret the facts of his life in search of the inner man. For all its intellectual sophistication, such work has to negotiate difficult obstacles, among which is our imperfect knowledge of the facts of Shakespeare's life. Are there, in spite of such absences, ways in which we can attempt to pluck out the heart of Shakespeare's mystery?

To start with, it is possible, for example, to assess his attitudes to work. We may deduce something about his ambition, his conscientiousness, his industry, by looking at the tasks he undertook. Early in his career he wrote the two long narrative poems *Venus and Adonis* and *The Rape of Lucrece*, published in 1593 and 1594 respectively. Maybe this is because he saw the

---

① Sir Stanley William Wells, a distinguished Shakespearean scholar, writer, professor and editor who has been honorary president of the Shakespeare Birthplace Trust, Professor Emeritus at Birmingham University, and general editor of the Oxford and Penguin Shakespeare. The reading material is adapted from the first part of his four-part lecture series "What Was Shakespeare Really Like". https://www. shakespeare. org. uk/explore−shakespeare/podcasts/what−was−shakespeare−really/what−manner−man−was−shakespeare/.

need for an alternative career while the theatres were closed because of plague. In his early years, at least, he worked as an actor—the 1616 Folio of his rival Ben Jonson's plays names him in the actor list of *Every Man in his Humour*, played at the Curtain in 1598, and as one of the 'principal tragedians' in Jonson's *Sejanus* in 1603, and he heads the list of actors in the 1623 First Folio of his own plays, but 'Less for making' is scribbled beside his name in a copy in the Glasgow University Library, which may suggest that as time passed his colleagues gave him time off from his acting duties so that he could write. He worked too as a theatre administrator, helping for two decades to manage a single theatre company, which suggests a high degree of business acumen, of stability of character, and of conscientiousness. Above all he worked as a playwright, producing an average of around two plays a year over two decades or more, but ceasing it would seem around 1613, three years before he died. And, as I shall discuss later, much serious reading lies behind his writings. He was a hard-working man for most of his life.

We may learn more about him too by thinking about how he got on with his colleagues, observing for instance that they stuck together over long periods of time and that he both received and made bequests to some of them. He was a true company man, writing with individual actors in mind for specific roles. He knew his colleagues' strengths and their limitations. As his leading actor and co-founder of the Lord Chamberlain's Men, Richard Burbage grew older, Shakespeare provided for him star roles that did not require him to appear youthful. It would be interesting to know how long Burbage went on playing Romeo and Hamlet; certainly, the central characters in plays written later in the careers of the playwright and his leading actor are less youthful than in the earlier plays. And it is clear from the first printed text of *Much Ado About Nothing* that he had Will Kemp and Abraham Cowley in mind for the roles of Dogberry and Verges.

Even without the aid of psychoanalytical techniques we can assess much from Shakespeare's writings about his mental qualities. We can say confidently that he was highly articulate, at least on the page; that he had a wide, flexible vocabulary which developed over the years. We can observe that the Latin that he learnt at school lies on the surface in his earlier writings but goes underground later. We can examine his vocabulary to see what it can tell us about his areas of knowledge such as the law, the court and the countryside, hunting, shooting and fishing, his familiarity with dialects and with languages other than English, and with various kinds of technical language. We can see how he deployed his vocabulary in his writings, his awareness of rhetorical devices and the development of his skill in using them, his innovative powers. We can observe, for example, that he uses highly specialized language of horse breeding in a speech by Biondello in *The Taming of the Shrew*, and that a speech in *Much Ado About Nothing* shows remarkable familiarity with women's clothing—the Duchess of Milan's wedding gown was made of 'cloth o' gold, and cuts, and laced with silver, set with pearls, down sleeves, side sleeves, and skirts, round underborne with a bluish tinsel'—and we may wonder where he got all this from. He clearly had an exceptional sense of verbal rhythm, an ear for the musical qualities of language, and a capacity to tussle with complex ideas. And of course, we know that he was capable of extreme wordplay, used sometimes to scintillatingly comic ends but also in profound explorations of torment and disgust in plays such as *Timon of Athens* and *Troilus and Cressida*, and in the *Sonnets*.

We can deduce much from Shakespeare's writings about his education, and we can relate this to what is known of the curriculum of the school that was available to him, sometimes, especially in his early plays, quoting directly from works of classical literature in the original language (for example, in

Titus Andronicus). We know a lot about the amount of reading he had to do for some, at least, of his plays. We can assess his knowledge of the Bible, and we may try to deduce which parts of it he found most to his taste. We can even deduce what he was reading at certain times: *The Book of Revelation*, for example, while he was composing *Antony and Cleopatra*. We can argue about whether his writings betray his religious leanings—was he a Protestant, did he have Roman Catholic sympathies, how did he feel both personally and professionally about Puritanism?—if I had to express my own views I should say that he was a conforming Church of England Protestant, did not have Roman Catholic sympathies, and profoundly disliked the Puritans.

We can see that he went on reading assiduously and widely throughout his working life, and we may make deductions from this about his sociability aided perhaps by Aubrey's remark that he 'was not a company keeper; lived in Shoreditch①; wouldn't be debauched, and, if invited to writ he was in pain.' He needed time to himself. We can see that he had a taste for or at least that he saw that he could make use in his own work of certain sorts of literature—the poetry of his contemporaries and predecessors such as Geoffrey Chaucer, Christopher Marlowe, and Sir Philip Sidney, works of English and classical history, Italianate romance, popular English fiction by writers including Greene and Lodge, philosophical writings including the essays of Montaigne, studies of contemporary issues such as *A Declaration of Egregious Popish Impostures* by Samuel Harsnett—who became Archbishop of York—and we can be certain from the date of publication of some of these books that he remained an assiduous reader for most, at least, of his life. We may note absences from the record, too, such as the small

---

① Shoreditch is a district in the East End of London. In the 16th century, Shoreditch was an important center of the Elizabethan Theatre, and it has been an important entertainment center since that time.

impact on his work of Spenser's *Faerie Queene*.

Still developing studies in authorship and dramatic collaboration suggest that in his earlier years Shakespeare was enough of a team player to collaborate with George Peele (on *Titus Andronicus*), and possibly with Nashe and Marlowe. From the founding of the Lord Chamberlain's Men in 1594 onwards we can see him continuing to plough his own furrow as an essentially romantic dramatist in face of the growing popularity of city comedy, led by Ben Jonson, and of satirical tragedy in the works of writers such as John Marston and Thomas Middleton, even though in his later years he found enough sympathy with Middleton to collaborate with him and to draw on his individual talents for the more satirical scenes of *Timon of Athens*; and we can perhaps more readily understand how he found a congenial collaborator in the more romantically inclined John Fletcher, a younger man who may have seen Shakespeare as a mentor.

Through study of texts on which Shakespeare collaborated with other writers we can think about what collaboration involved. It doesn't for example necessarily mean that he sat down in the same room as Marlowe or Middleton or Fletcher, and that they worked on both plot and dialogue in intimate communion. Ben Jonson boasts in the Prologue to *Volpone* that he wrote the play single-handed within the space of five weeks:

> Tis known, five weeks fully penned it
> From his own hand, without a coadjutor,
> Novice, journeyman, or tutor.

Here Jonson usefully identifies four different kinds of collaborator. 'Coadjutor' is an ecclesiastical term referring to a bishop's assistant, so here I suppose we may take it to apply to a more or less equal collaborator;

'novice' seems to imply a beginner or apprentice playwright, 'journeyman' a hack writer, and 'tutor' an experienced writer working alongside and advising a novice. George Peele, with whom it is now believed Shakespeare worked on the early *Titus Andronicus*, was eight years older than Shakespeare. Was he, as it were, the tutor and Shakespeare the novice? If Shakespeare really did collaborate with his almost exact contemporary Christopher Marlowe, were they genuine coadjutors or was the more experienced Marlowe in charge? Or did they perhaps devise plots together and then write their allotted scenes independently? In Shakespeare's later years, was he perhaps 'tutor' to his collaborator Thomas Middleton and John Fletcher, both of whom were about sixteen years younger than he?

Study of the structure of his plays can help us to identify qualities of mind that made him successful as a plotter, as someone who could construct a complex dramatic structure, who had a practical knowledge of the theatrical conditions of his time, of the limitations imposed by the fact that only male actors would appear in his plays, that he needed to lay out his plot so that an individual actor might be required to take more than one role. We can guess that such exigencies affected his plotting. Did Lady Montague, for instance, die before her time because there was no one left to play her in the final scene of *Romeo and Juliet*? We can sometimes identify limitations in his dramatic technique, and developments in it as he gained in experience. Even early in his career there is a great leap forward between the relatively amateurish plotting of *The Two Gentlemen of Verona* and the masterly construction of *The Comedy of Errors*.

We can see him as an observer of the life around him, as someone who knew, whether from direct experience or through his reading, about domestic life, about the law, and music, and philosophy, about plants and gardens, and about hunting and wild life. We can think about his sense of individual character, both by observing how he makes characters in his plays speak and behave and also by observing what he makes them say about other characters in their plays, their moral attitudes, their foibles and sensitivities. We can look at his portrayal of human idiosyncrasy, observing his sympathetic amusement at the ramblings of the Nurse in *Romeo and Juliet* and of Justice Shallow, at the immature illusions of the lords in *Love's Labour's Lost*, the affected language of Osric in *Hamlet*, the social pretensions of the Old Shepherd and his son in *The Winter's Tale*. We can try to assess his sensibility by examining how in his plays he imagines himself into his characters' attitudes to the life around them. We can observe, for example, that he was capable of empathizing with the suffering of animals: 'The poor beetle that we tread upon / In corporal sufferance finds a pang as great as when a giant dies' says Isabella in *Measure for Measure* (3.1.). And in *Pericles* (4.1.), Marina evinces the same kind of sensibility:

> Believe me, la, I never killed a mouse nor hurt a fly.
> I trod upon a worm against my will,
> But I wept for it.

We can wonder how common such empathy was at the time—I remember Terence Spencer saying that he had observed it only in Shakespeare and Montaigne.

We can think about the absences in the literary as well as the biographical record; about for instance the fact that in spite of his massive literary talent he wrote almost entirely for the theatre, that he appears not to have written masques for the court, or pageants for the City, or what we may call 'public' poems such as commendatory verses for other writers' work, or comments on national events, or tributes on the death of members of the royal family such as Queen Elizabeth in 1603 or Prince Henry in 1612—

both of which elicited extensive comment from fellow writers.

We can think about the implications for Shakespeare's personality of his choice of subject matter for his plays, of the fact that almost all of them are set in the past and (except of course for the English history plays) in foreign lands. And in relation to this we can consider how his choice of subject matter compares with that of his contemporaries—of his fondness for Italian sources, of the comparative absence from his plays of clear topical reference, of his general avoidance of direct contemporary satire. He was a Romantic, and his work always had a touch of the old-fashioned, even whilst bristling with dazzling new words, freshly-minted from his hyper-articulating imagination.

We can observe his sympathetic portrayal of morally dubious characters such as Bardolph and Doll Tearsheet, Parolles, Toby Belch, and even Falstaff, and we can contrast this with his evident dislike of such cold fish as Prince John and Angelo, Don John, Octavius Caesar, or Giacomo. Some characters in his plays, such as Richard III and Iago, may seem unmitigatedly evil, but other villains, such as Macbeth and even Edmund in *King Lear*, are portrayed with a degree of sympathy and understanding, and he is unmoralistic about, for example, the passions of Antony and Cleopatra.

We can, I think, deduce something about Shakespeare's personal opinions from the plays. He seems to me to have distrusted people, like Iago in *Othello*, and Goneril, Regan, and above all Edmund, in *King Lear*, who express a severely rationalistic view of life and of morality, and to have sympathized more easily with the skeptical irrationality of Gloucester and indeed of Hamlet: 'There are more things in heaven and earth, Horatio...' There is a speech by Lafeu in *All's Well that Ends Well*, unnecessary to the action, in which I think that for once we can hear Shakespeare speaking:

'They say miracles are past, and we have our philosophical persons to make modern and familiar things [that are] supernatural and causeless. Hence is it that we make trifles of terrors, ensconcing ourselves into seeming knowledge when we should submit ourselves to an unknown fear.' (2.3.1– 6) He is suggesting that 'clever', excessively rational people, try to reduce to a commonplace level matters that are beyond human understanding, reducing the mysteries of the universe to a series of scientific formulae, making 'trifles of terrors' instead of opening their imaginations to the fullness of experience—or, as he puts it, submitting themselves 'to an unknown fear'—that is, to the uncertainties of the unknown and unknowable. It is an exact description of the error that Lady Macbeth makes in thinking that she can ignore the promptings of imagination. Essentially, it seems to me, this identifies Shakespeare as someone who acknowledges the mystery of human life but is not bound by any dogma.

We can also, I suggest, discern something about the subconscious workings of Shakespeare's mind in images not directly demanded by the narrative, in a manner that was adumbrated by Caroline Spurgeon in her book *Shakespeare's Imagery and What It Tells Us* and, more subtly, by Edward Armstrong in his *Shakespeare's Imagination: A Study of the Psychology of Association and Inspiration*, where he discerns recurrent image-clusters that help to track the working of Shakespeare's subconscious mind.

And I notice a recurrent preoccupation with imagery of diminution, as in Edgar's description of Dover Cliff:

> The fishermen, that walk upon the beach,
> Appear like mice; and yond tall anchoring bark,
> Diminish'd to her cock; her cock, a buoy
> Almost too small for sight. (*The Tragedy of King Lear*, 4.5.)

It comes again elsewhere, as in Innogen's imagining of Posthumus's departure:

> I would have broke mine eye-strings; cracked them, but
> To look upon him, till the diminution
> Of space had pointed him sharp as my needle,
> Nay, followed him, till he had melted from
> The smallness of a gnat to air, and then
> Have turned mine eye and wept. (Cymbeline, 1.3.)

And maybe this preoccupation relates also to recurrent imagery of a coming together of opposites, as several times in *The Winter's Tale*, as when Camillo says of Leontes and Polixenes:

> they have seemed to be together, though absent, shook
> hands, as over a vast, and embraced, as it were, from the
> ends of opposed winds. (1.1.)

And in the Young Shepherd's:

> I am not to say it is a sea, for it is now the
> sky: betwixt the firmament and it you cannot thrust
> a bodkin's point. (*The Winter's Tale*, 3.3.)

And this observational quality is also present in *Othello*:

> For do but stand upon the foaming shore,
> The chidden billow seems to pelt the clouds;
> The wind-shaked surge, with high and monstrous mane,
> Seems to cast water on the burning bear,
> And quench the guards of the ever-fixed pole.(*Othello*, 2.1)

These are just a few instances of points in the plays where the poetic content seems to me to be determined as much by Shakespeare's subconscious mind as by his literary intentions.

In brief, it seems to me that Shakespeare led a life of external respectability and that he achieved personal popularity and worldly success, but the amazing degree of imaginative fecundity and emotional ferment to which his works bear abundant witness surely reflects a life of inner turmoil. His life is a tale of two cities (or one town and one city). In Stratford he is the prosperous and outwardly respectable family man. But he leads a double life, disappearing at frequent intervals to the metropolis. There he is the successful poet, actor, and playwright, leading member of the most successful theatre company of the age, a frequenter of the royal court and also of the Inns of Court. I see him as a man whose inner tensions were contained with stern self-discipline in an external appearance of harmony, but who found release in the creative energy that informs his plays and especially, I believe, in his *Sonnets*. In some of them, I believe, he delved deeply into his innermost self, discovering for himself what manner of man he was by giving voice to his most intimate being.

Activities

1. Shakespeare and Today

Direction: After reading the essay above, think about the following questions.

1) What does the name of Shakespeare mean to you?

2) What do you want to know about Shakespeare?

3) Shakespeare has been constantly reimagined and reshaped. For instance, *Shakespeare in Love*(《恋爱中的莎士比亚》, 又译为《莎翁情史》), the 7 Oscars winner at the 71st Academy Awards reveals the romantic facet of Shakespeare, while *Upstart Crow*(《新贵》), a British sitcom makes a satiric

parody on the life of William Shakespeare. Look at the following two posters and tell your partner which one fits your imagination about Shakespeare and why.

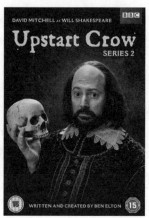

2. Shakespeare and China

Direction: In 2015, on a state visit to Great Britain, Chairman Xi Jinping introduced Tang Xianzu（汤显祖）, the 17th century Chinese playwright as "Shakespeare of the East". Make a comparison between Shakespeare and Tang Xianzu to see in what way Chinese traditional operas and Shakespeare's plays are similar to or different from each other.

3. Shakespeare and Beyond

Direction: Work within groups to check out the following facts about Shakespeare and make a short account about Shakespeare's life based on your findings.

Fact 1

Shakespeare's parents were John and Mary Shakespeare. John came to Stratford upon Avon from Snitterfield before 1532 as an apprentice glover and tanner of leathers. He prospered and began to deal in farm products and wool before being elected to a multitude of civic positions.

Fact 2

Shakespeare and Anne Hathaway had three children together—a son, Hamnet, who died in 1596, and two daughters, Susanna and Judith. His only granddaughter Elizabeth—daughter of Susanna—died childless in 1670. Shakespeare therefore had no descendants.

Fact 3

Apart from writing, Shakespeare was also an actor who performed many of his own plays as well as those of other playwrights. There is evidence that he played the ghost in *Hamlet* and Adam in *As You Like It*.

Fact 4

Shakespeare lived a double life. By the seventeenth century he had become a famous playwright in London but in his hometown of Stratford, where his wife and children were, and which he visited frequently, he was a well-known and highly respected businessman and property owner.

Fact 5

The first reference to Shakespeare as a writer came in 1592, by which time he was well established on the London theatrical scene. In 1593, his name appeared in print for the first time as the author of the narrative poem *Venus and Adonis*.

Fact 6

During his life, Shakespeare wrote at least 37 plays and 154 sonnets. In addition, there are a number of lost plays and problem plays. This means Shakespeare wrote an average of 1.5 plays a year since he first started writing in 1589.

Fact 7

Shakespeare has been credited by the *Oxford English Dictionary* with introducing almost 3,000 words to the English language. It is estimated that his vocabulary may range from 17,000 to 29,000.

Further Reading

BURGESS A, 2014. Shakespeare[M]. London: Random House.

DOBSON M, WELLS S, et al., 2015. The Oxford companion to Shakespeare[M]. Oxford: Oxford University Press.

DUNCAN J K, 2010. Shakespeare: an ungentle life [M]. London: Bloomsbury Academic.

GREENBLATT S, 2016. Will in the world [M]. New York: W. W. Norton.

SMITH E, 2020. This is Shakespeare[M]. London: Pantheon.

Unit 2 Why to Read Shakespeare?

章节概述

　　莎士比亚为什么值得我们一读再读？在现代化高速推进，科技日新月异，观念不断迭代的今天，回首四百年前的莎士比亚意义何在？

　　意大利文学家卡尔维诺（Italo Calvino）在《为什么读经典》（*Why Read the Classics*）一书中说：经典是那些所述永无止境的作品，它们带着记忆一路走向我们，留下经过不同文化的足迹①。卡尔维诺的话很好地解释了阅读莎士比亚的意义，因为莎士比亚正是这样的经典。

　　英国古典主义者德莱登（John Dryden）称莎士比亚有一颗通天之心，能够了解一切人物和激情。歌德曾以那个时代特有的激昂发表演讲，高呼："自然，自然！没有比莎士比亚的人物更自然的了！"②透过一个个鲜活的人物，每个读者都能从莎士比亚的作品中窥见自己，找到成长的经验。

　　莎士比亚是包罗万象的。雨果（Victor Hugo）认为莎士比亚的降临"使得艺术、科学、哲学或者整个社会焕然一新"，他的光辉照耀着全人类③。翻开莎士比亚的作品，如同打开了通往文艺复兴时代的大门。伊丽莎白时代的生活日常、科学发展，甚至大航海的每一个生物发现都历历在目。他的作品不仅滋养着文学书写，为哲学家的理论思考提供例证、模型和历史内容，也成为后世科学研究的样本，艺术创作的灵感。

　　莎士比亚是超越时代的。早在几个世纪以前，本・琼生（Ben Jonson）就预见了他的不朽，认为莎士比亚"不属于一个时代，而是属

---

① Calvino, Italo. *Why Read the Classics*. Boston: Houghton Mifflin Harcourt, 2014, p.5.

② Goethe, J. W. von. *Essays on Art and Literature*. Princeton: Princeton University Press, 1986, p.238.

③ 维克多・雨果：《雨果论文学》，柳鸣九译，上海：上海译文出版社，1980年，第168页。

于所有的时代"①。杜勃罗留波夫（Nikolay Dobrolyubov）把莎士比亚看作"黑暗王国的一线光明"，认为其代表着人类认识的最高阶段②。别林斯基（V. G. Belinsky）对莎士比亚的赞誉则更溢于言表："他的灵感的天眼，看到了宇宙脉搏的跃动。他的每一部剧本都是一个世界的缩影，包含着这个现在、过去及未来。"③

时至今日，莎士比亚的智慧之光和艺术魅力仍在世人的传说中熠熠生辉。正如赫尔德（J. G. Herder）所说，"如果说，有一个人使我心里浮现出这样一个庄严场面：高高地坐在一块岩石顶上！他脚下风暴雷雨交加，海在咆哮；但他的头部却被明朗的天空照耀着！那么，莎士比亚就是这样！——只是当然还得补充这一点，他的岩石宝座的最下面，有一大堆人在喃喃细语，他们在解释他，拯救他，判他的罪名，为他辩护，崇拜他，诬蔑他，翻译他，诽谤他，而他对他们的话却一点儿也听不见"④。

世界是一个舞台，打开莎士比亚便能看到世界。

Selected Reading

Why Read Shakespeare's Works?
Gary Taylor⑤

Twenty-five centuries ago, the Greeks measured both artistic and athletic achievement by counting superlatives. The ancient Greeks, who invented the Olympics, also invented dramatic festivals that pitted playwrights against

① 参见本·琼生为1623年莎士比亚第一对开本写的前言，原文为"He was not of an age, but for all times!"

② 杨周翰：《莎士比亚评论汇编》，北京：中国社会科学出版社，1979年，第498页。

③ 威廉·莎士比亚：《仲夏夜之梦》，傅光明译，天津：天津人民出版社，2019年，第197页。

④ Herder, J. G. *Shakespeare*. Princeton: Princeton University Press, 2008, p.34.

⑤ Gary Taylor: George Matthew Edgar Professor of English, Dahl and Lottie Pryor Professor of Shakespearean Literature at Florida State University. He was one of the General Editors of *The Oxford Shakespeare*, *The Oxford Middleton*, and the *New Oxford Shakespeare: Complete Works*. The reading material is adapted from the introduction of *New Oxford Shakespeare: Complete Works*.

each other, and recorded the winners in stone. Those competitions make it possible for us to say that Sophocles won more first prizes than any other Athenian tragedian.

Shakespeare is the poet of superlatives, who has for four centuries set the standard for the unsurpassable. That number, 'four centuries', is a mundane way of pointing to something beyond our personal experience and to the scale of a particular human singularity.

Shakespeare the best

Shakespeare's works are the most quoted, most taught, most translated, most anthologized, most performed, most broadcast on radio, most filmed, most televised, most internetted, and most admired. He created more varied roles for actors than any other playwright in English. He wrote more surviving plays than all the great play-wrights of ancient Athens (put together) or ancient Rome (put together). He mastered more dramatic genres than any of his predecessors. Most readers and writers and actors agree that Shakespeare wrote more of the best work in more genres than any other writer: tragedies, comedies, history plays, tragicomedies, and poems.

Shakespeare's history plays, and many of his tragedies, dramatize the struggle to be the exception, the king, the emperor, the one who rules them all. Marriage too can be a contest for supremacy: between Petruccio and Kate in *The Taming of the Shrew*, Adriana and Antipholus of Ephesus in *The Comedy of Errors*, Mr. and Mrs. Ford in *The Merry Wives of Windsor*, Leontes and Hermione in *The Winter's Tale*, Macbeth and his conjugal co-conspirator. All Shakespeare's comedies dramatize the search for, the eventual possession or recovery of, a uniquely beloved partner who will make possible 'the perfect' pair. In *The Comedy of Errors* and *Twelfth Night* that unique partner is a twin sibling. in *Pericles* and *The Winter's Tale* it is a lost daughter.

More often, it is a romantic match who promises 'the marriage of true minds' (Sonnet 116). *The Phoenix and the Turtle* are 'co-supremes' (a word Shakespeare invented), whose love produces 'Two distincts, division none'. The failure to achieve or sustain that desired perfect union creates the tragedies of Venus and Adonis, Romeo and Juliet, Troilus and Cressida, Antony and Cleopatra.

Shakespeare's titles, and his works, are dominated by proper names—including unique names like Coriolanus, created to represent 'his fame unparalleled' (5.2.17), and Cleopatra, that 'lass unparalleled' (43.305). The prologue to *Henry V* invokes 'the warlike Harry, like himself': the particularized proper one-of-a-kind, who can be compared to nothing but his own self. This kind of reflective, tautological self-comparison is an odd, recurrent mannerism of Shakespeare's style and thought: from 'you alone are you' (Sonnet 84) to 'I am that I am' (Sonnet 121) and 'Naught but itself can be its parallel' (*Cardenio* 3.1.17).

For his singularity, most of the most important, most talented, and best-educated writers and readers of the last four centuries have considered Shakespeare the best writer in English, or the best modern writer in any language, or the world's best playwright, or the best Western writer of the last thousand years, or the best writer ever, or the greatest genius of all time.

He was the man who of all modern and perhaps ancient poets had the largest and most comprehensive soul.
John Dryden, 1668

Shakespeare is above all writers, at least above all modern writers, the poet of nature; the poet that holds up to his readers a faithful mirror of manners and of life. His characters are not modified by the customs of particular places, unpractised by the rest of the world; by the peculiarities of studies or professions, which can operate but upon small numbers; or by the accidents of transient fashions or temporary opinions: they are the genuine progeny of common humanity, such as the world will always supply, and observation will always find. His persons act and speak by the influence of those general passions and principles by which all minds are agitated, and the whole system of life is continued in motion.

Samuel Johnson, 1765

[Shakespeare's histories] stand to the tragedies of French taste much as a large fresco stands to a miniature painting intended to adorn a ring.

Georg Lessing, 1768

He was not only a great poet, but a great philosopher... the greatest genius that perhaps human nature has yet produced, our *myriad-minded* Shakespeare...

S. T. Coleridge, 1813, 1817

He has left nothing to say, about nothing or anything.... The excellence of every art is its intensity, capable of making all disagreeables evaporate from their being in close relationship with beauty and truth. Examine *King Lear*, and you shall find this exemplified throughout... it struck me what quality went to form a man of achievement, especially in literature, and which Shakespeare possessed so enormously—I mean *negative capability*, that is, when a man is capable of being in uncertainties, mysteries, doubts, without any irritable reaching after fact and reason.

John Keats, 1817

Shakespeare is drama; and drama, which is based on the grotesque and the sublime in the same breath, tragedy and comedy, such drama is the appropriate form for... the literature of the present.

Victor Hugo, 1827

Now, literature, philosophy, and thought are Shakespearized. His mind is the horizon beyond which at present we do not see.

Ralph Waldo Emerson, 1846

Shakespeare, coming upon me unawares, struck me like a thunderbolt. The lightning flash of that discovery revealed to me at a stroke the whole heaven of art, illuminating it to its remotest corners. I recognized the meaning of grandeur, beauty, dramatic truth...

Hector Berlioz, 1870

The Tempest affects us, taking its complexity and its perfection together, as the rarest of all examples of literary art. There may be other things as exquisite, other single exhalations of beauty reaching as high a mark and sustained there for a moment... but nothing, surely, of equal length and variety lives so happily and radiantly as a whole... I see him, at the last, over *The Tempest*, as the composer, at the harpsichord or the violin, extemporizing in the summer twilight.

Henry James, 1907

Shakespeare the universal

A book can create its own world, or many worlds, a complete parallel universe. This may sound like something out of theoretical astrophysics or science fiction, and there is no reason we cannot apply modern science to past literature, just as we apply it to past geology or anthropology. But in fact, the theory of an infinite universe, consisting of many different worlds, was first articulated in 1584 in a book by the Italian philosopher Giordano Bruno (the last heretic to be burned at the stake by the Roman Inquisition). And the theory that fiction writers create an alternative world can be found in the most important Elizabethan defense of literature, *An Apology for Poetry*, written by Sir Philip Sidney, whose poems and prose indisputably influenced Shakespeare.

> Nature never set forth the earth in so rich tapestry as diverse poets have done, neither with pleasant rivers, fruitful trees, sweet-smelling flowers, nor whatsoever else may make the too-much-loved earth more lovely. Her world is brazen; the poets only deliver a golden.

Whether or not he had read Sidney's treatise (posthumously published in 1595), Shakespeare wrote something similar in *A Midsummer Night's Dream* (which most scholars believe was written in 1595 or 1596). But typically, Shakespeare says it better:

> The poet's eye, in a fine frenzy rolling,
> Doth glance from heaven to earth, from earth to heaven,
>
> And, as imagination bodies forth
> The forms of things unknown, the poet's pen
> Turns them to shapes, and gives to airy nothing
> A local habitation and a name. (7.12−17)

The Austrian philosopher Ludwig Wittgenstein wrote, in his notebooks, 'He is *not* true to life' and 'things *aren't like that*'—followed by the recognition that Shakespeare's art is governed by the logic of dreaming. Every reader is invited into Shakespeare's dreams, and contributes their own. For centuries,

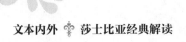

critics have agreed that 'immortal Shakespeare' created an alternative universe.

The great twentieth-century scientist J. B. S. Haldane once wrote in his book *Possible Worlds*, 'the universe is not only queerer than we suppose, but queerer than we can suppose.' To articulate that scepticism, Haldane turned to Shakespeare: 'I suspect that there are more things in heaven and earth than are dreamed of, or can be dreamed of, in any philosophy' (*Hamlet* 5.175).

Shakespeare does not offer us only a single alternative world. He created many. He is the greatest writer of sequels in the English language: his eight plays on the Wars of the Roses, his two plays on Mark Antony, his four Falstaff plays. But he could also create an entirely new world in a single short stand-alone play, like *The Tempest* (which inspired a cult science fiction film, *Forbidden Planet*).

Italian physicist Carlo Rovelli compares Einstein's general theory of relativity to other 'absolute masterpieces', including *King Lear*; Einstein reveals 'a reality which seems to be made of the same stuff which our dreams are made of, but which is nevertheless more real than our clouded quotidian dreaming', Rovelli writes, echoing Shakespeare's 'we are such stuff | As dreams are made on', in a speech about 'cloud-capped towers' and the nature of theatre (*Tempest* 4.1.148–58).

Apart from science and philosophy, the visual component of Shakespeare's work also connects him to centuries of art. He is just as strongly connected to the history of music. Shakespeare's verse, especially as spoken by trained actors, has often been described as musical. William Poel cast the plays musically, choosing actors to create a particular range and interaction of pitch and timbre. George Bernard Shaw believed that Shakespeare's greatest achievement was his word-music, which made his plays 'stand above all recorded music'. In 1930 T. S. Eliot said that Shakespeare's philosophy 'really has more in common with, let us say, the philosophy of Beethoven' than the treatises of philosophers.

By the 1630s, if not before, Shakespeare's words were being set to music, outside the performances of the King's Men, by professional composers like Henry Lawes. The sonnets are still being set to music. Rufus Wainwright's 2016 collection was performed by the BBC Symphony Orchestra, and described by reviewer Ian Gittins as a 'baroque Brechtian cabaret', where 'the florid romance of the sonnets dovetails exquisitely with Wainwright's own exuberant, rococo musical flourishes'.

Shakespeare's music equally thrives in *Hamilton*, which belongs to the history of Shakespeare's continuing influence, four centuries after his death. Accepting the Tony Award for best score for a new musical, Miranda read a sonnet (including the very Shakespearean tautology 'And love is love is love is love is love'). *Hamilton*'s protagonist, originally played by Miranda, quotes Macbeth's 'Tomorrow and tomorrow and tomorrow | Creeps in this petty pace from day to day' (5.5.19–20), but trusts that his audience will understand the reference to the Scottish tragedy 'without my having to name the play'. Having rhymed his line with Shakespeare's, he then proceeds to compare James Madison to Banquo, Thomas Jefferson to Macduff, and the United States Congress to Birnam Wood. Later in the same scene, his sister-in-law Angelica quotes Lady Macbeth's 'Screw your courage to the sticking place' (1.7.61). She does not call attention to her Shakespearean source, and Miranda admits in a note to the published script that he first heard the phrase in the Disney musical *Beauty and the Beast*, and as a child had no idea that it came from a much earlier play. We pick up scattered pieces of Shakespeare's imagination without realizing it. As Tom Stoppard said in 1980, 'a bit of

Shakespeare' gets added to 'a bit of me, a bit more of that, off with me, on with some Shakespeare'.

Shakespeare keeps surprising us: we turn the page and step through a door into another world. 'Shakespeare is in the water supply,' Stanley Wells wrote in 2003, 'and is likely to remain there until the pipes run dry.' Shakespeare will last as long as our civilization. But we might also say that Shakespeare's works are, themselves, the pipes that bind us together, the fibre-optic cables of our culture. His public works connect us. He created the infrastructure of our imaginations. Shakespeare is connectable, is 'relatable', to thousands of different fractions of our composite culture. No artist in the long history of our culture is so massively and intricately linked to so many other artists. Each of those connections, each of those interactions between Shakespeare and another artist, has stimulated, and often continues to stimulate, its own satellite system of critical and historical commentary.

Shakespeare the contemporary

Shakespeare has been dead for hundreds of years. But in the room Shakespeare vacated so long-ago, generations of men and women come and go, still in conversations with and about him, naming him, arguing about him, quoting him.

Virginia Woolf did love 'the volley, volume, tumble' of Shakespeare's words, which 'utterly outpace and outrace my own, seeming to start equal and then I see him draw ahead, do things I could not in my wildest tumult and utmost press of mind imagine'. Shakespeare was, Woolf confided in the wild tumult of her diary, in the characteristic superlatives that characterize Shakespeare and almost everything written about him, 'quicker than anybody else's quickest'.

Huxley did not imagine a future in which Shakespeare had simply become difficult to read; he imagined a world in which reading Shakespeare was forbidden. Likewise, in the future imagined by Ray Bradbury's *Fahrenheit 451*, there is only one copy of Shakespeare's works left in the country, because the government burns all books, on the principle that 'a book is a loaded gun in the house next door'. Books are, in that imagined future, intrinsically dangerous. George Orwell, in *Nineteen Eighty-Four*, involves various writers, such as Shakespeare, Milton, Swift, Byron, Dickens, and some others into his imagination. One night, the protagonist Winston Smith has a dream about the past, and particularly about the death of his parents, in which he realizes that 'Tragedy... belonged to the ancient time, to a time when there was still privacy, love, and friendship.' Then he wakes up 'with the word "Shakespeare" on his lips'.

All these classic modern novels imagine a future in which Shakespeare has become a precious relic. But why should we read plays and poems written more than 400 years ago? This question is particularly important in Shakespeare's case. When we read Shakespeare, we are reading a writer from our past who is writing about his past. The stories that he tells are even older than his past act of telling them: his pastness ranges from the fall of Troy to the sixteenth century. Why, in the twenty-first century, should we care about such musty stuff? The usual answer is that certain writers, like Shakespeare, preserve universal truths. That may be true. But what 'universal truth' tends to mean, in practice, is that certain statements or characters or events in Shakespeare's works coincide with our own experiences or prejudices.

Our past is someone else's present. What we think of as the distant past is actually happening to other people right now. So how do we know that what's past will stay safely in the past? How do we know that what's happening

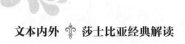

elsewhere won't start happening here? Shakespeare imagines the past imagining the future, not only in *Julius Caesar,* but in the prophecies that fill his English history plays: a spectator, or a reader, in the present, witnesses a person from the past anticipate the future. Past, present, and future are inextricably interconnected.

We should read Shakespeare precisely because his works are sharp reminders (like sharp inoculation needles) of how brutal and frail we are. His works are full of pain, and full of beauty, and painfully beautiful.

'I have more sympathy with one of Shakespeare's pick-purses,' William Hazlitt said in 1819, 'than I can possibly have with any member of the society.' Like Hazlitt, each of the billions of human beings currently crowded onto our little planet is an exception to some genetic or social norm, and every life has its exceptionally happy and exceptionally horrible moments. Consequently, any person can connect, at some point or in some way, to Shakespeare's incomparable fascination with the incomparable.

Reading the whole book is like getting to know the whole person. Most of the people we encounter play bit parts in our lives. But there is a much smaller number that we want to know more about, and there is a very small number that we would be delighted to know everything about. We learn the overall patterns of their behavior, but also the less obvious quirks; we puzzle over the apparent incompatibles; over time, with attention, we acquire a sense of the whole complex network of their being. Shakespeare is one of those writers who rewards the long, intense, intimate relationship created by rereading, and rereading, all their work. For a statistically surprising number of people, Shakespeare never gets boring. Their relationship with Shakespeare becomes an element of their identity.

Activities

1. Shakespeare and Today

Direction: Match the following popular quotations in Column A with Shakespeare's plays in Column B.

Column A	Column B
1. What is past is prologue.	*Richard II*
2. To be or not to be, that is a question.	*The Tempest*
3. You may my glories and my state depose but not my griefs; still am I king of those.	*A Midsummer Night's Dream*
4. All that glisters is not gold.	*Hamlet*
5. The course of true love never did run smooth.	*The Merchant of Venice*
6. All the world's a stage, and all the men and women merely players.	*As You Like It*
7. If music be the food of love, play on.	*Henry IV*
8. Parting is such sweet sorrow.	*Julius Caesar*
9. Uneasy lies the head that wears a crown.	*Twelfth Night*
10. Cowards die many times before their deaths; the valiant never taste of death but once.	*Romeo and Juliet*

2. Shakespeare and China

Direction: Read the poem excerpt below to see what characters of Shakespeare are referred to in the poem and talk about why people still read Shakespeare.

……多少人物的命运
留下了长远思索的命题：
一个青年知识分子的困惑，
一个老年父亲在荒野的悲啼，

一个武士丈夫的钟情和多疑，
另一个武士在生命边缘的醒悟，
都曾使过往岁月的无数旅人
停步，重新寻找人生的道路。

…………

你引起了评论千万篇，每一代
最大的才子为你用尽聪明，
而你最少书卷气，因为你
原是绿野的清风，溪水的声音。

因此你坦荡荡。四百年云烟过眼，
科学登了月，猜出了生命的密码，
却不能把你销蚀。有什么能代替
你笔下的人的哀乐，生的光华？

　　　　　——摘自《春天，想到了莎士比亚》，王佐良[①]

3. Shakespeare and Beyond

Direction: look at the following pictures and identify the plays that have inspired these artistic works.

_____

[①] 王佐良：《王佐良全集（第六卷）》，北京：外语教学与研究出版社，2016年，第628–629页。

_____

_____

_____

Further Reading

BARKAN L, 2022. Reading Shakespeare reading me [M]. New York: Fordham University Press.

BATE J, 2007. William Shakespeare complete works [M]. New York: The Modern Library.

HOLDERNESS G, 1988. The Shakespeare myth [M]. Manchester: Manchester University Press.

VICKERS B, 2004. William Shakespeare: the critical heritage [M]. London & New York: Rutledge.

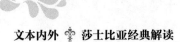

李伟民, 2019.莎士比亚戏剧在中国语境中的接受与流变[M].北京:中国社会科学出版社.

聂珍钊, 杜娟, 2020.莎士比亚与外国文学研究[M].北京:商务印书馆.

杨林贵, 乔雪瑛, 2020.世界莎士比亚研究选编 [M].北京:商务印书馆.

张冲, 2005.同时代的莎士比亚:语境、互文、多种视域 [M].上海:复旦大学出版社.

Unit 3 How to Read Shakespeare?

章节概述

1765 年的塞缪尔·约翰逊（Samuel Johnson）曾宣称，阅读莎士比亚不为其他，只为享受。但在几百年后的今天莎士比亚是否还能带给读者同样的愉悦与欲罢不能呢？毕竟，对于现代读者而言，莎士比亚的故事已年代久远，诗韵体的文法句法更是让人望而却步，加之典故、隐喻、双关语的使用，难免让阅读莎士比亚充满挑战。

不过，无数人正跨越时代的沟壑与莎士比亚结下不解之缘。那些不畏艰辛的人也在与莎士比亚的对话中收获了自己的精神财富。莎士比亚即生命，即世界。每一次的阅读都是一次发现之旅，感受新的世界，看到新的自己。那么，作为初学者究竟应该如何走近莎士比亚呢？

首先，不必畏惧。莎士比亚的确很难，但莎士比亚并非遥不可及。在莎士比亚所处的时代，戏剧不是阳春白雪的高雅艺术，而是大众文化的一部分。那时的剧院聚集了来自社会不同阶层的观众。他们在那里饮食、休闲、社交。而戏剧表演与斗熊、杂耍一样，不过是娱乐的一种方式。所以，莎士比亚的戏剧记录呈现的不过是世事种种，烟火年年。当大幕拉开，莎士比亚就是你我，而我们也都是他舞台上的人物。

其次，远观细品。如果把阅读莎士比亚比作一次寻宝探险，我们首先需要获得的是莎士比亚的宝藏地图，勾勒轮廓，形成对其作品内容、结构特点的整体认识；然后按图索骥，找到最经典的片段，如琢如磨，渐入佳境。在此过程中，遭遇困惑，不得其义是常有的事，我们要做的是把前人的阅读精要、经典的文本注释、传神的中文翻译当作寻宝的秘籍，研读思考，有所得而后继续前行。

再者，身临其境。莎士比亚的诗歌和戏剧都极具表演性。而理解表演最好的方式就是成为舞台的一部分。通过反复诵读、情感带入、角色演绎，看似艰深晦涩的段落表达也会在真实的语境中鲜活起来。当然，如果能把自己想象成导演，对诗歌剧本的理解则会更进一步。大到舞台设计、人物塑造，小到每句台词、每个动作的拿捏，都蕴含着对作品的不同阐释。此外，风格各异的广播剧，影视表演视频音频也能多角度辅助对原文的理解，帮助我们形成更为立体的认识。

最后，互动讨论。莎士比亚作品犹如一面镜子，折射出对社会、历史、人文的各种思考，同时又为每一个话题留下了无限的阐释空间。于是，一千个读者眼里有一千个哈姆雷特。在不断的切磋碰撞中，我们或可瞥见莎士比亚的不同侧面，进而构建起一个完整的形象。

Selected Reading

How to Read Shakespeare?
StageMilk Team[①]

It's one thing to know how great Shakespeare is and be told time and time again that all men should read his works, but it's another thing to actually sit down with a play in front of us and read. Shakespeare's language, through the passage of time, has grown archaic and difficult for us to access. There's no two ways around it. Shakespeare is *hard*. Anyone who says it's not is either lying or deluded. However, the challenge that accessing Shakespeare poses is not an excuse to not *try*! If we can push through our own fears and doubts about our ability to read and understand Shakespeare, we unlock the potential for us to experience some of the best writing in the world, and some of the best characters for us to play and build our craft as actors.

Reading Shakespeare is challenging. It targets all the different 'muscle

---

① StageMilk Team is made up of professional actors and writers from around the world, who are dedicated to promoting the understanding of drama and Shakespeare's plays in particular. The reading material is adapted from https://www.stagemilk.com/how-to-read-shakespeare/.

groups' of the craft: The mind, the voice, the body and the heart. Unlike some contemporary mediums, which only strengthen our ability to do that one specific thing, Shakespeare enables us to tackle anything which is placed in front of us.

Tackling Shakespeare gives us the power to tackle any text or story which comes our way. We have felt and experienced this fact, and we would like to share our thoughts about the fundamental question about starting off on a Shakespearean journey: How do we read Shakespeare?

Opening the first page of *The Merchant of Venice*, we are smacked in the face with the following speech from Antonio:

> In sooth, I know not why I am so sad:
> It wearies me; you say it wearies you;
> But how I caught it, found it, or came by it,
> What stuff 'tis made of, whereof it is born,
> I am to learn;
> And such a want-wit sadness makes of me,
> That I have much ado to know myself.

When we're met with language which is challenging to access right from the beginning of a play, it's going to be a real struggle for us to get through to the final scenes of the fifth act. So, let's talk about five ways we can enhance our ability to access Shakespeare's text, so we can enjoy the works and see what all the fuss is about.

#1 Start Small

The task of developing any skill requires us to start small. Studying and understanding Shakespeare requires this patient process from us, too. If you're new to Shakespeare, start with bite sized chunks of text before attempting to read entire plays.

Soliloquies, (speeches addressed directly to the audience) are a fantastic place to start this process. Some of Shakespeare's most famous moments are in his characters soliloquies, so by choosing one to read and practice your understanding of, you can rest easy knowing that there is tremendous value to this process.

Make the process of choosing a character's soliloquy really simple. Choose a play you have heard of and potentially know a few things about. Choose a character from that play who seems familiar to you, either because you have heard of them before or because they are a character which you can relate to.

One other thing to keep in mind when you're selecting the play/ scene/ character from Shakespeare you'd like to start reading is that there are certain plays which are more accessible to us than others. This is an undeniable fact. This is not to say you shouldn't work towards diving into Shakespeare's more complex work, like *Cymbeline*, *A Winter's Tale* or *King Lear*, but to begin with it's much more beneficial to start simple. The most popular of Shakespeare's plays, (*Romeo and Juliet*, *Macbeth*, *Hamlet*, *Othello*, etc.) are undeniably more accessible than some of the other plays in the canon. Don't worry yourself with preparing a monologue no-one has ever read before or reading a lesser known play because you want to try to be original, just tackle the first plays you come across.

In all of Shakespeare's plays are links and threads connecting them to the rest of his work. The more you read of Shakespeare, the more you'll be able to read and understand. All that's required from you is to start, and to start small.

#2 Read the Text Aloud

Shakespeare's plays were never made to be merely read or studied, they were made to be performed. I sometimes wonder what Shakespeare would think of the fact that in schools all around the world today young people have their heads buried in plays of his, riddled with analysis and footnotes. Perhaps he'd be delighted, perhaps he'd be mortified. One thing is for sure: this was never Shakespeare's intention. Shakespeare died decades before his works were compiled together and released in folios and quartos, so perhaps even people reading the plays for leisure would have been an odd concept to him.

What this means for us, is that in order to access Shakespeare we need to experience the words in as close to their natural way as possible. This means that the words need to be spoken out loud.

Shakespeare's audience was much more of an auditory culture, whereas we are primarily a visual one. We have so much visual stimulation in our lives today, from screens and films to vivid lighting in our homes. Vision was less of a primary sense for Shakespeare's audience than that of hearing. Listening to words being spoken in plays and poetry was a primary form of entertainment, and even though much of the population would have been illiterate, their ears would still have been far more attuned to the verse structures present in Shakespeare's plays than we are today.

So, once you have chosen your piece to dive into and dissect, start off by reading the text aloud. Read slowly, read quietly, don't place the pressure to perform on yourself. Simply just read the words for sense. Reading out loud will be more of an active process of dissecting the text than reading in your head. It will ensure your focus is entirely with the words. In addition to this, reading along will allow you to begin noticing the rhythms and structures tied into the words and enhance your ability to understand what is being said.

#3 Translate the Words!

As generations pass, language changes a LOT! How many words do you use, whether in person or over social media, that your parents would have no idea about? These words, slang, and abbreviations may not have

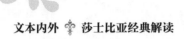

found their place in a dictionary yet, but that doesn't mean they won't, one day. Language is constantly changing and developing with the passing of time, which is why Shakespeare's English is so different to that which we use today. His language is archaic, and can be really difficult to access. So, that's why we make ourselves a simple translation!

When working professionally in Shakespeare, we will always be mining the text for meaning and understanding, and in the more complex sections and speeches, we may even write ourselves a modern translation of the text to ensure we truly comprehend what is being spoken. This is absolutely ok to do, and I'd encourage you to do this for yourselves. Let's take the same section we looked at above, for example:

> In sooth, I know not why I am so sad:
> It wearies me; you say it wearies you;
> But how I caught it, found it, or came by it,
> What stuff 'tis made of, whereof it is born,
> I am to learn;
> And such a want-wit sadness makes of me,
> That I have much ado to know myself.

Having selected this piece, and spoken the words out loud a few times, now I want to create a modern translation of the words to make sure I really know what is being said. The translation can be very simple and purely for sense, something like this:

> To be honest, I don't know why I'm so sad.
> You think you're tired of it? I'm tired of it!
> How I caught this sadness or came across it, ·
> what has caused it or given birth to it
> I am still trying to figure out

This sadness makes me feel like such a fool

that I have a lot of work to do to get to know myself better.

To create this translation, I read through the text slowly and out loud, trying to piece together the puzzle for myself. I also looked up some information about the text online, and read a few other translations which had been written. Most importantly, I translated the unfamiliar language which was preventing me from understanding the text. In the case of this speech, words like, 'sooth' and 'want-wit' were crucial for me to translate to something more modern, like 'truth' and 'fool', respectively.

A word of caution with this process. Translating Shakespeare is a useful device for sections of text which are really hindering your understanding of a play. There are many websites which provide their own translations of Shakespeare's text. It is important to remember that these translations (even the ones on this website!) are a huge **simplification** of the language, and will only serve to benefit your understanding, not necessarily your performance. Once you feel confident with the meaning of what is being said, go back to the original text and do your best to weave your new-found understanding into the original text on the page. The challenge and complexity of Shakespeare's text is all a part of its sophistication and marvel, and we should strive to embrace that challenge rather than find too many shortcuts and simplifications.

#4 Given Circumstances

As with any text, we're going to be hard pressed to understand what is going on if we don't understand the given circumstances of the story. This, in simple terms, means the 'who, what, when, where, and why' of the story. Who are the characters and relationships, what has happened between them up until this point/ what do they want/ what are they saying, when is the scene taking place, (time period and night or day), where are they and why

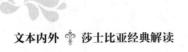

are they here. Answering all of these questions surrounding the moment you're trying to understand will greatly increase your ability to do so.

Now, much of this information will be revealed to you as you read the play, but you might also like to read complimentary resources to assist you with the process. Reading summaries of scenes, acts and plays is a tool I find really useful in understanding what is going on whilst I am reading.

I feel it's important to flag at this point the shame that some of us may feel when attempting to read Shakespeare. Some of us, (including myself) feel this obligation or this expectation to be able to fully understand Shakespeare as we're reading it for the first time, and if we're unable to do this then we feel that this reflects our intelligence. If this is your experience and you're putting this pressure on yourself to be able to immediately understand Shakespeare with no additional assistance, then please let me reassure you that you do not need to feel this way. Shakespeare is really difficult to dive into, even for experienced actors. The most experienced actors I have worked with, some of whom have been acting Shakespeare for 50+ years, still take the time to ensure they understand the language and what is happening in the scenes.

If an aid will make the process of reading Shakespeare more accessible and enjoyable for you, then use whatever assistance you like! Read along with scene and play summaries, read character descriptions, read translations. It's much better to search wide for the access to a script rather than giving up when you meet your first roadblock.

#5 Watch a Production

In addition to reading laterally from the play you've chosen—the summaries and translations helping you access the play—it's also incredibly useful to watch a production of the play. This task tackles a few of the points we've already raised: we're hearing the words spoken out loud, and the play is clearly anchored in its given circumstances. We're able to see the characters brought to life, speaking these words to each other across the space. Even though we may still miss some of the meaning of the language, (and filmed versions of Shakespeare have often been significantly abridged) we're definitely going to pick up the sense of the story more than we might while reading it silently to ourselves.

One step better than finding a film of the play to watch, is to watch a theatre production! This may be more difficult, especially if you've chosen a rarely performed Shakespeare play, but there's a high chance you'll be able to find at least a few options for live Shakespeare to watch in the near future in your hometown.

Shakespeare's works are still very much alive and present in our culture today, so there's nothing stopping you from watching his work, whether live or recorded, right away!

#6 Verse and Prose

The points we've covered so far will have enabled you to develop a strong understanding of the play your currently reading, so now let's dive a little bit deeper. Let's talk briefly about how Shakespeare writes.

Shakespeare writes in two different ways: he writes in *verse*, and he writes in *prose*. Prose, simply, is written word without metric structure. It is 'ordinary' writing that you would find in a novel, or an article, such as the one you are currently reading. Verse, by contrast, is written with a poetic structure. Verse is poetry.

Shakespeare will have his characters speaking in verse or prose, depending on a number of different factors. These factors include the character's status, intention and psychological state in a particular moment. Hamlet, for example, speaks soliloquies in verse, but while he is speaking to the other members of the Danish court, he will often speak in prose. This may go in line with his wish to appear unhinged whilst wearing his 'antic disposition' in order to distract Claudius from his vengeful desires.

The first step in understanding verse and prose and feeling the impact of it whilst you are reading is to be able to identify it on the page. Simply put, prose is written without a physical structure on the page, whereas verse has a structure to it. You can actually spot verse based on the formatting of the words on the page. Let me give you an example.

The following text is from one of Hamlet's soliloquies:

> O, that this too too solid flesh would melt
> Thaw and resolve itself into a dew!
> Or that the Everlasting had not fix'd
> His canon 'gainst self-slaughter! O God! God!
> How weary, stale, flat and unprofitable,
> Seem to me all the uses of this world!
> Fie on't! ah fie! 'tis an unweeded garden,
> That grows to seed; things rank and gross in nature
> Possess it merely. That it should come to this!

This soliloquy is written in verse, and we can see that from its formatting on the page. Each line begins with a capitalised letter. The physical length of each line is fairly uniform. Going a step deeper, Shakespeare used the poetic structure of Iambic Pentameter to base his verse on. This manifests in many ways throughout his works, but in the main, each line of Shakespeare will have 10 syllables—5 unstressed when spoken, and 5 stressed. If we were to speak a few lines from this speech with Iambic Pentameter from of mind, it would be stressed like this: (stressed syllables in bold)

> O, **that** this **too** too **solid flesh** would **melt**
> Thaw **and** re**solve** itself **into** a **dew**!

Prose is written with a noticeable lack of structure when it appears on the page. This is from another of Hamlet's speeches, however this time he is not addressing the audience, but two of his prying friends:

> I have of late,—but wherefore I know not,—lost all my mirth, forgone all custom of exercises; and indeed it goes so heavily with my disposition that this goodly frame, the earth, seems to me a sterile promontory; this most excellent canopy, the air, look you, this brave o'erhanging firmament, this majestical roof fretted with golden fire, why, it appears no other thing to me but a foul and pestilent congregation of vapours. What a piece of work is a man!

We can see that these words are without the same rigid structure that we had in the previous speech. The lines are long and uncapitalised and the syntax is sporadic. As you are working your way through your play of choice, keep an eye out for how Shakespeare plays with form. When are his characters speaking verse, and when are they speaking in prose? There are many further discussions about this topic, but for the moment, identifying whether the character is speaking casually or poetically may increase your understanding of what is going on in the scene.

Conclusion: Words, Words, Words

So, there you have it. You've begun your journey into the world of William Shakespeare. It's wonderful, believe me. It may be challenging at first, in fact I can promise you that it will be challenging, but so are all the worthwhile things in life.

Use these six steps: start small, read the words out loud, translate the text, understand the given circumstances, watch a production of the play and then begin noticing the style of the writing. By following this progression, you're infinitely more likely to continue your reading of the play and enjoy it, leading you to a deeper level of confidence and skill with tackling Shakespeare's works.

If all else fails, and you're really struggling to find the motivation and confidence to read Shakespeare, but you still want to be able to do it, then it is time to organize a reading party! Invite a few like-minded friends around, organize some chips and a beverage of choice, and read the play out loud whilst sitting around the living room. So much can be gained from reading with friends, and they will help you access and enjoy the work.

Activities

1. Shakespeare and Today

Direction: Shakespeare is not only known as a timeless playwright, but also as a prolific inventor of words that are still in use today. Look up in the dictionary the following words coined by Shakespeare and write down the meanings of them in the blanks.

Bandit (*Henry VI, Part 2. 1594*) _____

Critic (*Love's Labour Lost. 1598*) _____

Dauntless (*Henry VI, Part 3. 1616*) _____

Dwindle (*Henry IV, Part 1. 1598*) _____

Elbow v. (*King Lear. 1608*) _____

Green-Eyed (*The Merchant of Venice. 1600*) _____

Lackluster (*As You Like It. 1616*) _____

Lonely (*Coriolanus. 1616*) _____

Skim-milk (*Henry IV, Part 1. 1598*) _____

Swagger (*Midsummer Night's Dream. 1600*) _____

2. Shakespeare and China

Direction: The books shown in the picture below are known as the Four Great Chinese Classic Novels. Think about how they are related to shakespeare to make canons and accomplish the following tasks:

1) How would you translate the titles of the four books into English?

2) Could you introduce each of the four books with three sentences?

3) Give your foreign friends 5 tips on how to read Chinese Classics.

3. Shakespeare and Beyond

Direction: Shakespeare must have loved the prefix un- because he created or gave new meaning to more than 300 words that begin with it. Here are just a few. Work within groups to write a short dramatic dialogue by using them.

Unaware (*Venus & Adonis*. 1593)

Uncomfortable (*Romeo & Juliet*. 1599)

Undress (*Taming of the Shrew*. 1616)

Unearthly (*A Winter's Tale*. 1616)

Unreal (*Macbeth*. 1623)

Further Reading

CORCORAN N, 2018. Reading Shakespeare's soliloquies [M]. London:

Bloomsbury.

LOPEZ J, 2019. The Arden introduction to reading Shakespeare [M]. London: The Arden Shakespeare.

MALLIN E S, 2019. Reading Shakespeare in the movies [M]. New York: Palgrave Macmillan.

TRAUB V, 2016. The Oxford handbook of Shakespeare and embodiment [M]. Oxford: Oxford University Press.

WALKER J L, 2002. Shakespeare and the classical tradition [M]. London: Taylor & Francis.

Part Two Shakespeare's Sonnets

Unit 1 From Petrarch to Shakespeare

章节概述

　　十四行诗是一种包含十四行诗句的固定诗歌形式，最早起源于13世纪意大利的西西里诗派，英语单词"sonnet"来源于意大利语单词"sonetto"，本意为旋律或乐曲。意式十四行诗（Italian Sonnet）又被称为彼得拉克式十四行诗（Petrarchan Sonnet），主要原因是早期意大利文艺复兴时期的学者兼诗人弗朗西斯科·彼得拉克（Francesco Petrarca①）创作了大量的十四行诗，使得这一诗体在内容及结构上达到了艺术的完善，在影响上也超出了意大利本土范围，远播欧洲其他各国。

　　彼得拉克式十四行诗在结构上通常分为两个部分，即一个八行诗（octave）和一个六行诗（sestet）的诗节（stanza）。从内容上来说，第一个八行诗诗节会提出一个问题，而后续的六行诗诗节则着重探索该问题的答案。同时，彼得拉克式十四行诗的第九行经常通过使用风格、情感或立场的变化来表达一个明显的转折（volta），标志着诗歌内容从问题到答案的转变。在押韵方式方面，彼得拉克式十四行诗的第一个八行诗诗节的押韵方式统一为abbaabba，而后续的六行诗诗节押韵方式则灵活多变，彼得拉克本人通常使用cdecde或cdcdcd来押韵，而在英文创

① Petrarca转为英语拼写即Petrarch。

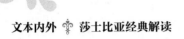
作的意式十四行诗中，也可见cddcdd、cddece、cddccd、cddcee、cdcdee等押韵方式。

　　彼得拉克的十四行诗在意大利及欧洲其他国家广泛流传，被许多文人翻译、模仿和推广。16世纪初叶，英国贵族托马斯·怀亚特爵士（Sir Thomas Wyatt）及萨里伯爵亨利·霍华德（Henry Howard, Earl of Surrey）开始将彼得拉克的十四行诗译为英文，并根据英文的发音及语法特点进行了十四行诗结构与韵律上的创新创作，由此揭开了十四行诗在英国蓬勃发展的序幕。英国文艺复兴时期的诗人们也开始使用这种诗歌形式，莎士比亚是其中最著名的一位，也是英国十四行诗创作艺术的集大成者，因此英式十四行诗（English Sonnet）也被称为莎士比亚式十四行诗（Shakespearean Sonnet）。

　　从结构上来说，莎士比亚式十四行诗将全诗分为四个诗节，由三个四行诗（quatrain）及一个对句（couplet）构成，押韵方式通常为abab cdcd efef gg。这样的诗歌结构从内容的表达上来说比彼得拉克式十四行诗更加灵活，因为三组四行诗或可以通过排比增强表达效果，或可以层层递进，表达某个观点或感情，或可以彼此对立，形成鲜明的对比。而且，整体来说，莎士比亚式十四行诗可分为8-4-2或8-6这两种结构单元，这样就可以使警言式的对句在结尾承担或总结归纳全诗，或陈述新的感情思想，或完全推翻前文内容的作用。这种警言式的对句结尾也可以说是全诗的点睛之笔，也是莎士比亚式十四行诗的一个突出特点。

　　随着英国文学的不断发展，除了彼得拉克式十四行诗和莎士比亚式十四行诗，也诞生了诸如斯宾塞式十四行诗（Spenserian Sonnet）、弥尔顿式十四行诗（Miltonic Sonnet）等多种十四行诗的形式。这些十四行诗在结构、内容、风格上略有差异。具体来说，斯宾塞式十四行诗由英国诗人埃德蒙·斯宾塞（Edmund Spencer）在16世纪发明，其结构与莎士比亚式十四行诗相同，由三个四行诗及一个对句构成。但押韵方式为abab bcbc cdcd ee，较莎式十四行诗更为复杂；而弥尔顿式十四行诗则由英国诗人约翰·弥尔顿（John Milton）在17世纪发明，其押韵方式与彼得拉克式十四行诗基本相同，但整首诗在结构上为一个十四行诗句整体（quatozain），并没有诗节之分。

今天，十四行诗仍然是一个十分受欢迎的诗歌形式，在世界各地的
文学作品中被广泛应用。虽然它最初是在意大利文艺复兴时期发展起来
的，但随着时间的推移，十四行诗已经成为一种全球性的文学形式，体
现了人们对诗歌的热爱和追求。

Selected Reading

Introduction of *A History of the Sonnet in England:*
"A Little World Made Cunningly" [1]
Jochen Petzold[2]

When Giacomo da Lentini invented the sonnet, he created a new poetic
form. As we will see as we look at sonnets through the centuries, there has
always been a certain readiness to experiment with this form, to try out
variations. However, distinct structural patterns have developed which are
reflected in their respective rhyme schemes, and I will use this section to
distinguish two basic types known as the **Italian sonnet** and the **English
sonnet**（also called the **Shakespearean sonnet**）.

While the two basic patterns primarily affect the internal subdivision（on the
level of syntax and semantics）and the rhyme scheme of the sonnet, there is
comparatively little variation in terms of the metrical structure. As stated
above, in Italian the typical sonnet line is the hendecasyllable, in French it is
the Alexandrine（a line of twelve syllables, often with a caesura before the

---

① This reading material is abridged from the "Introduction" of *A History of the Sonnet in England*:
   "*A Little World Made Cunningly*". Petzold, Jochen. *A History of the Sonnet in England: "A Little
   World Made Cunningly"*. Berlin: Erich Schmidt Verlag, 2021.
② Professor Dr. Jochen Petzold was working in the College of Languages, Literatures and Cultures
   at Universität Regensburg （德国雷根斯堡大学）when the book was published. His research
   field includes theory of poetry, genre theory, Victorian literature for children and young adults,
   etc.

sixth syllable). In English poetry, iambic lines are by far the most common, and most sonnets in English use the iambic pentameter as their basic measure, i.e., a line of ten or eleven syllables in which five syllables are stressed, namely the second, fourth, sixth, eighth, and tenth syllable. Inversions are fairly common, though, particularly at the beginning of a line (i.e., the first syllable is stressed, followed by two unstressed syllables), but other metres are rare.

The Italian Sonnet

Although the rhyme scheme underwent certain changes, two basic principles of the Italian sonnet have remained stable over the centuries: its fourteen lines are divided into two parts, the octave and the sestet, and these units are clearly distinguished by different rhyme schemes. Furthermore, octave and sestet are usually further subdivided into two quatrains and two tercets. The octave uses only two sets of end rhymes (each rhyming sound repeated four times), and while initially the rhyme scheme was that of alternate rhyme, *abab. abab*, embracing rhymes, *abba. abba*, soon became dominant. Petrarch uses the latter form in 303 (more than 95 per cent) of the 317 sonnets in his *Canzoniere* (cf. Barber 1977, p. 140), and Petrarch's great popularity during the Renaissance certainly helped to establish this as the Italian format of the octave. The sestet introduces new sets of end rhymes and allows for more variation, as two or three rhyming sounds can be used, either in an alternating or in an interlaced pattern. In Petrarch's *Canzoniere*, the most common rhyme scheme in the sestets is *cde. cde* (used in 121 sonnets), followed by *cdc. dcd* (116 sonnets) and *cde. dce* (64 sonnets); the use of couplets in Petrarch's sestet is so rare that it is deemed illegitimate by many theorists of the sonnet.

Typically, there is a break or turn, called *volta*, between the octave and the sestet, which introduces a discernible semantic shift. Hence, the sonnet consists of two parts of almost but not quite equal length, clearly distinguished by the rhyme scheme, leading to a division or development on the level of content, and many critics see this as the defining principle of the sonnet. The dynamics of the two unequal parts has been compared to the expansion and contraction of a breathing organism, or to the ebb and flow of waves. While this may sound somewhat esoteric to contemporary ears, there is general agreement that the Italian sonnet lends itself to a fairly balanced presentation of ideas, or to the exposition of a theme in the octave which is then commented upon in the sestet. The following poem may serve as a good example of the Italian sonnet form in English:

<blockquote>
I love thee, dear one, more than this can tell,   a
Or thou canst comprehend, who lov'st not me.   b
Thou canst not fathom half my misery,   b
Nor reach the bottom of my love's deep well.   a
Nor dost thou care to try it, for the knell   a
Of separation hath divided thee   b
From him who ne'er again that face may see,   b
Whose image in his heart must ever dwell.   a
Yet it is better so, for, wert thou mine,   c
No passionate embraces could suffice   d
To slake the ardour of my quenchless love,   e
Unless my essence were transfused with thine,   c
And both one being made, as Paradise   d
Beholds its happy angels do, above.   e

(Upward 1888, p. 2)
</blockquote>

It is the second poem in Allen Upward's (1863–1926) thirty SONNETS TO ELLA—a collection in the Petrarchan mould, exploring the speaker's unrequited love for Ella. Fittingly, then, it employs the rhyme scheme most frequently used by Petrarch, *abba. abba. cde. cde*. The presentation on the page reinforces the distinction in octave and sestet, and suggests the subdivision into two quatrains and two tercets. In the octave, the speaker focuses on the fact that his love for Ella is unrequited and will remain so, since they are separated. There is a slight shift between the quatrains, the first one emphasizing the greatness of the speaker's love, the second the fact of separation, but they clearly form a semantic unit. The *volta* is explicitly marked by the adversative conjunction "Yet" that starts the sestet and indicates a break or contradiction. In the sestet, the fact that the love is unrequited is paradoxically presented as positive, since no worldly passion could do justice to the purity of the speaker's love. Hence, Upward's poem is a typical Italian sonnet that utilizes the form to reinforce the semantic structure of the text, which presents a situation in the octave and comments on it in the sestet.

The sonnet form that divides the fourteen lines into an octave (rhymed *abba. abba*) and a sestet (using a different rhyme scheme) is by far the most common throughout Europe and has been productive ever since the proliferation of the sonnet in the sixteenth century. However, some critics further distinguish between Italian and French sonnets, as the French sonneteers developed a different rhyme scheme for the sestet. Petrarch hardly ever used an arrangement that results in one or more couplets in the sestet (*cdc. cdc* is used twelve times, *cdd. dcc* only four times). When the sonnet was adopted by the poets of the French Pléiade, they introduced one or two couplets into the sestet. Pierre de Ronsard (1528–1585), the most renowned poet of the Pléiade, wrote almost 700 sonnets. His two most frequent rhyme schemes in the sestet are *ccd. eed* (405 cases) and *ccd. ede* (188 cases), establishing these forms of the sestet as the norm in French sonneteering. Walter Mönch, who provides these statistics, suggests that in terms of their respective musicality, this creates a harsh contrast between the

French and the Italian sonnet (cf. 1955, p. 19). However, the rhyme pattern does not really support his claim that, due to the couplet, the French sestet is more likely to be epigrammatic, since it typically does not end in a concluding couplet—which arguably invites an epigrammatic turn or revelation at the end (see chapter 1.2.2). Rather, I would argue that the structural similarities outweigh the differences between the French and the Italian sonnet: both make use of an octave that is clearly identifiable as a unit and which is almost exclusively rhymed *abba.abba*; furthermore, both make use of a sestet that is differentiated from the octave by the introduction of new rhymes. Hence, both maintain the internal subdivision of eight and six lines that gives the sonnet its affinity to binary or dialectic representation.

The English or Shakespearean Sonnet

While the French and the Italian sonnets share many structural similarities, the English or Shakespearean sonnet uses an arrangement of the fourteen lines which is distinctly different, and which often changes the internal structure of the sonnet. It is a form that is primarily used by sonneteers writing in English, and while William Shakespeare did not invent the form, he used it in most of his sonnets. Therefore, this particular form of the sonnet was labelled the Shakespearean sonnet (or simply Shakespeare sonnet), presumably in an attempt to legitimize the form with the help of his reputation. I will say more about the circumstances that led to the development of this pattern in the next chapter; here, I want to focus on the form and its structural implications.

Whereas the Italian sonnet is made up of an octave and a sestet, the English sonnet consists of three quatrains, each using a new set of alternating rhymes, and a concluding couplet, creating the rhyme pattern *abab.cdcd.efef. gg*. This arrangement does not necessarily preclude the internal division into octave and sestet, but it certainly does not call for it. Instead, the three

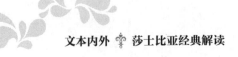

quatrains facilitate the development of a thought or argument in three distinct steps, leading to an epigrammatic conclusion in the final rhymed couplet, as in the following example, Shakespeare's sonnet 60:

> Like as the waves make towards the pebbled shore,   a
> So do our minutes hasten to their end,   b
> Each changing place with that which goes before,   a
> In sequent toil all forwards do contend.   b
> Nativity, once in the main of light,   c
> Crawls to maturity, wherewith being crowned,   d
> Crookèd eclipses 'gainst his glory fight,   c
> And Time that gave doth now his gift confound.   d
> Time doth transfix the flourish set on youth,   e
> And delves the parallels in beauty's brow,   f
> Feeds on the rarities of nature's truth,   e
> And nothing stands but for his scythe to mow.   f
> And yet to times in hope my verse shall stand,   g
> Praising thy worth, despite his cruel hand.   g
>
> (Shakespeare 2007, p. 231)

The internal subdivision of this sonnet is ideally represented by the rhyme scheme and the syntactical structure: the quatrains are three syntactical units, each ending in a full stop. They are thematically linked, but each provides a variation on the theme of time and its relationship to human life. In the first quatrain, the passing of time is described as an eternal process and its lethal implication for humans is only vaguely hinted at. The second quatrain makes these implications more explicit: time eventually 'crowns' the new-born child with maturity, but the further passage of time turns this gift of maturing into the curse of decay. This idea is then further developed in the third quatrain: the beauty of youth is pierced by time, which leads to beauty being marred by the wrinkles of old age. At the end of the third quatrain, the implication of mortality is made explicit: everything in nature must eventually succumb to the "scythe" of death. There is no octave-sestet structure, no volta after the eighth line. Rather, the first twelve lines of the sonnet develop one central idea, the power of time over individual life and beauty, each quatrain expanding the argument, logically concluding in the image of death in the twelfth line. The next line starts with "And yet", a phrase frequently used in sonnets to signal a change—in Upward's sonnet discussed above, the traditional volta after the octave was marked by "Yet". In Shakespeare's sonnet, the concluding couplet introduces a new idea, a counter-argument: while the living beauty of the addressee may decay, the poetry created by the speaker will provide a monument that outlasts time. This epigrammatic conclusion is facilitated by the rhyme scheme ending in the couplet, and it is typical of English (or Shakespearean) sonnets.

However, not all Shakespearean sonnets are as clearly structured in line with the rhyme scheme. In Shakespeare's sonnets, the concluding couplet does not always form a syntactical unit and sometimes the internal structure is more akin to the division into octave and sestet. For example, sonnet 81 treats a very similar topic to sonnet 60, but the internal structure is quite different:

Or I shall live your epitaph to make,   [whether...or
Or you survive me when I in earth am rotten,
From hence your memory death cannot take,
Although in me each part will be forgotten.
Your name from hence immortal life shall have,
Though I (once gone) to all the world must die;
The earth can yield me but a common grave,
When you intombèd in men's eyes shall lie:

Your monument shall be my gentle verse,

Which eyes not yet created shall o'er-read,

And tongues to be your being shall rehearse,

When all the breathers of this world are dead;

    You still shall live (such virtue hath my pen)

Where breath most breathes, even in the mouths of men.

(Shakespeare 2007, p. 273)

Here the first eight lines talk about the eventual death of both the speaker and his addressee, which will have different implications. The speaker insists that he will be forgotten, while the memory of the addressee will live on. The octave ends with the suggestion that the addressee will be "entombed in men's eyes", an image that may at first seem puzzling. However, the colon at the end of the eighth line already indicates that the following lines will provide a solution to the riddle (if it is one). As in the previously discussed sonnet, the speaker's verse will provide a lasting monument, to be taken in by the eyes of future readers and to be given breath and hence life when the poem is recited or read out. While the last two lines can be read as a kind of epigrammatic summing up, the punctuation indicates that the last six lines form a unit. Thus, although the rhyme scheme suggests an internal structure that leads up to a surprising conclusion provided in the rhyming couplet, the presentation of the topic is in this case more in line with the Italian form of the sonnet.

This example shows that the rhyme scheme can only provide an indication of a sonnet's internal structure. However, the form of the English (or Shakespearean) sonnet lends itself to an epigrammatic ending in a way that the Italian (or Petrarchan) sonnet does not, and since the English form was not particularly productive on the continent, it is responsible for a unique strain in English sonneteering.

There is a second type of sonnet practically unique to sonnets in the English language, the **Spenserian sonnet**. It is the form Edmund Spenser used in his dedicatory sonnets to *The Faerie Queene* (1590) and in the sonnet sequence AMORETTI (1595, see chapter 2.2.3). Like the Shakespearean sonnet, it is usually structured as three quatrains and a concluding couplet, but the quatrains are connected by an intricate rhyme scheme in which the second rhyme from one quatrain is used as the first rhyme in the next: *abab.bcbc.cdcd.ee.*

The Spenserian form did not prove particularly productive. One reason could be that it deviates from the Italian form without addressing the 'problem' of the scarcity of rhymes in the English language (as compared to Italian). In the Italian octave, each rhyme needs to appear four times; in the Shakespearean sonnet, every rhyme only appears twice, making the poet's task of fulfilling the demands of the form somewhat less difficult. However, Spenser's interlacing of the quatrains results in a pattern that also needs four occurrences of two of the rhymes; only the distribution over the fourteen lines is different. Furthermore, the rhyme scheme of Spenser's sonnets runs counter to an internal division into octave and sestet, but neither does it strengthen a subdivision into three quatrains and a couplet, since the rhyme binds the quatrains together. Whatever the reasons, the Spenserian sonnet is a rare occurrence in English sonneteering.

Formal Variation and the Sonnet in English

As we have seen, English sonneteering is unique in having produced two distinct versions of the sonnet. The Italian and the Shakespearean sonnets are established and generally recognized models, the Spenserian pattern providing a more unusual third possibility. Particularly in comparison with the sonnets of the Romance languages, where the octave rhyming *abba.abba* holds almost exclusive sway, English sonnets show more formal variety.

Nonetheless, the Italian sonnet is probably also the most frequent form in English language sonnets. In 1910, L. T. Weeks conducted a survey and statistical analysis of roughly six thousand sonnets from the sixteenth century to the twentieth. His method of selecting his corpus almost certainly gave precedence to 'established' authors and it cannot claim to be strictly representative of sonnet production in English. However, it is sufficiently large to warrant certain deductions. Of roughly 6,300 sonnets, almost 3,500 use the traditional octave rhyming *abba. abba* (55 per cent); in Weeks's sample, this is most frequently combined with sestets rhyming *cdc. dcd* (820) or *cde. cde* (775), i.e., more than 25 per cent of the sample follow exactly the most frequent patterns of Italian sonnets. By comparison, only 20 per cent of the sample follow the prototypical pattern of the Shakespearean sonnet (*abab. cdcd. efef. gg*). Hence, it seems fair to conclude that the 'English' sonnet is not the most frequent type of sonnet in English.

Throughout the centuries, poets have experimented with the form, creating subcategories of the sonnet. There are three aspects of the form that invite experimentation: the sonnet's length, the arrangement of quartets and tercets, and its rhyme scheme. Most deviations from the fourteen-line rule expand the sonnet. Thus, the **caudate sonnet** (or *sonetto caudato* in Italian) adds a 'tail' (Lat. *cauda*), usually of one or more units of a half-line followed by a couplet; in the **rinterzato sonnet** (layered sonnet), seven or eight shorter lines are integrated into the sonnet structure, leading to twenty-one or twenty-two lines; the **double sonnet** consists of twenty-eight lines, usually doubling the octave and sestet to sixteen and twelve lines respectively. The **curtal sonnet** is shortened to a sestet and a section of four and a half lines, thereby maintaining the proportion of octave to sestet (8:6 = 6:4,5).

If a sonnet has two quatrains and two tercets as its basic units, then these can be arranged differently from the octave-sestet division: In a **reversed sonnet** (also called *sonettessa*) the sestet precedes the octave, in an **alternating sonnet** the quatrains and tercets alternate, and in an **enclosed sonnet** the sestet is preceded and followed by a quatrain.

Not surprisingly, most variation exists on the level of the rhyme scheme. If the 'rules' of the prototypical Italian, French or English sonnets are ignored, fourteen lines allow for a considerable number of patterns. In the study referred to above, Weeks (who treated all sonnets as consisting of an octave and a sestet, regardless of their actual structure) found examples of thirty-five different patterns in the octave and twenty-nine different patterns in the sestet, leading to a total of 262 different combinations (in his sample not every octave pattern is combined with every sestet pattern). Some combinations are very rare, and certainly they do not all warrant a specific name. However, some forms stand out: The **terza rima sonnet** uses the interlaced rhyme scheme of the *terza rima*, ideally returning to the first rhyme (*aba. bcb. cdc. dad. aa*). The term **continuous sonnet** is used for sonnets that employ only two rhyme sounds. In the extreme form of the **iterative sonnet** the rhyme word itself is repeated, thus creating identical rhymes (also called tautological rhymes) in which each line ends on the same word. In a **chained sonnet** each new line starts by repeating the last word of the previous line.

All these alterations and experiments point to the fact that poets have never adhered to the so-called rules of the sonnet as strictly as some critics would have liked them to. In this book, I am not particularly concerned with 'sonnet legislation'; my approach is descriptive rather than prescriptive and we will encounter various experiments with the form.

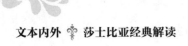

Activities

1. Shakespeare and Today

Direction: Traditionally, the sonnet was composed to express the feeling of love and romantic emotions. Nowadays, sonnets may vary greatly in themes and forms. Please read the following three sonnets, compare their forms with Petrarchan and Shakespearean sonnets and discuss the themes of these three sonnets.

How do I Love Thee?

By Elizabeth Barrett Browning（1850）

How do I love thee? Let me count the ways—

I love thee to the depth and breadth and height

My soul can reach, when feeling out of sight

For the end of Being and Ideal Grace.

I love thee to the level of everyday's

Most quiet need, by sun and candlelight—

I love thee freely, as men strive for Right, —

I love thee purely, as they turn from Praise；

I love thee with a passion, put to use

In my old griefs；and with my childhood's faith—

I love thee with the love I seemed to lose

With lost Saints'—I love thee with the breath,

Smiles, tear, of all my life! —and, if God choose,

I shall but love thee better after death.

Sonnet XVI in the "In Time of War" Sequence

By W. H. Auden（1939）

Here war is simple like a monument:

A telephone is speaking to a man；

Flags on a map assert that troops were sent;
A boy brings milk in bowls. There is a plan

For living men in terror of their lives,
Who thirst at nine who were to thirst at noon,
And can be lost and are, and miss their wives,
And, unlike an idea, can die too soon.
But ideas can be true, although men die,
For we have seen a thousand faces
Made active by one lie:

And maps can really point to places
Where life is evil now:
Nanking; Dachau.

LEGENDARY #1

New York City, 1987

By Nicole Sealey (2009)

You want me to say who I am and all of that?

—Pepper LaBeija

LaBeija, my house, is kept gold, swept clean—
fronts fantasy from top to plump bottom.
What I want to be, I be: crew-cut queen,
middle sex owed to manicured pink thumbs.
Catwalk as fierce as the fiercest real bitch,
I am high like fashion. And fame. I am
a man who likes men and a good cross-stitch,
whom homesick kids crown "legendary." Ma'am
of the ball, been walking now two decades
and *got more grand prizes than all the rest*.

61

The long and short: I'm a one-man parade,

elaborate drag, from manner to breasts.

Within ballrooms I am most opulent.

Inside this house I am most relevant.

2. Shakespeare and China

Direction: The sonnet has been one of the most popular forms adopted by Western poets to carry out literary creation through centuries. Can you introduce in detail and give examples of one or two of the most popular poetic forms in the history of Chinese literature?

3. Shakespeare and Beyond

Direction: Poetry, as one the major forms of literature with unique structures, has a long and varied history, evolving differentially across the globe. The 2016 Nobel Prize in Literature was awarded to the American singer-songwriter Bob Dylan "for having created new poetic expressions within the great American song tradition". Bob Dylan's songs are rooted in the rich tradition of American folk music and are influenced by the poets of modernism. Dylan's lyrics incorporated social struggles, political protest, love as well as religion. His writing is often characterized by refined rhymes and it paints surprising, sometimes surreal imagery. Try to find some of Bob Dylan's lyrics and have a discussion on the following questions: Can Dylan's lyrics be categorized as poetry? Why or why not?

Further Reading

BURT S, MIKICS D, 2011. The art of the sonnet [M]. London: Belknap of Harvard UP.

COUSINS A D, HOWARTH P, 2011. The Cambridge companion to the sonnet [M]. Cambridge; New York: Cambridge University Press.

HAFT L, 2000. The Chinese sonnet: meanings of a form [M]. Leiden, the Netherlands: Research School CNWS, Leiden U.

PETZOLD J, 2021. History of the sonnet in England [M]. Berlin: Erich Schmidt Verlag.

STEINMAN L M, 2008. Invitation to poetry: the pleasures of studying poetry and poetics [M]. Malden, MA: Blackwell Pub.

Unit 2 Sonnets by Theme

章节概述

　　人们在提及或讨论《莎士比亚十四行诗集》时，指的多是1609年由伦敦出版商托马斯·索普（Thomas Thorpe）独家印行的四开本（quarto）诗集。这本诗集收录了154首十四行诗及另一首长篇叙事诗《恋女的怨诉》（*A Lover's Complain*）。这些十四行诗可能是莎士比亚在1590年至1605年间创作完成，并可能做过修订。这部诗集从出版至今在读者及莎学界引发了巨大的兴趣和争论。除诗歌内容本身所引起的争议外，这本初版诗集卷首还刊印了一篇令人费解的献词（dedication）：

梁宗岱译文：

献给下面刊行的十四行诗的

唯一的促成者

W. H. 先生

祝他享有一切幸运，并希望

我们的永生的诗人

所预示的

不朽

得以实现。

对他怀着好意

并断然予以

出版的

　　　　　　　　　　　　　T. T.

TO. THE. ONLIE. BEGETTER. OF.
THESE. INSVING. SONNETS.
M'. W. H. ALL. HAPPINESSE.
AND. THAT. ETERNITIE.
PROMISED.
BY.
OVR. EVER-LIVING. POET.
WISHETH.
THE. WELL-WISHING.
ADVENTVRER. IN.
SETTING.
FORTH.

T. T.

Shake-Speare's Sonnets, quarto published by Thomas Thorpe, London, 1609, title page, Folger Library

　　由于这份献词是由出版商而非莎士比亚所作，且莎士比亚是否参与了1609年诗集的出版依旧未可知，所以献词中的 W. H. 先生身份成谜，对后续读者及学者就诗歌内容本身的解读及研究带来了一定的困扰。但也正是因为这种不确定性，使得有关莎士比亚十四行诗的解读、研究及翻译百花齐放、百家争鸣，未尝不是一种幸运。

目前，按照广泛流行的解读，莎士比亚的154首十四行诗如其戏剧一般，似乎有一条情节主线贯穿其中。按照大概的"故事"梗概，这些诗作可以分为两大组诗：第1首至第126首为第一组，内容提及或献给一位美貌的贵族男性青年，故被称为"The Fair Youth Sequence"；第127至第152首为第二组，内容提及或献给一位肤色较深的女性情人，故被称为"The Dark Lady Sequence"；最后两首及中间个别几首则与故事情节无关。

在前126首十四行诗中，莎士比亚刻画了一位年轻俊美、身居高位、举世瞩目、备受追捧的无名美少年。通过劝诫青年结婚生子，赞美青年异于常人且略带女性气质的美貌，描述自己的诗句能够让青年的美好永存以抗拒时间和死亡的蹂躏等多种凸显不同主题的诗句，莎士比亚表达了自己对这位无名美少年纯粹的友情式倾慕与柏拉图式的爱慕之情。

与之形成鲜明对比的是后续献给女性情人的诗作，在这26首十四行诗中，莎士比亚描述了一位与当时伊丽莎白一世时期大众对女性审美所持的主流看法截然相反的颇具魅力的女性。与传统的金发碧眼不同，这位女性情人肤色偏深，褐发黑眼，仪态欠佳，却充满了原始的诱惑力。而莎士比亚在这组诗中更多展现的是对这位女性情人的爱欲纠葛，由异性肉欲关系引发的复杂感情，甚至一种自我克制式的对异性的厌恶之情。

值得注意的是，莎士比亚的十四行诗基本都是以第一人称"我"来进行陈述，表达与"我"相关的强烈感情。不论是对真善美的执着，对爱情的渴望和追求，对友情的赞美和崇敬，对丑陋现实的不满与憎恶，还是对理想破灭的失望，以第一人称的角度进行叙述，可以使读者直接感受到莎士比亚拥有普通人面对人生中的问题时同样所有的激情与苦恼。再加上作者本身高超的诗歌结构和语言技巧的灵活运用，每一首十四行诗都具有自己独特的审美价值。虽然有些诗作中作者表达的非传统内容以及美少年与女性情人至今身份未明这一事实可能有时会让莎士比亚的十四行诗读来令人费解或难以捉摸，但不难看出的是莎士比亚十四行诗的永恒主题都是"爱"，朋友之爱、精神之爱、男女之爱、肉欲之爱等，同时诗句中也交织时间、变化、衰老、欲望、缺席、不忠、理想与现实等多重主题，"在否定中世纪黑暗时代的禁欲主义和神权的基础上，人文主义赞扬人的个性，宣称人生而平等，赋予了人和人的生存以全部重要性和新的意义。莎诗处处浸透了这种精神，处处充满对生活的歌颂与怀疑，对人的本质的歌颂与怀疑，对自我的歌颂与怀疑"[①]。莎士比亚想通过十四行诗表达的远不仅限于诗句当中的内容。所以即使在四百年后的今天，诸如"莎士比亚的十四行诗是关于什么的？"和"读者应该如何阅读并理解莎士比亚十四行诗？"等问题也依然值得我们探讨，莎士比亚十四行诗也会常读常新。

Selected Reading

SONNET 17

Who will believe my verse in time to come

If it were filled with your most high deserts?

Though yet, heaven knows, it is but as a tomb

Which hides your life and shows not half your

parts.

If I could write the beauty of your eyes

And in fresh numbers number all your graces,

The age to come would say, "This poet lies:

Such heavenly touches ne'er touched earthly

faces."

So should my papers, yellowed with their age,

Be scorned, like old men of less truth than

此处使用了跨行连续（enjambment）的诗歌写作技巧，跨行连续指的是诗歌中的句子或短语从一行诗连续到下一行诗，跨行连续的诗句在换行处不受标点符号的限制

明喻（simile），明喻是一种进行比较的修辞手法，在英语中通常使用"like"或"as"来表示两种不同事物之间的相似之处。此处将"我"的诗句比喻成一座坟墓

parts：n. attributes 特质，品质

numbers：n. lively verses 诗句

number：v. record 记录

夸张（hyperbole）

意象（imagery），意象是莎士比亚在诗歌中经常使用的一种文学手法，即使用生动的描述来引起读者的感官体验，在其脑海中创造一个具体的形象、图画或想法，使读者能够更好地体会作者想要表达的情感

明喻

---

① 威廉·莎士比亚，《莎士比亚十四行诗》，辜正坤译，北京：外语教学与研究出版社，2021年，第318页。

tongue,

And your true rights be termed a poet's rage

And stretchèd meter of an antique song.

But were some child of yours alive that time,

You should live twice—in it and in my rhyme.

> 头韵（alliteration），头韵指的是两个及以上连续的单词的初始辅音相同，带来一种发音的重复感

> rage: n. praises or hyperbole 夸张的描写

> stretchèd: a. overwrought 过于复杂的

译文1（曹明伦版）

在未来之日谁会相信我的诗文，	Who will believe my verse in time to come
即使通篇都是对你优点的赞歌？	If it were filled with your most high deserts?
唯有上天还知道它是一座坟茔，	Though yet, heaven knows, it is but as a tomb
埋着你的生命，难显你的本色。	Which hides your life and shows not half your parts.
纵然我能够写出你眼睛之漂亮，	If I could write the beauty of your eyes
用清词丽句绘尽你的俊秀婵娟，	And in fresh numbers number all your graces,
将来的人也会说"这诗人撒谎；	The age to come would say, "This poet lies:
神笔天工绝不刻画凡夫的容颜。"	Such heavenly touches ne'er touched earthly faces."
于是我这些被岁月染黄的诗章	So should my papers, yellowed with their age,
会被当做聒絮的老叟遭人嘲笑，	Be scorned, like old men of less truth than tongue,

你应得之赞美则成诗人的狂想，

被说成是一首夸张的古老歌谣：

　但如果那时你有个孩子活在凡尘，

　你将在他身上和我诗里双重永生。

And your true rights be termed a poet's rage

And stretchèd meter of an antique song.

　But were some child of yours alive that time,

　You should live twice—in it and in my rhyme.

译文2（屠岸版）

SONNET 18

Shall I compare thee to a summer's day?
Thou art more lovely and more temperate.
Rough winds do shake the darling buds of May,
And summer's lease hath all too short a date.
Sometime too hot the eye of heaven shines
And often is his gold complexion dimmed,
And every fair from fair sometime declines,
By chance or nature's changing course untrimmed.
But thy eternal summer shall not fade
Nor lose possession of that fair thou ow'st,
Nor shall Death brag thou wand'erst in his shade,
When in eternal lines to time thou grow'st.
　So long as men can breathe or eyes can see,
　So long lives this and this gives life to thee.

summer: 英国由于其地理位置偏北，所以夏季相对气候宜人，明媚动人，是英国四季中最美好的季节

暗喻（metaphor），又叫隐喻，在英文中指的是在不使用"like"或"as"等词的情况下，直接比较两个看似不同的事物

lease: n. fixed span of time 短暂一段时期内的拥有

指代太阳

his: 即为 its

头韵

All beautiful things will lose their beauty at some point.

untrimmed: a. rendered ordinary 变为普通的

possession: n. the state of having, owning or controlling something. 依法拥有的财产，这里是与前文的 lease 相对

ow'st: v. own 拥有

the beauty you own

这里的 So long 及下一句的 So long 构成重复（repetition）

this: 指代这首十四行诗

译文1（辜正坤版）

或许我可用夏日把你来比方，	Shall I compare thee to a summer's day?
但你比夏日更可爱也更温良。	Thou art more lovely and more temperate.
夏风狂作常摧落五月的娇蕊，	Rough winds do shake the darling buds of May,
夏季的期限也未免还不太长。	And summer's lease hath all too short a date.
有时天眼如炬人间酷热难当，	Sometime too hot the eye of heaven shines
但转瞬金面如晦，云遮雾障。	And often is his gold complexion dimmed,
每一种美都终究会凋残零落，	And every fair from fair sometime declines,
难免见弃于机缘与天道无常。	By chance or nature's changing course untrimmed.
但你永恒的夏季却不会终止，	But thy eternal summer shall not fade
你优美的形象也永不会消亡，	Nor lose possession of that fair thou ow'st,
死神难夸口说你身陷其罗网，	Nor shall Death brag thou wand'erst in his shade,
只因你借我诗行可长寿无疆。	When in eternal lines to time thou grow'st.
只要人眼能看，人口能呼吸，	So long as men can breathe or eyes can see,
我诗必长存，使你万世流芳。	So long lives this and this gives life to thee.

译文2（曹明伦版）

SONNET 66

Tired with all these, for restful death I cry,

As, to behold desert a beggar born,

And needy nothing trimmed in jollity,

And purest faith unhappily forsworn,

And gilded honor shamefully misplaced,

And maiden virtue rudely strumpeted,

And right perfection wrongfully disgraced,

And strength by limping sway disablèd,

And art made tongue-tied by authority,

And folly (doctor-like) controlling skill,

And simple truth miscalled simplicity,

And captive good attending captain ill.

    Tired with all these, from these would I be gone,

    Save that to die I leave my love alone.

merit born in poverty 优秀的人生于贫困

在这首十四行诗中，莎士比亚大量运用了首语重复（anaphora）这种手法，在英语中，首语重复指的是在连续的句子或短语的开头重复使用一个单词或短语，目的是强调想表达的内容或感情

worthlessness adorned with finery 无才之人被华丽的服饰所修饰

forsworn：v. swear falsely 背叛

the most solemn oaths broken 最庄严的誓言被破坏

crudely prostituted 被迫卖淫

feeble leaders 虚弱的领导者

learning silienced a. 被迫沉默的

doctor-like：a. folly, feigning erudition, dominating true wisdom or ability 假装博学的

simplicity：n. stupidity 愚蠢

to：were I to 的省略形式

译文 1（屠岸版）

对这些都倦了，我召唤安息的死亡，——	Tired with all these, for restful death I cry,
譬如，见到天才注定了做乞丐， 见到草包穿戴得富丽堂皇，	As, to behold desert a beggar born, And needy nothing trimmed in jollity,
见到纯洁的盟誓遭恶意破坏，	And purest faith unhappily forsworn,
见到荣誉被可耻地放错了位置，	And gilded honor shamefully misplaced,

见到暴徒糟蹋了贞洁的处子，	And maiden virtue rudely strumpeted,
见到不义玷辱了至高的正义，	And right perfection wrongfully disgraced,
见到瘸腿的权贵残害了壮士，	And strength by limping sway disablèd,
见到文化被当局封住了嘴巴，	And art made tongue-tied by authority,
见到愚蠢（像博士）控制着聪慧，	And folly (doctor-like) controlling skill,
见到单纯的真理被瞎称作呆傻，	And simple truth miscalled simplicity,
见到善被俘去给罪恶将军当侍卫，	And captive good attending captain ill.
对这些都倦了，我要离开这人间，	Tired with all these, from these would I be gone,
只是，我死了，要使我爱人孤单。	Save that to die I leave my love alone.

译文2（辜正坤版）

SONNET 99

The forward violet thus did I chide:

"Sweet thief, whence didst thou steal thy sweet that smells

If not from my love's breath? The purple pride

Which on thy soft cheek for complexion dwells

In my love's veins thou hast too grossly dyed."

> forward: a. early 提早开花的
>
> sweet: n. fragrance, perfume 香味，芬芳
>
> the purple color you are so proud of 你引以为傲的紫色
>
> grossly: adv. obviously 明显地

The lily I condemnèd for thy hand, ——————— blamed for stealing the whiteness of your hand 责备它偷取了你秀手的洁白

And buds of marjoram had stol'n thy hair.

The roses fearfully on thorns did stand, ——————— grew on thorny stems 生长在带刺的花茎上

One blushing shame, another white despair; ——————— 指第三朵玫瑰是粉色的

A third, nor red nor white, had stol'n of both, ——————— to: prep. in addition to 另外

And to his robb'ry had annexed thy breath, ——————— added the crime of stealing your breath for his perfume 还增加了从你的呼吸中偷取芬芳的罪行

But for his theft in pride of all his growth ——————— in punishment for 为了某事而惩罚

A vengeful canker ate him up to death. ——————— the glory of its prime 在它拥有最繁盛的美好时

    More flowers I noted, yet I none could see,

But sweet or color it had stol'n from thee. ——————— that had not stolen its scent or color from you 没有一朵不是从你那里窃取了香味或颜色

译文1（梁宗岱版）

我对孟浪的紫罗兰这样谴责：	The forward violet thus did I chide:
"温柔贼，你哪里偷来这缕温馨，	"Sweet thief, whence didst thou steal thy sweet that smells
若不是从我爱的呼息？ 这紫色	If not from my love's breath? The purple pride
在你的柔颊上抹了一层红晕，	Which on thy soft cheek for complexion dwells
还不是从我爱的血管里染得？"	In my love's veins thou hast too grossly dyed."
我申斥百合花盗用了你的手， 茉沃兰的蓓蕾偷取你的柔发；	The lily I condemnèd for thy hand, And buds of marjoram had stol'n thy hair.
站在刺上的玫瑰花吓得直抖，	The roses fearfully on thorns did stand,
一朵羞得通红，一朵绝望到发白，	One blushing shame, another white despair;

另一朵，不红不白，从双方偷来；

还在赃物上添上了你的呼息，

但既犯了盗窃，当它正昂头盛开，

一条怒冲冲的毛虫把它咬死。

　　我还看见许多花，但没有一朵

不从你那里偷取芬芳和婀娜。

A third, nor red nor white, had stol'n of both,

And to his robb'ry had annexed thy breath,

But for his theft in pride of all his growth

A vengeful canker ate him up to death.

　　More flowers I noted, yet I none could see,

　　But sweet or color it had stol'n from thee.

译文 2（曹明伦版）

SONNET 130

My mistress' eyes are nothing like the sun；
Coral is far more red than her lips' red；
If snow be white, why then her breasts are dun；
If hairs be wires, black wires grow on her head.
I have seen roses damasked, red and white,
But no such roses see I in her cheeks；
And in some perfumes is there more delight
Than in the breath that from my mistress reeks.
I love to hear her speak, yet well I know
That music hath a far more pleasing sound.
I grant I never saw a goddess go；
My mistress when she walks treads on the ground.

传统的情诗中，将眼睛比喻为太阳十分常见，诗人后续也反向运用了一些在传统情诗中常见的比喻用来讽刺之前的十四行诗歌颂爱情的陈词滥调

dun：a. grayish brown 暗褐色的

伊丽莎白一世时期的诗人经常在诗作中将女性的秀发比作金线

damasked：a. dappled 有花色的

这里的 such, roses, see, cheeks 使用了辅音韵（consonance）。英文当中辅音韵指的是在一行文本中重复相同的辅音。在使用辅音韵时，重点是辅音发出的声音，而不一定是字母本身。此外，相似的辅音可以出现在单词的开头、中间或结尾，作者可以安排这些辅音押韵的单词连续出现，以强化艺术语言来吸引读者

And yet, by heaven, I think my love as rare
As any she belied with **false compare**.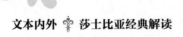

woman misrepresented by untrue comparisons 假意奉承

译文 1（辜正坤版）

我情人的眼睛一点不像太阳，

即便珊瑚也远比其朱唇红亮，

雪若算白，她胸膛褐色苍苍，

若美发如金，她满头黑丝长。

曾见过似锦玫瑰，红白相间，

却见不到她脸上有这样晕光；

有若干种香味叫人闻之欲醉，

我情人口里却吐不出这芬芳。

我喜欢聆听她声音，我明白

悦耳音乐比她的更甜美铿锵。

我承认从没有见过仙女步态，
反正我爱人只能在地上徜徉。

老天在上，所谓美女盖世无双，

My mistress' eyes are nothing like the sun;

Coral is far more red than her lips' red;

If snow be white, why then her breasts are dun;

If hairs be wires, black wires grow on her head.

I have seen roses damasked, red and white,

But no such roses see I in her cheeks;

And in some perfumes is there more delight

Than in the breath that from my mistress reeks.

I love to hear her speak, yet well I know

That music hath a far more pleasing sound.

I grant I never saw a goddess go;
My mistress when she walks treads on the ground.

　And yet, by heaven, I think my love as rare

与我爱人相比,至多旗鼓相当。   As any she belied with false compare.

译文2（曹明伦版）

Activities

1. Shakespeare and Today

Direction: 2016 marked the 400th anniversary of William Shakespeare's Death and people around the world held a series of commemorative activities, including seminars, reciting, performances, celebration parades, etc. The following sonnet titled "Lines Composed on April 23, 2016, on the 400th Anniversary of His Death", was written by the poet Wilude Scabere on April 23, 2016, playing against Shakespeare's Sonnet 18. What do you think about this modern sonnet? Do you think it is a good example of how contemporary poems drawing on earlier traditions? Why or why not?

Shall I compare his language to a grave?

It is more lively and more flowery.

His rough-shook words refuse to be death's slave.

No tomb's as showy or so showery.

A sepulchre, though hard as rock, erodes,

and shrines do often lose their lustre's prime,

while monuments, though nice, make poor abodes,

and sadly catacombs decay in time.

But Shakespeare's language will not go away.

Unceasingly, his lines play in the mind.

They pop up even on a summer's day.

Unlike a crypt, they will not stay behind.

Alas, poor Oracle, his song goes on,

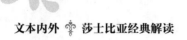

despite all efforts of oblivion.

2. Shakespeare and China

Direction: A number of great translators have translated Shakespeare's sonnets into different versions. However, poetry translation has always been one of the most difficult practices in literary translation. Choose one of the selected sonnets from above to comment on the merits of each Chinese version, and try to identify certain techniques in poetry translation.

3. Shakespeare and Beyond

Direction: Love is the eternal theme in Shakespeare's sonnets. Do you think poetry is the ideal vehicle for love? Have you ever written a love poem? Do you have a favorite love poem or any other form of expression to convey love?

Further Reading

BOADEN J, ABRAHAM W, 2013. Portraits of Shakespeare, and on the sonnets of Shakespeare [M]. Cambridge: Cambridge University Press.

KINGSLEY-SMITH J, 2023. Shakespeare's global sonnets: translation, appropriation, performance [M]. Cham: Springer International AG.

SMITH B R, 2010. Phenomenal Shakespeare [M]. Chichester, U.K.: John Wiley & Sons.

VENDLER H H, 1997. The art of Shakespeare's sonnets [M]. Cambridge, Mass.: Belknap of Harvard UP.

WILDE O, 1905. The portrait of Mr. W.H.: a problem of the Shakespeare sonnets [M]. Connecticut: Literary Collector.

Unit 3 Sonnets by Meter

章节概述

从结构上来说，莎士比亚的绝大多数十四行诗采用了抑扬五步格（iambic pentameter）的格律及 abab cdcd efef gg 的押韵方式，但也有几首例外。例如，第 145 首的格律为抑扬四步格（iambic tetrameter）；第 99 首包含十五行而不是十四行诗句，押韵方式为 ababa cdcd eeee ff；第 126 首则只有十二行诗句，押韵方式为 aabb ccdd eeff。那什么是抑扬五步格呢？为什么莎士比亚会选择抑扬五步格这种格律呢？

抑扬五步格,是一种常用于传统英文诗歌和诗剧中的格律。中文诗歌中，构成一行诗的最小单位为汉字，而在英文诗歌中，构成一行诗的最小单位却不是单词，而是音步（foot）。一个音步由两个或三个甚至更多的音节（syllable）组成，这些音节可以是轻音节（unstressed syllable）或重音节(stressed syllable)，按照一定的规律排布，构成不同种类的音步。例如，当一个音步由一个轻音节和一个重音节构成时，重音在后为抑扬格（iamb），重音在前则为扬抑格（trochee）；当一个音步由两个轻音节和一个重音节构成时，当重音在前时为扬抑抑格（dactyl），重音在后为抑抑扬格（anapest）。通常一行诗的音步类型相同，所以当一行诗句中有几个这样的音步，便称为几步诗。常见的英文诗歌有四步诗（tetrameter）、五步诗（pentameter）、八步诗（octameter）等。抑扬五步格便指的是一行诗句中含有五个由抑扬格构成的音步。抑扬五步格由乔叟（Geoffrey Chaucer）于 14 世纪率先引入英语，是英语诗歌中最常见的格律，常用于无韵诗（blank verse）、英雄双韵体（heroic couplet）等押韵诗节中。除了莎士比亚在十四行诗及戏剧中大量使用抑扬五步格，弥尔顿的《失乐园》（*Paradise Lost*）及威廉·华兹华斯（William Wordsworth）的《序曲》（*The Prelude*）等其他诗歌作品

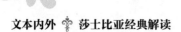
也使用了这种格律。如果用x表示轻音节，/表示重音节，那么抑扬五步格就可以在诗句中这样来区分：

So long as men can breathe, or eyes can see,

x / x / x / x /   x /

So long lives this, and this gives life to thee.

x / x / x / x / x /

—Sonnet 18 by William Shakespeare

那么为何莎士比亚会选择大量使用抑扬五步格呢？英语中有大量的单词，其发音都是一轻一重，如 adore, excite, above, around, appear, besides, attack, supply, believe, return 等，所以用英语写诗，采用抑扬格就显得十分便利。对于剧作家而言，使用抑扬格可以让角色在表演中模仿人们日常讲话的节奏，使文本和对话显得生动自然，不那么僵硬。同时，抑扬五步格有一种悦耳的基本节奏，非常类似心跳的声音 da DUM da DUM da DUM da DUM da DUM，听来抑扬顿挫，读之朗朗上口。所以莎士比亚不仅在他的十四行诗中使用了抑扬五步格，他在戏剧中也经常运用这种格律来撰写台词。

莎士比亚的诗作除了收录在1609年出版的四开本中的154首十四行诗，还包括三首长篇叙事诗，即《维纳斯与阿多尼》（*Venus and Adonis*）、《鲁克丽丝受辱记》（*The Rape of Lucrece*）和《恋女的怨诉》（*A Lover's Complaint*）以及一首寓言诗《凤凰与斑鸠》（*The Phoenix and the Turtle*）。其中，《维纳斯与阿多尼》由199个六行诗诗节构成，采用抑扬五步格，押韵方式为ababcc；《鲁克丽丝受辱记》由265个七行诗诗节构成，采用抑扬五步格，押韵方式为ababbcc；《恋女的怨诉》由47个七行诗诗节构成，采用抑扬五步格，押韵方式为ababbcc；《凤凰与斑鸠》由13个四行诗诗节及5个三行诗诗节构成，采用扬抑四步格（trochaic tetrameter），四行诗诗节的押韵方式为abbc，三行诗诗节的押韵方式为aaa。除此之外，在戏剧《罗密欧与朱丽叶》（*Romeo and Juliet*）、《亨利五世》（*Henry V*）和《爱的徒劳》（*Love's Labour's Lost*）

中，莎士比亚也采用了十四行诗的创作方式。

在伊丽莎白一世时期，虽然十四行诗的创作在结构、主题和表达上多有限制，但莎士比亚仍能通过鲜活的语言、简单的文字为我们呈现出即时、复杂的人类情感，从不同的切入点向读者传递出人文主义情怀以及对真善美的追求，这可能也就是为什么莎士比亚被后人称为"不朽的吟游诗人"的原因。

Selected Reading

SONNET 116

Let me not to the marriage of true minds

Admit impediments. Love is not love

Which alters when it alteration finds

Or bends with the remover to remove.

Oh no, it is an ever-fixèd mark,

That looks on tempests and is never shaken;

It is the star to every wand'ring bark,

Whose worth's unknown, although his height be taken.

Love's not Time's fool, though rosy lips and cheeks

Within his bending sickle's compass come;

Love alters not with his brief hours and weeks,

But bears it out even to the edge of doom.

    If this be error and upon me proved,

    I never writ, nor no man ever loved.

> echos the words of the marriage service in the *Book of Common Prayer*, where the couple and the congregation are asked to declare if they know of any impediment to the marriage. 指法律规定的阻碍婚姻的条件

> is inclined to cease if abandoned by the object of love or to be unfaithful in response to infidelity from the object of love. 因一方放弃、改变或背叛这份爱而改变

> an unmoving sea mark, such as a lighthouse or a beacon that provides constant reference point for the sailors. 指海上位置不变的灯塔

> 指北极星

> value cannot be fully known or measured 灯塔的价值不可被完全估量

> 这里使用了元音韵（assonance），在英文诗歌中元音韵指的是一行诗句中有两个及以上的单词中元音发音相似或相同

> height above the horizon can be scientifically measured 但灯塔的高度可以被计算出来

> fool: n. plaything 玩物

> its

> I am proved to have committed it 证明我犯了错

79

译文1（梁宗岱版）

我绝不承认两颗真心的结合	Let me not to the marriage of true minds
会有任何障碍；爱算不得真爱，	Admit impediments. Love is not love
若是一看见人家改变便转舵，	Which alters when it alteration finds
或者一看见人家转弯便离开。	Or bends with the remover to remove.
哦，决不！爱是亘古长明的塔灯，	Oh no, it is an ever-fixèd mark,
它定睛望着风暴却兀不为动；	That looks on tempests and is never shaken;
爱又是指引迷舟的一颗恒星，	It is the star to every wand'ring bark,
你可量它多高，它所值却无穷。	Whose worth's unknown, although his height be taken.
爱不受时光的播弄，尽管红颜	Love's not Time's fool, though rosy lips and cheeks
和皓齿难免遭受时光的毒手；	Within his bending sickle's compass come;
爱并不因瞬息的改变而改变，	Love alters not with his brief hours and weeks,
它巍然矗立直到末日的尽头。	But bears it out even to the edge of doom.
我这话若说错，并被证明不确，	If this be error and upon me proved,
就算我没写诗，也没人真爱过。	I never writ, nor no man ever loved.

译文2（辜正坤版）

SONNET 64

When I have seen by Time's fell hand defaced

The rich proud cost of outworn buried age,

When sometime lofty towers I see down razed,

And brass eternal slave to mortal rage;

When I have seen the hungry ocean gain

Advantage on the kingdom of the shore

And the firm soil win of the wat'ry main,

Increasing store with loss, and loss with store;

When I have seen such interchange of state,

Or state itself confounded to decay,

Ruin hath taught me thus to ruminate

That Time will come and take my love away.

   This thought is as a death, which cannot choose

   But weep to have that which it fears to lose.

When I have 为首语重复	
fell：a. fierce 猛烈的，破坏性大的	
splendid extravagance 富丽堂皇	
sometime：adv. once 曾经	
razed to the ground 夷为平地	
seen as the most durable substances 被视为最耐久的物质	
death's destructive fury or frenzy 死亡毁灭性的狂怒	
main：n. ocean 大海	
each side alternately winning and losing, each loss being the other side's gain 沧海桑田	
overthrown and ruined 变为废墟	

译文 1（梁宗岱版）

当我眼见前代的富丽和豪华	When I have seen by Time's fell hand defaced
被时光的手毫不留情地磨灭；	The rich proud cost of outworn buried age,
当巍峨的塔我眼见沦为碎瓦，	When sometime lofty towers I see down razed,
连不朽的铜也不免一场浩劫；	And brass eternal slave to mortal rage;

当我眼见那欲壑难填的大海	When I have seen the hungry ocean gain
一步一步把岸上的疆土侵蚀,	Advantage on the kingdom of the shore
汪洋的水又渐渐被陆地覆盖,	And the firm soil win of the wat'ry main,
失既变成了得,得又变成了失;	Increasing store with loss, and loss with store;
当我看见这一切扰攘和废兴,	When I have seen such interchange of state,
或者连废兴一旦也化为乌有;	Or state itself confounded to decay,
毁灭便教我再三这样地反省:	Ruin hath taught me thus to ruminate
时光终要跑来把我的爱带走。	That Time will come and take my love away.
哦,多么致命的思想!它只能够	This thought is as a death, which cannot choose
哭着去把那刻刻怕失去的占有。	But weep to have that which it fears to lose.

译文2（曹明伦版）

SONNET 73

That time of year thou mayst in me behold

When yellow leaves, or none, or few do hang

Upon those boughs which shake against the cold,

Bare ruined choirs where late the sweet birds sang.

In me thou seest the twilight of such day

> the branches are compared to chancels(choirs), the parts of churches reserved for singers 树枝被比喻为教堂中专为唱诗班预留的高坛

> late: adv. recently 最近

As after sunset fadeth in the west,

Which by and by black night doth take away,

Death's second self, that seals up all in rest.

In me thou seest the glowing of such fire

That on the ashes of his youth doth lie,

As the deathbed whereon it must expire,

Consumed with that which it was nourished by.

　　This thou perceiv'st, which makes thy love more strong,

　　To love that well which thou must leave ere long.

> 莎士比亚在这首十四行诗中使用了象征（symbolism）这种手法，用 sunset fadeth 及 black night 象征死亡或终结

> 指黑夜

> seals people up in sleep as if in a coffin 人们沉睡在梦中就像沉睡在死亡中一样

> the fire is smothered by the ashes of the substance on which it fed 火焰最终被助其燃烧的灰烬所熄灭

> 可以指诗人或生命或青春

> leave：v. lose 失去

译文1（屠岸版）

你从我身上能看到这个时令：	That time of year thou mayst in me behold
黄叶落光了,或者还剩下几片	When yellow leaves, or none, or few do hang
没脱离那乱打冷颤的一簇簇枝梗——	Upon those boughs which shake against the cold,
不再有好鸟歌唱的荒凉唱诗坛。	Bare ruined choirs where late the sweet birds sang.
你从我身上能看到这样的黄昏：	In me thou seest the twilight of such day
落日的回光沉入了西方的天际,	As after sunset fadeth in the west,
死神的化身——黑夜,慢慢地临近,	Which by and by black night doth take away,
挤走夕辉,把一切封进了安息。	Death's second self, that seals up all in rest.

你从我身上能看到这种火焰：

它躺在自己青春的余烬上燃烧，

像躺在临终的床上，一息奄奄，

跟供它养料的燃料一同毁灭掉。

　　看出了这个，你的爱会更加坚贞，

　　好好地爱着你快要失去的爱人！

In me thou seest the glowing of such fire

That on the ashes of his youth doth lie,

As the deathbed whereon it must expire,

Consumed with that which it was nourished by.

　　This thou perceiv'st, which makes thy love more strong,

　　To love that well which thou must leave ere long.

译文2（梁宗岱版）

SONNET 20

A woman's face with Nature's own hand painted

> created by Nature herself 由自然创造

Hast thou, the master-mistress of my passion;

> 本诗虽描绘的是一位男性，但是其美貌与风采却征服了男女两性

A woman's gentle heart, but not acquainted

With shifting change, as is false women's fashion;

> 跨行连续

An eye more bright than theirs, less false in rolling,

> rolling: v. wondering 眼光漫不经心地移动

> hue: n. attractive appearance 美丽的外表

Gilding the object whereupon it gazeth;

A man in hue, all hues in his controlling,

> one with the form of a man, but whose facial beauty has the power to enthral both men and women 虽然性别为男，但容颜所具有的双性之美足以迷住所有男女

Which steals men's eyes and women's souls amazeth.

And for a woman wert thou first created,

> as; to be

Till Nature as she wrought thee fell a-doting,

> a-doting: a. behaved foolishly 变得入迷的

And by addition me of thee defeated————— deprived me of you 使我失去你

By adding one thing to my purpose nothing.——— irrelevant to my purposes 和我的目的无关

    But since she pricked thee out for women's pleasure, —— pricked：v. choose 选择

    Mine be thy love and thy love's use their treasure.————— let me have your love in heart and women can have sexual relations with you 让我拥有你的心灵之爱而女人们可以享受你的肉体之美

译文1（曹明伦版）

你有大自然亲手妆扮的女性的脸，	A woman's face with Nature's own hand painted
你哟,我苦思苦恋的情郎兼情妇；	Hast thou, the master-mistress of my passion;
你有女性的柔情,但却没有沾染	A woman's gentle heart, but not acquainted
时髦女人的水性杨花和朝秦暮楚；	With shifting change, as is false women's fashion;
你眼睛比她们的明亮,但不轻佻,	An eye more bright than theirs, less false in rolling,
不会把所见之物都镀上一层黄金；	Gilding the object whereupon it gazeth;
你集美于一身,令娇娃玉郎拜倒,	A man in hue, all hues in his controlling,
勾住了男人的眼也惊了女儿的心,	Which steals men's eyes and women's souls amazeth.
大自然开始本想造你为红颜姝丽,	And for a woman wert thou first created,
但塑造之中她却为你而堕入情网,	Till Nature as she wrought thee fell a-doting,

心醉神迷之间她剥夺了我的权利，把一件对我无用的东西加你身上。

但既然她为女人的欢愉把你塑成，

就把心之爱给我，肉体爱归她们。

And by addition me of thee defeated

By adding one thing to my purpose nothing.

But since she pricked thee out for women's pleasure,

Mine be thy love and thy love's use their treasure.

译文2（梁宗岱版）

SONNET 144

Two loves I have, of comfort and despair,

Which like two spirits do suggest me still:

The better angel is a man right fair,

The worser spirit a woman colored ill.

To win me soon to hell my female evil

Tempteth my better angel from my side,

And would corrupt my saint to be a devil,

Wooing his purity with her foul pride.

And whether that my angel be turned fiend

Suspect I may, but not directly tell;

But being both from me, both to each friend,

I guess one angel in another's hell.

　　Yet this shall I ne'er know, but live in doubt,

　　Till my bad angel fire my good one out.

loves：n. lovers 爱人

明喻

suggest：v. entice 引诱

still：adv. constantly 经常地，不断地

fair：a. light, arractive, beautiful 美丽的，白皙的，道德高尚的

ill：a. dark, ugly, unattractive 深肤色的，丑陋的，毫无魅力的

unpleasant vanity 丑陋的虚荣

away from me 离我而去

drive him out 将他赶走

译文 1（梁宗岱版）

两个爱人像精灵般把我诱惑，	Two loves I have, of comfort and despair,
一个叫安慰，另外一个叫绝望：	Which like two spirits do suggest me still:
善的天使是个男子，丰姿绰约；	The better angel is a man right fair,
恶的幽灵是个女人，其貌不扬。	The worser spirit a woman colored ill.
为了促使我早进地狱，那女鬼	To win me soon to hell my female evil
引诱我的善精灵硬把我抛开，	Tempteth my better angel from my side,
还要把他迷惑，使沦落为妖魅，	And would corrupt my saint to be a devil,
用肮脏的骄傲追求纯洁的爱。	Wooing his purity with her foul pride.
我的天使是否已变成了恶魔，	And whether that my angel be turned fiend
我无法一下子确定，只能猜疑；	Suspect I may, but not directly tell;
但两个都把我扔下，互相结合，	But being both from me, both to each friend,
一个想必进了另一个的地狱。	I guess one angel in another's hell.
可是这一点我永远无法猜透，	Yet this shall I ne'er know, but live in doubt,
除非是恶的天使把善的撵走。	Till my bad angel fire my good one out.

译文 2（曹明伦版）

Activities

1. Shakespeare and Today

Direction: Rap is defined as rapid singing and speaking that uses rhyme, slang language, and musical, usually electronic, accompaniment. Poetry is commonly defined as writing or spoken words that express feelings and ideas, sometimes using rhyme and rhythm. Although they have different subject matter, rap and poetry are capable of speaking on the same subjects. For example, songs like "Heartless" by Kanye West and "Nothing Lasts Forever" by J. Cole discuss heartbreak. So too do poems like "Never Give All the Heart" by W. B. Yeats and "I Am Not Yours" by Sara Teasdale. Although rap and poetry have different forms, they both use verses, refrains, rhyming words, rhythm, and meter. Although rap and poetry use different types of language, some poems use complex language while others are far simpler. The same can be said for rap. However, there is a difference in the percentage of jargon and slang language used in rap versus poetry. Find a rap song that you like and compare it with one of Shakespeare's sonnets to see the similarities and differences.

2. Shakespeare and China

Direction: Imagery is probably one of the most frequently used literary devices not only in Shakespeare's sonnets, but also in Chinese poems. Based on your previous knowledge of Chinese poetry, can you give a few examples of imagery in Chinese poems?

3. Shakespeare and Beyond

Direction: Suppose you are a novice sonneteer and just begin to practice sonnet writing, Shakespearean sonnet is probably a good start, because of its most regular and straightforward rhyme scheme and structure. Now, choose a subject matter, whether it is love, frustration or hatred, remember the structure of three quatrains plus a couplet, the iambic pentameter as well as the rhyming scheme of abab cdcd efef gg, grab your pen, and try to compose your first Shakespearean sonnet.

Further Reading

CALLAGHAN D, 2007. Shakespeare's sonnets ［M］. Blackwell Introductions to Literature. Somerset: Blackwell.

KINGSLEY-SMITH J, 2019. The afterlife of Shakespeare's sonnets ［M］. New York, NY: Cambridge University Press.

晋学军, 徐悦, 2016. 律诗律译:以莎士比亚十四行诗为例 ［M］. 武汉: 武汉大学出版社.

龙娟, 2020. 情伴歌咏, 爱随诗吟:中西经典爱情诗歌的比较与探索 ［M］. 成都: 四川大学出版社.

罗益民, 2016. 莎士比亚十四行诗版本批评史 ［M］. 北京: 科学出版社.

Part Three The Histories

Unit 1 History and History Plays

章节概述

　　如何定义历史是一个值得探究的问题。历史有着双重含义，其一是人类社会过去发生的事件，其二则是对过去发生事件的文字记录的研究与阐释。中文中的"历史"古称"史"。在甲骨文中"史"即"事"，指事件。而在许慎的《说文解字》中，历史已然具有了书写和以正视听的功能：史，"记事者也。从又持中；中，正也"①。英文中的"History"源自古希腊语：ἱστορία（Historia），原义为"调查、探究、知识"，同样显示出超越事件本身的叙事性。希罗多德的《历史》（*Historia*）便得名于此。

　　待到莎士比亚时代，历史书写逐渐成为一种潮流，重修历史几乎成为都铎王朝的一项国家工程，编年史的地位由此得以建立。1548 年，爱德华·霍尔（Edward Hall）依据波利多尔（Polydore Vergil）书中对理查二世至亨利八世的描写，编写出版了《兰开斯特与约克两大望族的联合》（*The Union of the Two Noble and Illustre Families of Lancastre and Yorke,* also known as *Hall's Chronicle*）。1577 年，拉斐尔·霍林谢德（Raphael Holinshed）出版了《英格兰、苏格兰和爱尔兰编年史》（*Chronicles of England, Scotlande and Irelande*）。层出不穷的编年史体现

---

① 许慎：《说文解字》，汤可敬译注，北京：中华书局，2018 年，第 623 页。

出了伊丽莎白时期英国对构建自身历史的热望。然而，真正让英国历史深入人心的并不是编年史，而是莎士比亚。

通过对旧有剧本、编年史、民间传说以及民谣的借用，莎士比亚以戏剧的形式重现了英国王朝的更迭。他对历史的创造性演绎不仅使自己一举成名，让英国历史家喻户晓，更是确立了历史剧作为新兴戏剧文体的地位。

事实上，莎士比亚之前并无真正的历史剧。文艺复兴时期流行的古典戏剧体系，以亚里士多德、贺拉斯理论为基础，主要由悲剧和喜剧构成。悲剧用深奥的诗句揭示出古代神与英雄的陨落。喜剧则通过幽默讽刺，将日常生活戏剧化。虽然在莎士比亚时期，受历史撰写热潮的影响，以历史为题材的戏剧并不少见，但历史剧作为概念提出却是源于莎士比亚。1623年，莎士比亚的作品第一次以对开本的形式出版发行，而历史剧也第一次与悲剧、喜剧比肩，作为独立剧种登台亮相。

第一对开本①收录了莎士比亚的37部剧，首次对莎剧进行了悲剧、喜剧、历史剧的具体分类。根据这一分类，莎士比亚的历史剧特指以英格兰王朝历史为背景的十部戏剧，包括《约翰王》《理查二世》《亨利四世（上）》《亨利四世（下）》《亨利五世》《亨利六世（上）》《亨利六世（中）》《亨利六世（下）》《理查三世》《亨利八世》。以苏格兰或古罗马为背景的历史题材剧如《麦克白》《尤利乌斯·凯撒》《安东尼和克莉奥佩特拉》《科里奥拉努斯》等则不在此列。甚至以凯尔特时期古不列颠国王为原型的《李尔王》也被排除在外。

莎士比亚的历史剧延续了都铎神话的书写模式，采用奇迹剧、道德剧等传统教化戏剧惯用的"分幕结构"（episodic structure），强化了从中世纪的传奇英雄亚瑟王至亨利七世的神话谱系关系。通过两个四联剧外加穿插的形式，莎士比亚的历史剧演绎出一部横跨金雀花王朝、兰开斯特王朝、约克王朝、都铎王朝，历经堕落、中兴、分裂，而最终被都

---

① 莎士比亚的许多剧本在他生前都未正式出版，1623年，他的同事将所能找到的剧本结集出版，取名为《威廉·莎士比亚先生的喜剧、历史剧和悲剧》（*Mr. William Shakespeare's Comedies, Histories, & Tragedies*），内含36部剧本，其中18部是首次出版。由于此全集是以对开本的形式印制，因此西方通称第一版为"第一对开本"（the First Folio），这也是目前学界最为认可的一个版本。

铎明君拯救的神话史诗。莎士比亚首先在第一四联剧（《亨利六世（上、中、下）》和《理查三世》）中讲述了英国王朝历史的后半部分，然后通过第二四联剧（《理查二世》、《亨利四世（上、下）》和《亨利五世》）追叙了历史的前半部分，最后以《亨利八世》的盛世预言为整个历史剧系列画上了完美的句号。

莎士比亚的创作生涯以历史剧《亨利六世》开始，以历史剧《亨利八世》结束。历史剧由此构成了莎士比亚作品的重要组成部分，也塑造了大众对英国王朝历史的基本认知。时至今日，从《空王冠》《白王后》《理查二世》等一系列影视剧的风靡中，我们仍不难窥见莎士比亚历史剧深远的影响。与此同时，莎

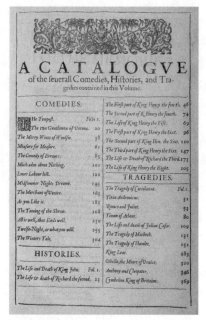

Mr. William Shakespeare's Comedies, Histories & Tragedies produced in 1623 (also known as The First Folio) is the first published collection of Shakespeare's plays. It groups his plays into categories for the first time. https://www.bl.uk/collection-items/shakespeares-first-folio（image credit: British Library）

士比亚的历史剧也推动了历史观的改变。莎士比亚不仅以人文主义挑战了传统的神造历史观，也为后世探索历史及书写历史提供了另类的教材和启迪。

莎士比亚的过去没有过去，莎士比亚的历史剧也没有成为历史。时光或可湮没一切，也能留存永恒，一如他在诗中所写：

> 毁灭性的战争会把塑像掀翻，
> 兵燹会根除石筑的碑塔楼台，
> 可无论是战神的利剑或狼烟
> 都难毁这追忆你的生动记载。
> 面对死亡和忘却一切的恶意，

你将信步前行；对你的赞颂，

将永远闪烁在后世子孙眼里，

直到世界末日使一切都告终。

——《十四行诗第55首》[1]

Selected Reading

The Histories and History
Robert J. Watt[2]

When Shakespeare's First Folio（第一对开本）reached the bookstalls in 1623, it became the first collection printed in the prestigious folio format to feature plays exclusively from the commercial stages. It was also the first collection to construct and advertise history as a clearly defined dramatic genre. The Folio divides its plays into three theatrical genres, which are indicated by the 'Catalogue' and also by the title of the collection—*Master William Shakespeare's Comedies, Histories, and Tragedies.* The Folio selectively collects plays of English kings as 'Histories', excluding the Scottish history of *Macbeth* and classical histories, such as *Julius Caesar*, and arranges them according to the historical order of English kings, rather than the order of composition. By doing so, the collection effectively publishes its own statement about the parameters of the genre: the history plays' proper subject is English monarchical history after the Conquest.

---

① 莎士比亚：《莎士比亚十四行诗全集》，曹明伦译，桂林：漓江出版社，1995年，第79页。

② Robert J. Watt is a distinguished Shakespearean scholar. The reading material is adapted from his introduction to *Shakespeare's History Plays*（Watt, R. J. C. *Shakespeare's History Plays*. New York: Routledge, 2002, pp. 1–17）. Meanwhile it also partly refers to *Publishing the History Play in the Time of Shakespeare* by Amy Lidster（Lidster, Amy. *Publishing the History Play in the Time of Shakespeare*. Cambridge: Cambridge University Press, 2022, pp. 7–8）.

Shakespeare's Histories

The Shakespeare's Histories tell of the country's history at a time when the English nation was struggling with its own sense of national identity and experiencing a new sense of power. Queen Elizabeth had brought stability and a relative freedom from war to her decades of rule. She had held at bay the Roman Catholic powers of the Continent, notably Philip Ⅱ of Spain, and fought off Philip's attempts to invade her kingdom with the great Spanish Armada（西班牙无敌舰队）of 1588. Chronicle history was popular at that time because it flattered the patriotic spirit of the English. When converted into dramatic form, chronicle history gave opportunities for striking action and enabled the playwrights to freely mingle the comic and the tragic. Shakespeare thus followed the theatrical fashions of the time.

Shakespeare's history plays composed mainly in 1590s consist 10 plays: *King John*, *Richard Ⅱ*, *Henry Ⅳ* (*Part Ⅰ*, *Part Ⅱ*), *Henry Ⅴ*, *Henry Ⅵ* (*Part Ⅰ*, *Part Ⅱ*, *Part Ⅲ*), *Richard Ⅲ*, and *Henry Ⅷ*. The plays could roughly be put into two tetralogies. The first tetralogy (*Henry Ⅵ* (*Part Ⅰ*, *Ⅱ*, *Ⅱ*); *Richard Ⅲ*) addresses the fall of the House of Lancaster at around 1422-1485. The second tetralogy (*Richard Ⅱ*, *Henry Ⅳ* (*Part Ⅰ*, *Part Ⅱ*), *Henry Ⅴ*) moves back in time to examine the rise of Lancastrians, covering English history from about 1398 to 1420. Altogether the histories represent what happened before Tudor Dynasty: the split of England during the Wars of the Roses and the eventual unification by Henry Tudor.

King John portrays an incredibly unpopular king who is systematically betrayed, abdicated and eventually killed. King John with the aid of his mother, has usurped the royal title of his nephew Arthur, the king of France. As a result, a war demanding that Arthur be placed on the throne breaks out which however turns out to be an exercise in futility on all sides. This first of the history plays is probably the least performed in modern times, although it was a favorite play of Victorian era England.

Richard Ⅱ follows with another bloody succession battle in the

Plantagenet dynasty. The previous monarch, Edward III, passed over his younger sons to bring his grandson Richard II to the throne, leaving Richard to a lifetime battle with his uncles and cousins.

Henry IV (*Part I*, *II*) is probably the best-known history play about Henry Era, which continues the battles of King Henry IV after his supplanting of Richard II on the throne and tells how his son Young Hal, a lazy drunkard at the beginning, finally renounces his former life and becomes King Henry V.

Henry V is a chronicle of the Battle of Agincourt, where a small English army overcame tremendous odds against a French force, and Henry's victory resulted in his marriage and alliance with France.

Henry VI (*Part I*, *II* and *III*) mainly treat the Wars of Roses between the houses of Lancaster and York. The sequent plays begin at the funeral of Henry V, as political fractions are forming around the boy king Henry VI. *Part I* covers the early part of King Henry's reign and ends with events immediately preceding the beginning of the civil war that dominates *Part II* and *III*. With the Henry VI trilogy (leading up to the devastating portrayal of evil in *Richard III*), Shakespeare analyzes the harrowing process by which England suffered through decades of civil war.

Richard III details the end of the Plantagenet reign and the rise of the Tudor Dynasty by painting Richard III as an unredeemable character overrun by flaws and ego. Having killed King Henry VI and the prince of Wales in *Henry VI*, Richard sets out to kill all who stand between him and the throne of England. However, Richard's claim to the throne is eventually challenged by an army led by Henry Tudor, earl of Richmond. After a desperate fight at the Battle of Bosworth, Richard is killed, and Richmond becomes King Henry VIII.

Henry VIII, the last of the history plays was first performed in 1613, and covers part of the reign of Elizabeth I's father, Henry VIII. The play ends with a final celebration and the prophecy of England's glory under the future

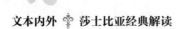

Queen Elizabeth Ⅰ. *Henry Ⅷ* is more notable for a tragic coincidence. At a performance at The Globe Theater in 1613, a cannon misfired, setting the roof of the stage ablaze and destroying the entire theater. Because of this, the play is often considered "cursed" by theater professionals.

Although some of the material of the history plays would have been common knowledge in Shakespeare's day, he is believed to have taken most of his information from Raphael Holinshed's *Chronicles of England, Scotland and Ireland and Edward Hall's Chronicle—The Union of the Two Noble and Illustre Families of Lancastre and Yorke*. The history plays are not considered to be completely historically accurate, as Shakespeare left out or added details, characters and motivations. Nevertheless, in a time of little wide-spread education, the history plays gave English citizens access to an action-packed version of their own history that remains popular in modern day.

Shakespeare and History

The term "history", of course, applied to both dramatic and non-dramatic texts. The *OED* outlines history as a sequence of past events—real or imaginary—such as those relating to the life of an individual, group of people, or nation; a branch of knowledge and enquiry into past events; and any account of such events[1]. "History" is, as David Scott Kastan describes, a "radically ambiguous" term that applies both to past events and to accounts of them[2]. It does not refer exclusively or self-evidently to those based on historical records or an accepted historical tradition, but also applies to entirely fictional events in a range of forms. The terms "history" and "story" were used interchangeably, and one of the dominant meanings of "story" during the period was a narrative of events that were believed to have taken

---

① See "history, n.", Oxford English Dictionary Online.

② Kastan, David Scott. *Shakespeare and the Shapes of Time*. Basingstoke: Palgrave Macmillan, 1982, p. 11.

place in the past, an application that further limits the precision and usefulness of these terms in isolation. For these reasons, understanding "history" is a process of understanding how certain people have preferred to use and treat it.

In the early stage of human civilization, it was assumed that God made history. That is, divine providence was held to foresee and plan all that occurred. That providential view was being overthrown in Shakespeare's time by the Machiavellian view that human beings, not God, are the agents of historical causation. The conflict between these two theories of history can be seen as underlying much of the excitement of the history plays. Yet in Shakespeare the issue is of further interest because the plays may be proposing just that it is people, not God, who make things happen.

In drama the relation between man and history centers on character and action. As Catherine Belsey puts it, "man is the origin and source of meaning, of action, and of history"[1]. Hence there is an acute issue for representations of action which are also versions of history.

In the nineteenth century, a character-based literary criticism and a "great man" theory of historical causation were closely allied. In the light of this view, which still survives residually, plays are important because they delineate character: character is Important because it gives rise to historical action. The close conjunction can be seen in Thomas Carlyle, principal exponent of the "great man" theory of history, who began his lectures "On Heroes and Hero-Worship" in 1840 with the claim that "Universal History... Is at bottom the History of... Great Men", and went on to assert that "it is in... Portrait-painting, delineating of men and things, especially of men, that Shakespeare is great."[2] Drama by its nature focuses on individuals, and drama about historic or heroic events may tend to glamorize them.

---

[1] Belsey, Catherine. *Critical Practice*. London: Methuen, 1980, p. 7.

[2] Carlyle, Thomas. *On Heroes, Hero-Worship, and the Heroic in History*. London: Chapman and Hall, 1872, pp. 1, 42, 97, 228. (Lecture 1, 5 May 1840 and Lecture 3, 12 May 1840)

Fortunately, however, drama also has some immunity from the crude view that history is simply the result of the doings of heroes, if only because drama invariably represents conflict among a plurality of characters.

The humanistic view of history was further developed in the 20th century. In 1944 E. M. W. Tillyard published his book *Shakespeare's History Plays*. In it he treats history as if it were an extended Morality play, "by which events evolve under a law of justice and of which Elizabeth's England was the acknowledged outcome." ① The course of history is equated with "nature's course". That course is distorted by a crime, Henry Bolingbroke's usurpation of Richard Ⅱ's throne, and the plays are seen as recounting a long struggle to restore the true course. Although the perfect king Henry Ⅴ, "by his politic wisdom and his piety postpones the day of reckoning", the curse imposed by the usurpation is then realized in the time of Henry Ⅵ in "the dreaded form of a child being king".② The final crisis and resolution come in Richard Ⅲ: with the removal of the monster Richard at the end of the play, "God had guided England into her haven of Tudor prosperity".③ This makes of history "a dramatic and philosophical sweep" and makes the plays an embodiment of the "Tudor myth" —the idea propagated by Henry Ⅶ that "the union of the two houses of York and Lancaster through marriage was the providential and happy ending of an organic piece of history".④

According to Tillyard, a human society should be organized to exhibit the order which characterizes the universe itself. Shakespeare's history plays therefore present disorder as an abhorrent departure from a natural state of order, which should be corrected or otherwise punished.

The problematizing of the concept of history itself is one feature that characterizes recent work and sets it apart from what went before. In

---

① Tillyard, E. M. W. *Shakespeare's History Plays*. Harmondsworth: Penguin, 1966, p. 325.

② Tillyard, E. M. W. *Shakespeare's History Plays*. Harmondsworth: Penguin, 1966, pp. 66–67.

③ Tillyard, E. M. W. *Shakespeare's History Plays*. Harmondsworth: Penguin, 1966, p. 210.

④ Tillyard, E. M. W. *Shakespeare's History Plays*. Harmondsworth: Penguin, 1966, pp. 65, 36.

consequence, "history" has been largely replaced by "histories" and "story" has ceased to be history's less authoritative cousin. Such developments place Shakespeare's histories at the center of one of the most interesting and important cultural shifts of our times.

While Tillyard saw the plays as reflecting the concerns of Shakespeare's contemporary world, a number of modern critics have chosen to see the plays instead as conscious acts of historiography, serious attempts to interpret the past, not merely about the 1590s in disguise.

From History to Historiography

If history can mean both what happened and what is written about what happened, the term historiography unambiguously refers to the latter: the writing of history, and the theories and assumptions with which history is written. In this sense, Shakespeare should be taken seriously as a historiographer.

In her book *Stages of History*, Rackin discusses the move away from a providential view of history and identifies "three great innovations, all originating in Italy" which "were changing English historiography during the second half of the sixteenth century—a new interest in causation, a recognition of anachronism, and a questioning of textual authority."[1] She claims that what happens in this period is the emergence of historiography itself—the beginning of an awareness that there is more than one way of writing any history, or as she says, "the recognition that history was not necessarily identical with historiography."[2]

This stress on Shakespeare as a fascinated theoretician of historical writing may or may not be wholly convincing, but it is certainly in contrast

---

[1] Rackin, Phillis. *Stages of History: Shakespeare's English Chronicles*. London: Routledge, 1991, p. 5.

[2] Rackin, Phillis. *Stages of History: Shakespeare's English Chronicles*. London: Routledge, 1991, p. 13.

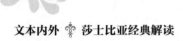

with another school of critics. For them, Shakespeare's history plays are not about history at all. Rather, the plays represent the social and political issues, and even particular events, of the years in which Shakespeare wrote them. Accounts of Shakespeare's part in performing Richard Ⅱ complete with its controversial deposition scene the night before the Earl of Essex's actual attempt to overthrow the Queen on 8 February 1601 can still make startling reading. Classic old-historicist studies in this mode, linking the plays to actual contemporary events, are now less favored than they once were. Instead there is a tendency to see the plays as not merely touching on specific events but representing key conflicts in Shakespeare's period.

Shakespeare's history plays, accounting for nearly one-third of his work as a dramatist, were written almost exclusively in and around the 1590s, the decade after the Spanish Armada, the later years of Queen Elizabeth's reign. That brief period produced around eighty popular plays on English historical subjects. Soon after 1600, the history play became virtually unwritable, hastening into obsolescence along with two other major Elizabethan genres, romantic comedy and Petrarchan poetry.

The reasons why the genre arose, flourished and disappeared are far from agreed. The old view that the upsurge in history plays was part of patriotic euphoria caused by the Armada is shaky. Why the young playwright would commemorate a great national victory with a penetrating and dispiriting analysis of how England lost her French possessions and collapsed into civil war is not clear. Such questions about the social origins of literary form are among the most interesting, and the hardest, faced by criticism. And there too is the possibility of interesting work to be done.

Although history plays fell out of favor in Shakespeare's own day, they have been of deep interest since, and never more so than in the last few decades. What Stephen Greenblatt eloquently says of our relationship to the Renaissance as a whole is also true of our period's relation to the history plays: we see in them

"...the shaping of crucial aspects of our sense of self and society and the natural world, but we have become uneasy about our whole way of constituting reality. Above all, perhaps, we sense that the culture to which we are as profoundly attached as our face is to our skull is nonetheless a construct, a thing made, as temporary, time conditioned, and contingent as those vast European empires from whose power Freud drew his image of repression. We sense too that we are situated at the close of the cultural movement initiated in the Renaissance and that the places in which our social and psychological world seems to be cracking apart are those structural joints visible when it was first constructed. In the midst of the anxieties and contradictions attendant upon the threatened collapse of this phase of our civilization, we respond with passionate curiosity and poignancy to the anxieties and contradictions attendant upon its rise."[1]

Shakespeare's history plays are for our times.

Activities

1. Shakespeare and Today

Direction: Have a discussion with your partners and answer the following questions:

1) *How do Shakespeare's history plays help reshape the concept of history?*

2) *What can Shakespeare's history plays tell us about the present?*

2. Shakespeare and China

Direction: Britain's Royal Shakespeare Company will embark on its first major tour of China, presenting the Bard's history plays in medieval England to a new and potentially vast audience. If you were the director of RSC,

---

[1] Greenblatt, Stephen. *Renaissance Self-Fashioning: From More to Shakespeare*. Chicago: University of Chicago Press, 1980, pp. 174–175.

which play would you choose for the debut and how would you publicize it so as to make it more appealing to Chinese audience?

3. Shakespeare and Beyond

Direction: Despite the difference in name, plot and context, Shakespeare's histories do have something in common. For instance, Shakespeare's histories mostly dramatize the Hundred Years' War between France and England and the War of the Roses, though not always in a historically accurate manner. Can you find some other common features? What are they?

Further Reading

GRENE N, 2007. Shakespeare's serial history plays [M]. Cambridge: Cambridge University Press.

HOLLAND P, 2015. Shakespeare survey 63: Shakespeare's English histories and their afterlives [M]. Cambridge: Cambridge University Press.

LIDSTER A, 2022. Publishing the history play in the time of Shakespeare [M]. Cambridge: Cambridge University Press.

RACKIN P, 1991. Stages of history: Shakespeare's English chronicles [M]. London: Routledge.

WATT R J, 2002. Shakespeare's history plays [M]. New York: Routledge.

Unit 2 Richard Ⅲ

章节概述

《理查三世》创作于1592—1594年，是莎士比亚第一对开本中最长的一部剧①，也是语言表达最为考究的一部剧，整部剧98%由诗韵体构成。尽管如此，《理查三世》仍是莎士比亚历史剧中最受欢迎的一部。

早在1623年第一对开本出版前，《理查三世》已有6个版本问世（1597, 1598, 1602, 1605, 1612, 1622），堪称伊丽莎白时期印刷次数最多的剧本之一。当然，《理查三世》也是演出场次最多的历史剧。自1594年首演以来，《理查三世》就从未淡出观众的视野。无论英国还是美国，但凡剧院开张，《理查三世》总是榜上有名。《理查三世》在美国尤其受到青睐，其公演次数远远超过其他莎剧。它的上演甚至戏剧性地改变了美国历史——美国总统林肯正是被扮演理查三世的演员约翰·布斯（John Wilkes Booth）刺杀身亡的。

时至今日《理查三世》仍以它独特的艺术魅力和文化价值吸引着无数的追随者。继劳伦斯·奥利弗（Laurence Olivier）以理查三世的角色斩获柏林国家电影节银熊奖后，包括伊恩·麦凯伦（Ian McKellen）和本尼迪克特·康伯巴奇（Benedict Cumberbatch）在内的多位世界知名演员，都以精湛的演技再现了理查三世的形象。英国广播公司于20世纪80年代、2012年和2016年先后拍摄过几个不同版本的莎士比亚英国历史剧系列，《理查三世》都是其中不可或缺的一部分。2015年，中国国家话剧院受邀前往英国伦敦莎士比亚环球剧院演出，同样将《理查三世》列为首选剧目。

《理查三世》的故事最早来源于托马斯·莫尔爵士（Sir Thomas

---

① 《哈姆雷特》通常被认为是莎士比亚戏剧中最长的一部剧，但第一对开本收录的《哈姆雷特》不同于之前的四开本，长度比《理查三世》略短。

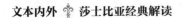

More）的《理查三世史》（*History of King Richard Ⅲ*,1513）。莫尔爵士在亨利八世时期曾担任宫廷文史官。他的记录被爱德华·霍尔和拉斐尔·霍林谢德收入编年史，也因此成为莎士比亚创作的主要素材。此外，历史组诗《治世通鉴》（*The Mirror for Magistrates*,1559）及无名剧作《理查三世的真实悲剧》（*The True Tragedie of Richard the Third*,1594）也在一定程度上为莎士比亚的情节设置提供了参考。

第一四联剧收尾之作《理查三世》，讲述了在玫瑰战争末期约克家族战胜兰开斯特家族，从亨利六世手中夺取王位后，理查如何在纷繁复杂的政治斗争中，以奸诈的权谋机断，扫除障碍，从哥哥爱德华四世手中篡夺王位，并最终在众叛亲离中走向毁灭的故事。

《理查三世》之所以备受瞩目，在于它塑造出了一个传世的"反英雄"形象。剧中的主人公理查三世是一个典型的马基雅维利主义者。攫取权力、掌控世界似乎是他唯一的人生目标。为了达到目的，他参与杀害了兰开斯特家族的亨利六世及其儿子。而后制造谣言离间哥哥爱德华四世与克莱伦斯。在克莱伦斯被暗杀，爱德华四世病逝后，他又伺机剪除王后党羽的势力，并将爱德华两个年幼的王子投入伦敦塔，秘密杀害。对于宫廷里的大臣，他同样毫不留情，稍有不从就大开杀戒，即便是心腹同谋最终也难逃厄运。对于理查三世而言，亲情、友情、爱情都不过是他通往权力道路的筹码。

在《理查三世》中，我们不难看到塞内加戏剧及伊丽莎白时代复仇剧、道德剧的影响。但与同时代剧作不同的是，《理查三世》并没有采用传统的平行结构，进行简单的善恶二元对立，而是将理查三世置于聚光灯下，以类似于蒙太奇的手法细致刻画出他的外在与内心世界。整部剧5幕25场中，理查出场的就有14场。其台词总数占到全剧的32%，是所有人物中台词最多的一个，仅长篇独白就有10段。其中，开篇第一幕第一场的独白尤为传神，可谓其可悲人生的极致缩影。通过对理查形象的凸显，莎士比亚摒弃了群像式的历史剧创作模式，第一次以"明星剧"的形式，将个人命运写进了历史的集体记忆。

与克里斯托弗·马洛（Christopher Marlowe）笔下的帖木儿（Tamburlaine）、巴拉巴斯（Barabas）等人物不同，莎士比亚的理查三世虽为反派，却被赋予了更为复杂的人性特点。在剧中，他可以是阴险的谋划者、能言善辩的演说家，也可以是正义的兄弟、深情的爱慕者、潜心问道的虔诚信徒。正如《亨利六世（下）》中的一段独白所言，他"比蜥蜴更会变色"，"比普罗透斯更会变形"①（第三幕，第二场）。理查三世无疑是个恶人，但同时也是一个在伤痛、仇恨、屈辱、恐惧中苦苦挣扎的人；他巧舌如簧，诡诈善变，看似冷酷无情，实则孤独无助，甚至不堪一击。在其强悍的外表之下隐藏的是他错乱的身份和脆弱的内心。表演是他唯一的铠甲。一旦停止，其虚妄的世界也便随之坍塌，余下的只有无处安放的自我。从这个意义上讲，他在摧毁别人时也摧毁了自己，在搅动历史的同时也为历史所吞噬。

在莎士比亚的演绎下，理查三世幻化成了一个无形的幽灵，在不同的叙事中游荡、变化、生长、往复。在经历了从历史事件到编年史，再到历史剧的变化后，理查三世犹如一面镜子映照出关于过去的种种猜想。爱德华·卡尔（Edward H. Carr）认为，历史是历史学家与事实之间连续不断的交互，是现在和过去间永不停息的对话②。莎士比亚的《理查三世》即是如此，它讲述着理查的历史、都铎王朝的历史，也记录下了关于历史的历史。

Selected Reading

Act Ⅰ, i

Enter Richard, Duke of Gloucester, solus.

RICHARD

Now is the winter of our discontent

Made glorious summer by this son of York:

And all the clouds that loured upon our house

In the deep bosom of the ocean buried.

> noun+of+noun 表隐喻：将约克与兰开斯特两大家族间的宿怨比作严冬

> son of York 指理查的哥哥爱德华四世，其父为约克公爵。同时 son 与 sun 谐音，一方面因为太阳是约克家族的象征，一方面又与前文炎炎夏日相呼应

> loured: v. look angry or sullen 面露愠色，此处为拟人用法

> house: 双关语，既指房屋，又指约克家族（House of York）

---

① 莎士比亚：《莎士比亚全集》（第六卷），朱生豪译，北京：人民文学出版社，1978年，第280页。

② Carr, Edward Hallett. *What Is History*. Michigan: Michigan University Press, 1962, pp. 3–36.

Now are our brows bound with victorious wreaths,

Our bruisèd arms hung up for monuments,

Our stern alarums changed to merry meetings,

Our dreadful marches to delightful measures.

Grim-visaged war hath smoothed his wrinkled front,

And now, instead of mounting barbèd steeds

To fright the souls of fearful adversaries,

He capers nimbly in a lady's chamber

To the lascivious pleasing of a lute.

But I, that am not shaped for sportive tricks,

Nor made to court an amorous looking glass:

I, that am rudely stamped, and want love's majesty

To strut before a wanton ambling nymph:

I, that am curtailed of this fair proportion,

Cheated of feature by dissembling nature,

Deformed, unfinished, sent before my time

Into this breathing world, scarce half made up,

And that so lamely and unfashionable

That dogs bark at me as I halt by them—

Why, I, in this weak piping time of peace,

Have no delight to pass away the time,

Unless to see my shadow in the sun

And descant on mine own deformity.

And therefore, since I cannot prove a lover,

To entertain these fair well-spoken days,

I am determinèd to prove a villain

And hate the idle pleasures of these days.

Plots have I laid, inductions dangerous,

正常语序为：our brows（额头）are bound with victorious wreaths 后面几行结构相同，省略了 are

visaged：a. having an appearance of a specific kind（文学表达）有……面容的。这里是指有着狰狞面容的战争之神也舒展了眉宇

capers：v. to leap or prance about in a playful manner 轻盈舞蹈

lascivious：a. lewd, lustful 令人意乱情迷的
pleasing：n. joy 愉悦

sportive tricks：调情示爱的行为

court an amorous looking glass：顾影自怜

want：v. lack（古英语）缺乏

strut：v. to walk with a proud gait 趾高气扬地行走

nymph：n. (in Greek and Roman mythology) a spirit of nature in the form of a young woman 希腊和罗马神话中的自然女神，文学作品中常用以指代美丽的女子

amble：v. to walk at a slow, relaxed pace 原指马缓步前行，这里用以形容女子步履蹁跹

curtailed of：deprived of 被剥夺

piping time of peace：歌舞升平之时

shadow：一方面表现出理查的形单影只，一方面也暗示出他的无足轻重

descant on：ponder/comment on; talk tediously about 念念不忘，絮絮叨叨

By drunken prophecies, libels, and dreams,

To set my brother Clarence and the King

In deadly hate, the one against the other.

And if King Edward be as true and just

As I am subtle, false, and treacherous,

This day should Clarence closely be mewed up,

About a prophecy which says that 'G'

Of Edward's heirs the murderer shall be.

Dive, thoughts, down to my soul.

Here Clarence comes.

> mewed up: caged, imprisoned 被关进笼子，这里指将克莱伦斯投入监狱

> 克莱伦斯的名字为 George，所以名字里含有字母 G。但事实上，理查的名字里也含有字母 G，因为理查也称葛罗斯特公爵（Duke of Gloucester）

译文 1（朱生豪版）

第一幕第一场

葛罗斯特上。

葛罗斯特

现在我们严冬般的宿怨已给这颗约克的红日照耀成为融融的夏景：那笼罩着我们王室的片片愁云全都埋进了海洋深处。现在我们的额前已经戴上胜利的花圈：我们已把战场上折损的枪矛高挂起来留作纪念；当初的尖厉的角鸣，已变为欢庆之音；杀气腾腾的进军步伐一转而为轻歌妙舞。那面目睁狞的战神也不再横眉怒目；如今他不想再跨上征马去威吓敌人们战栗的心魄，却只顾在贵

Act I , i

Enter Richard, Duke of Gloucester, solus.

RICHARD

Now is the winter of our discontent

Made glorious summer by this son of York；

And all the clouds that loured upon our house

In the deep bosom of the ocean buried.

Now are our brows bound with victorious wreaths,

Our bruisèd arms hung up for monuments,

Our stern alarums changed to merry meetings,

Our dreadful marches to delightful measures.

Grim-visaged war hath smoothed his wrinkled front,

妇们的内室里伴随着春情逸荡的琵琶声轻盈地舞蹈。可是我呢，天生我一副畸形陋相，不适于调情弄爱，也无从对着含情的明镜去讨取宠幸；我比不上爱神的风采，怎能凭空在嫋娜的仙姑面前昂首阔步；我既被卸除了一切匀称的身段模样，欺人的造物者又骗去了我的仪容，使得我残缺不全，不等我生长成形，便把我抛进这喘息的人间，加上我如此跛跛踬踬，满叫人看不入眼，甚至路旁的狗儿见我停下，也要狂吠几声；说实话，我在这软绵绵的歌舞升平的年代，却找不到半点赏心乐事以消磨岁月，无非背着阳光窥看自己的阴影，口中念念有词，埋怨我这废体残形。因此，我既无法由我的春心奔放，趁着韶光洋溢卖弄风情，就只好打定主意以歹徒自许，专事仇视眼前的闲情逸致了。我这里已设下圈套，搬弄些是非，用尽醉酒诳言、毁谤、梦呓，唆使我三哥克莱伦斯和大哥皇上之间结下生死仇恨：为的是有

And now, instead of mounting barbèd steeds
To fright the souls of fearful adversaries,
He capers nimbly in a lady's chamber
To the lascivious pleasing of a lute.
But I, that am not shaped for sportive tricks,
Nor made to court an amorous looking glass:
I, that am rudely stamped, and want love's majesty
To strut before a wanton ambling nymph：
I, that am curtailed of this fair proportion,
Cheated of feature by dissembling nature,
Deformed, unfinished, sent before my time
Into this breathing world, scarce half made up,
And that so lamely and unfashionable
That dogs bark at me as I halt by them—
Why, I, in this weak piping time of peace,
Have no delight to pass away the time,
Unless to see my shadow in the sun
And descant on mine own deformity.
And therefore, since I cannot prove a lover,
To entertain these fair well-spoken days,
I am determinèd to prove a villain
And hate the idle pleasures of these days.
Plots have I laid, inductions dangerous,
By drunken prophecies, libels, and dreams,
To set my brother Clarence and the King
In deadly hate, the one against the other.
And if King Edward be as true and just

人传说爱德华的继承人之中有个 G 字起头的要弑君篡位，只消爱德华的率直天真比得上我的机敏阴毒，管叫他今天就把克莱伦斯囚进大牢。且埋藏起我的这番心念，克莱伦斯来了。

译文 2 （辜正坤版）

As I am subtle, false, and treacherous,
This day should Clarence closely be mewed up,
About a prophecy which says that 'G'
Of Edward's heirs the murderer shall be.
Dive, thoughts, down to my soul.
Here Clarence comes.

Act I , ii

Enter the corse *of Henry the Sixth on a bier, with Halberds to guard it, Lady Anne being the mourner, accompanied by Gentlemen.*

> corse: n.中古英语，同 corpse 尸体

Enter Richard, Duke of Gloucester

ANNE Foul devil, for God's sake, hence, and trouble us not,
For thou hast made the happy Earth thy hell,
Filled it with cursing cries and deep exclaims.
If thou delight to view thy heinous deeds,
Behold this pattern of thy butcheries.

> pattern：n. example 例证，指亨利六世的尸体

She points to the corpse.

......

ANNE Thou wast the cause and most accursed effect.

> effect：n. agent 罪魁，在下文理查用到了 effect 的另一含义"后果"，以此巧妙化解了安对他的指责

RICHARD Your beauty was the cause of that effect.

Your beauty, that did haunt me in my sleep

To undertake the death of all the world,

So I might live one hour in your sweet bosom.

ANNE If I thought that, I tell thee, homicide,

These nails should rend that beauty from my cheeks.

RICHARD These eyes could never endure that beauty's wrack.

You should not blemish it, if I stood by.

As all the world is cheerèd by the sun,

So I by that: it is my day, my life.

> So I by that: so am I cheered by the sun, 理查将安的美比作太阳, 称之为他的白昼与生命

ANNE Black night o'ershade thy day, and death thy life.

RICHARD Curse not thyself, fair creature: thou art both.

ANNE I would I were, to be revenged on thee.

RICHARD It is a quarrel most unnatural

To be revenged on him that loveth thee.

ANNE It is a quarrel just and reasonable

To be revenged on him that killed my husband.

RICHARD He that bereft thee, lady, of thy husband,

Did it to help thee to a better husband.

ANNE His better doth not breathe upon the earth.

RICHARD He lives that loves thee better than he could.

ANNE Name him.

RICHARD Plantagenet.

> Plantagenet: 普兰塔琪纳特 (也指金雀花王朝), 亨利六世和理查的父亲约克公爵都曾以此为姓

ANNE Why, that was he.

RICHARD The selfsame name, but one of better nature.

ANNE Where is he?

RICHARD Here. (*Spits at him*)

Why dost thou spit at me?

ANNE Would it were mortal poison for thy sake.

> 虚拟语气表愿望，意为"但愿是针对你的致命毒药"

RICHARD Never came poison from so sweet a place.

ANNE Never hung poison on a fouler toad.

Out of my sight, thou dost infect mine eyes.

RICHARD Thine eyes, sweet lady, have infected mine.

ANNE Would they were basilisks, to strike thee dead.

> basilisk：巴西利斯克（西方传说的蛇怪）的蛇毒

RICHARD I would they were, that I might die at once,

For now they kill me with a living death.

Those eyes of thine from mine have drawn salt tears,

Shamed their aspects with store of childish drops：

These eyes, which never shed remorseful tear—

No, when my father York and Edward wept,

To hear the piteous moan that Rutland made

When black-faced Clifford shook his sword at him,

> Rutland：理查年幼的弟弟鲁特兰，在《亨利六世（下）》中被支持兰开斯特家族的克列福（Clifford）勋爵残忍杀害

Nor when thy warlike father, like a child,

Told the sad story of my father's death,

And twenty times made pause to sob and weep,

That all the standers-by had wet their cheeks

Like trees bedashed with rain: in that sad time,

My manly eyes did scorn an humble tear.

And what these sorrows could not thence exhale,

Thy beauty hath, and made them blind with weeping.

I never sued to friend nor enemy:

My tongue could never learn sweet smoothing word.

But now thy beauty is proposed my fee,

My proud heart sues and prompts my tongue to speak. *She looks scornfully at him*

Teach not thy lip such scorn, for it was made

For kissing, lady, not for such contempt.

If thy revengeful heart cannot forgive,

Lo, here I lend thee this sharp-pointed sword,

Which if thou please to hide in this true breast.

And let the soul forth that adoreth thee,

I lay it naked to the deadly stroke

And humbly beg the death upon my knee.

He lays his breast open;

she offers at [it] with his sword

Nay, do not pause, for I did kill King Henry—

But 'twas thy beauty that provokèd me.

Nay, now dispatch; 'twas I that stabbed young Edward

—But 'twas thy heavenly face that set me on.

She falls the sword

Take up the sword again, or take up me.

ANNE Arise, dissembler. Though I wish thy death,

fee：n. 诉讼费，与后文的 sue 均为法律用语。在莎士比亚作品中存在大量法律指涉

set me on：与前文 provoke 同义，指引发

take up：这行中第一个 take up 意为"拿起"，第二个意为"接纳某人"，而安选择了 take up 的第三个含义"扶起"，所以后文才会出现"Arise"（站起身来）

I will not be thy executioner.

RICHARD Then bid me kill myself, and I will

do it. (*Takes his sword back*)

ANNE I have already.

RICHARD That was in thy rage:

Speak it again and, even with the word,

This hand, which for thy love did kill thy love,

Shall for thy love kill a far truer love.

To both their deaths shalt thou be accessory.

ANNE I would I knew thy heart.

RICHARD 'Tis figured in my tongue.

ANNE I fear me both are false.

> I fear me：相当于I am afraid

RICHARD Then never was man true.

ANNE Well, well, put up your sword.

RICHARD Say, then, my peace is made.

ANNE That shalt thou know hereafter.

RICHARD But shall I live in hope?

ANNE All men I hope, live so.

译文1（朱生豪版）

第一幕第二场	Act I , ii
役使们簇拥亨利六世棺具上，安夫人送殡致哀	*Enter the corse of Henry the Sixth on a bier, with Halberds to guard it, Lady Anne being the mourner, accompanied by Gentlemen.*
	Enter Richard, Duke of Gloucester
安　恶魔，上天不容，走开些，莫来寻麻烦；	**ANNE** Foul devil, for God's sake, hence, and trouble us not,

你已经把快乐世界变成了地狱，使人间充满了怒咒痛号的惨声。

你如果愿意欣赏你残害忠良的劣迹，就请一看你自己屠刀杀人的这具模型。（手指尸体）
…………

安 祸根就是你，而干出这样滔天罪行的也是你。

葛罗斯特 原是你的天姿国色惹起了这一切；你的姿色不断在我睡梦中萦绕，直叫我顾不得天下生灵，只是一心想在你的酥胸边取得一刻温暖。

安 早知如此，我告诉你，凶犯，我一定亲手抓破我的红颜。

葛罗斯特 我怎能漠视美容香腮受到摧残；有我在身边就不会容许你加以毁损：正如太阳照耀大地，鼓舞世人。你的美色就是我的白昼和生命。

安 让黑夜掩盖你的白昼，死亡吞没你的生命！

葛罗斯特 莫诅咒你自身，你

For thou hast made the happy Earth thy hell,

Filled it with cursing cries and deep exclaims.

If thou delight to view thy heinous deeds,

Behold this pattern of thy butcheries.

She points to the corpse.

......

ANNE Thou wast the cause and most accursed effect.

RICHARD Your beauty was the cause of that effect.

Your beauty, that did haunt me in my sleep

To undertake the death of all the world,

So I might live one hour in your sweet bosom.

ANNE If I thought that, I tell thee, homicide,

These nails should rend that beauty from my cheeks.

RICHARD These eyes could never endure that beauty's wrack.

You should not blemish it, if I stood by.

As all the world is cheerèd by the sun,

So I by that: it is my day, my life.

ANNE Black night o'ershade thy day, and death thy life.

RICHARD Curse not thyself, fair

正是白昼，又是生命，可人儿。

安 但愿能这样，正好报你的仇。

葛罗斯特 要在爱你的人身上报仇，好一场离奇古怪的争执。

安 为了在杀害我夫君的人身上雪恨复仇，正是一番公允合理的争论。

葛罗斯特 夫人，那使你丧失夫君的人为的就是要帮你另配一个更好的夫君。

安 比他还好的人，世上已经找不到了。

葛罗斯特 这个人却在人间，他爱你更为深厚。

安 讲出他的姓名来。

葛罗斯特 普兰塔琪纳特。

安 正是他。

葛罗斯特 和他同名，品质却在他之上。

安 这个人在哪儿？

葛罗斯特 在这儿。（她啐他）你为什么唾我？

安 对付你，我巴不得能喷出毒液来！

葛罗斯特 这样甜蜜的嘴里哪儿喷得出毒液。

安 哪儿还有比你更臭更烂的毒蛤蟆。我见不得你！你会使

creature: thou art both.

ANNE I would I were, to be revenged on thee.

RICHARD It is a quarrel most unnatural To be revenged on him that loveth thee.

ANNE It is a quarrel just and reasonable To be revenged on him that killed my husband.

RICHARD He that bereft thee, lady, of thy husband,
Did it to help thee to a better husband.

ANNE His better doth not breathe upon the earth.

RICHARD He lives that loves thee better than he could.

ANNE Name him.

RICHARD Plantagenet.

ANNE Why, that was he.

RICHARD The selfsame name, but one of better nature.

ANNE Where is he?

RICHARD Here. (*Spits at him*)
Why dost thou spit at me?

ANNE Would it were mortal poison for thy sake.

RICHARD Never came poison from so sweet a place.

ANNE Never hung poison on a fouler toad.

我双目都遭殃。

葛罗斯特 甜蜜的夫人，是你的媚眼殃及了我的官能。

安 但愿我目光如蛇怪，好致你死命！

葛罗斯特 这样才好，好让我死得痛快；

无奈你秋波一转竟害得我活不成，死不了。你那双迷魂的眼睛叫我一见，就不由得不泪珠盈盈，像孩童般顾不得人们的耻笑；我的眼里何曾流过什么真情的泪；

当黑脸的克列福挥动长刀指向弱小的鲁特兰,逼得他哀号悲鸣，这时间我父约克和哥哥爱德华都忍不住哭泣起来，而我却没有流泪；

再说，当你那英勇的父亲像一个孩童般追述着我父亲如何惨遭杀害，他曾多次泣不成声，

闻者都不禁泪流满颊，好比树身淋着雨水一样：在那个悲哀的时日，我还是虎视眈眈，不

Out of my sight, thou dost infect mine eyes.

RICHARD Thine eyes, sweet lady, have infected mine.

ANNE Would they were basilisks, to strike thee dead.

RICHARD I would they were, that I might die at once,

For now they kill me with a living death.

Those eyes of thine from mine have drawn salt tears,

Shamed their aspects with store of childish drops:

These eyes, which never shed remorseful tear—

No, when my father York and Edward wept,

To hear the piteous moan that Rutland made

When black-faced Clifford shook his sword at him,

Nor when thy warlike father, like a child,

Told the sad story of my father's death,

And twenty times made pause to sob and weep,

That all the standers-by had wet their cheeks

Like trees bedashed with rain: in that sad time,

屑抛出一滴弱泪；

当年那些伤心事都打不动我的心，

可是，今天我却为你的美色热泪盈眶。

我从不向友人求情，向敌人讨饶；我的舌头学不会一句甜蜜话；可是今天却是你的红颜为我付出了讼费，逼得我压住傲气而向你苦苦申诉。（她向他横眉怒目，表示轻蔑）

何必那样噘起轻慢的朱唇呢，夫人，天生你可亲吻的香腮，不是给你做侮蔑之用的。如果你还是满心仇恨，不肯留情，那末我这里有一把尖刀借给你；单看你是否想把它藏进我这赤诚的胸膛，解脱我这向你膜拜的心魂，我现在敞开来由你狠狠地一戳，我双膝跪地恳求你恩赐，了结我这条生命。

（打开胸膛；她持刀欲砍）

快呀，别住手；是我杀了亨利王；也还是你的美貌引起我来。莫停住，快下手；也是我

My manly eyes did scorn an humble tear.

And what these sorrows could not thence exhale,

Thy beauty hath, and made them blind with weeping.

I never sued to friend nor enemy:

My tongue could never learn sweet smoothing word.

But now thy beauty is proposed my fee,

My proud heart sues and prompts my tongue to speak. *She looks scornfully at him*

Teach not thy lip such scorn, for it was made

For kissing, lady, not for such contempt.

If thy revengeful heart cannot forgive,

Lo, here I lend thee this sharp-pointed sword,

Which if thou please to hide in this true breast.

And let the soul forth that adoreth thee,

I lay it naked to the deadly stroke

And humbly beg the death upon my knee.

He lays his breast open;

she offers at [it] with his sword

Nay, do not pause, for I did kill King Henry—

But 'twas thy beauty that provokèd me.

刺死了年轻的爱德华；又还是你的天姿鼓舞了我。

（她又作砍势，但立即松手，刀落地）

拾起那把刀来，不然挽我起来。

安　站起来，假殷勤。我虽巴不得你死，倒不想做你的刽子手。

葛罗斯特　那末吩咐我自杀，我一定照办。

安　我已经讲过了。

葛罗斯特　那是你在盛怒之下说的；再说一遍，只消你金口一开，我这只手，为了爱你曾经杀过你的旧欢，现在还是为了爱你，可以再杀一个爱得你更加真切的情郎。这样，新欢旧爱先后被杀，而你却都是从犯。

安　我倒很想看看你这颗心。

葛罗斯特　我的心就挂在我的嘴唇边。

安　我怕你竟是心口全非。

葛罗斯特　那世上就没有一个真心人了。

安　好啦，好啦，把你的刀收起来。

Nay, now dispatch; 'twas I that stabbed young Edward
—But 'twas thy heavenly face that set me on.

She falls the sword

Take up the sword again, or take up me.

ANNE Arise, dissembler. Though I wish thy death,
I will not be thy executioner.

RICHARD Then bid me kill myself, and I will do it.(*Takes his sword back*)

ANNE I have already.

RICHARD That was in thy rage:
Speak it again and, even with the word,
This hand, which for thy love did kill thy love,
Shall for thy love kill a far truer love.
To both their deaths shalt thou be accessory.

ANNE I would I knew thy heart.

RICHARD 'Tis figured in my tongue.

ANNE I fear me both are false.

RICHARD Then never was man true.

ANNE Well, well, put up your sword.

葛罗斯特 那末就算是和解了。

安 这还得等着瞧。

葛罗斯特 但是我可否就在希望中求生呢?

安 人人都靠希望生存，我想。

译文2（辜正坤版）

RICHARD Say, then, my peace is made.

ANNE That shalt thou know hereafter.

RICHARD But shall I live in hope?

ANNE All men I hope, live so.

Activities

1. Shakespeare and Today

Direction: Answer the following questions and see how the story of Richard Ⅲ *is still related to people today.*

1）What makes Richard a villain? Are people born evil?

2）What animals is Richard compared to by people around him?

3）What comprises a person's self-identity? Do you think Richard has a clear understanding of himself?

4）Why is Richard so ambitious? When can ambition become dangerous?

2. Shakespeare and China

Direction: Both Yanzi and Richard Ⅲ were once humiliated and denied due to their physical deformity, but they responded differently. Read the following story excerpted from The Spring and Autumn Annals of Master Yan（《晏子春秋》）*and think about in what way a man's choice may decide his fate.*

晏子使楚，以晏子短，楚人为小门于大门之侧而延晏子。晏子不入，曰："使狗国者，从狗门入；今臣使楚，不当从此门入。"傧者更道从大门入，见楚王。王曰："齐无人耶?"晏子对曰："临淄三百闾，张袂成阴，挥汗成雨，比肩继踵而在，何为无人?"王曰："然则子何为使乎?"晏子对曰:"齐命使,各有所主,其贤者使使贤王,不肖者使使不肖王。婴最不肖,故直使楚矣。"

晏子将至楚,楚闻之,谓左右曰:"晏婴,齐之习辞者也,今方来,吾欲辱之,何以也?"左右对曰:"为其来也,臣请缚一人,过王而行,王曰:'何为者也?'对曰:'齐人也。'王曰:'何坐?'曰:'坐盗。'"

晏子至,楚王赐晏子酒,酒酣,吏二缚一人诣王。王曰:"缚者曷为者也?"对曰:"齐人也,坐盗。"王视晏子曰:"齐人固善盗乎?"晏子避席对曰:"婴闻之,橘生淮南则为橘,生于淮北则为枳,叶徒相似,其实味不同。所以然者何? 水土异也。今民生长于齐不盗,入楚则盗,得无楚之水土使民善盗耶?"王笑曰:"圣人非所与熙也,寡人反取病焉。"[1]

3. Shakespeare and Beyond

Direction: Read the following report on the latest archeological discovery of Richard III's remains in Leicester and try to adapt the play Richard III *into a new version based on the facts released.*

The discovery of the remains of Richard III beneath a car parking lot in the English city of Leicester in 2012 sparked excitement around the world. In the years since it was exhumed, the King's skeleton has given up plenty of secrets—and research continues to find out more.

Richard III was not hunchbacked

For the archaeologists searching for Richard's remains, the sight of the freshly-uncovered skeleton's twisted spine was the moment the hairs began to stand up on the back of their necks; tests later revealed the King suffered from idiopathic adolescent-onset scoliosis. While the skeleton's curved vertebrae are striking, experts say it would have only meant his right shoulder was slightly higher than the other.

He was blue-eyed and blond

The most famous portraits of Richard III depict him as dark-haired and

---

[1] 晏子:《晏子春秋》,徐文翔导读注译,长沙:岳麓书社,2021年,第214-215页。

steely eyed, but they were painted some 25 to 30 years after his death, and DNA tests on the remains suggest he was blue-eyed and blond.

He dined on peacock and heron

It is perhaps not surprising that a monarch would have a taste for the finer things in life, but heron—really? Well yes—in the medieval period wildfowl such as heron, egret and even swan would have featured heavily on the high-protein menus of the aristocracy.

He had worms when he died

Something in that rich diet made Richard III sick: Scientists from the University of Cambridge and the University of Leicester found evidence the King was suffering from a roundworm infection when he died.

He was killed by a blow to the head

Richard III was the last English King to die in battle, at Bosworth on August 22, 1485. In his *Anglica Historia,* the Italian Polydore Vergil, recorded that "King Richard alone was killed fighting manfully in the thickest press of his enemies." When archaeologists studied the remains unearthed in Leicester, they found evidence of 11 wounds inflicted at or around the time of his death: nine to his skull and two to other parts of his body. The position of the injuries suggest that Richard had lost both his horse and his helmet when he was set upon by opposition troops[1].

Further Reading

ANDERSON J H, 1984. Biographical truth: the representation of historical persons in Tudor-Stuart writing [M]. New Haven: Yale University Press.

BALDWIN D, 2013. Richard III [M]. Stroud, Gloucestershire: Amberley Publishing.

COLLEY S, 1992. Richard's himself again: a stage history of Richard

---

[1] https://www.cnn.com/2015/03/22/europe/richard-iii-burial-5-things/index.html.

III [M]. Westport, Conn.: Greenwood Press.

CONNOLLY A, 2013. Richard III: a critical reader, Arden early modern drama guides[M]. London: Bloomsbury Arden Shakespeare.

PRESCOTT P, 2006. The Shakespeare handbooks: Richard III [M]. Basingstoke: Palgrave Macmillan.

Unit 3 Henry Ⅳ

章节概述

　　《亨利四世（上、下）》创作于1596—1598年，是莎士比亚历史剧中最精彩的二联剧。其故事主要来源于英国编年史家拉斐尔·霍林斯赫德所著的《英格兰、苏格兰和爱尔兰编年史》，以及塞缪尔·丹尼尔（Samuel Daniel）《内战前四篇》（*The First Four Books of the Civil War*）中的部分内容。出于剧情设置需要，莎士比亚在创作中大胆地修改了部分历史事实。比如，霍茨波（Hotspur or Henry Percy）和亨利王子（Prince Henry）在剧中被塑造为同龄人，但历史上两人的年龄实际相差悬殊。

　　《亨利四世（上、下）》与《理查二世》《亨利五世》一起构成了莎士比亚历史剧的第二四联剧，展现了作为玫瑰战争一方的兰开斯特家族的崛起。《亨利四世（上、下）》延续了《理查二世》的故事情节，主要讲述亨利·波林勃洛克（Henry Bullingbrook）取代理查二世成为亨利四世后的跌宕人生。

　　亨利四世以不正当的方式登上王位后，终日寝食难安，时刻担心着权力的旁落。他原本计划通过朝谒圣地洗刷罪过、重获人心，不料先行到来的却是来自苏格兰、威尔士的进攻，以及支持者们的反戈一击。

　　内忧外患生死存亡之际，一向放浪形骸、不务正业的亨利王子却出人意料地选择了回归正道。他毅然投入捍卫国家与荣誉的战斗，并凭借过人的胆识与谋略，击退叛军、铲除奸佞，最终赢得了父亲的信任。殚精竭虑的亨利四世病逝后，亨利王子顺利登上王位，成为后来叱咤风云的亨利五世。

　　对于莎士比亚时代的观众而言，《亨利四世》恰如其分地演绎出了他们对于时代的焦虑，也满足了他们对王位顺利交接的想象。而对于后世的读者与观众，《亨利四世》的魅力则在于其无法超越的丰富内涵。

《亨利四世》的故事勾勒出了一幅精彩纷呈的社会图景。从温莎城堡到伦敦酒肆，从城市法官到乡绅保甲，从王公贵族到妓女强盗，从纵酒享乐到浴血疆场，其涉及面之广，远非其他的历史剧可比。整个二联剧俨然一幅细腻的时代画卷，充分展现出了16世纪90年代英格兰王朝治下的人间百态、世事万千。

为了最大限度地呈现历史的捭阖与人生的悲欢，莎士比亚在《亨利四世（上、下）》中融合了各种戏剧之长。乔纳森·贝特（Jonathan Bate）曾借用《哈姆雷特》中波洛涅斯（Polonius）的话对《亨利四世》进行点评，认为它不仅是历史剧，也是田园剧、喜剧与悲剧。

作为历史剧，它呈现出王朝的更迭、权力的争夺，以及文艺复兴时期针对秩序、信用、荣誉等价值理念的争论。作为田园剧，《亨利四世》让夏禄法官格洛斯特郡的果园散发出尤为迷人的气息。那里闲适的下午茶不仅赋予了剧本剑拔弩张外的另一种节奏，也让观众借以窥见16世纪斯特拉福德小镇上的乡村生活。

作为喜剧，《亨利四世》塑造出了西方文学中堪称经典的喜剧人物——福斯塔夫。他是骑士，却没有骑士精神。他生为贵族，却破落如乞丐。他嗜酒好色，爱慕虚荣，贪生怕死，却又凭借着他的荒唐、机智与幽默，赢得了无数人的喜爱，其中也包括伊丽莎白一世。其结果是，福斯塔夫成为唯一同时存在于莎士比亚历史剧与喜剧中的人物。继《亨利四世》之后，在《温莎的风流娘们儿》中，他再次成为逗乐的主角。英国散文家莫尔根认为，福斯塔夫的复杂性堪比哈姆雷特与夏洛克，他是"一个矛盾的综合体：他既是青年，又是老年；既有冒险精神，又游手好闲"[1]。恩格斯则给予了他更高的礼遇，以福斯塔夫式的背景命名了他所代表的"五光十色的平民社会"[2]。

当然《亨利四世》也是一部悲剧。它无情地见证了一个青年从昂扬到疯狂，一个不合时宜的父亲仓促而悲凉的诀别，以及无数人在历史洪

---

[1] Morgan, Maurice. *An Essay on the Dramatic Character of Sir John Falstaff*. London: T. Davies, 1777, p. 146.

[2] 贺祥麟等：《莎士比亚研究文集》，西安：陕西人民出版社，1982年，第111页。

流中的挣扎与消逝。

　　《亨利四世》让人在成功中看到隐患，在对峙中坚守，在笑声中嗟叹，哀而不伤。而最令人折服的一点则在于其跨越时代的包容性。在历史叙事之外，《亨利四世》也是关于战争、家庭、责任、选择的故事。其中关于父子关系的反思，时至今日仍具有启发意义。在这部二联剧中，父与子是成对出现的。亨利四世与亨利王子、诺森伯兰与霍茨波是父子关系；亨利王子与霍茨波都是名为亨利的儿子，却有着不同的成长路径；而亨利四世与福斯塔夫则呈现出两种迥异的父亲形象。《亨利四世》剧名指向的是作为父王的亨利四世，但真正的主角却是亨利王子。透过亨利王子，《亨利四世》提出的问题是：什么样的人堪当时代重任？什么样的教育能成就未来的主人？而面对家国命运，什么又是对的选择？

　　在《亨利四世（下）》第四幕第一场中，莎士比亚创造性地将history 用作动词，从而使历史成为一个动态的选择。同样的历史在不同的时代有着不同的讲述，同样的讲述也可以在不同的时代激发出不同的思考。四百年前，莎士比亚选择以《亨利四世》演绎出时代的焦虑、人间的悲喜；四百年后，我们选择以《亨利四世》开启对世界的别样审视。时空流转，世事变迁，在不断的选择中，历史得以继续。

Selected Reading

Part 1, Act Ⅰ, ii

PRINCE HENRY

I know you all, and will awhile uphold

The unyoked humour of your idleness.

Yet herein will I imitate the sun,

Who doth permit the base contagious clouds

To smother up his beauty from the world,

That when he please again to be himself,

> uphold：v. support, maintain a practice 支持；继续

> unyoked humour: 不羁的天性。源于古希腊的体液说（humourism），该学说在莎士比亚时代极为流行。这一学说认为人体是由四种体液（humour）——血液、黏液、黄胆汁和黑胆汁构成，不同体液构成不同的气质及行为方式

> 太阳常被视为皇权的象征

> 伊丽莎白时代的人们认为，云可以传染疾病

Being wanted, he may be more wondered at,

By breaking through the foul and ugly mists

Of vapors that did seem to strangle him.

If all the year were playing holidays,

To sport would be as tedious as to work;

> sport: v. to amuse oneself 娱乐

But when they seldom come, they wished-for come,

> 物以稀为贵

And nothing pleaseth but rare accidents.

> falsify: v. to prove false 证明……是错误的

So, when this loose behavior I throw off

And pay the debt I never promisèd,

By how much better than my word I am,

> reformation: n. the act or process of changing and improving 改过自新

By so much shall I falsify men's hopes;

And like bright metal on a sullen ground,

> foil: n. sth that serves as a contrast 原意为展示珠宝的衬布，这里指反衬
> set off: to make sth distinct 衬托

My reformation, glittering o'er my fault,

Shall show more goodly and attract more eyes

> offend: v. to transgress 故意胡作非为，以犯众怒

Than that which hath no foil to set it off.

I'll so offend to make offence a skill,

> skill: n. ability 技能，这里指策略

Redeeming time when men think least I will.

> redeeming time: 弥补失去的时间

译文1（辜正坤版）

<table>
<tr><td>第一部分第一幕第二场</td><td>Part 1, Act I, ii</td></tr>
<tr><td>亨利王子</td><td>PRINCE HENRY</td></tr>
<tr><td>我深知众卿所作所为，</td><td>I know you all, and will awhile uphold</td></tr>
<tr><td>暂与你们的懒散德性</td><td>The unyoked humor of your idleness.</td></tr>
<tr><td>相呼相应，放浪无行。</td><td></td></tr>
<tr><td>为此我要效仿太阳，</td><td>Yet herein will I imitate the sun,</td></tr>
<tr><td>让恶云暂蔽其威光，</td><td>Who doth permit the base contagious clouds</td></tr>
<tr><td>一旦云垒破雾障散，</td><td>To smother up his beauty from the world,</td></tr>
<tr><td>他重现真身，因为久仰，</td><td>That when he please again to be himself,</td></tr>
</table>

世人倍加礼赞他的辉煌。	Being wanted, he may be more wondered at,
	By breaking through the foul and ugly mists
	Of vapors that did seem to strangle him.
倘若天天皆佳节喜庆,	If all the year were playing holidays,
游乐就会乏味如劳作;	To sport would be as tedious as to work;
为其稀有,众人渴求;	But when they seldom come, they wished-for come,
事物罕见,兴味盎然;	And nothing pleaseth but rare accidents.
一旦我收敛放荡行状,	So, when this loose behavior I throw off
还清我从未承诺要还的欠账,	And pay the debt I never promisèd,
我之所为必远胜我之所言,	By how much better than my word I am,
一举破除世人于我的成见。	By so much shall I falsify men's hopes;
如金银衬于暗底而耀眼,	And like bright metal on a sullen ground,
我一旦幡然改进,	My reformation, glittering o'er my fault,
则愈显今之上进,	Shall show more goodly and attract more eyes
更赢天下人之羡钦;	
此道助我,相反相成:	Than that which hath no foil to set it off.
犯过实为日后补过矫正,	I'll so offend to make offence a skill,
在人们最难料时弃旧图新。	Redeeming time when men think least I will.

译文2（朱生豪版）

Part 1, Act II, iv

FALSTAFF ...But tell me, Hal, art not thou horrible afeard? Thou being heir apparent, could the world pick thee out three such enemies again as that fiend Douglas, that spirit Percy, and

> horrible afeard: 中古英语用法,相当于 horribly afraid

> spirit: n. supernatural being 超人,暗含勇猛之意。这里列举了亨利四世及亨利王子面临的三重威胁:苏格兰的宿敌道格拉斯(Douglas)、倒戈的潘西(Percy),以及威尔士大英雄葛兰道厄(Glendower)

127

that devil Glendower? Art not thou horrible afraid? Doth not thy blood thrill at it?

PRINCE HENRY Not a whit, I lack some of thy instinct.

> a whit: a little bit 一丁点

> thy instinct: 指贪生怕死是福斯塔夫的本能。福斯塔夫的话语中提到的 horrible afeard, thrill at it 都显示出他的怯懦本性

FALSTAFF Well, thou wilt be horribly chid tomorrow when thou comest to thy father: if thou love me, practise an answer.

PRINCE HENRY Do thou stand for my father, and examine me upon the particulars of my life.

FALSTAFF Shall I? Content. (*He sits down*) This chair shall be my state, this dagger my sceptre, and this cushion my crown.

> state: n. throne 皇位宝座

PRINCE HENRY Thy state is taken for a joined-stool, thy golden sceptre for a leaden dagger, and thy precious rich crown for a pitiful bald crown.

> taken for: seen to be 看上去是……

> an: 中古英语，意为 if

FALSTAFF Well, an the fire of grace be not quite out of thee, now shalt thou be moved. —Give me a cup of sack to make mine eyes look red, that it may be thought I have wept, for I must speak in passion, and I will do it in King Cambyses' vein.

> the fire of grace: 原为清教用语，指上帝救赎的恩泽，这里指慈悲天良

> *Life of Cambyses, King of Persia* 是托马斯·普利斯顿（Thomas Preston）于 1558—1569 年创作的一部悲剧，讲述了波斯国王 Cambyses 的故事，以夸张的文风著称。这里 in King Cambyses' vein 意为 in Cambyses' style, 即极尽夸张

PRINCE HENRY Well, here is my leg.

FALSTAFF And here is my speech. (*As King*) Stand aside, nobility.

HOSTESS QUICKLY O Jesu, this is excellent sport, i' faith!

> 在上述普利斯顿创作的剧中，王后曾伤心而泣。这里福斯塔夫扮演国王，戏称桂嫂为王后。不同的是，桂嫂是笑出的眼泪

FALSTAFF (*as King*) Weep not, sweet queen; for trickling tears are vain.

HOSTESS QUICKLY O the Father, how he holds his countenance!

FALSTAFF For God's sake, lords, convey my tristful queen,

For tears do stop the floodgates of her eyes.

HOSTESS QUICKLY O Jesu, he doth it as like one of these harlotry players as ever I see!

FALSTAFF Peace, good pint-pot; peace, good tickle-brain. Harry, I do not only marvel where thou spendest thy time, but also how thou art accompanied, for though the camomile, the more it is trodden the faster it grows, yet youth, the more it is wasted the sooner it wears. That thou art my son, I have partly thy mother's word, partly my own opinion, but chiefly a villanous trick of thine eye and a foolish hanging of thy nether lip, that doth warrant me. If then thou be son to me, here lieth the point: why, being son to me, art thou so pointed at? Shall the blessed sun of heaven prove a micher and eat blackberries? A question not to be asked. Shall the son of England prove a thief and take purses? A question to be asked. There is a thing, Harry, which thou hast often heard of and it is known to many in our land by the name of pitch: this pitch, as ancient writers do report, doth defile; so doth the company thou keepest. For, Harry, now I do not speak to thee in drink but in tears, not in pleasure but in passion, not in words only, but in woes also. And yet there is a virtuous man whom I have often noted in thy company, but I know not his

> tristful: a. melancholy 忧郁哀伤的。这里福斯塔夫在故意模仿 *King Cambyses* 在剧中的夸张用词

> pint-pot: n.品脱壶，装酒容器；tickle-brain: n.（俚语）烈酒。这句用的是下里巴人世俗的表达，与福斯塔夫现在扮演的国王身份形成巨大反差。而后的 marvel 又回到了浮夸的文风上。这种文风的突转显示出福斯塔夫实则不了解国王应有的样子，他对国王浅薄的认识完全来自剧场表演

> camomile: n. chamomile 春黄菊，民间谚语中，春黄菊越被踩踏长得越快

> 民间谚语中常将吃乌梅与游手好闲的人（micher）相联系

name.

PRINCE HENRY What manner of man, an it like your majesty?

> 相当于 if it pleases

FALSTAFF A goodly portly man, i' faith, and a corpulent; of a cheerful look, a pleasing eye and a most noble carriage; and, as I think, his age some fifty, or, by 'r lady, inclining to three score; and now I remember me, his name is Falstaff. If that man should be lewdly given, he deceives me; for, Harry, I see virtue in his looks. If then the tree may be known by the fruit, as the fruit by the tree, then peremptorily I speak it, there is virtue in that Falstaff: him keep with, the rest banish. And tell me now, thou naughty varlet, tell me, where hast thou been this month?

PRINCE HENRY Dost thou speak like a king? Do thou stand for me, and I'll play my father.

FALSTAFF Depose me? If thou dost it half so gravely, so majestically, both in word and matter, hang me up by the heels for a rabbit-sucker or a poulter's hare.

PRINCE HENRY Well, here I am set.

FALSTAFF And here I stand. Judge, my masters.

PRINCE HENRY Now, Harry, whence come you?

FALSTAFF My noble lord, from Eastcheap.

PRINCE HENRY The complaints I hear of thee are grievous.

FALSTAFF 'Sblood, my lord, they are false:

> 'Sblood (an inappropriately strong oath for the imagined situation) 一种不合时宜的赌咒发誓

nay, I'll tickle ye for a young prince, i' faith.

PRINCE HENRY Swearest thou, ungracious boy? Henceforth ne'er look on me. Thou art violently carried away from grace: there is a devil haunts thee in the likeness of an old fat man; a tun of man is thy companion. Why dost thou converse with that trunk of humours, that bolting-hutch of beastliness, that swollen parcel of dropsies, that huge bombard of sack, that stuffed cloak-bag of guts, that roasted Manning-tree ox with the pudding in his belly, that reverend Vice, that grey Iniquity, that father Ruffian, that Vanity in years? Wherein is he good, but to taste sack and drink it? Wherein neat and cleanly, but to carve a capon and eat it? Wherein cunning, but in craft? Wherein crafty, but in villainy? Wherein villainous, but in all things? Wherein worthy, but in nothing?

FALSTAFF I would your grace would take me with you: whom means your grace?

PRINCE HENRY That villainous abominable misleader of youth, Falstaff, that old white-bearded Satan.

FALSTAFF My lord, the man I know.

PRINCE HENRY I know thou dost.

FALSTAFF But to say I know more harm in him than in myself, were to say more than I know. That he is old, the more the pity, his white hairs do witness it; but that he is, saving your reverence, a whoremaster, that I utterly

ye: 口语中的 you,福斯塔夫的用词非常口语化。与之形成鲜明对比的是,亨利王子接下来的表达大量使用比喻、排比、矛盾修辞法,遣词造句处处彰显高贵气质

for: 口语用法,相当于 as

neat and cleanly: deft and skillful 灵巧利落

take me with you: let me catch up with you 这里福斯塔夫已经跟不上王子的语言表述,无法理解王子的意思

deny. If sack and sugar be a fault, God help the wicked! if to be old and merry be a sin, then many an old host that I know is damned: if to be fat be to be hated, then Pharaoh's lean kine are to be loved. No, my good lord; banish Peto, banish Bardolph, banish Poins: but for sweet Jack Falstaff, kind Jack Falstaff, true Jack Falstaff, valiant Jack Falstaff, and therefore more valiant, being, as he is, old Jack Falstaff, banish not him thy Harry's company, banish not him thy Harry's company: banish plump Jack, and banish all the world.

> Pharaoh's lean kine：法老王的瘦牛。在《创世纪》(Genesis, 41:18–21) 中，法老王曾梦见7头瘦牛吃掉了7头肥牛，预示着7年灾荒。

PRINCE HENRY I do, I will.

译文1（辜正坤版）

第一部分第二幕第四场	Part 1, Act Ⅱ, iv

福斯塔夫 ……不过，哈尔，告诉我，你不怕得心惊肉跳吗？身为王位的当然继承人，此生此世遇到的仇敌有比恶魔道格拉斯、恶神潘西和魔怪葛兰道厄更恐怖的吗？你难道不惊恐？听了刚才那个凶讯，你难道不骇得热血骤冷？

FALSTAFF ...But tell me, Hal, art not thou horrible afeard? Thou being heir apparent, could the world pick thee out three such enemies again as that fiend Douglas, that spirit Percy, and that devil Glendower? Art not thou horrible afraid? Doth not thy blood thrill at it?

亨利王子 毫无惧怕，我缺乏你的那种本能。

PRINCE HENRY Not a whit, I lack some of thy instinct.

福斯塔夫 嘿，你明天去见你的父王，将会被苛责一顿的；如果你爱我的话，我们还

FALSTAFF Well, thou wilt be horribly chid tomorrow when thou comest to thy father: if thou love me, practise an

是来练习练习你该怎样应答吧。

亨利王子 你就扮作我的父亲吧，这样你可以详细查问我生活中的细枝末节。

福斯塔夫 要我来扮？好吧，这把椅子就算我的王座，这把短剑就是我的权杖，这个垫子就是我的王冠。

亨利王子 你的王座是一个折叠凳，你的金权杖是一把铅剑，你的璀璨的王冠是一个可怜的秃顶！

福斯塔夫 好啦，如果你还有几分优雅风度的话，此刻你应动几分真情。给我一杯萨克酒喝，使我的眼睛发红，让人家看起来我刚刚哭过，因为我说话必须充满激情，用冈比西斯王的激昂腔调。

亨利王子 好，那我就跪下了。

福斯塔夫 我要讲话了。各位贵客靠边站。

老板娘奎克莉 这真好玩哟。

福斯塔夫 不要洒泪，酒店女王，几滴清泪，徒沾衣裳。

老板娘奎克莉 啊，瞧这父王满脸正经的样子！

福斯塔夫 看在上帝份

answer.

PRINCE HENRY Do thou stand for my father, and examine me upon the particulars of my life.

FALSTAFF Shall I? Content. (*He sits down*) This chair shall be my state, this dagger my sceptre, and this cushion my crown.

PRINCE HENRY Thy state is taken for a joined-stool, thy golden sceptre for a leaden dagger, and thy precious rich crown for a pitiful bald crown.

FALSTAFF Well, an the fire of grace be not quite out of thee, now shalt thou be moved. —Give me a cup of sack to make mine eyes look red, that it may be thought I have wept, for I must speak in passion, and I will do it in King Cambyses' vein.

PRINCE HENRY Well, here is my leg.

FALSTAFF And here is my speech. (*As King*) Stand aside, nobility.

HOSTESS QUICKLY O Jesu, this is excellent sport, i' faith!

FALSTAFF (*as King*) Weep not, sweet queen; for trickling tears are vain.

HOSTESS QUICKLY O the Father, how he holds his countenance!

FALSTAFF For God's sake, lords,

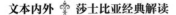

上，各位贤卿，陪送哀伤的皇后回宫去，因为泪水已经堵塞了她的双眼。

老板娘奎克莉 啊，太精彩啦，他演得像我见过的街头戏子一样！

福斯塔夫 安静，你这提啤酒壶的，安静，你这卖老烧酒的。——哈利，我不仅惊讶于你在何处厮混，而且惊讶于你同谁厮混，虽然春黄菊越遭践踏越易滋长，年华光阴却虚抛不再来。你是我的儿子，这一则是你的母亲的说法，一则是我自己的看法，但主要是你那邪乎的眼神和下唇下垂的蠢态使我坚信此言不虚。如果你是我的儿子，那么就有一个问题：为什么做了我的儿子却被世人如此訾议？难道天上的尊贵太阳成了浪荡公子，成天嚼乌梅子，这个问题不言自明。难道英格兰的亲王会去做贼偷别人的钱袋？这是一个必须问的问题。哈利，有个东西你常有所闻，吾国之人也多有所知，这东西名叫沥青：据古时文人所言，这沥青逢物则玷污。交友也一样。哈利，此刻我对你所言非酒后之语，乃泣

convey my tristful queen,
For tears do stop the floodgates of her eyes.

HOSTESS QUICKLY O Jesu, he doth it as like one of these harlotry players as ever I see!

FALSTAFF Peace, good pint-pot; peace, good tickle-brain. Harry, I do not only marvel where thou spendest thy time, but also how thou art accompanied, for though the camomile, the more it is trodden the faster it grows, yet youth, the more it is wasted the sooner it wears. That thou art my son, I have partly thy mother's word, partly my own opinion, but chiefly a villanous trick of thine eye and a foolish hanging of thy nether lip, that doth warrant me. If then thou be son to me, here lieth the point: why, being son to me, art thou so pointed at? Shall the blessed sun of heaven prove a micher and eat blackberries? A question not to be asked. Shall the son of England prove a thief and take purses? A question to be asked. There is a thing, Harry, which thou hast often heard of and it is known to many in our land by the name of pitch: this pitch, as ancient writers do report, doth defile; so doth the company thou keepest. For,

泪之劝诫：非戏言，乃真情；非只言辞，乃内心忧戚直露。然而在你朋辈之中，有一人德行弥高，常令我刮目，不知此人姓甚名谁。

亨利王子　此人令陛下如此见爱，请问他是何模样？

福斯塔夫　此人体格伟岸，胖大敦实，笑容满面，眉目和悦，气质高贵，依我看，他年届五十左右，或许近于六十；我记起啦，他名叫福斯塔夫。如果此人竟干诲淫诲盗之事，那我就是有眼无珠，因为，哈利，我看他的面相就知道他德行可嘉。如若见果而知其树，见树而知其果，我敢断言，这个福斯塔夫肯定隆德在身：你且与他为友，勿与其他人等交往。告诉我，你这不肖之子，告诉我你这个月在哪里厮混？

亨利王子　你这番言辞像一个国王吗？现在你来扮我，我扮我的父亲。

福斯塔夫　要废黜我？如果你的言谈举止能赶得上我一半的庄重威风，你把我倒吊起来，像倒挂一个兔崽子或野兔

Harry, now I do not speak to thee in drink but in tears, not in pleasure but in passion, not in words only, but in woes also. And yet there is a virtuous man whom I have often noted in thy company, but I know not his name.

PRINCE HENRY What manner of man, an it like your majesty?

FALSTAFF A goodly portly man, i' faith, and a corpulent; of a cheerful look, a pleasing eye and a most noble carriage; and, as I think, his age some fifty, or, by 'r lady, inclining to three score; and now I remember me, his name is Falstaff. If that man should be lewdly given, he deceives me; for, Harry, I see virtue in his looks. If then the tree may be known by the fruit, as the fruit by the tree, then peremptorily I speak it, there is virtue in that Falstaff: him keep with, the rest banish. And tell me now, thou naughty varlet, tell me, where hast thou been this month?

PRINCE HENRY Dost thou speak like a king? Do thou stand for me, and I'll play my father.

FALSTAFF Depose me? If thou dost it half so gravely, so majestically, both in word and matter, hang me up by the heels for a rabbit-sucker or a poulter's

亨利王子 好，我在王位上坐定了。

福斯塔夫 我就站着。各位评评吧。

亨利王子 喷，哈利，你从哪来啊？

福斯塔夫 父王在上，儿从依斯特溪泊来。

亨利王子 我听到人们对你怨诽声声。

福斯塔夫 说实话，陛下，他们全在信口开河。——我来扮演亲王给你看看，肯定叫你开心。

亨利王子 你怎么出口就伤人呢，没教养的孩子？从今往后，不要面见我了。你已经完全不成体统，一个魔鬼扮成一个胖老头附在你身上了，一个臃肿如大酒桶的家伙成了你的挚友。你为什么要结交那个藏垢纳污的箱子，盛满兽性的容器，肿胀的大脓包，硕大的酒囊，塞满五腑六脏的大皮囊，一肚子香肠填料的曼宁特里烤牛，德高望重的罪恶化身，满头白发的罪孽魁首，倚老卖老的无赖，年深月久的虚荣之最？他除了尝酒喝酒，还

hare.

PRINCE HENRY Well, here I am set.

FALSTAFF And here I stand. Judge, my masters.

PRINCE HENRY Now, Harry, whence come you?

FALSTAFF My noble lord, from East-cheap.

PRINCE HENRY The complaints I hear of thee are grievous.

FALSTAFF 'Sblood, my lord, they are false: nay, I'll tickle ye for a young prince, i' faith.

PRINCE HENRY Swearest thou, ungracious boy? Henceforth ne'er look on me. Thou art violently carried away from grace: there is a devil haunts thee in the likeness of an old fat man; a tun of man is thy companion. Why dost thou converse with that trunk of humours, that bolting-hutch of beastliness, that swollen parcel of dropsies, that huge bombard of sack, that stuffed cloak-bag of guts, that roasted Manning-tree ox with the pudding in his belly, that reverend Vice, that grey Iniquity, that father Ruffian, that Vanity in years? Wherein is he good, but to taste sack

有什么本事？他除了用刀切鸡、大饱口福，还有何能耐？他除了机关算尽，有何聪慧可言？他除了作恶，有何谋略运筹？他的所作所为，哪一桩不伤天害理？哪一桩足可称道？

福斯塔夫 祈望陛下明示所指何人？

亨利王子 那可憎可恶、误人子弟的福斯塔夫，那须发已白的老撒旦啊。

福斯塔夫 陛下，此人我认识。

亨利王子 我知道你认识。

福斯塔夫 可是，说我知道他的弊病比我自己的弊病多，无异于说我知道我所不知道的事情。他老了，这是足可惋惜的，他的满头白发可以为证。然而，要说他是一个奸邪之徒，恕我直言，我是要断然否认的。如果喝几杯加糖的萨克酒就算过失，愿上天拯救失足者；如果人老了寻点开心也算罪过，那我认识的许多老者都要下地狱；如果胖子该遭人恨，那么法老的瘦牛该惹人喜爱了。不，英明的殿下，罢黜皮多，罢黜巴道夫，罢黜波因斯，可是，可爱的杰克·福斯

and drink it? Wherein neat and cleanly, but to carve a capon and eat it? Wherein cunning, but in craft? Wherein crafty, but in villainy? Wherein villainous, but in all things? Wherein worthy, but in nothing?

FALSTAFF I would your grace would take me with you: whom means your grace?

PRINCE HENRY That villainous abominable misleader of youth, Falstaff, that old white-bearded Satan.

FALSTAFF My lord, the man I know.

PRINCE HENRY I know thou dost.

FALSTAFF But to say I know more harm in him than in myself, were to say more than I know. That he is old, the more the pity, his white hairs do witness it; but that he is, saving your reverence, a whoremaster, that I utterly deny. If sack and sugar be a fault, God help the wicked! if to be old and merry be a sin, then many an old host that I know is damned: if to be fat be to be hated, then Pharaoh's lean kine are to be loved. No, my good lord; banish Peto, banish Bardolph, banish Poins: but for sweet Jack Falstaff, kind Jack Falstaff, true Jack Falstaff, valiant Jack Falstaff, and therefore more valiant, being, as he is,

塔夫，善良的杰克·福斯塔夫，忠心耿耿的杰克·福斯塔夫，勇武的杰克·福斯塔夫，老而弥勇的杰克·福斯塔夫——不能罢黜他，不能褫夺哈利的挚友，万万不能：没有了胖杰克就没有了整个世界啊。

old Jack Falstaff, banish not him thy Harry's company, banish not him thy Harry's company: banish plump Jack, and banish all the world.

亨利王子 我要，我一定要罢黜他。

PRINCE HENRY I do, I will.

译文2（朱生豪版）

Activities

1. Shakespeare and Today

Direction: Discuss the following questions with your partner.

1）What prompts King Henry to consider a holy crusade at the beginning of the play? Why would Prince Hal banish Falstaff? Knowing the mistakes of the past will help ensure they are not repeated. Think about how the way to deal with the past decides the life of today and tomorrow.

2）Both King Henry Ⅳ and Falstaff play the role of father figures in the play. What positives and negatives do they each possess as father figures? How is the father-son relationship represented in the modern litcrature?

2. Shakespeare and China

Direction: Leadership is one of main themes of Henry Ⅳ, *which concerns not only monarch and state running but the management of personal life as well. Translate the following quotations from* The Analects of Confucius *into English and think about how these words of wisdom may apply in our own life.*

1）季康子问政于孔子，孔子对曰："政者，正也。子帅以正，孰敢不正?"（《论语·季氏》）

2）子曰："益者三友，损者三友。友直，友谅，友多闻，益矣。友便辟，友善柔，友便佞，损矣。"（《论语·季氏》）

3）季文子三思而后行，子闻之，曰："再，斯可矣。"（《论语·公冶长》）

4）子曰："一朝之忿，忘其身，以及其亲，非惑与?"（《论语·颜渊》）

5）子曰："过而不改，是谓过矣。"（《论语·卫灵公》）

3. Shakespeare and Beyond

Direction: Food transcends mere sustenance assuming a role of cultural and social indicator. Through the lens of food, one may gain insights into a person's taste, character and position or a society's ethos, heritage and daily practice. Find out what food is mentioned in Henry Ⅳ *and analyze its function in the play.*

Further Reading

BRISTOL D, 2008. The Oxford Shakespeare: Henry Ⅳ [M]. Oxford: Oxford University Press.

BULLOUGH G, 1975. Narrative and dramatic sources of Shakespeare [M]. New York: Columbia University Press.

BRISTOL M, 1985. Carnival and theatre: plebeian culture and the structure of authority in renaissance England [M]. London: Methuen.

ELDEN S, 2018. Shakespearean territories [M]. Chicago: University of Chicago Press.

GREENBLATT S, 1988. Shakespearean negotiations [M]. Berkeley: University of California Press.

Part Four   Shakespeare's Comedies

Unit 1 Comedy and Laughter

章节概述

　　作为一种戏剧类型，喜剧通常以夸张的剧情结构、滑稽的人物形象、诙谐的对白台词交织出一种喜剧性矛盾，如丑与美、假与真、恶与善等，并通过对戏剧的各个环节加以可笑化处理，使内容与形式、愿望与行动、动机与效果、本质与现象相悖逆而产生出滑稽戏谑的喜剧效果。让观众在笑的同时得以审视时代，读懂内心，获得精神的力量与认知的成长。

　　欧洲喜剧发源于古希腊。当代英语中"喜剧"一词Comedy源自希腊语 Komoidia（狂欢歌舞）。吉尔伯特·默雷①（Gilbert Murray）在《古希腊文学史》（*The Literature of Ancient Greek*）中提到，喜剧诞生自古希腊农民在葡萄和谷物收割节的化妆游戏，并随后在雅典（Athens）及西西里（Sicilia)的锡拉库萨（Syracuse）逐步成为一种艺术形式。亚里士多德（Aristotle）也在其《诗学》（*Poetics*）的第二章中提到过古希腊的墨伽拉②人（Magara）自称首创喜剧。

　　从古希腊、古罗马、中世纪到文艺复兴时期的欧洲，喜剧不断发展衍变，但对其本质的探讨从未停止。亚里士多德认为喜剧模仿低劣的

---

① 吉尔伯特·默雷（1866—1957），英国著名学者，希腊学专家，以翻译评述古希腊戏剧闻名。
② 墨伽拉，希腊一座古老的港口城市，距首都雅典42公里。

人，他们不是无恶不作的歹徒。他们或其貌不扬，或言行滑稽，或产生谬误，但不会给人带来痛苦或造成伤害。多纳图斯①（Donatus）理解的喜剧是关于城市公民的各种性格和经历的故事。人们从故事里认识到生活中的好与坏，善与害。因此，喜剧是对生活的模仿，是反映习俗的镜子，是表现真理的意象。博韦的樊尚②（Vincent de Beauvais）在其百科全书《大宝鉴》（*The Speculum Maius*）中，强调了喜剧是一种诗，是一个悲哀的开端和幸福的结尾的故事。

如果说，悲剧通过毁灭人生最宝贵的东西而让人痛彻心扉，喜剧则将那些日常的、普遍的琐碎撕破，让人拨云见日，看清真正的意义和价值，明了某些根深蒂固甚至我们曾苦苦坚守的东西也许并无价值，甚至还可能是丑陋不堪的，从而更深刻地理解生命和生活。那些包含着喜剧性矛盾的众多现象分散在生活的角角落落，通过戏剧化的提炼、浓缩、集中、夸张，而被典型化，从而激发起人们的惊奇感、优越感及笑声。

喜剧最直接的艺术效果是让观众发笑。黑格尔（G.W.F. Hegel）认为喜剧的笑是（感性）形式压倒理性（内容）。康德（Immanuel Kant）认为在一切引起撼动人心的大笑里必然有某种荒谬悖理的东西存在。马克思（Karl Heinrich Marx）认为笑是人对社会或艺术中的喜剧现象的一种主观态度，是对丑的东西的一种情绪上的反映。事物不协调状态下其内容与形式之间的喜剧性矛盾，便成为笑的根源。而这种笑极具审美价值，不只是情绪的表达，更隐含着观众对创作者的理解及自身的价值判断。

莎士比亚作为欧洲喜剧的代表人物，其喜剧主要创作于1592—1602年这十年间，这也是莎士比亚创作思想走向成熟的十年。众多的喜剧作品不仅折射了伊丽莎白时期的人文主义精神，更传递出莎士比亚对社会、对人生、对爱情等的深刻思考。莎翁的喜剧作品主要包括《错误的喜剧》（*The Comedy of Errors*）、《仲夏夜之梦》（*A Midsummer Night's Dream*）、《威尼斯商人》（*The Merchant of Venice*）、《无事生非》（*Much Ado About Nothing*）、《第十二夜》（*Twelfth Night*）、《皆大欢喜》

① 多纳图斯，公元4世纪前后罗马修辞家和文法学家。
② 博韦的樊尚（1190—1264），中世纪时期法国一位百科全书编纂者，曾编著了中世纪时期最大的一部百科全书《大宝鉴》（The *Speculum Maius*）。

（*As You Like It*）、《温莎的风流娘儿们》（*The Merry Wives of Windsor*）等共14部。其中《仲夏夜之梦》《威尼斯商人》《皆大欢喜》《第十二夜》被公认为莎翁四大喜剧。

莎士比亚创作的喜剧几乎都以爱情为主题。从悲情的故事开始，历经曲折，终以获得真爱及婚姻为欢喜结局。莎士比亚擅长营造灵巧轻快的故事风格，以饱含机智、嘲讽、戏谑、逗笑的语言，错综复杂、不落俗套的情节，呈现出一个又一个闪烁着人文主义理想光芒的爱情故事。如《仲夏夜之梦》中，赫米娅与拉山德反抗家长和雅典亲王的干涉，在城外几里的小树林中，得到仙人的帮助收获甜美的爱情。在《威尼斯商人》中，鲍西娅追求爱情自由，她不在意门第和财富，更看重爱人的品德与才能。在《温莎的风流娘儿们》中，"穿裙子的英雄们"以实际行动对父权制度做出挑战。在《第十二夜》中，勇敢聪慧的少女薇奥拉努力争取人格独立和爱情幸福。这些喜剧作品无不充满着对自由的渴望和对生活的热爱，同时也突显出这样一群美丽、智慧、坚强的女性角色，她们在历史的长河中，不断走向成熟。

人生是跌宕的，人性是复杂的。细细品读，我们会清晰地从喜剧欢快的氛围中感到丝丝的落寞。笑的同时，内心的某个地方被悄悄刺痛。细细地看那伤口，我们才明白，原来自己与故事里那个人，那群人，有着太多的相似。此刻，我在笑他；彼时，可有人在笑我？

Selected Reading

Exploring the Nature of Shakespearean Comedy[①]
Denton Jaques Snider

The Tragic and the Comic fade into each other by almost insensible gradations, and the greatest beauty of a poetical work often consists in the harmonious blending of these two elements. Not only in the same drama

---

[①] This material is abridged from *The System of Shakespeare's Drama* by Denton Jaques Snider (1841—1925) who was a writer, educator and literary critic. He was one of the original members of the St. Louis Philosophical Society and produced many commentaries on Shakespeare's plays.

may both exist in perfect unison, but even in the same character. Great actors generally have a similar quality, and frequently it is hard to tell whether their impersonations be more humorous or more pathetic. This happy transfusion and interchange of tragic and comic coloring is one of the characteristics of supreme art; it brings the relief along with the pain; it furnishes the reconciliation along with the conflict.

Shakespeare seems to have taken a special delight in its employment. No principle of his procedure is better known or more fully appreciated. His tragedies never fail of having their comic interludes; his comedies have, in nearly every case, a serious thread, and sometimes a background with a tragic outlook. Life is not all gloom or all delight; the cloud will obscure the sun, but the sun will illumine the cloud—at least around the edges.

Still, the Comic is not the Tragic, however subtle may be their intertwining, and however rapid their interaction. They rest upon diverse, and in some respects opposite, principles. Criticism must seek to explain the difference between them for the understanding, and must not rest content with a vague appeal to the feeling of beauty. Tragic earnestness springs from the deep ethical principle which animates the individual. He, however, assails another ethical principle, and thereby falls into guilt. The tragic character, moreover, must have such strength and intensity of will that it can never surrender its purpose.

A reconciliation is impossible; death alone can solve the conflict. In Comedy also there is a collision with some ethical principle on the part of the individual; he intends a violation, but does not realize his intention; he is foiled through external deception, or breaks down through internal weakness; to him is wanting that complete absorption in some great purpose which is the peculiar quality of the tragic hero. The common realm of Tragedy and Comedy, therefore, is the ethical world and its collision. Their essential difference lies in the different relation of the leading characters to this ethical world.

Here we are brought face to face with the point which must be settled—what constitutes the Comic Individual? A single person does not make a comedy; it requires several who are in action and counteraction. The comic individual is, in one form or another, the victim of deception. He fights a shadow of his own mind, or pursues an external appearance; his end is a nullity, his plan an absurdity; he is always deceived; he really is not doing that which he seems to be doing. His object may be a reasonable one, his purpose may be a lofty one, but he is inadequate to its fulfillment; the delusion is that he believes in his own ability to accomplish what he wills. His object also may be an absurd one; he pursues it, however, with the same resolution. It may be called a foible, a folly, a frailty—still the essential characteristic is that the individual is pursuing an appearance, and thus is the victim of deception, though he may even be conscious of the absurd and delusive nature of his end.

The two limitations of this sphere are to be carefully noticed. The Comic Individual must not succeed in violating the ethical principles which he conflicts with; these are the highest, the most serious, interests of man, and cannot even be endangered without exciting an apprehension, which destroys every comic tendency. Successful seduction, adultery, treason—in fine, the violations of State and Family—are not comic; nor is villainy, which attains its purpose. Such an intention of wrong-doing may exist, but it must never come to realization; it must not only be thwarted, but also punished. The delusion, therefore, ought not to go so far as to produce a violation of ethical principles.

Nor, on the other hand, ought it to transgress the limits of sanity—a madman is not a comic character. Reason must be present in the individual, though his end be absurd. A rational man acting irrationally is the incongruity which calls forth the laugh—is the contradiction upon which Comedy reposes. There must be, in the end, a restoration from delusion, and often a punishment, both of which are precluded by the notion of insanity.

Many readers feel that Don Quixote is too much of a lunatic. In general, therefore, the Comic Individual must not be a criminal, nor must he be a madman.

We are now to take a glance at the instrumentalities of Comedy—at the means which renders the Individual comic. His deceptions can arise from two sources—from the senses and from the mind. It thus may have an external cause, namely, the situation in which he is placed; or it may have an internal origin, namely, his caprice, his imagination, his understanding. Here we have the two essential kinds of Comedy—that of Situation and that of Character. The former seeks its instrumentalities outside of the individual; he is determined by them externally; hence freedom almost disappears in this form of the drama. But, in Comedy of Character, the Individual is self-determined; his situation, in its essential points, is the consequence of his own action—of his own folly or weakness; he is not plunged into it from without, by fate or by accident. In this sphere the Individual will find a realm of freedom.

In Comedy of Situation, therefore, a person is placed in circumstances over which he has little or no control, and is made to pursue absurd and nugatory objects without any direct fault of his own. His deception is brought about through the senses; his mistakes arise from false appearances which hover around him—in general, that which is phantom seems reality. He now follows up his delusions as ends; he meets and collides with others who have similar ends, or with others who have rational ends. The result is an infinite complication of mistakes and deceptions, which is the peculiar nature of Comedy of Situation, or, as is more commonly called from its intricacy, Comedy of Intrigue.

The special forms of this sensuous deception ought also to be classified. In the first place, things may be disguised. The natural and artificial objects which ordinarily surround a man may be so changed that he imagines himself a different person, or in a strange world; sudden transition into a new country, or into a new condition of life, may be made to appear actual, though wholly unreal. Christopher Sly, the drunken tinker, who, being suddenly surrounded by the luxury of a palace, comes to consider himself a lord, is an example. But this phase is quite subsidiary—it is a mere setting for other and greater effects.

The second, and chief, instrumentality of Comedy of Situation is the mistake in personality, or, as it is sometimes called Mistaken Identity. One person is taken for another; thus two persons lose their relations to the society around them, and this society loses its relation to them. The effect is wonderful. The whole world seems to be converted into a dream—into fairyland; the natural order of things is turned upside down; the ordinary mediations of life are perverted or destroyed. A man with a strong head, it is true, may preserve his equilibrium in the confusion; such a one, however, is not a comic character.

You go upon the street; you are taken for somebody else; are familiarly addressed by persons whom you have never before seen, and about matters of which you have never before heard; presents are given you; payment is demanded of you for unknown articles; you are met by a woman who calls herself your wife, and, when you indignantly repudiate her, the law is invoked; you are dragged before a court of justice, where her claim is successfully established by many witnesses, and finally, you are in danger of being lynched by an angry populace. The other person for whom you are taken has also corresponding difficulties; his relations in life are thrown into serious confusion; his business is crossed; his dear wife seems to have gone astray; still, the disturbing influence is to him a total mystery. Society, too, is drawn into the same whirl of delusion. Law, Family, State— the highest institutions of man—become the wild sport of accident. Such a condition of things cannot last long, but, while it does last, there is fun for those who are in the secret. What is the matter? Mistaken Identity, which, however, the parties caught in the complication must not think of, else the spell is broken.

The mistakes of identity are produced mainly in two ways—by Natural Resemblance and by Disguise. The first is an accident, and lies outside of the knowledge of the individuals who happen to be like one another. They are, therefore, the unconscious victims of an external influence; they are involved in a confusion of which nobody knows the origin. But Disguise is intentional—at least on the part of one person, namely, he who has disguised himself. All the other characters of the play may be victimized by the mask, and take the appearance for the reality; or a part of them may be in the secret, and enjoy the sport with the audience.

One individual, however, is not deceived—is free; has a conscious purpose of his own, which he is realizing. Disguise has a thousand shapes; it is the most common artifice, not merely of Comedy, but of the Drama generally. It may run through a whole play and constitute the main point of interest, or it may be employed for a subordinate object in a single scene. Its manifold forms show the originality of the writer of Comedy. Here is his province—the creation of novel disguises and situations. They all, however, have the one common characteristic—deception through a false appearance.

But Disguise has its limits, which will be manifested often beneath the most adroit concealment. The person in mask is usually supposed to be the master of the complications which he weaves around himself, and so he is ordinarily portrayed. But an unsuspected resemblance may come in and disturb his plans. Thus Viola, in *Twelfth Night*, notwithstanding her disguise, is lost in the comic labyrinth by the appearance of her brother, whom she supposed to be drowned. But the true dissolution of Disguise is manifested when character reveals itself beneath the mask, and the internal nature of man shows itself stronger than any external covering. Then the Disguise becomes nothing—it quite disappears. Rosalind, in *As You Like It*, betrays herself when she faints at the story of the bloody handkerchief; both her sex and her love shine out beneath her doublet and hose. The disguised mother at a masquerade will be apt to manifest some peculiar interest in her daughter, and thus reveal both herself and the daughter. The same may be said of many other relations of life. This has a supreme comic effect; it is the climax of Comedy of Situation, and, at the same time, the transition into a deeper principle. The external Disguise has melted away before the internal Character.

It will thus be seen that Comedy of Situation is logically incomplete, and is inadequate to express the more profound comic elements of human nature. Moreover, it is wanting in freedom. That man should be represented as placed in a world of deception and appearance, which cajoles him and leads him astray without any fault on his part, does not satisfy reason or true Aesthetic feeling. Mistakes through sensuous delusion may be very laughable, but they lack the highest comic principle.

We all think that a person ought not to be responsible for that which is external and accidental. Such is sometimes the reality, however, though by no means the deepest and truest reality of human existence. Man must be reached by his own act; he must himself be the cause of his own difficulties. Thus he is moved from within, is self-determined, and is to blame for his follies. Anything short of freedom will not completely satisfy us; it conflicts too strongly with our rational nature.

From these observations it will easily be inferred that, in Comedy of Situation, there can be but little portraiture of character. A person may be caught in a train of ludicrous circumstances, be his disposition what it may. A man's hat blows off on a windy day; is followed by his wig; he runs to pick them out of the mud. He is, no doubt, a laughable object to the bystanders, but such an occurrence is not determined by his character, nor designates it in any way. His behavior under the trying ordeal may reveal certain traits; still, this is not inherent in the situation, but points beyond, namely, to the inner nature of the man.

Thus we arrive at the necessity of the second grand division of Comedy, as manifested in the Individual. From its essential principle it will be best named Comedy of Character. Now, the Individual has truly an absurd end; his deed is internal in its origin; it springs from himself, and cannot be laid to his surroundings. His purpose is still a delusive appearance, which, however, is the product of his own brain. He may even be aware of its insubstantial nature, and yet pursue it; or, he may not be aware of that fact. Here rise up at once before us the two leading phases of Comedy and Character—the Involuntary and the Voluntary.

In the first of these spheres the Individual loses sight of his true relations to the external world, to other individuals, to society. This delusion is not brought about through any disguise of what is real, but through his own folly or infatuation; it does not result from any external deception, but from self-deception. The objects and persons around him have not been changed; the disguise has now gone into his mind—has become internal, and casts its shadow upon his judgment. The mistake, therefore, is not of the senses, but rather of the understanding. This phase of comic development is thus seen to be quite different from Comedy of Situation, though the latter ultimately may reach the judgment through sensuous deception. A servant, forgetting his place, falls in love with his mistress of noble blood—like Malvolio; a stupid clown seeks the hand of a beautiful and wealthy heiress—like Aguecheek.

The ethereal, poetic Titania, Queen of fairyland, becomes infatuated with the gross, prosaic Bottom, fool of fools. All these persons have lost their true relation in the world, and are in pursuit of their own subjective delusions, which, after making them dupes, vanish into nothing. Their purposes break to pieces in the very act of realization. Here are to be reckoned the comic effects of love requited and unrequited, the characters absorbed by a single passion—as avarice or jealousy—odd people, whimsical people, monomaniacs—indeed, most of the delineations of Comic Literature. Still, the limitation before mentioned must not be forgotten, which is liable to be transgressed just at this point. The individual must not be portrayed as devoid of sanity, even in his wildest delusions; otherwise, responsibility ceases—we think his acts are not his own; pity takes the place of merriment. The contradiction which excites the laugh is that the deed be irrational, but the doer rational; both elements must be present.

These absurd ends are pursued in earnest; the character is not usually conscious of their nature. Still, he ought to know better; his conduct deserves to be punished with shouts of laughter. But he may be quite aware of the ridiculousness of what he is doing, and nevertheless do it, and do it seriously. It is possible to be indifferent to the jeers of the world; or, a man may be driven by a passion which is stronger than the fear of ridicule. In this case, however, the result is almost the same as if the comic quality of the act were not known to him. In fact, there is almost every shade from a naive unconsciousness to complete consciousness. With the latter stage a new realm begins to make its appearance.

It is manifest that, in the phase just considered, the Comic Individual has not yet attained perfect freedom—he is still ignorant of a certain element of the nature of his deed; or, he is forced to do what he knows to be ridiculous in order to accomplish his deeper purpose. There is a chasm between his will and his action which is not yet bridged over. Now comes the last and highest development of Comedy—the Comic Individual is not only conscious, but voluntary. He pursues his delusion, knowing that it is a delusion, and because it is a delusion. His purpose is absurd; he intends it to be absurd, and enjoys its absurdity. His delight is in his own tricks and follies; he makes a comedy for his own amusement.

The tinge of seriousness in the character now disappears; the earnest pursuit of a false appearance or delusion has been left behind forever. He performs his own play and is his own audience at the same time; he knows and wills himself to be deceived, and then he steps back, as it were, and laughs at himself, as a spectator would do. Who can assail him? He is complete, for he takes into himself all sides; he is free, for he realizes everything which lies in his intention, and his deed has nothing in it which is alien to what he purposes. Here is the climax of Comic Art; only the greatest geniuses have been able to reach such an elevation. The nicest balance must be maintained; the least swerving to the right or to the left causes a rapid descent into lower regions.

But the highest point is the termination; Comedy can go no further. Its very excellence pushes it beyond its limits, and into dissolution. When the Individual becomes conscious that his action is absurd and contradictory, every effort of the mind is usually directed to getting rid of the contradiction. That rational man can be consciously and purposely irrational, is the supreme absurdity, and, hence, this is just the absurdity upon which the supreme comic character reposes. But the logical process cannot stop at such a fine point of transition. When a person has sense enough to find out that he has no sense, he is already quite sensible.

A famous sage of antiquity may be cited. The great saving of Socrates was that, while previous philosophers thought they knew something, but did not know anything, he knew that he knew nothing. This he justly considered to be quite an advance upon former wisdom. To be conscious of our ignorance is much better than to be simply ignorant; such a consciousness already goes far towards lifting us beyond the assault of folly. At this point, therefore, the comic form begins to dissolve; men will no longer pursue a delusive purpose when they become aware of its true nature.

Let us now recapitulate the various principles which have been elaborated. Comedy exhibits the external or internal deception of the Individual, who, however, must not proceed in his delusion to a serious ethical violation, nor transgress the limits of sanity. To bring about his deception there are two instrumentalities—Situation and Character. The first lies in the senses, the second in the mind. Furthermore, Situation has two elements—the relation of the Comic Individual to the physical world on the

one hand, and his relation to the persons therein on the other hand; both these relations become false appearances through Natural Resemblance and Intentional Disguise. Comedy of Character has also two main forms—the Involuntary and the Voluntary; the former exhibits man as the unwilling, and for the most part unconscious, victim of some whim, delusion, contradiction; while the latter shows a similar conduct as proceeding from conscious volition.

The relation of the Comic Individual to his audience is also worthy of mention. In the pure Comedy of Situation the audience is always presupposed, and must fully comprehend the nature and cause of the deception; it thus stands entirely above the persons in the play, to whom the matter is of the most serious import. The laugh belongs to the man who is not caught in the dilemma. There is thus between the hearer and actor a chasm which gradually becomes smaller, as we approach Comedy of Character, till, finally, it is wholly filled up and smoothed away in the highest form of the latter. For the Voluntary Comic Individual knows and laughs at his own absurdities—he is both actor and spectator. He has reached the serene height of the happy gods, which can be disturbed by nothing from without. Here is seen the true plastic element of Comedy, as far as such a term can be applied to this realm of art.

Activities

1. Shakespeare and Today

Direction: Shakespeare creates a group of "heroines in dress" in his comedies. They are courageous and smart, charming and steadfast. They are constantly in struggle for identity and in pursuit of true love. Following them, modern women go on fighting for better opportunities, better life and better contribution to the world. Make a comparison between women in the modern world and women in Shakespeare's comedies to see in what ways they are similar and different.

2. Shakespeare and China

Direction: The Handan Dream（《邯郸记》）*is one Chinese comic play from Tang Xianzu*（汤显祖）, *in which Lusheng*（卢生）, *a young scholar yet in destitute, was led into a dreamy world by Immortal Lü Dongbin*（吕洞宾）, *in which he experienced numerous ups and downs on his way of life. When he woke up from the dream, the meal was not done yet. Are there any comic features from the play that inspire you most?*

3. Shakespeare and Beyond

Direction: Shakespeare utilizes these characters of fools, also sometimes equated with the word "clown" throughout his plays to a variety of differing ends. You can see **Touchstone**（As You Like It, *Shakespeare's first use of a fool*）, **Feste** （Twelfth Night）, **Bottom** （A Midsummer Night's Dream）, **Dogberry**（Much Ado About Nothing）, *etc. Pick out more characters of fool from Shakespeare's comedies and make comparisons.*

Further Reading

BATE J, 2016. The genius of Shakespeare［M］. New York: Picador.

CHAMPION L S, 1973. The evolution of Shakespeare's comedy［M］. Cambridge, MA: Harvard University Press.

GREENBLATT S, 2016. Will in the world: how Shakespeare became Shakespeare［M］. New York: W W Norton & Company.

MASLEN R W, 2006. Shakespeare and comedy［M］. London: Arden Shakespeare.

李伟民，2020. 中国莎士比亚喜剧研究［M］. 北京: 商务印书馆.

Unit 2 A Midsummer Night's Dream

章节概述

　　城市与树林，白昼与黑夜，清醒与梦境。交替更迭中，情与爱，喜与悲变幻莫测。这就是莎士比亚喜剧的巅峰之作——《仲夏夜之梦》。西方文化中，仲夏夜多指夏至前的那个夜晚。夏至是太阳运行的转折点，传说中，这一夜会有精灵现身。莎士比亚将故事的主要情节安排在这个充满神秘色彩的夏至前夜的小树林中，将神话世界与现实矛盾交织在一起，为整个故事披上了梦幻的薄纱。

　　《仲夏夜之梦》创作于1594年岁末，并首演于1595年，讲述了一个有情人终成眷属的爱情故事。全剧以雅典统治者忒修斯公爵的婚姻为主线，由两对青年男女的爱情纠葛、仙王和仙后的矛盾和解及雅典一群工匠为忒修斯婚礼献演戏剧等情节共同编织成一场妙趣横生的喜剧。

　　故事中的雅典有一条法律。女儿的婚姻要听命于父母，否则要么被处死，要么终生囚于修道院之中。贵族小姐赫米娅 与青年人拉山德相爱，却偏偏遭到父亲的阻挠。赫米娅不愿遵从父亲的意愿嫁给贵族青年狄米特律斯，便决定与拉山德私奔。他们约好在离雅典城一里格（约3英里）的一片树林里汇合并逃离雅典。赫米娅的好友海丽娜偏偏爱着狄米特律斯，她把这一消息透露给狄米特律斯，并一前一后追到树林。同时，一群雅典城的工匠也来到树林排练为忒修斯公爵婚礼助兴的戏剧。

　　在小树林里还住着可爱的小精灵们。仙王奥布朗和仙后提泰妮娅正在为一个换儿（Changeling boy）闹别扭。为了捉弄仙后，仙王命令随从迫克去采一种神奇的花汁。将花汁滴在仙后的眼睛上，她醒来就会狂热地爱上第一眼看到的人或动物。仙王还安排迫克将一些花汁滴到狄米特律斯的眼里，以帮助海丽娜获得渴望的爱情。可是迫克却把拉山德误认为狄米特律斯而滴下了花汁，所有的混乱就此开始。拉山德醒来后看到海丽娜，便不停地向她求爱而将赫米娅抛在一边。仙王发现后，又将花汁滴入狄米特律斯的眼中。狄米特律斯醒来看到海丽娜，便和拉山德争先恐后地向她表白。与此同时，仙后在魔汁的作用下爱上了一个排戏的工匠波顿，而波顿在魔法的作用下变成了一头驴子。仲夏夜的树林里，欢闹痴狂的故事中形式与内容、本质与现象形成巨大反差。当一个个剧中人因不知情而全力应对着各种情形时，观众们却因知情而捧腹大笑。笑声中，我们看到了爱情该有的模样；笑声中，我们深深理解了人文主义对个性解放与爱情自由的宣言。

该剧创作于伊丽莎白一世统治时期。政权相对稳固，社会比较稳定，英国文艺复兴运动和人文主义运动进入繁盛阶段，人们开始认识到自身存在的价值和意义。《仲夏夜之梦》便是这样一部集中体现文艺复兴精神和人文主义思想的喜剧。

《仲夏夜之梦》的情节揭露了莎士比亚时期社会生活中根深蒂固的父权思想。无论是勇敢追求爱情的赫米亚和海丽娜，奋力维护自身权益的仙后提泰妮娅，还是被忒修斯用剑征服却对豪门婚姻并无太多热情的希波吕忒，无不展现了女性的自我觉醒与成长。正如西蒙·德·波伏娃（Simon de Beauvior）①曾写下的：女人不是生来即为女人，而是不断成为女人②。

---

① 西蒙娜·德·波伏娃（1908—1986），法国著名女作家，女权主义者。其《第二性》一书被认为是西方妇女理解自我成长及自我价值的必读之书。

② 该句英语表达为 One is not born a woman, but rather becomes one。

Selected Reading

Act I , i

LYSANDER How now, my love! why is your cheek so pale?

How chance the roses there do fade so fast?

> chance: v. 表示出现某一情况
> 正常语序：How does it chance that...

HERMIA Belike for want of rain, which I could well

Beteem them from the tempest of my eyes.

> belike: adv. probably 可能

> beteem: v. allow/permit 允许

> 正常语序：the torrent of tears which is ready to pour from my eyes 我眼中的滂沱泪雨

LYSANDER Ay me, for aught that I could ever read,

Could ever hear by tale or history,

The course of true love never did run smooth.

But either it was different in blood—

> aught: pron. anything 任何事物

> 这句话的意思是 There was inequality in the matter of birth. 人生来就贵贱有别

HERMIA O cross! Too high to be enthralled to low.

> 这句话的意思是 How one of higher rank could be the slave of love to one beneath him. 地位高的无法因爱而臣服

LYSANDER Or else misgraffèd in respect of years—

HERMIA O spite! Too old to be engaged to young.

LYSANDER Or else it stood upon the choice of merit—

> merit: n. admirable quality 优秀品质
> the choice of merit 的意思是 "什么是优点也要基于别人的认可"

HERMIA O hell! To choose love by another's eyes.

LYSANDER Or, if there were a sympathy in choice,

> sympathy: n. agreement 一致的意见

War, death, or sickness did lay siege to it,

> it: 这里指爱情

Making it momentary as a sound,

Swift as a shadow, short as any dream:

Brief as the lightning in the collied night,

That in a spleen unfolds both heaven and earth,

And ere a man hath power to say 'Behold!'

> ere: pron. before 在……以前
>
> hath: vt. have 的第三人称单数现在时形式

The jaws of darkness do devour it up:

So quick bright things come to confusion.

> confusion: n. ruin 毁灭，莎士比亚戏剧中多见这种用法

HERMIA If then true lovers have been ever

crossed,

It stands as an edict in destiny.

Then let us teach our trial patience,

Because it is a customary cross,

As due to love as thoughts and dreams and

sighs,

Wishes and tears, poor fancy's followers.

> poor fancy's follower 即 poor love's follower 可怜的追爱的人

LYSANDER A good persuasion. Therefore,

hear me, Hermia.

I have a widow aunt, a dowager

Of great revenue, and she hath no child.

From Athens is her house removed seven leagues,

> leagues: n. 里格，一种长度单位，1 里格约等于 3 英里

And she respects me as her only son.

There, gentle Hermia, may I marry thee,

And to that place the sharp Athenian law

Cannot pursue us. If thou lov'st me then

Steal forth thy father's house tomorrow night,

And in the wood, a league without the town,

> without: prep. outside 在……的外面

Where I did meet thee once with Helena,

To do observance to a morn of May,

> 五月的第一个清晨，即欧洲传统节日 "五朔节"

There will I stay for thee.

HERMIA My good Lysander!

I swear to thee, by Cupid's strongest bow,

By his best arrow with the golden head,

By the simplicity of Venus' doves,

By that which knitteth souls and prospers love,

And by that fire which burned the Carthage queen,

When the false Troyan under sail was seen,

By all the vows that ever men have broke,

In number more than ever women spoke,

In that same place thou hast appointed me,

Tomorrow truly will I meet with thee.

LYSANDER Keep promise, love. Look, here comes Helena.

> knitteth 源自 knit，knitteth souls 即将心灵联结在一起
> prosper v. 繁盛，prospers love 即让爱意浓厚

> 迦太基女王 Dido，因特洛伊勇士伊尼亚斯的背弃而引火自焚

> 不忠实的特洛伊人

译文1（辜正坤版）

第一幕第一场	Act I, i

拉山德 亲爱的，怎么啦？脸色这么苍白？

你颊上的玫瑰怎么谢得这么快？

赫米娅 怕是缺少雨露滋养，我有的是滂沱泪雨来把它们浇灌。

拉山德 我曾涉猎的群书，听过的故事和史实，都说真爱路上无坦途，要么是贵贱有别——

赫米娅 哦，倒霉！门第太高无法为爱臣服。

LYSANDER How now, my love! why is your cheek so pale?

How chance the roses there do fade so fast?

HERMIA Belike for want of rain, which I could well

Beteem them from the tempest of my eyes.

LYSANDER Ay me, for aught that I could ever read,

Could ever hear by tale or history,

The course of true love never did run smooth.

But either it was different in blood—

HERMIA O cross! Too high to be enthralled to low.

拉山德　或是生不逢时，年齿悬殊——

赫米娅　哦，头疼！老少参差难成佳偶。

拉山德　再不，就是得听任亲朋拿主张——

赫米娅　嗨，见鬼！得按旁人的眼光挑爱人。

拉山德　即便挑对了人，

战争、死亡、疾病也可能将爱重重围困；

令它像声音一样转瞬即逝，

又飘忽如影，短促如梦；

疾如暗夜闪电，

刹那间照亮天地，

不等人说"看哪！"

就被黑夜的巨口吞噬，

光明就此迅速地殒于黑暗。

赫米娅　如果真心相爱之人总要遭受阻挠，

如果这就是命运的裁断，

是屡见不鲜的磨难。

像思念、梦想和叹息，

像憧憬和眼泪，时时与爱为伴。

那我们两个可怜的追梦人，就耐心忍受考验吧。

LYSANDER　Or else misgraffèd in respect of years—

HERMIA　O spite! Too old to be engaged to young.

LYSANDER　Or else it stood upon the choice of merit—

HERMIA　O hell! To choose love by another's eyes.

LYSANDER　Or, if there were a sympathy in choice,

War, death, or sickness did lay siege to it,

Making it momentary as a sound,

Swift as a shadow, short as any dream:

Brief as the lightning in the collied night,

That in a spleen unfolds both heaven and earth,

And ere a man hath power to say 'Behold!'

The jaws of darkness do devour it up:

So quick bright things come to confusion.

HERMIA　If then true lovers have been ever crossed,

It stands as an edict in destiny.

Then let us teach our trial patience,

Because it is a customary cross,

As due to love as thoughts and dreams and sighs,

Wishes and tears, poor fancy's followers.

拉山德　很有道理。且听我说，赫米娅，

我有个寡居的姑妈，

她进项颇丰，膝下却无人承欢，

因而视我为独子，百般钟爱。

她家离雅典不过七里格，

温柔的赫米娅，到那儿我就能娶你了。

在那儿，雅典的严刑酷法

对我们鞭长莫及。如果你爱我，

明晚就偷偷离开父亲家，

到离城一里格的树林去，

就是依五朔节风俗

我与你和海丽娜清早会面的地方，

我会在那儿等你。

赫米娅　好拉山德，

凭丘比特最硬的弯弓，

和他最锐利的金头箭，

凭维纳斯鸟的纯洁，

凭结合心灵、加深爱意的一切，

凭迦太基女王目睹背信的特洛伊人扬帆离去，

点燃的自焚之火，

凭天下男人背的誓，

它的数目超出古往今来女子的言辞，

我对你发誓，明日我一定在你

LYSANDER A good persuasion. Therefore, hear me, Hermia.

I have a widow aunt, a dowager

Of great revenue, and she hath no child.

From Athens is her house removed seven leagues,

and she respects me as her only son.

There, gentle Hermia, may I marry thee,

And to that place the sharp Athenian law

Cannot pursue us. If thou lov'st me then

Steal forth thy father's house tomorrow night,

And in the wood, a league without the town,

Where I did meet thee once with Helena,

To do observance to a morn of May,

There will I stay for thee.

HERMIA My good Lysander!

I swear to thee, by Cupid's strongest bow,

By his best arrow with the golden head,

By the simplicity of Venus' doves,

By that which knitteth souls and prospers love,

And by that fire which burned the Carthage queen,

When the false Troyan under sail was seen,

By all the vows that ever men have broke,

说的地方，
等着与你见面。

In number more than ever women spoke,

In that same place thou hast appointed me,

Tomorrow truly will I meet with thee.

拉山德 亲爱的，一言为定。瞧，海丽娜来了。

LYSANDER Keep promise, love. Look, here comes Helena.

译文 2（朱生豪版）

Act Ⅱ , i

OBERON Well, go thy way: thou shalt not from this grove

Till I torment thee for this injury.

My gentle Puck, come hither. Thou rememb'rest

Since once I sat upon a promontory,

And heard a mermaid on a dolphin's back

Uttering such dulcet and harmonious breath ——— breath: n. singing 歌声

That the rude sea grew civil at her song,

And certain stars shot madly from their spheres —— certain: adv. surely 确确实实

To hear the sea-maid's music.

ROBIN I remember.

OBERON That very time I saw, but thou couldst not,

Flying between the cold moon and the earth, —— certain: adj. specific 某一个特定的

Cupid, all armed; a certain aim he took

At a fair vestal, thronèd by the west, —— vestal: n. woman vowed to chastity 贞女，很多评论家认为这里意指王座上的伊丽莎白一世

And loosed his love-shaft smartly from his bow,

As it should pierce a hundred thousand hearts. —— as: adv. as if 好像

But I might see young Cupid's fiery shaft

Quenched in the chaste beams of the wat'ry

moon;

And the imperial votress passèd on,

In maiden meditation, fancy-free.

Yet marked I where the bolt of Cupid fell.

It fell upon a little western flower,

Before milk-white, now purple with love's

wound,

And maidens call it love-in-idleness.

Fetch me that flower; the herb I showed thee once:

The juice of it on sleeping eyelids laid

Will make or man or woman madly dote

Upon the next live creature that it sees.

Fetch me this herb, and be thou here again

Ere the leviathan can swim a league.

ROBIN I'll put a girdle round about the earth

In forty minutes.

OBERON Having once this juice,

I'll watch Titania when she is asleep,

And drop the liquor of it in her eyes.

The next thing then she waking looks upon,

Be it on lion, bear, or wolf or bull,

On meddling monkey, or on busy ape,

She shall pursue it with the soul of love.

And ere I take this charm off from her sight,

As I can take it with another herb,

I'll make her render up her page to me.

But who comes here? I am invisible,

And I will overhear their conference.

> imperial votress: 童贞女王

> fancy-free: untouched by thoughts of love 不受爱情的影响

> 正常语序为：Yet I marked where the bolt of Cupid fell 我注意到丘比特的金箭掉落的地方

> milk-white in the past 在过去是乳白色的

> love-in-idleness 多翻译为"爱懒花"，为欧洲常见的三色堇花

> ere: pron. before 在……前

> 这里指海怪利维坦，犹太神话中的一种海兽

> take it: take off the magic power 解除魔力

> another herb: 爱懒花魔汁的解毒药

> render up: give 交出

> page: n. little boy 小男孩

译文1（朱生豪版）

| 第二幕第一场 | Act Ⅱ, i |

奥布朗 好，去你的吧！为着这次的侮辱，我一定要在你离开这座林子之前给你一些惩罚。我的好迫克，过来。你记得有一次我坐在一个海岬上，望见一个美人鱼骑在海豚的背上，她的歌声是那样婉转而谐美，镇静了狂暴的怒海，好几个星星都疯狂地跳出了它们的轨道，为要听这海女的音乐。

OBERON Well, go thy way: thou shalt not from this grove

Till I torment thee for this injury.

My gentle Puck, come hither. Thou rememb'rest

Since once I sat upon a promontory,

And heard a mermaid on a dolphin's back

Uttering such dulcet and harmonious breath

That the rude sea grew civil at her song,

And certain stars shot madly from their spheres

To hear the sea-maid's music.

迫克① 我记得。

ROBIN I remember.

奥布朗 就在那个时候，你看不见，但我能看见持着弓箭的丘比特在冷月和地球之间飞着；他瞄准了坐在西方宝座上的一个童贞女，很灵巧地从他的弓上射出他的爱情之箭，好像它能刺透十万颗心的样子。否则我也许可以看见小丘比特的火箭在如水冷洁的月光中熄灭，那位童贞的女王心中一尘不染，在纯洁的思念中安然无

OBERON That very time I saw, but thou couldst not,

Flying between the cold moon and the earth,

Cupid, all armed; a certain aim he took

At a fair vestal, thronèd by the west,

And loosed his love-shaft smartly from his bow,

As it should pierce a hundred thousand hearts.

But I might see young Cupid's fiery

---

① Robin别称Puck，朱生豪版将其译为迫克。

恙；但是我看见那支箭却落在西方一朵小小的花上，它本来是乳白色的，现在已因爱情的创伤而被染成紫色，少女们把它称作"爱懒花"。去给我把那花采来。我曾经给你看过它的样子；它的汁液如果滴在睡着的人的眼皮上，无论男女，醒来一眼看见什么生物，都会发疯似的对它恋爱。给我采这种花来；在鲸鱼还不曾游过三英里路之前，必须回来复命。

迫克 我可以在四十分钟内环绕世界一周。（下）

奥布朗 这种花汁一到了手，我便留心着等提泰妮娅睡了的时候把它滴在她的眼皮上；她一醒来第一眼看见的东西，无论是狮子也好，熊也好，狼也好，公牛也好，或者好事的狒猴、忙碌的无尾猿也好，她都会用最强烈的爱情追求它。我可以用另一种草解去这种魔

shaft

Quenched in the chaste beams of the wat'ry moon;

And the imperial votress passèd on,

In maiden meditation, fancy-free.

Yet marked I where the bolt of Cupid fell.

It fell upon a little western flower,

Before milk-white, now purple with love's wound,

And maidens call it love-in-idleness.

Fetch me that flower; the herb I showed thee once:

The juice of it on sleeping eyelids laid

Will make or man or woman madly dote

Upon the next live creature that it sees.

Fetch me this herb, and be thou here again

Ere the leviathan can swim a league.

ROBIN I'll put a girdle round about the earth

In forty minutes.

OBERON Having once this juice,

I'll watch Titania when she is asleep,

And drop the liquor of it in her eyes.

The next thing then she waking looks upon,

Be it on lion, bear, or wolf or bull,

On meddling monkey, or on busy ape,

She shall pursue it with the soul of love.

And ere I take this charm off from her

力，但第一我先要叫她把那个孩子让给我。可是谁到这儿来啦？他们看不见我，让我听听他们的谈话。

sight,

As I can take it with another herb,

I'll make her render up her page to me.

But who comes here? I am invisible,

And I will overhear their conference.

译文2（辜正坤版）

Activities

1. Shakespeare and Today

Direction: In a soliloquy from Act Ⅰ, i, the forlorn Helena laments that "love looks not with the eyes, but with the mind". In Act Ⅲ, ii, the enchanted Bottom speaks that "reason and love keep little company together". In the end of the play, proud Theseus derides that "the lunatic, the lover and the poet are of imagination all compact". Swamped with the overloaded modern life, will people be more rational or irrational for love? Why?

2. Shakespeare and China

Direction: Shakespeare creates a fairy world in which you might become someone else, you might fall in love with someone you detest and you might forsake the one you swear to love forever. Chuang Tzu（庄周）, a Chinese ancient philosopher had once dreamt of turning into a butterfly. How to interpret the identity transition between the real and unreal world?

不知周之梦为胡蝶与，胡蝶之梦为周与?

周与胡蝶，则必有分矣。此之谓物化。

——《庄子·齐物论》

3. Shakespeare and Beyond

Direction: Shakespeare loves to sprinkle his stories with botanic images not just to present an oasis of dream and passion but depict characters more vividly and convey their feelings more clearly. Work together to track down more botanical terms from A Midsummer Night's Dream *and his other plays.*

 三色堇	**Act Ⅱ, i**, line 168-171 **Oberon** Yet marked I where the bolt of Cupid fell. It fell upon a little western flower, Before milk-white, now purple with love's wound, And maidens call it love-in-idleness.
 野蔷薇	**Act Ⅱ, i**, line 254-257 **Oberon** I know a bank where the wild thyme blows, When oxlips and nodding violet grows, Quite over-canopied with luscious woodbine, With sweet musk-roses and white eglantine.
 结果的双季开花 樱桃树	**Act Ⅲ, ii**, line 209-212 **Helena** So we grew together Like to a double cherry, seeming parted, But yet a union in partition, Two lovely berries moulded on one stem, So with two seeming bodies but one heart.

Further Reading

ALXENDER L, 2008. Shakespeare's comedy of love [M]. London: Rutledge.

BARBER C L, 2011. Shakespeare's festive comedy: a study of dramatic form and its relation to social custom [M]. New Jersey: Princeton University.

波伏娃，1998. 第二性 [M]. 陶铁柱，译. 北京：中国书籍出版社.

傅光明，2018. 戏梦—莎翁：莎士比亚的喜剧世界[M].天津：天津人民出版社.

威尔斯，2019. 莎士比亚植物志 [M].王睿，译. 北京：人民文学出版社.

Unit 3　Twelfth Night

章节概述

《第十二夜》（或《各遂所愿》）是莎士比亚在1600—1602年创作的一部著名喜剧，也是他最后一部早期喜剧。这个时期，无论是戏剧创作还是思想深度，莎士比亚都进入一个相当成熟的阶段。他的喜剧不仅对人生、对爱情有了更深刻的理解和诠释，其剧情中还刻意存留了一些那个时代独有历史风貌。全剧共五幕十八场，暗流涌动、悲喜交织的情节及个性鲜明的众多人物，都表现了莎士比亚深深的人文主义情怀。

故事的主角是长得一模一样的双胞胎兄妹西巴斯辛和薇奥拉。他们在一次航海事故中失散，并各自侥幸脱险，流落到美丽的伊利里亚。薇奥拉以为哥哥身遭不幸，便化名西萨里奥女扮男装在当地统治者奥西诺公爵门下当侍童。奥西诺公爵派薇奥拉替自己向年轻貌美的伯爵小姐奥丽维娅求婚。不料伯爵小姐拒绝了公爵的爱意，却对女扮男装的薇奥拉情有独钟，而薇奥拉却在心底偷偷地爱着公爵。年轻的他们在爱而不得中饱受煎熬。不久，薇奥拉的兄长西巴斯辛与救他的船长安东尼奥也来到伊利里亚，碰巧遇到了奥丽维娅。伯爵小姐以为这就是她爱的那个俊朗少年西萨里奥，便大胆求婚，西巴斯辛也欣然接受。最终，真相大白，兄妹历经生死终得以团圆，奥西诺公爵也爱上了聪慧勇敢的薇奥拉。整个故事延续了莎士比亚喜剧最典型的爱情架构，从哀伤的起点一路向前，历经磨难终于抵达快乐美满的爱情终点。在伊利里亚蔚蓝的大海及芳香四溢的百花映衬下，全剧弥漫着浓郁迷人的浪漫气息。

在欧洲，每年圣诞节后的第十二天，即1月6日是基督教"主显节"，用以纪念耶稣诞生后，东方三贤到伯利恒①（Bethlehem）朝拜圣婴的故事。"第十二夜"就是"主显节"之夜，人们会举行盛大的庆祝活动。到了莎士比亚时期，"第十二夜"的宗教色彩已逐渐淡化，而演变为一个世俗气息浓郁的狂欢之夜。莎士比亚将这部剧命名为《第十二夜》，正是为了契合这样一个特别的日子。虽然故事里的世界与现实相去甚远，但在这个特别的日子，走进莎翁笔下的伊利里亚，看故事里的他们错爱、失爱又获爱，我们在笑声中明白，在这个世界里，所有的出乎意料、所有的荒诞离奇都无须追问缘由。

其实，爱和快乐本就不需要理由。爱情让人怦然心动，刻骨铭心，却也可以毫无道理可言，就像伯爵小姐因兄长离世而悲伤地远离爱情，却又无法自拔地对薇奥拉一见钟情，她说："如今怎么办？怎么这么快就染上爱情这种瘟疫？"但爱与快乐又有着无数的理由，就像薇奥拉深深隐藏起对公爵的爱慕，并义不容辞、竭尽全力帮自己所爱的人追求幸福。当薇奥拉说出"我定全力成全您的心愿——但此事甚难！"时，她的内心是苦涩的，更是温暖的，因为真正的爱情也许不只是拥有，更是付出。

奥西诺公爵与薇奥拉、奥丽维娅与西巴斯辛大团圆的结局让我们欣喜，但细细品味，我们又会产生些许的疑惑。奥西诺公爵拉起薇奥拉的手，意味着放弃了长久以来对奥丽维娅的爱情渴望。奥丽维娅表白西巴斯辛，但心中爱的其实是女扮男装的薇奥拉，毕竟世上没两片完全相同的叶子，西巴斯辛并不完全等于那个让她心动的西萨里奥。那么薇奥拉呢？直到剧终，她都未换回那一身女儿装。奥西诺公爵说："当你还是一个男人的时候，你便是西萨里奥。等你换了别样的衣裙，你才是奥西诺心上情人。"那么薇奥拉的爱情会圆满吗？

我们不妨把《第十二夜》当作一个狂欢节日的故事，随主人公们去浪漫一程吧。

---

① 伯利恒，巴勒斯坦中部城市，相传为耶稣降生地，被认为是基督教圣地。

Selected Reading

Act I, i

Illyria: 亚得里亚海东部国家，现克罗地亚，全剧故事在这里发生

Enter Orsino Duke of Illyria, Curio, and other Lords

ORSINO If music be the food of love, play on,

Give me excess of it, that surfeiting,

The appetite may sicken, and so die.

sicken, and so die: 使……患病，并消亡

That strain again, it had a dying fall:

a dying fall: 旋律愈来愈低沉

O, it came o'er my ear like the sweet sound

That breathes upon a bank of violets,

stealing and giving odour: 这里作伴随状语，指甜美的乐声唤着紫罗兰的芳香，也将花香撒向四方

Stealing and giving odour. Enough, no more,

'Tis not so sweet now as it was before.

O spirit of love, how quick and fresh art thou

That, notwithstanding thy capacity,

Receiveth as the sea: 作定语从句，修饰 capacity，指如海洋一般吞纳万物的容纳力，"th" 为古英语中动词第三人称词尾

Receiveth as the sea. Nought enters there,

Of what validity and pitch soe'er,

正常语序为：No matter what validity and pitch it bears 不论它怎样珍贵高档

But falls into abatement and low price

abatement and low price: 指一种毫无价值的状态

Even in a minute. So full of shapes is fancy

That it alone is high fantastical.

正常语序为：Fancy is so full of shapes. fancy 这里指爱情，句子意思为：爱情是如此充满变幻

CURIO Will you go hunt, my lord?

ORSINO What, Curio?

high fantastical: 即 highly fantastical, 非常奇妙的

CURIO The hart.

ORSINO Why so I do, the noblest that I have.

这是奥西诺公爵回应随从的话，"是的，我正在经历着一场如狩猎般的追逐，被捕猎的我高贵的心"

O, when mine eyes did see Olivia first,

Methought she purged the air of pestilence.

methought: 这里作插入语，据我看，我想

That instant was I turned into a hart,

And my desires, like fell and cruel hounds,

fell: adj. fierce, cruel 残暴的，凶恶的

E'er since pursue me.

Enter Valentine

How now, what news from her?

VALENTINE So please my lord, I might not be admitted,

But from her handmaid do return this answer:

The element itself, till seven years' heat,

Shall not behold her face at ample view,

But like a cloistress she will veilèd walk,

And water once a day her chamber round

With eye-offending brine—all this to season

A brother's dead love, which she would keep fresh

And lasting in her sad remembrance.

ORSINO O, she that hath a heart of that fine frame

To pay this debt of love but to a brother,

How will she love when the rich golden shaft

Hath killed the flock of all affections else

That live in her—when liver, brain and heart,

These sovereign thrones, are all supplied, and filled

Her sweet perfections with one self king!

Away before me, to sweet beds of flowers.

Love thoughts lie rich when canopied with bowers.

[*Exeunt*]

> 正常语序为: The outer world(the air and sky around and above) itself shall not see her face completely till it has been warmed by the sun during seven annual revolutions. 在七个寒暑不曾过去之前，就是青天也不能窥见她的全貌

> season: v. 给……加调味料，这里指奥丽薇娅要通过这样的方式让自己对亡兄的爱保持常新，永不消失

> 正常语序为: her love for her dead brother

> 传说中爱神丘比特的金箭

> 正常语序为: When the organs of her being, the thrones of all noble thought and feeling, which constitute her rare perfection, shall be occupied by one and the same king. 她的肝、脑和心，这些至高无上的御座，被一个且是唯一的君王占据，并充满她一切可爱的品性

> before me: lead the way, precede me 前面带路

> bower: n. arbour 树荫遮蔽之处，亦可理解为凉亭

译文1（辜正坤版）

<table>
<tr><td colspan="2" align="center">第一幕第一场</td><td colspan="2" align="center">Act I, i</td></tr>
</table>

第一幕第一场	Act I, i
伊利里亚公爵奥西诺、丘里奥与其他贵族上	*Enter Orsino Duke of Illyria, Curio, and other Lords*
奥西诺 若音乐是爱情的食粮，奏吧，	**ORSINO** If music be the food of love, play on,
多多给我奏响，直到过量，	Give me excess of it, that surfeiting,
欲望才会腻烦，才会死亡。	The appetite may sicken, and so die.
那首曲子再来一遍，它调子渐消。	That strain again, it had a dying fall:
啊，如天籁掠过我的耳旁，	O, it came o'er my ear like the sweet sound
吹拂着一片紫罗兰，	That breathes upon a bank of violets,
窃来又送出芳香。够了，停！	Stealing and giving odour. Enough, no more,
现在已不如原先动听。	'Tis not so sweet now as it was before.
啊，爱情，你那么活泼有生机，	O spirit of love, how quick and fresh art thou
尽管你的容量	That, notwithstanding thy capacity,
像大海一样。沦陷其中的万物，	Receiveth as the sea. Nought enters there,
无论再珍贵高档，	Of what validity and pitch soe'er,
无不瞬间贬值缩水。	But falls into abatement and low price
因此爱情变幻多端，	Even in a minute. So full of shapes is fancy
它本身就有很多花样。	That it alone is high fantastical.
丘里奥 要去打猎吗，殿下？	**CURIO** Will you go hunt, my lord?
奥西诺 猎什么，丘里奥？	**ORSINO** What, Curio?
丘里奥 鹿。	**CURIO** The hart.
奥西诺 我正在打猎啊，不过猎的是我的心。	**ORSINO** Why so I do, the noblest that I have.

啊，我初见奥丽维亚，
感觉四周气息因她清新甜美。

那一刻我变成了一头鹿，
我的情欲如凶猛残暴的猎犬，

从此把我追逐。
瓦伦丁上
如何？她那里可有消息？

瓦伦丁　启禀殿下，我没能进去。
但她的侍女传回了她的答复：

老天亦不能瞧见她的全貌，

除非经过七个夏天。
她要像修女般蒙着面纱走路，
每天要用伤眼的咸泪水

洒遍她的闺房——这都为了不忘
亡兄的爱，她要使之鲜活，

长久保存在自己的悲伤记忆中。

奥西诺　啊，她的心底如此美好，
仅对兄长就有如此爱意。
她的爱可以想象，如果珍贵的金箭

O, when mine eyes did see Olivia first,
Methought she purged the air of pestilence.

That instant was I turned into a hart,
And my desires, like fell and cruel hounds,

E'er since pursue me.

Enter Valentine

How now, what news from her?

VALENTINE　So please my lord, I might not be admitted,

But from her handmaid do return this answer:

The element itself, till seven years' heat,

Shall not behold her face at ample view,

But like a cloistress she will veilèd walk,

And water once a day her chamber round

With eye-offending brine—all this to season

A brother's dead love, which she would keep fresh

And lasting in her sad remembrance.

ORSINO　O, she that hath a heart of that fine frame

To pay this debt of love but to a brother,

How will she love when the rich golden shaft

173

把她心中所有其他情感	Hath killed the flock of all affections else
都消灭——肝、脑和心	That live in her—when liver, brain and heart,
这些至高无上的王座，全被	These sovereign thrones, are all supplied, and filled
她对一位君王宝贵完美的爱占领！	Her sweet perfections with one self king!
前面走，到美丽的花园。	Away before me, to sweet beds of flowers.
凉亭之下情思最烂漫。	Love thoughts lie rich when canopied with bowers.
众人下	[*Exeunt*]

译文2（朱生豪版）

Act V, i

Enter Sebastian

SEBASTIAN I am sorry, madam, I have hurt your kinsman.

But, had it been the brother of my blood,

> 虚拟语气，正常语序为：if it were not the brother of my own
> 如果这不是我的兄长

I must have done no less with wit and safety.

You throw a strange regard upon me, and by that

> regard: n. look 凝视，看

I do perceive it hath offended you.

> hath: have 的第三人称单数

Pardon me, sweet one, even for the vows,

We made each other but so late ago.

> so late ago: a combination of 'so lately' and 'so short a time ago' 不久之前

ORSINO One face, one voice, one habit, and two persons,

A natural perspective, that is and is not!

SEBASTIAN Antonio, O my dear Antonio!

How have the hours racked and tortured me,

Since I have lost thee!

ANTONIO Sebastian are you?

SEBASTIAN Fear'st thou that, Antonio?

ANTONIO How have you made division of

yourself?

An apple cleft in two is not more twin

Than these two creatures. Which is Sebastian?

OLIVIA Most wonderful!

SEBASTIAN Do I stand there? I never had a

brother,

Nor can there be that deity in my nature

Of here and every where. I had a sister,

Whom the blind waves and surges have devoured.

Of charity, what kin are you to me?

What countryman? What name? What parentage?

VIOLA Of Messaline. Sebastian was my father,

Such a Sebastian was my brother too,

So went he suited to his watery tomb.

If spirits can assume both form and suit

You come to fright us.

SEBASTIAN A spirit I am indeed.

But am in that dimension grossly clad

Which from the womb I did participate.

Were you a woman, as the rest goes even,

I should my tears let fall upon your cheek,

And say 'Thrice-welcome, drowned Viola!'

VIOLA My father had a mole upon his brow.

perspective 一词在莎翁作品中多次出现，莎学家们多认为该词指一种透视镜，这里可以理解为 mirror，指双胞胎兄妹形如一人，如镜中的影子一般

正常语序为：that is and that is not 是这样，又不是这样

正常语序为：Are you so astonished that you doubt my being Sebastian 难道你不相信是我吗

deity: n. 神，神性

here and every where: 这里副词做名词用，指四处现身

我的兄长也叫同一个名字——西巴斯辛

suited: adj. dressed 这样的着装，此处作状语

正常语序为：if spirits have the power to assume both the form and dress of a man
assume: v. take on a certain form 呈现……的样子

go even（with sth）：相吻合

正常语序为：I should let my tears fall upon your cheek 我一定会让我的眼泪滴在你的脸上

SEBASTIAN And so had mine.

VIOLA And died that day when Viola from her birth

Had numbered thirteen years.

SEBASTIAN O, that record is lively in my soul!

He finished indeed his mortal act

That day that made my sister thirteen years.

VIOLA If nothing lets to make us happy both

But this my masculine usurped attire,

Do not embrace me till each circumstance

Of place, time, fortune, do cohere and jump

That I am Viola—which to confirm,

I'll bring you to a captain in this town,

Where lie my maiden weeds, by whose gentle help

I was preserved to serve this noble count.

All the occurrence of my fortune since

Hath been between this lady and this lord.

SEBASTIAN So comes it, lady, you have been mistook.

But nature to her bias drew in that.

You would have been contracted to a maid,

Nor are you therein, by my life, deceived,

You are betrothed both to a maid and man.

ORSINO Be not amazed; right noble is his blood.—

If this be so, as yet the glass seems true,

I shall have share in this most happy wreck. —

Boy, thou hast said to me a thousand times

mortal act: 人离世前在世间的活动

lets to: hinders, stop 阻止

正常语序为: this dress of a man, which I have put on without having any right to 我这身本无权穿着的男装

cohere and jump: agree and tally in proving that I am Viola
jump: v.相吻合，相符合

weeds: n. clothes 这种用法在莎剧中较常见

I was preserved: 我就得以留在这里

count: n.伯爵

to her bias: according to her likes or dislikes 介词短语作状语，按照自己的喜好

have been contracted: 订婚

the glass: the mirror, 指双胞胎兄妹仿佛镜子里的身影一般

Thou never **shouldst** love woman **like to** me.

VIOLA And all those sayings will I overswear;

And those swearings keep as true in soul

As **doth** that **orbèd continent** the fire

That severs day from night.

ORSINO Give me thy hand，

And let me see thee in thy woman's weeds.

VIOLA The captain that did bring me first on shore

Hath my maid's garments. He upon some action

Is now **in durance**, at Malvolio's suit,

A gentleman, and follower of my lady's.

OLIVIA He shall **enlarge** him...

> shouldst: 古英语中 shall 的第二人称单数过去式，表示"将"的意思
>
> like to: as much as 像我爱一个女人那样
>
> doth: 古英语中 do 的第三人称单数
>
> orbèd continent: 球形的天体，此处指太阳，蕴藏着昼夜不熄的烈火
>
> in durance: imprisoned 身处牢狱之中
>
> enlarge: v. elease 释放

译文1（辜正坤版）

第五幕第一场

西巴斯辛上

西巴斯辛 抱歉，小姐，我伤了你的族人。

然而，即使那是我的同胞兄弟，为了适当的自卫我也不会留情。

你用奇怪的眼神看我，由此我明白这件事冒犯了你。

原谅我，亲爱的，就算为了

不久前我们对彼此发的誓言。

奥西诺 一副面孔，一个嗓音，一样装扮，却是两个人。

Act V, i

Enter Sebastian

SEBASTIAN I am sorry, madam, I have hurt your kinsman.

But, had it been the brother of my blood, I must have done no less with wit and safety.

You throw a strange regard upon me, and by that

I do perceive it hath offended you.

Pardon me, sweet one, even for the vows,

We made each other but so late ago.

ORSINO One face, one voice, one habit, and two persons,

自然的透镜，是又不是！

西巴斯辛 安东尼奥，啊，亲爱的安东尼奥！

这几个钟头让我痛苦、备受煎熬，

自打我找你不到！

安东尼奥 你是西巴斯辛？

西巴斯辛 你有疑虑吗，安东尼奥？

安东尼奥 你是如何把自己分开的？

一个分成两半的苹果也比不上这两个双胞胎这样相像。哪个是西巴斯辛？

奥丽维亚 太妙了！

西巴斯辛 站在那儿的是我吗？我从来都没有兄弟。

我也没有什么神灵特性可以四处现身。我有个妹妹，

无情的波涛和海浪已把她吞没。

请好心告诉我，你和我有什么亲戚关系？

和我一个国家吗？叫什么名字？父母是谁？

薇奥拉 我来自梅萨林。我的父亲叫西巴斯辛。

我哥哥也叫作西巴斯辛。

他葬身水墓的时候也是这样打扮。

A natural perspective, that is and is not!

SEBASTIAN Antonio, O my dear Antonio!

How have the hours racked and tortured me,

Since I have lost thee!

ANTONIO Sebastian are you?

SEBASTIAN Fear'st thou that, Antonio?

ANTONIO How have you made division of yourself?

An apple cleft in two is not more twin Than these two creatures. Which is Sebastian?

OLIVIA Most wonderful!

SEBASTIAN Do I stand there? I never had a brother,

Nor can there be that deity in my nature Of here and every where. I had a sister,

Whom the blind waves and surges have devoured.

Of charity, what kin are you to me?

What countryman? What name? What parentage?

VIOLA Of Messaline. Sebastian was my father,

Such a Sebastian was my brother too, So went he suited to his watery tomb.

如果鬼魂有外貌能穿衣，
你一定是鬼魂来吓我们的。
西巴斯辛　我确实是鬼魂，
但是却被血肉深深包裹，
这是从在子宫里我就具有的。
若你是女人，因为别的一切都符合，
我该让眼泪落在你脸颊，

说一声："三倍欢迎，溺水的薇奥拉！"
薇奥拉　我父亲眉间有颗痣。

西巴斯辛　我父亲也有。
薇奥拉　辞世那天是薇奥拉出生以来
数到第十三年。
西巴斯辛　啊，这件事深深烙在我心中！
他确实在那天完结了人间行动
正值我妹妹十三岁生日。

薇奥拉　如果阻止我们俩高兴的事情
只有我的这身盗用男装。
别拥抱我，直到所有情况

包括地点、时间和遭遇都连贯，
说明我是薇奥拉——为了证实

If spirits can assume both form and suit
You come to fright us.
SEBASTIAN　A spirit I am indeed.
But am in that dimension grossly clad
Which from the womb I did participate.
Were you a woman, as the rest goes even,
I should my tears let fall upon your cheek,
And say 'Thrice-welcome, drowned Viola!'
VIOLA　My father had a mole upon his brow.
SEBASTIAN　And so had mine.
VIOLA　And died that day when Viola from her birth
Had numbered thirteen years.
SEBASTIAN　O, that record is lively in my soul!
He finished indeed his mortal act
That day that made my sister thirteen years.
VIOLA　If nothing lets to make us happy both
But this my masculine usurped attire,
Do not embrace me till each circumstance
Of place, time, fortune, do cohere and jump
That I am Viola—which to confirm,

我要带你去见这城里的一位船长，

我的女装留在那里，是他好心帮助

我才得以服侍这位高贵的公爵。

自此有关我命运的一切事情

都发生在这位小姐和这位公爵之间。

西巴斯辛 一切都清楚了，小姐，你弄错了。

都是造化根据她的偏好造成的。

你原打算与一位少女订婚，

至于我，你也不算受骗，

你和少女和汉子都订了婚。

奥西诺 勿惊慌；他的血统还挺高贵。——

如果事情如此，透视镜看起来也真，

我要从这次最幸运的沉船中分一杯羹，——

孩子，你对我说过一千次

你永不会爱女人像爱我一样多。

薇奥拉 我可以一遍遍为那些话发誓；

所有那些誓言都存在心中，真

I'll bring you to a captain in this town,

Where lie my maiden weeds, by whose gentle help

I was preserved to serve this noble count.

All the occurrence of my fortune since

Hath been between this lady and this lord.

SEBASTIAN So comes it, lady, you have been mistook.

But nature to her bias drew in that.

You would have been contracted to a maid,

Nor are you therein, by my life, deceived,

You are betrothed both to a maid and man.

ORSINO Be not amazed; right noble is his blood.—

If this be so, as yet the glass seems true,

I shall have share in this most happy wreck.—

Boy, thou hast said to me a thousand times

Thou never shouldst love woman like to me.

VIOLA And all those sayings will I overswear;

And those swearings keep as true in

实得	soul
就像那个天体火球	As doth that orbèd continent the fire
让白昼和黑夜分明。	That severs day from night.
奥西诺 把你的手给我，	**ORSINO** Give me thy hand,
让我看看身着女装的你。	And let me see thee in thy woman's weeds.
薇奥拉 最先把我救上岸的船长	**VIOLA** The captain that did bring me first on shore
存着我的女装。他因涉诉讼，	Hath my maid's garments. He upon some action
现在正被羁押。告他的马伏里奥	Is now in durance, at Malvolio's suit,
	A gentleman, and follower of my lady's.
是这位小姐的随从跟班。	
奥丽维亚 他会释放他的……	**OLIVIA** He shall enlarge him...

译文2（朱生豪版）

Activities

1. Shakespeare and Today

Direction: Mutual learning among civilizations is an important driving force for advancement of human civilization and peaceful development of the whole world. Twelfth Night *and some other Shakespearean plays provide great possibilities for artists to recreate and represent on different stages all over the world. Watch the Chinese traditional Yue Opera* Twelfth Night *and see whether you can resonate to the story as well as the original one.*
（https://www.bilibili.com/video/av986950012/）

2. Shakespeare and China

Direction: Mulan is a Chinese girl who disguised herself into a male soldier and fought in the frontline so that her old father could stay safe at home.

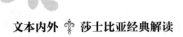

Make a comparison between Mulan and Viola to see in what ways the two girls are similar to or different from each other.

　　旦辞爷娘去，暮宿黄河边，不闻爷娘唤女声，但闻黄河流水鸣溅溅。
　　旦辞黄河去，暮至黑山头，不闻爷娘唤女声，但闻燕山胡骑鸣啾啾。
　　……

　　万里赴戎机，关山度若飞。朔气传金柝，寒光照铁衣。
　　将军百战死，壮士十年归。

——《木兰辞》

3. Shakespeare and Beyond

Direction: Shakespeare chooses the names of his characters carefully and often the names have hidden meanings. Work together to explore more secrets behind the character names in his plays. Following are examples for you.

– **Shylock** (*The Merchant of Venice*) is from the Hebrew Shallach (cormorant), or from Shiloh (Genesis 49:10, although the word means 'messiah') with connotations of wary secrecy and hoarding.

– **Oberon** (*A Midsummer Night's Dream*) is derived from Lord Berners's prose translation of the medieval French poem *Huon de Bordeaux*(《波尔多的荣恩》), and as well is indebted to the story of Zeus in Greek mythology.

– **Juliet** (*Romeo and Juliet*) is derived from the French name "Juliette", which translates to "youthful", for the youth and beauty of the fourteen-year-old Juliet in the story.

– **Cesario** (*Twelfth Night*) suggests untimely birth, as in "Caesarean section", a baby "from his mother's womb untimely ripped", through which Shakespeare suggests a quite unusual circumstance of identity disorder in love.

Further reading

BRYSON B, 2016. Shakespeare: the world as a stage [M]. UK: William Collins.

DRMITRIU C, 2011. Shakespeare dictionary of plays and characters [M]. Shanghai: Shanghai Bookstore Publishing House.

KERMODE F, 2001. Shakespeare's language [M]. London: Penguin Books Ltd.

ROU R P, 2011. The Shakespeare guide to Italy [M]. New York: Harper Perennial.

康拉德，2021. 莎士比亚：悲喜世界与人性永恒的舞台[M]. 齐彦婧，译. 北京：北京燕山出版社.

Part Five Shakespeare's Tragedies

Unit 1 The Origin of Tragedy

章节概述

　　西方悲剧从古希腊悲剧发展至今已有两千五百多年历史。希腊悲剧起源于民间的酒神崇拜和祭祀活动，题材大都取自神话。"悲剧"一词，希腊文的原意是"山羊之歌"。祭神者披上羊皮毛，模拟酒神狄俄倪索斯的伴侣——萨提尔（它是具有人形而又长着羊耳朵羊尾巴的一种半人半羊神）；这种祭仪中还保留着许多远古时代的习俗痕迹，比如以清脆的长笛和低沉的羯鼓声乐伴奏，饮宴狂舞，杀牲献祭。古希腊最著名的悲剧诗人有三位：埃斯库罗斯（Aeschylus）、索福克勒斯（Sophocles）和欧里庇得斯（Euripides）。在埃斯库罗斯之前，戏剧只有一位演员，演出由独白和旁白组成。埃斯库罗斯将演员发展为两人，可以用对话方式表演。此后，对话成了戏剧的主体部分。因对古希腊悲剧艺术发展做出的开创性贡献，埃斯库罗斯被誉为"悲剧之父"。希腊悲剧的主题常涉及命运。在诗人们看来，"人们的命运是生前注定的，无法加以改变；但是他们也尊重人类的自由意志，并在人类的自由意志和命运的冲突中建立悲剧主题，教导人们怎样积极地从事生活和斗争。"[1]他们的代表作《被缚的普罗米修斯》《俄狄浦斯王》《美狄亚》对后世产生了深远的影响。

---

[1]廖可兑：《西欧戏剧史》，北京：中国戏剧出版社，2001年，第9页。

第一个为悲剧下定义的人是亚里士多德。"悲剧是对一个严肃、完整、有一定长度的行动的摹仿,它的媒介是经过'装饰'的语言,以不同的形式分别被用于剧的不同部分,它的摹仿方式是借助人物的行动,而不是叙述,通过引发怜悯和恐惧使这些情感得到疏泄。"[1]这是西方第一个完整的悲剧定义。他认为,悲剧应该描写英雄人物殒命的故事,环境因素让他们的命运发生逆转,从而置他们于死地。所有的剧作都应该奉行时间、地点和行动相一致的原则,即著名的"三一"定律。在悲剧的效果上,亚里士多德提出了"净化说",认为悲剧使人产生怜悯和恐惧并让压抑的心情得到疏通。通过情绪的放纵和宣泄最终人们心情恢复平静,达到心灵的净化。

古罗马时期的悲剧创作虽不如古希腊那样繁荣,也有着悠久的发展历程和卓越的成就。塞内加(Lucius Annaeus Seneca)是这一时期著名的悲剧创作家和哲学家。他所处的时代政治极其残酷。他本人命运多舛,这使他产生了悲观的世界观和绝望的思想。在他看来,世界被盲目无情的命运支配,任何人都无法和命运抗争。他认为悲剧情节应该简单,没有什么复杂的矛盾和冲突。悲剧英雄应该性格单纯、反抗暴力、勇往直前,直到毁灭自己为止。塞内加的悲剧作品辞藻华丽,常写鬼神巫师,渲染恐怖事件,充斥着暴力和谋杀。它们深刻地影响了伊丽莎白时代的第一批戏剧大家,以及比他们稍晚一点的同时代人、他们的直接后继者莎士比亚。

经过漫长而黑暗的中世纪后,悲剧以及整个戏剧创作迎来了文艺复兴的曙光。14世纪中叶的文艺复兴运动起源于意大利,继而席卷全欧洲。这时的人文主义者们提倡"人道",反对"神道";提倡"人权",反对"神权";提倡"个性解放",反对"禁欲主义"。这一时期迎来了戏剧史上最璀璨的星辰——莎士比亚。

莎士比亚共创作了11部悲剧。著名的"四大悲剧"——《哈姆雷特》《奥赛罗》《李尔王》《麦克白》——均完成于他戏剧创作的高峰期(1601—1607)。莎士比亚悲剧借用已有题材描写久远年代或异国的故事,但都深刻地反映了16世纪末17世纪初英国的社会现实。

---

[1] 亚里士多德:《诗学》,陈中梅译注,北京:商务印书馆,2009年,第63页。

莎士比亚的悲剧通常围绕王公贵族、帝王将相展开。他们的行动虽然出自本人的意志和内心，但因为性格上的缺陷，他们的选择往往使他们走向不幸的结局，其故事常常以死亡而终结。

莎士比亚的悲剧有丰富的主题，其中最突出的是理想和现实的冲突，对死亡的思考和对命运无常的无可奈何。就像古希腊悲剧一样，英雄意志逃不脱命运的桎梏。莎士比亚擅长以大量的笔墨描写人物剧烈的内心冲突。他的语言汪洋恣肆，一泻千里，既富含哲理，又机智俏皮，具有无与伦比的表现力。

莎士比亚悲剧在时空律法上摆脱了古典戏剧的束缚，也在人物塑造上体现了文艺复兴时期创作的多样化和生命力。在欣赏莎士比亚的悲剧时，观众可以跟随剧情体味到同情和恐惧，从而意识到世界的不确定性以及很多人们习以为常的准则的脆弱。这也是悲剧的力量，让观众在平凡的生活中品味到美与崇高感，经历苦痛中的升华。

Selected Reading

What Is a Tragedy?[①]
Stanley Wells

People like labels. When we think about plays there's a natural tendency to group them into categories according to their subject matter and the way in which it is treated. The commonest dramatic categories are tragedy and comedy, terms which refer to the plays' overall tone and substance, and we may subdivide them respectively into domestic tragedies, heroic tragedies, and love tragedies; or into romantic comedies, farcical comedies, and sentimental comedies; and so on. Putting it simplistically, by comedies we mean plays that aim to make us laugh and that have a more or less happy ending—often marriage—and when we speak of tragedies we mean plays

---

① Stanley Wells, *Shakespeare's Tragedies: A Very Short Introduction*, London: Oxford University Press, 2017.

that end unhappily, usually with the death of one or more of their central characters.

Around half of Shakespeare's thirty-seven or so plays are tragedies in the most basic sense of the word, that is to say, plays leading up to the death of their central character or characters. He wrote them throughout his career, interspersing them with other plays that are primarily comic in tone. No doubt he varied the categories partly because, at least after the first few years when he worked as a freelance, in 1594 he became the house dramatist of a single company of actors, the Lord Chamberlain's, later the King's Men, who would expect him to provide variety of entertainment for playgoers who would often pay repeated visits to the same playhouse though it was also because he responded to internal as well as external pressures, seeking to deepen his exploration in dramatic form of matters of life and death. Hamlet, for example, is far more self-questioning than Romeo; Macbeth's career of self-destruction is portrayed with more inwardness than Richard III's; and Lear's descent into madness is charted with more psychological plausibility than Titus Andronicus's.

In this book I shall devote a chapter to each of the plays generally classed as tragedies, in the order in which Shakespeare wrote them, except for those classed in the Folio as histories, which will form the subject of a separate volume. In keeping with the aims of this series, hope to be genuinely introductory that is, to assume readers who, while they may have heard of some or all of these plays, have had no close experience of them either on the page or on the stage—and also to give readers a sense of why it's worth taking an interest in them. I shall write about each play's plot and structure, its origins, its literary and theatrical style, its place in Shakespeare's development, its impact, and the opportunities and challenges it has offered to performers over the centuries.

In 1623 the compilers of the first collected edition of plays by Shakespeare, known as the First Folio, grouped the plays not simply as comedies and tragedies, but as comedies, histories, and tragedies. Under histories' they included only plays that tell stories based on English history: those based on Greek, Roman, Scottish, and ancient British history—all of which end with the deaths of one or more of their central characters—they called tragedies. They found it difficult to pigeonhole certain plays. Although *Cymbeline*, normally regarded nowadays as a comedy (if of a rather peculiar kind), has historical elements, they printed it among the tragedies; and they squeezed in *Troilus and Cressida*, which Bart van Es, in his volume in the Very Short Introduction series devoted to the comedies, discusses as a 'problem comedy.'

The Folio's overall grouping of the plays is illogical in that two of its categories—tragedies and comedies—refer to dramatic form, whereas the other, histories, refers to subject matter. In 1598 the first published list of plays by Shakespeare had, more logically, recognized only two categories: comedies and tragedies. This is in *Palladis Tamia*—The Treasury of the Muses—by Francis Meres, who wrote:

> As Plautus and Seneca are accounted the best for comedy and tragedy among the Latins, so Shakespeare among the English is the most excellent in both kinds for the stage; for comedy, witness his *Gentlemen of Verona*, his *Errors*, his *Love Labours Lost*, his *Love's Labour's Won*, his *Midsummer Night's Dream*, and his *Merchant of Venice*: for tragedy his *Richard the II*, *Richard the III*, *Henry the IV*, *King John*, *Titus Andronicus* and his *Romeo and Juliet*.

There is a puzzle here: no play called *Love's Labour's Won* exists; it may be lost, or perhaps it was an alternative title for a play that survives. But that is by the by. What is relevant to discussion of Shakespeare's tragedies is that Meres lists under this heading plays relating to events of English and Roman history (along with the non-historical *Romeo and Juliet*) that the Folio hives off under the separate category of histories. In other words Meres is categorizing plays by their form, as derived from classical drama, whereas the Folio prints separately certain plays that dramatize historical events whether or not these plays shape the events they tell into stories that are primarily tragic or comic in tone.

This categorization—grouping some plays by their form, others by their subject matter—has permanently—and in my opinion regrettably—affected discussion of them. The events of history can be dramatically represented in a variety of ways; to give examples only from Shakespeare, he shapes the events of the reigns of Richard Ⅱ and Richard Ⅲ into the form most obviously associated with tragedy culminating in the death of a central character, but he dramatizes the happenings of the reigns of Henry Ⅳ and Henry Ⅴ over three plays which include the death of Henry Ⅳ but do not make this a climactic event, which include many complexly comic episodes involving Shakespeare's most famous comic character. Sir John Falstaff, and which culminate not, as we should expect in a tragedy with the death of Henry Ⅴ but, as in a comedy, with his successful wooing of the Princess of France and with the hope of unification of their two kingdoms.

It is also worth remembering that most of Shakespeare's comedies include elements that may be considered to be tragic in nature—near-rape of a heroine in *The Two Gentlemen of Verona*, the death threats that hang over Egeon in *The Comedy of Errors*, over Antonio in *The Merchant of Venice*,

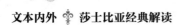

over Claudio in *Measure for Measure*, and over Prospero in *The Tempest*, and the apparent deaths of Hero in *Much Ado About Nothing*, of Hermione in *The Winter's Tale*, and of Innogen in *Cymbeline*, to give only a few examples. The genre—or sub-genre—of tragi-comedy was developing during the later part of Shakespeare's career, and he adopted some of its conventions.

Just as Shakespeare's comedies often verge on tragedy, so his tragedies frequently offer a wittily ironic perspective on the action such as is provided by Aaron the Moor in *Titus Andronicus* and by the Fool in *King Lear* as well as other elements associated with comedy such as the satire on the citizens in both *Julius Caesar and Coriolanus*, the Porter in *Macbeth*, and the clowns in *Othello* and *Antony and Cleopatra*. And *Hamlet* is shot through with comedy almost from start to finish. This suggests that when Shakespeare set about looking for a story to dramatize he was more concerned to find one that offered possibilities for variety of dramatic effect than for one that would fit neatly into the traditional kinds of drama. No one has expressed this more eloquently than Samuel Johnson when he wrote, in the 1765 Preface to his edition of Shakespeare,

Shakespeare's plays are not in the rigorous and critical sense either tragedies or comedies, but compositions of a distinct kind; exhibiting the real state of sublunary nature, which partakes of good and evil, joy and sorrow, mingled with endless variety of proportion and innumerable modes of combination; and expressing the course of the world, in which the loss of one is the gain of another; in which, at the same time, the reveller is hasting to his wine and the mourner burying his friend; in which the malignity of one is sometimes defeated by the frolick of another; and many mischiefs and many benefits are done and hindered without design.

Is it possible, nevertheless, to arrive at a more precise definition which would distinguish tragedies from plays that simply have unhappy endings? As a dramatic form tragedy originated in Ancient Greece with the work of writers such as Sophocles, Euripides, and Aeschylus, whose practice was famously defined in a treatise known as *The Poetics*, by Aristotle (385—322 BC), which has had a profound influence on later thought. Aristotle considered that all plays should obey the so-called unities of time, place, and action, and that tragedies should depict the downfall of heroic figures as the result of circumstances leading to a reversal in their fortunes causing their death. This supposedly led to a catharsis, or purging, of pity and terror in the spectator. Though there is no evidence that Shakespeare had read Aristotle, the point in *King Lear* at which Albany, calling for the dead bodies of Goneril and Regan to be brought before him, says 'This justice of the heavens, that makes us tremble, / Touches us not with pity' (*King Lear*, 5.3.226−7) may seem to invoke the Aristotelian notion of catharsis.

In Shakespeare's time, as in ours, the word 'tragedy' could be applied in a very broad sense outside the drama, to events that had disastrous consequences for those who endured them, and to narrations, whether dramatic or not, of such events. Certainly however, Shakespeare knew about tragedy as a dramatic form. We cannot be sure that he knew any of the great tragedies of classical antiquity at first hand, but he was certainly aware of, and influenced by, their derivatives, the Roman tragedies of Seneca (c. 4 BC—AD 65), which had been translated into English by Jasper Heywood and others and published in 1581, five years after the building of the first important London playhouse—the Theatre. Seneca's plays, deadly serious, full of sensationalism, intended to be recited or read rather than acted, rhetorical, moralistic, and bombastic, full of accounts of horrible deeds and often featuring ghosts and witches, exerted an enormous influence in their printed form (not through performance) on the first great wave of Elizabethan dramatists, such as Thomas Kyd, Christopher Marlowe, George

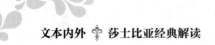

Peele, and Robert Greene, and, partly through their work, on their slightly later contemporary and immediate successor, Shakespeare.

Seneca is one of the only two playwrights of any period mentioned by name anywhere in Shakespeare's writings—the other is the comic dramatist Plautus (c.254—184 BC), whose plays, along with those of his successor Terence (c190—159 BC), were taught, and even performed, in the grammar schools of Shakespeare's time. In *Hamlet* Polonius names Seneca and Plautus as typical of the extremes of tragic and comic writing—'Seneca cannot be too heavy, nor Plautus too light' (*Hamlet*, 2.2.401-2). Interestingly, these are the dramatists with whom, only two or three years before Shakespeare wrote *Hamlet*, the literary chronicler Francis Meres had compared Shakespeare himself (as discussed earlier).

Certainly, some of Shakespeare's plays reflect a knowledge of classical practice. His most classically derived play has the word 'comedy', Roman in origin, in its title: *The Comedy of Errors* is based on Plautus's *Menaechmi* (*The Menaechmus Twins*) and obeys (more or less) the so-called classical unities of place, time, and action—meaning that the action is limited to a single plot enacted in a single location over only one day. (The other play in which Shakespeare comes close to this is *The Tempest.*) Even here, however, Shakespeare complicates the story by adding a plot based on a medieval romance which he was to use again towards the end of his career in one of his least classically constructed plays, *Pericles*.

Shakespeare uses the words 'tragedy' and 'tragic' in his writings a number of times, but always with a very general sense of, as the classic *Shakespeare Lexicon* by Alexander Schmidt puts it, 'a dramatic representation of a serious action' or 'a mournful and dreadful event.' In fact, what may be his first 'representation of a serious action' is in non-dramatic form. This is his long narrative poem *The Rape of Lucrece*, published in 1594 as a companion piece to the wittily comic (though ultimately elegiac) *Venus and Adonis* of 1593. Both poems tell classically derived stories based on poems by the Roman poet Ovid, one of Shakespeare's favourite writers to whom he refers, and whom he quotes, many times throughout his career.

Lucrece relates the tragic tale of the rape of this Roman matron by Tarquin, a close friend and fellow-warrior of her husband. Collatine, and of her consequent suicide. Lucrece is the tragic victim, but the poem's portrayal of the tormented state of mind and inner struggles to withstand temptation of her ravisher, driven by lust to betray her husband whom he calls 'my kinsman, my true friend' (1. 237), bestows on Tarquin the status of a later tragic hero such as Macbeth, who imagines 'withered murder' moving towards his victim 'with Tarquin's ravishing strides' (*Macbeth*, 2.1.52–6). Lucrece, bemoaning her fate, makes a theatrical reference as she invokes 'Night, image of hell, …Black stage for tragedies and murders fell', lines which would have reminded Shakespeare's readers of the black stage hangings used for tragic plays and referred to in the first line of *Henry Ⅵ*, Part One: 'Hung be the heavens with black'—in a playhouse of the time 'the heavens' referred to the canopy over the stage.

In amplifying Ovid's tale, relatively brief in its original telling, Shakespeare resorts to frequent use of 'sententiae', moral statements commenting on the action which help to give dignity and high seriousness to his dramatic tragedies, too. These plays have features in common which may help us to know what Shakespeare understood by tragedy. All of them end in the death of one or more of the central characters: all, like *Lucrece*, contain a certain amount of moral commentary and philosophical reflection (but then, so do his comedies.) But when we have said this we start having to make exceptions, saying for example 'all of them—except *Romeo and Juliet* and

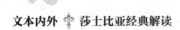

Othello—are set in the more or less distant past', or 'all of them—except Romeo and Juliet again, and perhaps Othello—focus on high-born characters whose fate involves national destiny.'

This has caused some critics to despair of ever defining what Shakespeare meant by tragedy, so that for example the critic Kenneth Muir said, in a British Academy lecture of 1958, 'There is no such thing as Shakespearian tragedy. There are only Shakespeare's tragedies.' This statement, though attractively terse—and quotable—is perhaps a little glib. Wide-ranging and varied in effect though Shakespeare's tragedies are, most of them portray one or more central characters with a degree of inwardness and with a suggestion that the disasters leading to their downfall are inextricably bound up with their personalities. (*Romeo and Juliet* is perhaps an exception (again), in that here the lovers' fate seems to be determined rather by external forces than by their own characters.) The same is true, however, of characters in some of his plays written in comic form, most notably Angelo in *Measure for Measure* and Leontes in *The Winter's Tale*, even though they are eventually redeemed. The Folio's categorization is reflected in the fact that in this series of Very Short Introductions the plays are divided into its three groupings. For this reason, writing on the tragedies, I shall limit myself to those that are not based on English history.

It is the absence of a definable theory of tragedy in Shakespeare plays that go under this label that encourages me to write about each play individually rather than adopting a thematic approach. In doing so I hope to give a sense of each play's uniqueness, of what makes it enjoyable and meaningful to readers and playgoers today, of the influence that it has exerted, and the pleasure that it has given.

Activities

1. Shakespeare and Today

Direction: It is said that literature is our best vaccine against trauma. Then how about tragedy? Do we ever get pleasure in tragedy? How does catharsis take place in reading a tragedy? Please make a comment based on your reading of Shakespeare.

2. Shakespeare and China

Direction: Hamlet and Macbeth are Shakespeare's two most discussed tragic figures with distinct strength and flaws in their characters. What distinguish them from other male protagonists like Othello or Romeo? Are there similar characters in Chinese literature? Please give some examples and explain how they are related to each other.

3. Shakespeare and Beyond

Direction: The Three-Character Classic (《三字经》) *begins with "Man on earth, Good at birth* (人之初, 性本善). *" What is your opinion? Human nature has always been an important theme of literature. Shakespeare's tragedy makes the most profound reflection on human nature. What do you think may curb or stimulate the darkness in human nature? What is the role of literature in building up a harmonious society?*

Further Reading

MCEACHERN C, 2002. The Cambridge companion to Shakespearean tragedy [M]. London: Cambridge University Press.

MCELROY B, 2017. Shakespeare's mature tragedies [M]. New Jersey: Princeton University Press.

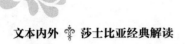

NEILL M, 2016. Oxford handbook of Shakespearean tragedy [M]. London: Oxford University Press.

SADOWSKI P, 2003. Dynamism of character in Shakespeare's mature tragedies [M]. London: Associated University Press.

SMITH E, 2004. Shakespeare's tragedies [M]. MA: Blackwell Publishing House.

WELLS S, 2017. Shakespeare's tragedies: a very short introduction [M]. London: Oxford University Press.

Unit 2 The Tragedy of Hamlet

章节概述

《哈姆雷特》创作于 1600 到 1601 年间，1603 年首次出版，1623 年收入第一对开本。《哈姆雷特》的故事最早大约在 10 世纪出现在斯堪的纳维亚半岛。12 世纪末丹麦历史学家萨克索将该故事录入《丹麦史》。约在 1570 年，法国作家贝尔福雷将该故事译成法语，收于《悲剧故事集》。约在 1590 年，英国剧作家托马斯·基德将这个故事搬上舞台。

"来者何人？"这句著名的诘问揭开了史上最伟大的悲剧之一的序幕。丹麦国王老哈姆雷特驾崩，他的弟弟继承了王位。新国王娶了已成寡妇的王后葛特鲁德。在威丁堡求学的年轻王子被紧急召回。哈姆雷特对于父亲的蹊跷离世和母亲的仓促改嫁甚感悲苦。他父亲的鬼魂现身并告诉他自己系谋杀身死，而凶手正是现任国王克劳狄斯。哈姆雷特发誓要为父王报仇。从此以后，哈姆雷特开始了装疯卖傻的生活，他拒绝了奥菲利娅的爱情，还暗中观察国王的一举一动。与此同时，克劳狄斯和御前大臣，也即奥菲利娅的父亲波洛涅斯也对哈姆雷特的种种古怪行为心存疑虑，派专人监视他。哈姆雷特邀请了一个巡回演出的戏班来到王宫，设计并上演了一出国王被兄弟谋害并篡位的戏中戏，确认了克劳狄斯的罪行。随后在葛特鲁德的卧室，母子暴发激烈争吵，哈姆雷特误将幕后偷听的波洛涅斯刺死。失去爱情和父亲的奥菲利娅在沉重打击下变得疯癫并不慎溺亡。敌我双方展开了激烈的较量。在一系列的延宕和痛苦的思想斗争后，哈姆雷特终于刺死了克劳狄斯，完成了复仇的使命。但是，他和母亲葛特鲁德，以及年轻的雷欧提斯也都命丧黄泉。挪威王子福丁布拉斯继承了丹麦王权，恢复了国家秩序。

《哈姆雷特》吸收了伊丽莎白时代通俗戏剧的各种因素：幽灵、说教的父亲式人物、戏中戏、哑剧、时事讽刺、暴死、求爱、充满音乐性

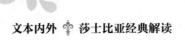

的疯狂场景、"小丑"的喜剧套路、决斗以及多个角色死亡的结局。莎士比亚借用反讽、讽刺、挖苦等手法，赋予了这部悲剧一种喜剧性的视角。

《哈姆雷特》既是一部政治剧，也是一部记录个体心路历程的戏剧。此剧有一个首要主题，那就是人们如何对待死亡。哈姆雷特发誓为父报仇，但这项任务之艰巨让他近乎疯狂。哈姆雷特的犹豫不只是找不到复仇方法时产生的矛盾心理，而且是他感悟到人的渺小、人的不完美，以及生的虚无时那迷惘与忧虑心态的外现，同时也是欧洲文艺复兴晚期信仰失落时人们进退两难的矛盾心理的象征性表述。

《哈姆雷特》展现了莎士比亚高超的戏剧艺术技巧。首先是人物形象的塑造。哈姆雷特性格内敛，长于沉思和自省，但严峻的局势却要求他立即采取果断行动。哈姆雷特的延宕是他的思想逻辑与行动逻辑背道而驰造成的张力的反映，心理内涵丰富而复杂。哈姆雷特的内心独白表达出他对社会与人生、生与死、爱与恨、理想与现实等方面的哲学探索，折射出他内心的矛盾、苦闷、困惑、迷惘和恐惧，有效地刻画了人物性格，推动了剧情的发展。其次是高超的情节结构艺术。哈姆雷特为父复仇是剧情主线，作者同时还安排了雷欧提斯和福丁布拉斯为父复仇这两条辅线，辅线与主线交错发展而又主次分明。三条线索起到了互成对比、激化矛盾的作用，使戏剧场面不断转换，造成戏剧高潮，产生动人心魄的艺术效果，共同表现全剧的主题。主人公的内心斗争与外部斗争相互辉映，个人抒情场面与敌我对峙交锋场面交错进行，使剧情张弛有度、跌宕起伏。最后是精彩的戏剧语言。剧中人物众多，但他们的对白都充满个性，语言贴合各自的身份、性别、年龄和性格。《哈姆雷特》的文体以无韵诗体为主，穿插了格律体和散文体。时而优雅深邃，时而粗俗直白的表达极大地增强了人物台词的表现力。

《哈姆雷特》作为西方文学史上最伟大的一部悲剧，既有古典的和谐与宏大，又有现代的混乱与骚动，其影响已远超出文学领域而渗入社会文化生活的方方面面。"一千个读者，就有一千个哈姆雷特。"这就是莎士比亚悲剧的魅力所在。

Selected Reading

Act III, i

Enter Hamlet

HAMLET To be, or not to be, that is the question:

Whether 'tis nobler in the mind to suffer

The slings and arrows of outrageous fortune,

Or to take arms against a sea of troubles,

And by opposing end them? To die, to sleep—

No more—and by a sleep to say we end

The heartache and the thousand natural shocks

That flesh is heir to: 'tis a consummation

Devoutly to be wished. To die, to sleep:

To sleep, perchance to dream: ay, there's the rub,

For in that sleep of death what dreams may come

When we have shuffled off this mortal coil,

Must give us pause: there's the respect

That makes calamity of so long life,

For who would bear the whips and scorns of time,

The oppressor's wrong, the proud man's contumely,

The pangs of disprized love, the law's delay,

The insolence of office and the spurns

That patient merit of the unworthy takes,

When he himself might his quietus make

With a bare bodkin? Who would these fardels bear,

To grunt and sweat under a weary life,

But that the dread of something after death,

> sling: n. a long, thin piece of rope with a piece of leather in the middle for throwing stones 吊索，投石器

> outrageous: a. very shocking and extremely unfair or offensive 骇人的，无法容忍的

> consummation: n. the point at which sth. is complete 结束，中止

> perchance: ad. (old use or literary) perhaps, by chance（诗、文）偶然，可能

> shuffle: v. to get away 逃避责任，（古英语）躲闪

> calamity: n. a terrible and unexpected event that causes a lot of damage or suffering 灾难，灾祸

> contumely: n. disrespectful and offensive behavior or language 侮辱，无礼，傲慢

> insolence: n. rude and disrespectful behavior 傲慢，傲慢无礼的行为

> spurn: n. to refuse to accept sth. 蔑视，摒弃

> quietus: n. death, the end of sth. 解除，偿清，生命的终止

> bodkin: n. a long thick needle without a point 锥子，长发夹

> fardel: n. parcel, burden 包裹，重担，负担

The undiscovered country from whose bourn

bourn: n. boundary, dividing line
界限，边界

No traveller returns, puzzles the will,

And makes us rather bear those ills we have

Than fly to others that we know not of?

Thus conscience does make cowards of us all；

And thus the native hue of resolution

Is sicklied o'er with the pale cast of thought,

And enterprises of great pith and moment

With this regard their currents turn awry,

And lose the name of action. Soft you now,

nymph: n. goddess, young woman
女神

The fair Ophelia.—Nymph, in thy orisons

orison: n.（old use）a prayer 祈祷

Be all my sins remembered.

OPHELIA Good my lord,

How does your honour for this many a day?

HAMLET I humbly thank you；well, well, well.

OPHELIA My lord, I have remembrances of yours,

That I have longèd long to re-deliver:

I pray you now receive them.

HAMLET No, no: I never gave you aught.

aught: n. 任何事物（相当于 anything）

OPHELIA My honoured lord, I know right well you did,

And with them words of so sweet breath composed

As made the things more rich；their perfume lost,

Take these again, for to the noble mind

Rich gifts wax poor when givers prove unkind.

There, my lord.

HAMLET Ha, ha! Are you honest?

OPHELIA My lord?

HAMLET Are you fair?

OPHELIA What means your lordship?

HAMLET That if you be honest and fair, your honesty should admit no discourse to your beauty.

OPHELIA Could beauty, my lord, have better commerce than with honesty?

> commerce: n. relationships and communication between people 此处指关系，互动

HAMLET Ay, truly, for the power of beauty will sooner transform honesty from what it is to a bawd than the force of honesty can translate beauty into his likeness: this was sometime a paradox, but now the time gives it proof. I did love you once.

> bawd: n. whore, a woman who manages bawdy house 鸨母，妓女

> paradox: n. a strange situation that involves two opposing ideas 矛盾，悖论

OPHELIA Indeed, my lord, you made me believe so.

HAMLET You should not have believed me, for virtue cannot so inoculate our old stock but we shall relish of it: I loved you not.

> inoculate: to protect someone against disease, usually by injecting v. 接种，打预防针

> relish: v. great enjoyment of sth. 享受，喜欢，期盼

OPHELIA I was the more deceived.

HAMLET Get thee to a nunnery. Why wouldst thou be a breeder of sinners? I am myself indifferent honest, but yet I could accuse me of such things that it were better my mother had not borne me: I am very proud, revengeful, ambitious, with more offences at my beck than I have thoughts to put them in, imagination to give them shape, or time to act them in. What should such fellows as I do crawling between heaven and earth? We are arrant knaves all: believe none of us. Go thy ways to a nunnery. Where's your father?

> beck: n. order, requirement 命令，要求

> arrant knaves: devil, villain 此处指十足的流氓、恶棍

OPHELIA At home, my lord.

HAMLET Let the doors be shut upon him, that he may play the fool nowhere but in's own house. Farewell.

OPHELIA O, help him, you sweet heavens!

HAMLET If thou dost marry, I'll give thee this plague for thy dowry: be thou as chaste as ice, as pure as snow, thou shalt not escape calumny. Get thee to a nunnery: go, farewell. Or if thou wilt needs marry, marry a fool, for wise men know well enough what monsters you make of them. To a nunnery, go, and quickly too. Farewell.

dowry: n. property and money that a woman gives to her husband when they marry 嫁妆，陪嫁

calumny: n. an untrue and unfair statement 诽谤，恶语中伤

OPHELIA O Heavenly powers, restore him!

HAMLET I have heard of your paintings too, well enough. God has given you one face and you make yourself another: you jig, you amble and you lisp, and nickname God's creatures, and make your wantonness your ignorance. Go to, I'll no more on't; it hath made me mad. I say we will have no more marriages: those that are married already, all but one shall live: the rest shall keep as they are. To a nunnery, go.

jig: n. to move up and down, to walk in a slow, relaxed way（使）上下动，此处指蹦跳

amble: v. 原指马缓行，从容漫步。此处指走路扭捏作态

lisp: v. to speak without clear or correct pronounciation 咬着舌说话，口齿不清地说。此处指说话拿腔拿调

Exit Hamlet

OPHELIA O, what a noble mind is here o'erthrown!

The courtier's, soldier's, scholar's eye, tongue, sword,

Th'expectancy and rose of the fair state,

The glass of fashion and the mould of form,

Th'observed of all observers, quite, quite down!

And I, of ladies most deject and wretched,

That sucked the honey of his music vows,

Now see that noble and most sovereign reason

Like sweet bells jangled out of tune and harsh,

That unmatched form and feature of blown

youth

Blasted with ecstasy. O, woe is me,

T'have seen what I have seen, see what I see!

> deject: a. unhappy, disappointed, or sad 沮丧的，情绪低落的
>
> wretched: a. very unhappy or ill 可怜的，悲惨的
>
> jangle: v. to make a sharp sound by hitting metal objects at each other 发出金属撞击声，叮当声
>
> blown: a. 灿烂的，绽放的，同 "blooming"

译文1（朱生豪版）

第三幕第一场	ACT III, i
哈姆雷特上。	*Enter Hamlet*
哈姆雷特 生存还是毁灭，这是一个值得考虑的问题；默然忍受命运的暴虐的毒箭，或是挺身反抗人世的无涯的苦难，在奋斗中结束了一切，这两种行为，哪一种是更勇敢的？死了，睡着了，什么都完了；要是在这一种睡眠之中，我们心头的创痛，以及其他无数血肉之躯所不能避免的打击，都可以从此消失，那正是我们求之不得的结局。死了，睡着了；睡着了也许还会做梦；嗯，阻碍就在这儿：因为当我们摆脱了这一具朽腐的皮囊以后，在那死的睡眠里，究竟将要做些什么梦，那不能不使我们踌躇	**HAMLET** To be, or not to be, that is the question: Whether 'tis nobler in the mind to suffer The slings and arrows of outrageous fortune, Or to take arms against a sea of troubles, And by opposing end them? To die, to sleep— No more—and by a sleep to say we end The heartache and the thousand natural shocks That flesh is heir to: 'tis a consummation Devoutly to be wished. To die, to sleep: To sleep, perchance to dream: ay, there's the rub,

顾虑。人们甘心久困于患难之中，也就是为了这个缘故。谁愿意忍受人世的鞭挞和讥嘲，压迫者的凌辱，傲慢者的冷眼，被轻蔑的爱情的惨痛，法律的迁延，官吏的横暴，和俊杰大才费尽辛勤所换来的鄙视，要是他只要用一柄小小的刀子，就可以清算他自己的一生，谁愿意负着这样的重担，在烦劳的生命的迫压下呻吟流汗？倘不是因为惧怕不可知的死后，惧怕那从来不曾有一个旅人回来过的神秘之国，是它迷惑了我们的意志，使我们宁愿忍受目前的折磨，不敢向我们所不知道的痛苦飞去？这样，重重的顾虑使我们全变成了懦夫，决心的赤热的光彩，被审慎的思维盖上了一层灰色，伟大的事业在这一种考虑之下，也会逆流而退，失去了行动的意义。且慢！美丽的奥菲利娅！——女神，在你的祈祷之中，不要忘记替我忏悔我的罪孽。

For in that sleep of death what dreams may come

When we have shuffled off this mortal coil,

Must give us pause: there's the respect

That makes calamity of so long life,

For who would bear the whips and scorns of time,

The oppressor's wrong, the proud man's contumely,

The pangs of disprized love, the law's delay,

The insolence of office and the spurns

That patient merit of the unworthy takes,

When he himself might his quietus make

With a bare bodkin? Who would these fardels bear,

To grunt and sweat under a weary life,

But that the dread of something after death,

The undiscovered country from whose bourn

No traveller returns, puzzles the will,

And makes us rather bear those ills we have

Than fly to others that we know not of?

Thus conscience does make cowards of us all;

And thus the native hue of resolution

Is sicklied o'er with the pale cast of thought,

And enterprises of great pith and moment

With this regard their currents turn awry,

And lose the name of action. Soft you now,

The fair Ophelia. —Nymph, in thy orisons

Be all my sins remembered.

OPHELIA Good my lord,

How does your honour for this many a day?

HAMLET I humbly thank you; well, well, well.

OPHELIA My lord, I have remembrances of yours,

That I have longèd long to re-deliver:

I pray you now receive them.

HAMLET No, no: I never gave you aught.

OPHELIA My honoured lord, I know right well you did,

And with them words of so sweet breath composed

As made the things more rich; their perfume lost,

Take these again, for to the noble mind

奥菲利娅 我的好殿下，您这许多天来贵体安好吗？

哈姆雷特 谢谢你，很好，很好，很好。

奥菲利娅 殿下，我有几件您送给我的纪念品，我早就想把它们还给您；请您现在收回去吧。

哈姆雷特 不，我不要，我从来没有给你什么东西。

奥菲利娅 殿下，我记得很清楚您把它们送给我，那时候您还向我说了许多甜蜜的言语，使这些东西格外显得贵重；现在它们的芳香已经消散，请您拿了回去吧，因为送礼的人要是变了心，礼物虽贵，也会失去了价值。拿去吧，殿下。

哈姆雷特　哈哈！你贞洁吗？

奥菲利娅　殿下！

哈姆雷特　你美丽吗？

奥菲利娅　殿下是什么意思？

哈姆雷特　要是你既贞洁又美丽，那么顶好不要让你的贞洁跟你的美丽来往。

奥菲利娅　殿下，美丽跟贞洁相交，那不是再好没有吗？

哈姆雷特　嗯，真的；因为美丽可以使贞洁变成淫荡，贞洁却未必能使美丽受它自己的感化；这句话从前像是怪诞之谈，可是现在时间已经把它证实了。我的确曾经爱过你。

奥菲利娅　真的，殿下，您曾经使我相信您爱我。

哈姆雷特　你当初就不应该相信我，因为美德不能熏陶我们罪恶的本性；我没有爱过你。

奥菲利娅　那么我真是受了骗了。

哈姆雷特　进尼姑庵去吧；为什么你要生一群罪人出来呢？我自己还不算是一个顶坏的

Rich gifts wax poor when givers prove unkind.

There, my lord.

HAMLET Ha, ha! Are you honest?

OPHELIA My lord?

HAMLET Are you fair?

OPHELIA What means your lordship?

HAMLET That if you be honest and fair, your honesty should admit no discourse to your beauty.

OPHELIA Could beauty, my lord, have better commerce than with honesty?

HAMLET Ay, truly, for the power of beauty will sooner transform honesty from what it is to a bawd than the force of honesty can translate beauty into his likeness: this was sometime a paradox, but now the time gives it proof. I did love you once.

OPHELIA Indeed, my lord, you made me believe so.

HAMLET You should not have believed me, for virtue cannot so inoculate our old stock but we shall relish of it: I loved you not.

OPHELIA I was the more deceived.

HAMLET Get thee to a nunnery. Why wouldst thou be a breeder of sinners? I am myself indifferent honest, but yet I

人；可是我可以指出我的许多过失，一个人有了那些过失，他的母亲还是不要生下他来的好。我很骄傲，有仇必报，富于野心，还有那么多的罪恶，连我的思想里也容纳不下，我的想象也不能给它们形象，甚至于我没有充分的时间可以把它们实行出来，像我这样的家伙，匍匐于天地之间，有什么用处呢？我们都是些十足的坏人；一个也不要相信我们。进尼姑庵去吧。你的父亲呢？

奥菲利娅　在家里，殿下。

哈姆雷特　把他关起来，让他只好在家里发发傻劲。再会！

奥菲利娅　哎哟，天啊！救救他！

哈姆雷特　要是你一定要嫁人，我就把这一个诅咒送给你做嫁奁：尽管你像冰一样坚贞，像雪一样纯洁，你还是逃不过谗人的诽谤。进尼姑庵去吧，去；再会！或者要是你必须嫁人的话，就嫁给一个傻瓜吧；因为聪明人都明白你们会叫他们变成怎样的怪物。进尼姑庵去吧，去；越快越好。再会！

could accuse me of such things that it were better my mother had not borne me: I am very proud, revengeful, ambitious, with more offences at my beck than I have thoughts to put them in, imagination to give them shape, or time to act them in. What should such fellows as I do crawling between heaven and earth? We are arrant knaves all: believe none of us. Go thy ways to a nunnery. Where's your father?

OPHELIA　At home, my lord.

HAMLET　Let the doors be shut upon him, that he may play the fool nowhere but in's own house. Farewell.

OPHELIA　O, help him, you sweet heavens!

HAMLET　If thou dost marry, I'll give thee this plague for thy dowry: be thou as chaste as ice, as pure as snow, thou shalt not escape calumny. Get thee to a nunnery: go, farewell. Or if thou wilt needs marry, marry a fool, for wise men know well enough what monsters you make of them. To a nunnery, go, and quickly too. Farewell.

奥菲利娅　天上的神明啊，让他清醒过来吧！

哈姆雷特　我也知道你们会怎样涂脂抹粉；上帝给了你们一张脸，你们又替自己另外造了一张。你们烟行媚视，淫声浪气，替上帝造下的生物乱取名字，卖弄你们不懂事的风骚。算了吧，我再也不敢领教了；它已经使我发了狂。我说，我们以后再不要结什么婚了；已经结过婚的，除了一个人以外，都可以让他们活下去；没有结婚的不准再结婚，进尼姑庵去吧，去。（下）

奥菲利娅　啊，一颗多么高贵的心是这样殒落了！朝臣的眼睛，学者的辩舌，军人的利剑，国家所瞩望的一朵娇花；时流的明镜，人伦的雅范，举世瞩目的中心，这样无可挽回地殒落了！我是一切妇女中间最伤心而不幸的，我曾经从他音乐一般的盟誓中吮吸芬芳的甘蜜，现在却眼看着他的高贵无上的理智，像一串美妙的银铃失去了谐和的音调，无比的青春美貌，在疯狂中凋谢！啊！我好苦，谁料过去的繁华，变作今朝的泥土！

OPHELIA　O Heavenly powers, restore him!

HAMLET　I have heard of your paintings too, well enough. God has given you one face and you make yourself another: you jig, you amble and you lisp, and nickname God's creatures, and make your wantonness your ignorance. Go to, I'll no more on't; it hath made me mad. I say we will have no more marriages: those that are married already, all but one shall live: the rest shall keep as they are. To a nunnery, go.

Exist Hamlet

OPHELIA　O, what a noble mind is here o'erthrown!

The courtier's, soldier's, scholar's eye, tongue, sword,

Th'expectancy and rose of the fair state,

The glass of fashion and the mould of form,

Th'observed of all observers, quite, quite down!

And I, of ladies most deject and wretched,

That sucked the honey of his music vows,

Now see that noble and most sovereign reason

Like sweet bells jangled out of tune and harsh,

That unmatched form and feature of blown youth

Blasted with ecstasy. O, woe is me,

T'have seen what I have seen, see what I see!

译文2 （辜正坤版）

Act V, i

Enter Hamlet and Horatio afar off

......

HAMLET Has this fellow no feeling of his business that he sings at grave-making?

HORATIO Custom hath made it in him a property of easiness.

HAMLET 'Tis e'en so: the hand of little employment hath the daintier sense.

> dainty: a. small, pretty, and delicate讲究的，优雅的

FIRST CLOWN (*sings*) But age with his stealing steps

Hath caught me in his clutch,

And hath shipped me intil the land,

As if I had never been such.

[*Throws up a skull*]

HAMLET That skull had a tongue in it and could sing once: how the knave jowls it to th'ground, as if it were Cain's jaw-bone, that did the first murder. It might be the pate of a politi-

> knave: n. villain, hooligan 无赖，流氓
>
> jowl: v. to throw, beat, or attack 扔，打，袭击
>
> Cain: 该隐，《圣经》里的第一个谋杀犯，他杀死了其弟亚伯。
>
> pate: n. head 头，脑袋

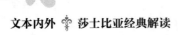

cian, which this ass o'er-offices, one that could circumvent God, might it not?

> circumvent: v. to avoid a problem in a clever or dishonest way, to trick 欺骗，战胜

HORATIO It might, my lord.

HAMLET Or of a courtier, which could say 'Good morrow, sweet lord! How dost thou, good lord?' This might be my lord Such-a-One, that praised my lord Such-a-One's horse when he meant to beg it, might it not?

HORATIO Ay, my lord.

HAMLET Why, e'en so, and now my lady Worm's, chapless, and knocked about the mazzard with a sexton's spade: here's fine revolution, if we had the trick to see't. Did these bones cost no more the breeding, but to play at loggats with'em? Mine ache to think on't.

> mazzard: n. head 头，脑袋

> loggats: 即 loggets，旧时英国的一种向木桩抛木块的游戏

FIRST CLOWN (*sings*) A pickaxe and a spade, a spade,

For and a shrouding sheet:

O, a pit of clay for to be made

For such a guest is meet.

[*Throws up another skull*]

HAMLET There's another. Why may not that be the skull of a lawyer? Where be his quiddities now, his quillets, his cases, his tenures, and his tricks? Why does he suffer this rude knave now to knock him about the sconce with a dirty shovel, and will not tell him of his action of battery? Hum. This fellow might be in's time a great buyer of land, with his statutes, his recognizances, his fines, his double vouchers, his re-

> quiddity: n. sophism, quibbling 诡辩

> tenure: n. the legal right to use a piece of land, position, honor（土地）的保有权，职位，荣誉

> voucher: n. a kind of ticket used for a particular purpose; a receipt 票券，收据，担保

coveries: is this the fine of his fines and the re-covery of his recoveries, to have his fine pate full of fine dirt? Will his vouchers vouch him no more of his purchases, and double ones too, than the length and breadth of a pair of inden-tures? The very conveyances of his lands will hardly lie in this box; and must the inheritor him-self have no more, ha?

......

HAMLET How long will a man lie i' th'earth ere he rot?

FIRST CLOWN I'faith, if he be not rotten before he die—as we have many pocky corpses now-a-days, that will scarce hold the laying in— he will last you some eight year or nine year: a tanner will last you nine year.

HAMLET Why he more than another?

FIRST CLOWN Why, sir, his hide is so tanned with his trade that he will keep out water a great while, and your water is a sore decayer of your whoreson dead body. Here's a skull now: this skull has lain in the earth three-and-twenty years.

HAMLET Whose was it?

FIRST CLOWN A whoreson mad fellow's it was: whose do you think it was?

HAMLET Nay, I know not.

FIRST CLOWN A pestilence on him for a mad rogue! A poured a flagon of Rhenish on my head once. This same skull, sir, this same skull, sir,

> indenture: n. a formal contract 契约，合同

> conveyance: n. the act of taking sth. from one place to another; a legal document that gives land, property from one person to an-other 运送，传达；产权转让证书

> pocky: a. suffering smallpox or syphilis 水痘的，梅毒的

> tanner: n. someone whose job is to make animal skin into leather by tanning 制革工，硝皮匠

> whoreson: a. illegitimate, abomi-nable 私生的，令人憎恶的

> pestilence: n. a disease that spreads quickly and kills large numbers of people 瘟疫，有害的事物

was Yorick's skull, the King's jester.

HAMLET This?

FIRST CLOWN E'en that.

HAMLET Let me see,—Alas, poor Yorick! I knew him, Horatio: a fellow of infinite jest, of most excellent fancy. He hath borne me on his back a thousand times—and how abhorred my imagination is! My gorge rises at it. Here hung those lips that I have kissed I know not how oft. —Where be your gibes now, your gambols, your songs, your flashes of merriment that were wont to set the table on a roar? No one now to mock your own jeering? Quite chop-fallen? Now get you to my lady's chamber and tell her, let her paint an inch thick, to this favour she must come. Make her laugh at that.—Prithee, Horatio, tell me one thing.

HORATIO What's that, my lord?

HAMLET Dost thou think Alexander looked o'this fashion i' th'earth?

HORATIO E'en so.

HAMLET And smelt so? Puh!

[*Places the skull on the ground or throws it down*].

HORATIO E'en so, my lord.

HAMLET To what base uses we may return, Horatio! Why may not imagination trace the noble dust of Alexander till he find it stopping a bung-hole?

HORATIO 'Twere to consider too curiously

> jester: n. a man employed to entertain people with jokes, stories（中世纪宫廷或贵族家中的）小丑，弄臣；爱开玩笑的人

> abhor: v. to hate a kind of behavior or way of thinking 痛恨，憎恶

> gorge: n. anger and fury 厌恶，气愤

> gibe: n. an unkind remark to ridicule someone 同 jibe 讥讽，嘲讽话

> gambol: n. an action that involves a risk 赌博，投机，冒险

> bung-hole: n. a hole for emptying or filling 桶孔，封塞孔

to consider so.

HAMLET No, faith, not a jot, but to follow him thither with modesty enough, and likelihood to lead it, as thus: Alexander died, Alexander was buried, Alexander returneth into dust; the dust is earth; of earth we make loam, and why of that loam whereto he was converted might they not stop a beer-barrel?

loam: n. good quality soil 肥土，泥团

Imperious Caesar, dead and turned to clay,

Might stop a hole to keep the wind away.

O, that that earth, which kept the world in awe,

Should patch a wall t'expel the winter's flaw!

But soft, but soft, aside: here comes the king.

译文1（朱生豪版）

第五幕第一场	Act V, i
哈姆雷特及霍拉旭上；立远处	*Enter Hamlet and Horatio afar off*
…………	......

哈姆雷特 这家伙难道对于他的工作一点没有什么感觉，在掘坟的时候还会唱歌吗？

HAMLET Has this fellow no feeling of his business that he sings at grave-making?

霍拉旭 他做惯了这种事，所以不以为意。

HORATIO Custom hath made it in him a property of easiness.

哈姆雷特 正是；不大劳动的手，它的感觉要比较灵敏一些。

HAMLET 'Tis e'en so: the hand of little employment hath the daintier sense.

甲丑 （唱）

FIRST CLOWN（*sings*）

谁料如今岁月潜移，

But age with his stealing steps

老景催人急于星火，

Hath caught me in his clutch,

两腿挺直，一命归西，

And hath shipped me intil the land,

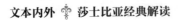

世上原来不曾有我。（掷起一骷髅）

哈姆雷特 那个骷髅里面曾经有一条舌头，它还会唱歌哩；瞧这家伙把它摔在地上，好像它是第一个杀人凶手该隐的颚骨似的！它也许是一个政客的头颅，现在却让这蠢货把它丢来踢去；也许他生前是个偷天换日的好手，你看是不是？

霍拉旭 也许是的，殿下。

哈姆雷特 也许是一个朝臣，他会说："早安，大人！您好，大人！"也许他就是某大人，嘴里称赞某大人的马好，心里却想把它讨了来，你看是不是？

霍拉旭 是，殿下。

哈姆雷特 啊，正是；现在却让蛆虫伴寝，他的下巴也脱掉了，一柄工役的锄头可以在他头上敲来敲去。从这种变化上，我们大可看透了生命的无常。难道这些枯骨生前受了那么多的教养，死后却只好给人家当木块一般抛着玩吗？想起来我的骨头都痛了。

甲丑 （唱）

锄头一柄，铁铲一把，
殓衾一方掩面遮身；

As if I had never been such. [*Throws up a skull*]

HAMLET That skull had a tongue in it and could sing once: how the knave jowls it to th'ground, as if it were Cain's jaw-bone, that did the first murder. It might be the pate of a politician, which this ass o'er-offices, one that could circumvent God, might it not?

HORATIO It might, my lord.

HAMLET Or of a courtier, which could say 'Good morrow, sweet lord! How dost thou, good lord?' This might be my lord Such-a-One, that praised my lord Such-a-One's horse when he meant to beg it, might it not?

HORATIO Ay, my lord.

HAMLET Why, e'en so, and now my lady Worm's, chapless, and knocked about the mazzard with a sexton's spade: here's fine revolution, if we had the trick to see't. Did these bones cost no more the breeding, but to play at loggats with'em? Mine ache to think on't.

FIRST CLOWN (*sings*)

A pickaxe and a spade, a spade,
For and a shrouding sheet:

挖松泥土深深掘下，

掘了个坑招待客人。（掷起另一骷髅）

哈姆雷特 又是一个；谁知道那不会是一个律师的骷髅？他的玩弄刀笔的手段，颠倒黑白的雄辩，现在都到哪儿去了？为什么他让这个放肆的家伙用龌龊的铁铲敲他的脑壳，不去控告他一个殴打罪？哼！这家伙生前也许曾经买下许多地产，开口闭口用那些条文、具结、罚款、证据、赔偿一类的名词吓人；现在他的脑壳里塞满了泥土，这就算是他所取得的罚款和最后的赔偿了吗？除了两张契约大小的一方地面以外，谁能替他证明他究竟有多少地产？这一撮黄土，就是他所有的一切了吗，吓？

…………

哈姆雷特 一个人埋在地下，要经过多少时候才会腐烂？

甲丑 假如他不是在未死以前就已经腐烂——就如现在多的是害杨梅疮死的尸体，简直抬

O, a pit of clay for to be made

For such a guest is meet. [*Throws up another skull*]

HAMLET There's another. Why may not that be the skull of a lawyer? Where be his quiddities now, his quillets, his cases, his tenures, and his tricks? Why does he suffer this rude knave now to knock him about the sconce with a dirty shovel, and will not tell him of his action of battery? Hum. This fellow might be in's time a great buyer of land, with his statutes, his recognizances, his fines, his double vouchers, his recoveries: is this the fine of his fines and the recovery of his recoveries, to have his fine pate full of fine dirt? Will his vouchers vouch him no more of his purchases, and double ones too, than the length and breadth of a pair of indentures? The very conveyances of his lands will hardly lie in this box; and must the inheritor himself have no more, ha?

……

HAMLET How long will a man lie i'th'earth ere he rot?

FIRST CLOWN I'faith, if he be not rotten before he die—as we have many pocky corpses now-a-days, that will scarce

都抬不下去——他大概可以过八九年；一个硝皮匠在九年以内不会腐烂。

哈姆雷特 为什么他要比别人长久一些？

甲丑 因为，先生，他的皮硝得比人家的硬，可以长久不透水；尸体一碰到水，是最会腐烂的。这儿又是一个骷髅，这骷髅已经埋在地下二十三年了。

哈姆雷特 它是谁的骷髅？

甲丑 是个婊子养的疯小子；你猜是谁？

哈姆雷特 不，我猜不出。

甲丑 这个遭瘟的疯小子！他有一次把一瓶葡萄酒倒在我的头上。这一个骷髅，先生，是国王的弄人郁利克的骷髅。

哈姆雷特 这就是他！

甲仆（丑） 正是他。

哈姆雷特 让我看。（取骷髅）唉，可怜的郁利克！霍拉旭，我认识他，他是一个最会开玩笑，非常富于想象力的家伙。他曾经把我负在背上一千次；现在我一想起来，却忍不住心头作呕。这儿本来有两片嘴

hold the laying in—he will last you some eight year or nine year: a tanner will last you nine year.

HAMLET Why he more than another?

FIRST CLOWN Why, sir, his hide is so tanned with his trade that he will keep out water a great while, and your water is a sore decayer of your whoreson dead body. Here's a skull now: this skull has lain in the earth three-and-twenty years.

HAMLET Whose was it?

FIRST CLOWN A whoreson mad fellow's it was: whose do you think it was?

HAMLET Nay, I know not.

FIRST CLOWN A pestilence on him for a mad rogue! A poured a flagon of Rhenish on my head once. This same skull, sir, this same skull, sir, was Yorick's skull, the King's jester.

HAMLET This?

FIRST CLOWN E'en that.

HAMLET Let me see,—Alas, poor Yorick! I knew him, Horatio: a fellow of infinite jest, of most excellent fancy. He hath borne me on his back a thousand times—and how abhorred my imagination is! My gorge rises at it. Here hung those lips that I have kissed

唇，我不知吻过它们多少次。——现在你还会挖苦人吗？你还会蹦蹦跳跳，逗人发笑吗？你还会唱歌吗？你还会随口编造一些笑话，说得满座捧腹吗？你没有留下一个笑话，讥笑你自己吗？这样垂头丧气了吗？现在你给我到小姐的闺房里去，对她说，凭她脸上的脂粉搽得一寸厚，到后来总要变成这个样子的；你用这样的话告诉她，看她笑不笑吧。霍拉旭，请你告诉我一件事情。

霍拉旭　什么事情，殿下？

哈姆雷特　你想亚历山大在地下也是这副形状吗？

霍拉旭　也是这样。

哈姆雷特　也有同样的臭味吗？呸！（掷下骷髅）

霍拉旭　也有同样的臭味，殿下。

哈姆雷特　谁知道我们将来会变成一些什么下贱的东西，霍拉旭！要是我们用想象推测下去，谁知道亚历山大的高贵的尸体，是不是塞在酒桶口上的泥土？

霍拉旭　那未免太想入非非了。

I know not how oft. —Where be your gibes now, your gambols, your songs, your flashes of merriment that were wont to set the table on a roar? No one now to mock your own jeering? Quite chop-fallen? Now get you to my lady's chamber and tell her, let her paint an inch thick, to this favour she must come. Make her laugh at that.—Prithee, Horatio, tell me one thing.

HORATIO　What's that, my lord?

HAMLET　Dost thou think Alexander looked o'this fashion i'th'earth?

HORATIO　E'en so.

HAMLET　And smelt so? Puh!

[*Places the skull on the ground or throws it down*]

HORATIO　E'en so, my lord.

HAMLET　To what base uses we may return, Horatio! Why may not imagination trace the noble dust of Alexander till he find it stopping a bung-hole?

HORATIO　'Twere to consider too curiously to consider so.

哈姆雷特　不，一点不，这是很可能的；我们可以这样想；亚历山大死了；亚历山大埋葬了；亚历山大化为尘土；人们把尘土做成烂泥；那么为什么亚历山大所变成的烂泥，不会被人家拿来塞在啤酒桶的口上呢？

恺撒死了，他尊严的尸体
也许变了泥把破墙填砌；
啊！他从前是何等的英雄，
现在只好替人挡雨遮风！
可是不要做声！不要做声！站开，国王来了。

HAMLET No, faith, not a jot, but to follow him thither with modesty enough, and likelihood to lead it, as thus: Alexander died, Alexander was buried, Alexander returneth into dust; the dust is earth; of earth we make loam, and why of that loam whereto he was converted might they not stop a beer-barrel?

Imperious Caesar, dead and turned to clay,

Might stop a hole to keep the wind away.

O, that that earth, which kept the world in awe,

Should patch a wall t'expel the winter's flaw!

But soft, but soft, aside: here comes the king.

译文2（辜正坤版）

Activities

1. Shakespeare and Today

Direction: Students will be divided in two groups, each working on one side of the puzzle: To be or not to be? If they were given a chance to speak to Hamlet face to face, what would they say about Hamlet's delay and overthinking? Would they urge him to take a quick revenge or would they persuade him to give up? Why?

2. Shakespeare and China

Direction: Please make a comparative reading of the two songs/lyrics in A Dream of Red Mansion *and* Hamlet. *Try to explain what the writers want to say about fate and death.*

《好了歌》	
世人都晓神仙好，惟有功名忘不了！	But age with his stealing steps
古今将相在何方？荒冢一堆草没了。	Hath caught me in his clutch,
世人都晓神仙好，只有金银忘不了！	And hath shipped me intil the land,
终朝只恨聚无多，及到多时眼闭了。	As if I had never been such.
世人都晓神仙好，只有姣妻忘不了！	A pickaxe and a spade, a spade,
君生日日说恩情，君死又随人去了。	For and a shrouding sheet:
世人都晓神仙好，只有儿孙忘不了！	O, a pit of clay for to be made
痴心父母古来多，孝顺儿孙谁见了？	For such a guest is meet.
（《红楼梦》）	(*Hamlet*)

3. Shakespeare and Beyond

Direction: Thomas Eliot, a famous writer and critic, once said, "Hamlet is Mona Lisa in literature." What did he imply about the play and its main character? Is it possible to find a link between a painting and a literary work? Can you draw some examples from Chinese art?

Further Reading

BRADLEY A C, 1992. Shakespearean tragedy: lectures on *Hamlet*, *Othello*, *King Lear* and *Macbeth* [M]. New York: Macmillan Publishing House.

EVERETT B, 1989. Young Hamlet: essays on Shakespeare's tragedies

［M］. New York: Oxford University Press.

LEE J, 2000. Shakespeare's Hamlet and the controversies of self ［M］. Oxford: Clarendon Press.

LEWIS R, 2017. Hamlet and the vision of darkness ［M］. Princeton: Princeton University Press.

ZAMIR T, 2018. Shakespeare's Hamlet: philosophical perspectives ［M］. New York: Oxford University Press.

Unit 3 The Tragedy of Macbeth

章节概述

《麦克白》约发表于1606年，1623年收入第一对开本。故事取材于16世纪英国历史学家霍林希德的《编年史》。《麦克白》是莎士比亚篇幅最短、情节发展最快，也是最血腥暴力的一部悲剧。读者在感受鲜血、黑暗、死亡、疾病等恐怖意象带来的强烈情感冲击的同时，也体验了该剧在情节、主题、语言、人物塑造上摄人心魄的艺术魅力。

苏格兰国王邓肯手下的两位将领麦克白和班柯从战场上凯旋，途中三位女巫向他们欢呼致意。她们预言麦克白将成为考多尔爵士和苏格兰国王，而班柯的子子孙孙将继承未来的王权。该预言的第一部分很快应验，因为邓肯嘉奖了麦克白为王室立下的战功，册封他为考多尔爵士。麦克白夫人受此鼓舞，并趁丈夫野心正盛之际，怂恿他谋杀了到他们城堡来做客的邓肯。邓肯的儿子马尔康和道纳本逃亡到英格兰。麦克白如愿做了国王，他为确保自己的地位又杀害了班柯。但班柯的鬼魂在一个宴会上出现在麦克白面前。惊魂未定的麦克白向三女巫求助。她们警告他提防逃到英格兰的贵族麦克杜夫，但同时向他保证，任何由女人生出的人都伤害不了他。麦克白下令谋杀了麦克杜夫的妻子和儿子。在英格兰，马尔康考验了麦克杜夫的忠诚，他们共同起兵讨伐暴君。麦克白对女巫的预言深信不疑，认为自己战无不胜。在讨伐大军日益逼近时，他得到了麦克白夫人自杀的消息。他和麦克杜夫在战场上相遇。当他得知麦克杜夫不是自然分娩而是剖宫产出的时候，他意识到他必须面对死亡，并最终殒命于麦克杜夫的剑下。马尔康加冕为苏格兰国王。

在这部剧里，麦克白的弑君行为像是打开了潘多拉的魔盒，打破了天地间原有的秩序：黑夜不羁、风暴骤起、大地颤动、万马齐喑。王位既得，麦克白开始了巩固其地位的一系列谋杀，但他也陷入了深深的恐惧和自责。他像一艘船在命运的狂风暴雨中飘荡；也像个输红了眼的赌徒在自我的权欲和别人的怂恿下越陷越深，难以自拔。"巫婆的指示使他沉溺于迷信的畏惧与屏息的悬望，从此他迫不及待地去证实她们的预言，并用邪恶、血污的手撕开了那遮掩着尚未分晓的将来的帷幕。"[①]最终，麦克白众叛亲离，而他的夫人则由于饱受精神折磨而患上了梦游之症，后以自杀结束了自己的生命。全剧以麦克白败在麦克杜夫手下，殒命战场而告终。《麦克白》让我们见证了高昂的激情、无羁的野心、结盟与背叛，是一出关于梦想如何变成噩梦，特别是贤德、忠勇之士如何蜕变成十恶不赦的杀人狂魔的悲剧。

相较于迟疑不定的麦克白，麦克白夫人有着顽强的意志力和狠辣的性格。她拥有一种可以忍受各种痛苦的坚毅品质，能抓住梦想成真的机会。她的与众不同或许并不在于其残忍狠毒，而是在于其处变不惊的头脑和意志。麦克白夫人在怂恿麦克白弑君篡位时说过极富煽动性的一段话："现在你有了大好的机会，你又失去勇气了。我曾经哺乳过婴孩，知道一个母亲是怎样怜爱那吮吸她乳汁的子女；可是我会在他看着我的脸微笑的时候，从他的柔软的嫩嘴里摘下我的乳头，把他的脑袋砸碎，要是我也像你一样，曾经发誓下这样的毒手的话。"[②]麦克白夫人的敢想敢做和心狠手辣令读者毛骨悚然，而这奸恶的形象正是通过女性特有的语言表现出来。出场不多但句句惊人的麦克白夫人也成了文学史上的经典人物。

这部剧早已超越了它原本的时代，不断地投射出人类的本能和欲望。

Selected Reading

Act I, vii

Hautboys. Torches. Enter a Sewer and divers

---

① 张薇：《莎士比亚精读》，上海：上海大学出版社，2009年，第221页。
② 威廉·莎士比亚：《麦克白：汉英对照》，朱生豪译，南京：译林出版社，2013年，第20页。

Servants with dishes and service over the stage.

Then enter Macbeth

MACBETH If it were done when 'tis done, then 'twere well

It were done quickly: if th'assassination

Could **trammel** up the consequence and catch

> trammel: v. to limit or prevent free movement 束缚，拘束，阻碍

With his **surcease** success: that but this blow

> surcease: n. stop, death 停止，死亡

Might be the be-all and the end-all—here,

But here, upon this bank and **shoal** of time,

> shoal: n. a small hill of sand 浅滩，沙洲

We'd jump the life to come. But in these cases

We still have judgement here, that we but teach

Bloody instructions, which, being taught, return

To plague th'inventor: this even-handed justice

Commends th' ingredients of our poisoned **chalice**

> chalice: n. a gold or silver decorated cup used to hold wine in Christian religious services 圣餐杯，酒杯

To our own lips. He's here in double trust:

First, as I am his kinsman and his subject,

Strong both against the deed: then, as his host,

Who should against his murderer shut the door,

Not bear the knife myself. Besides, this Duncan

Hath borne his faculties so meek, hath been

So clear in his great office, that his virtues

Will plead like angels, trumpet-tongued, against

The deep damnation of his taking-off:

And pity, like a naked new-born babe,

Striding the blast, or heaven's **cherubin**, horsed

> cherubin: n. (biblical) one of the angels that guard the seat where god sits 智天使（天堂乐园的守护者）

Upon the sightless couriers of the air,

Shall blow the horrid deed in every eye,

That tears shall drown the wind. I have no **spur**

> spur: n. a fact or event that makes you try harder to do sth. 冲动，心血来潮，激励

To prick the sides of my intent, but only

Vaulting ambition, which o'erleaps itself

And falls on th'other.—

Enter Lady[Macbeth]

How now? What news?

LADY MACBETH He has almost supped.

Why have you left the chamber?

> sup: v. to drink sth., esp. slowly in small amounts; (old use) to eat supper（小口地）喝，呷；吃晚餐

MACBETH Hath he asked for me?

LADY MACBETH Know you not he has?

MACBETH We will proceed no further in this business:

He hath honoured me of late, and I have bought

Golden opinions from all sorts of people,

Which would be worn now in their newest gloss,

Not cast aside so soon.

> gloss: n. shiny brightness on a surface 光彩，能产生光泽的物质

LADY MACBETH Was the hope drunk

Wherein you dressed yourself? Hath it slept since?

And wakes it now, to look so green and pale

At what it did so freely? From this time

Such I account thy love. Art thou afeard

To be the same in thine own act and valour

As thou art in desire? Wouldst thou have that

Which thou esteem'st the ornament of life,

And live a coward in thine own esteem,

Letting 'I dare not' wait upon 'I would',

Like the poor cat i'th'adage?

> adage: n. proverb; a well-known phrase that says sth. wise about human experience 格言，谚语，箴言

MACBETH Prithee, peace.

I dare do all that may become a man:

Who dares do more is none.

LADY MACBETH What beast was't, then,

That made you break this enterprise to me?

When you durst do it, then you were a man:

durst: v. dare, to be brave to do sth. 敢于，向……挑战

And to be more than what you were, you would

Be so much more the man. Nor time nor place

Did then adhere, and yet you would make both:

They have made themselves, and that their fitness

now

Does unmake you. I have given suck, and know

How tender 'tis to love the babe that milks me:

I would, while it was smiling in my face,

Have plucked my nipple from his boneless gums,

And dashed the brains out, had I so sworn as

you

Have done to this.

MACBETH If we should fail?

LADY MACBETH We fail?

But screw your courage to the sticking-place

And we'll not fail. When Duncan is asleep—

Whereto the rather shall his day's hard journey

Soundly invite him—his two chamberlains

wassail: n. banquet, wine for a banquet 酒宴，祝酒时用的酒

Will I with wine and wassail so convince,

That memory, the warder of the brain,

warder: n. jailor; someone who guards the prisoners 看守，守卫，典狱官

Shall be a fume, and the receipt of reason

A limbeck only: when in swinish sleep

limbeck: n. distiller 蒸馏器
swinish: a. like a pig; greedy 猪的，猪一般的；贪婪的

Their drenchèd natures lies as in a death,

What cannot you and I perform upon

Th'unguarded Duncan? What not put upon

His spongy officers, who shall bear the guilt

quell: v. n. put down, murder 镇压，谋杀

Of our great quell?

MACBETH Bring forth men-children only,

For thy undaunted mettle should compose

Nothing but males. Will it not be received,

When we have marked with blood those sleepy two

Of his own chamber and used their very daggers,

That they have done't?

LADY MACBETH Who dares receive it other,

As we shall make our griefs and clamour roar

Upon his death?

> clamour: n. very loud noise 喧闹，吵闹 v. to demand sth. loudly 强烈要求

MACBETH I am settled, and bend up

Each corporal agent to this terrible feat.

Away, and mock the time with fairest show:

False face must hide what the false heart doth know.　　　*Exeunt*

译文 1（朱生豪版）

第一幕第七场	ACT I, vii
高音笛奏乐；室中遍燃火炬。一司膳及若干仆人持肴馔食具上，自台前经过。麦克白上。	*Hautboys. Torches. Enter a Sewer and divers Servants with dishes and service over the stage. Then enter Macbeth*
麦克白　要是干了以后就完了，那么还是快一点干；要是凭着暗杀的手段，可以攫取美满的结果;要是这一刀砍下去，就可以完成一切，终结一切，解决一切——在这人世上，仅仅在这人世上，在时间的激流浅滩上，那么来生我也就顾不	**MACBETH** If it were done when 'tis done, then 'twere well It were done quickly: if th'assassination Could trammel up the consequence and catch With his surcease success: that but this blow Might be the be-all and the end-all—here,

到了。可是在这种事情上，我们往往可以看见冥冥中的裁判；教唆杀人的人，结果反而自己被人所杀；把毒药投入酒杯里的人，结果也会自己饮鸩而死。他到这儿来是有两重的信任：第一，我是他的亲戚，又是他的臣子，按照名分绝对不能干这样的事；第二，他是我的客人，我应当保障他的身体的安全，怎么可以自己持刀行刺？而且，这个邓肯秉性仁慈，处理国政，从来没有过失，要是把他杀死了，他的生前的美德，将要像天使一般发出喇叭一样清澈的声音，向世人昭告我的弑君重罪；"怜悯"像一个赤裸身体在狂风中飘荡的婴儿，又像一个御气而行的天婴，将要把这可憎的行为揭露在每一个人的眼中，使眼泪淹没了叹息。没有一种力量可以鞭策我前进，可是我的跃跃欲试的野心，却不顾一切地驱着我去冒颠簸的危险。

But here, upon this bank and shoal of time,

We'd jump the life to come. But in these cases

We still have judgement here, that we but teach

Bloody instructions, which, being taught, return

To plague th'inventor: this even-handed justice

Commends th' ingredients of our poisoned chalice

To our own lips. He's here in double trust:

First, as I am his kinsman and his subject,

Strong both against the deed: then, as his host,

Who should against his murderer shut the door,

Not bear the knife myself. Besides, this Duncan

Hath borne his faculties so meek, hath been

So clear in his great office, that his virtues

Will plead like angels, trumpet-tongued, against

The deep damnation of his taking-off:

And pity, like a naked new-born babe,

Striding the blast, or heaven's cherubin, horsed

Upon the sightless couriers of the air,

Shall blow the horrid deed in every eye,

That tears shall drown the wind. I have no spur

To prick the sides of my intent, but only

Vaulting ambition, which o'erleaps itself

And falls on th'other.—

Enter Lady[*Macbeth*]

How now? What news?

麦克白夫人上。

麦克白 啊！什么消息？

麦克白夫人 他快要吃好了；你为什么跑了出来？

麦克白 他没有问起我？

麦克白夫人 你不知道他问起过你吗？

麦克白 我们还是不要进行这一件事情。他最近给我极大的尊荣；我也好容易从各种人的嘴里博到了无上的美誉，我的名声现在正在发射最灿烂的光彩，不能这么快就把它丢弃了。

麦克白夫人 难道你把自己沉浸在里面的那种希望，只是醉后的妄想吗？它现在从一场睡梦中醒来，因为追悔自己的孟浪而吓得脸色这样苍白吗？从

LADY MACBETH He has almost supped. Why have you left the chamber?

MACBETH Hath he asked for me?

LADY MACBETH Know you not he has?

MACBETH We will proceed no further in this business:

He hath honoured me of late, and I have bought

Golden opinions from all sorts of people,

Which would be worn now in their newest gloss,

Not cast aside so soon.

LADY MACBETH Was the hope drunk

Wherein you dressed yourself? Hath it slept since?

And wakes it now, to look so green and

这一刻起，我要把你的爱情看作同样靠不住的东西。你不敢让你在自己的行为和勇气上跟你的欲望一致吗？你宁愿像一只畏首畏尾的猫儿，顾全你所认为生命的装饰品的名誉，不惜让你在自己眼中成为一个懦夫，让"我不敢"永远跟随在"我想要"的后面吗？

麦克白 请你不要说了。只要是男子汉的事，我都敢做；没有人比我有更大的胆量。

麦克白夫人 那么当初是什么畜生使你把这一种企图告诉我呢？是男子汉应当敢作敢为；要是你做了你本不能做的事，那才更是一个男子汉。那时候，无论时间和地点都不曾给你下手的方便，可是你却居然会决意实现你的愿望；现在你有了大好的机会，你又失去勇气了。我曾经哺乳过婴孩，知道一个母亲是怎样怜爱那吮吸她乳汁的子女；可是我会在他看着我的脸微笑的时候，从他的柔软的嫩嘴里摘下我的乳头，把他的脑袋砸碎，要是我

pale

At what it did so freely? From this time
Such I account thy love. Art thou afeard
To be the same in thine own act and
valour
As thou art in desire? Wouldst thou
have that
Which thou esteem'st the ornament of
life,
And live a coward in thine own esteem,
Letting 'I dare not' wait upon 'I would',
Like the poor cat i'th'adage?

MACBETH Prithee, peace.

I dare do all that may become a man:
Who dares do more is none.

LADY MACBETH What beast was't,
then,
That made you break this enterprise to
me!
When you durst do it, then you were a
man:
And to be more than what you were,
you would
Be so much more the man. Nor time
nor place
Did then adhere, and yet you would
make both:
They have made themselves, and that
their fitness now
Does unmake you. I have given suck,

也像你一样，曾经发誓下这样的毒手的话。

and know

How tender 'tis to love the babe that milks me:

I would, while it was smiling in my face,

Have plucked my nipple from his boneless gums,

And dashed the brains out, had I so sworn as you

Have done to this.

麦克白　假如我们失败了——

麦克白夫人　我们失败！只要你集中你的全副勇气，我们绝不会失败。邓肯赶了这一天辛苦的路程，一定睡得很熟；我再去陪他那两个侍卫饮酒作乐，灌得他们头脑昏沉，记忆化成了一阵烟雾；等他们烂醉如泥，像死猪一样睡去以后，我们不就可以把那毫无防卫的邓肯随意摆布了吗？我们不是可以把这一件重大的谋杀罪案，推在他的酒醉的侍卫身上吗？

MACBETH If we should fail?

LADY MACBETH We fail?

But screw your courage to the sticking-place

And we'll not fail. When Duncan is asleep—

Whereto the rather shall his day's hard journey

Soundly invite him—his two chamber-lains

Will I with wine and wassail so convince,

That memory, the warder of the brain,

Shall be a fume, and the receipt of reason

A limbeck only: when in swinish sleep

Their drenchèd natures lies as in a death,

What cannot you and I perform upon

Th'unguarded Duncan? What not put upon

麦克白　愿你所生育的全是男孩子，因为你的无畏的精神，只应该铸造一些刚强的男性。要是我们在那睡在他寝室里的两个人身上涂抹一些血迹，而且就用他们的刀子，人家会不会相信真是他们干下的事？

麦克白夫人　等他的死讯传出以后，我们就假意装出号啕痛哭的样子，这样还有谁敢不相信？

麦克白　我的决心已定，我要用全身的力量，去干这件惊人的举动。去，用最美妙的外表把人们的耳目欺骗；奸诈的心必须罩上虚伪的笑脸。（同下）

His spongy officers, who shall bear the guilt

Of our great quell?

MACBETH　Bring forth men-children only,

For thy undaunted mettle should compose

Nothing but males. Will it not be received,

When we have marked with blood those sleepy two

Of his own chamber and used their very daggers,

That they have done't?

LADY MACBETH　Who dares receive it other,

As we shall make our griefs and clamour roar

Upon his death?

MACBETH　I am settled, and bend up

Each corporal agent to this terrible feat.

Away, and mock the time with fairest show:

False face must hide what the false heart doth know.　　*Exeunt*

译文2（辜正坤版）

ACT V, v

Enter Macbeth, Seyton, and Soldiers with Drum and Colours

MACBETH Hang out our banners on the outward walls:

The cry is still 'They come.' Our castle's strength

Will laugh a siege to scorn: here let them lie

Till famine and the ague eat them up.

> ague: n. plague, contagious disease 瘟疫，发冷

Were they not forced with those that should be ours,

We might have met them dareful, beard to beard,

And beat them backward home.

A cry within of women

　　What is that noise?

SEYTON It is the cry of women, my good lord.

[*Exit or goes to the door*]

MACBETH I have almost forgot the taste of fears:

The time has been my senses would have cooled

To hear a night-shriek, and my fell of hair

Would at a dismal treatise rouse and stir

As life were in't. I have supped full with horrors:

Direness, familiar to my slaughterous thoughts,

> direness: n. the state of being bad or terrible 可怕，悲惨；dire 的名词形式

Cannot once start me.—

[*Seyton re-enters or comes forward*]

　　Wherefore was that cry?

[*To Seyton*]

SEYTON The Queen, my lord, is dead.

MACBETH She should have died hereafter:

There would have been a time for such a word.

Tomorrow, and tomorrow, and tomorrow,

Creeps in this petty pace from day to day

To the last syllable of recorded time:

And all our yesterdays have lighted fools

The way to dusty death. Out, out, brief candle.

Life's but a walking shadow, a poor player

That struts and frets his hour upon the stage

And then is heard no more. It is a tale

> strut: v. to walk proudly with head high 趾高气扬地走，昂首阔步

> fret: v. to feel worried, to make something weaker by rubbing 烦恼，发愁，使磨损

Told by an idiot, full of sound and fury,

Signifying nothing.

Enter a Messenger

Thou com'st to use thy tongue: thy story quickly.

MESSENGER Gracious my lord,

I should report that which I say I saw,

But know not how to do't.

MACBETH Well, say, sir.

MESSENGER As I did stand my watch upon

the hill,

I looked toward Birnam, and anon methought

The wood began to move.

> anon: ad. (literary) soon 不久，很快，立刻

MACBETH Liar and slave!

MESSENGER Let me endure your wrath if't

be not so.

> wrath: n. anger, fury 愤怒，盛怒

Within this three mile may you see it coming:

I say, a moving grove.

> grove: n. a small group of trees, wood 树丛，小树林

MACBETH If thou speak'st false,

Upon the next tree shall thou hang alive

Till famine cling thee: if thy speech be sooth,

I care not if thou dost for me as much.—

I pull in resolution, and begin

To doubt th'equivocation of the fiend

That lies like truth. 'Fear not, till Birnam Wood

Do come to Dunsinane', and now a wood

Comes toward Dunsinane.—Arm, arm, and out!

If this which he avouches does appear,

There is nor flying hence nor tarrying here.—

I'gin to be aweary of the sun,

And wish th' estate o' th' world were now

undone.—

Ring the alarum bell! Blow wind, come wrack,

At least we'll die with harness on our back.

Exeunt

> equivocation: n. words without clear or direct meaning 含糊话，模棱两可的话

> fiend: n. a very cruel or wicked person, devil 魔鬼，恶魔

> avouch: n. a strong statement or promise 断言，保证

> tarry: v. to linger or stay in a place 逗留，耽搁，徘徊

> wrack: n. (同 rack) an act to damage or ruin sth. 毁灭，破坏

译文1（朱生豪版）

第五幕第五场

旗鼓前导，麦克白、西登及兵士等上。

麦克白 把我们的旗帜挂在城墙外面；到处仍旧是一片"他们来了"的呼声；我们这座城堡防御得这样坚强，还怕他们围攻吗？让他们到这儿来，等饥饿和瘟疫来把他们收拾去吧。倘不是我们自己的军队也倒了戈跟他们联合在一起，我尽可以挺身出战，把他们赶回老家去。（内妇女哭声）那是什么声音？

ACT V, v

Enter Macbeth, Seyton, and Soldiers with Drum and Colours

MACBETH Hang out our banners on the outward walls:

The cry is still 'They come.' Our castle's strength

Will laugh a siege to scorn: here let them lie

Till famine and the ague eat them up.

Were they not forced with those that should be ours,

We might have met them dareful, beard to beard,

西登　是妇女们的哭声，陛下。（下）

麦克白　我简直已经忘记了恐惧的滋味。从前一声晚间的哀叫，可以把我吓出一身冷汗，听着一段可怕的故事，我的头发会像有了生命似的竖起来。现在我已经饱尝无数的恐怖；我的习惯于杀戮的思想，再也没有什么悲惨的事情可以使它惊悚了。

西登重上。

麦克白　那哭声是为了什么事？

西登　陛下，王后死了。

麦克白　迟早总是要死的，总要有听到这个噩耗的一天。明天，明天，再一个明天，一天接着一天地蹑步前进，直到最后一秒钟的时间；我们所有的昨天，不过替傻子们照亮了到死亡的土壤中去的路，熄灭了吧，熄灭了吧，短促的烛光！

And beat them backward home.

A cry within of women

　　What is that noise?

SEYTON　It is the cry of women, my good lord.

[*Exit or goes to the door*]

MACBETH　I have almost forgot the taste of fears:

The time has been my senses would have cooled

To hear a night-shriek, and my fell of hair

Would at a dismal treatise rouse and stir

As life were in't. I have supped full with horrors:

Direness, familiar to my slaughterous thoughts,

Cannot once start me. —

[*Seyton re-enters or comes forward*]

　　Wherefore was that cry?

[*To seyton*]

SEYTON The queen, my lord, is dead.

MACBETH　She should have died hereafter:

There would have been a time for such a word.

Tomorrow, and tomorrow, and tomorrow,

Creeps in this petty pace from day to day

人生不过是一个行走的影子，一个在舞台上指手画脚的拙劣的伶人，登场片刻，就在无声无臭中悄然退下；它是一个愚人所讲的故事，充满着喧哗和骚动，却找不到一点意义。

一使者上。

To the last syllable of recorded time:
And all our yesterdays have lighted fools
The way to dusty death. Out, out, brief candle.
Life's but a walking shadow, a poor player
That struts and frets his hour upon the stage
And then is heard no more. It is a tale
Told by an idiot, full of sound and fury,
Signifying nothing.

Enter a Messenger

麦克白　你要来拨弄你的唇舌；有什么话快说。

使者　陛下，我应该向您报告我以为我所看见的事，可是我不知道应该怎样说起。

麦克白　好，你说吧。

使者　当我站在山头守望的时候，我向勃南一眼望去，好像那边的树木都在开始行动了。

麦克白　说谎的奴才！

使者　要是没有那么一回事，我愿意悉听陛下的惩处；在这三英里路以内，您可以看见它向这边过来；一座活动的树林。

Thou com'st to use thy tongue: thy story quickly.

MESSENGER Gracious my lord,
I should report that which I say I saw,
But know not how to do't.

MACBETH Well, say, sir.

MESSENGER As I did stand my watch upon the hill,
I looked toward Birnam, and anon methought
The wood began to move.

MACBETH Liar and slave!

MESSENGER Let me endure your wrath if't be not so.
Within this three mile may you see it coming:
I say, a moving grove.

麦克白　要是你说了谎话，我要把你活活吊在树上，让你饿死；要是你的话是真的，我也希望你把我吊死了吧。我的决心已经有些动摇，我开始怀疑起那魔鬼所说的似是而非的暧昧的谎话了："不要害怕，除非勃南森林会到邓斯纳恩来。"现在一座树林真的到邓斯纳恩来了。披上武装，出去！他所说的这种事情要是果然出现，那么逃走固然走不了，留在这儿也不过坐以待毙。我现在开始厌倦白昼的阳光，但愿这世界早一点崩溃。敲起警钟来！吹吧，狂风！来吧，灭亡！就是死我们也要捐命沙场。（同下）

MACBETH If thou speak'st false,

Upon the next tree shall thou hang alive

Till famine cling thee: if thy speech be sooth,

I care not if thou dost for me as much.—

I pull in resolution, and begin

To doubt th'equivocation of the fiend

That lies like truth. 'Fear not, till Birnam Wood

Do come to Dunsinane', and now a wood

Comes toward Dunsinane.—Arm, arm, and out!

If this which he avouches does appear,

There is nor flying hence nor tarrying here.—

I'gin to be aweary of the sun,

And wish th'estate o'th'world were now undone.—

Ring the alarum bell! Blow wind, come wrack,

At least we'll die with harness on our back. *Exeunt*

译文2（辜正坤版）

Activities

1. Shakespeare and Today

Direction: Where precisely do dark forces come from? Why does Macbeth commit horrific acts? Does the supernatural stand for something vicious in the play? Or does it simply forecast what is going to happen? Make a research of the adaptation of Macbeth *in Chinese literature and art, see if there is any change and revision in the new cultural environment? Is it successful and why?*

2. Shakespeare and China

Direction: Lady Macbeth was considered the most evil and cruelest woman in Shakespeare's plays, but her undaunted determination and ability to act dwarf men around her, making her an awesome and respectable character on stage. Are there similar women images in Chinese literature? Please make an analysis.

3. Shakespeare and Beyond

Direction: Madness is a typical theme in Shakespeare's tragedies. There are famous cases of madness in both Hamlet *and* Macbeth, *namely, the madness of Hamlet, the madness of Ophelia, and the madness of Lady Macbeth. Please explain what causes their madness and what distinguishes their madness? Michel Foucault（米歇尔·福柯）points out in* Madness and Civilization *that how a society deals with madness can help measure how civilized a society is. What do you think about it? Please have a discussion in the class.*

Further Reading

CAMPBELL L B, 2009. Shakespeare's tragic heroes: slaves of passion [M]. London: Cambridge University Press.

CRAIG L H, 2001. Of philosophers and kings: political philosophy in Shakespeare's Macbeth and King Lear [M]. Toronto: University of Toronto Press.

KINNEY A F, 2001. Lies like truth: Shakespeare, Macbeth, and the cultural moment [M]. Detroit: Wayne State University Press.

MORRIS I, 2010. Shakespeare's god: the role of religion in the tragedies [M]. London: Routledge.

WILLS G, 1996. Witches and Jesuits: Shakespeare's Macbeth [M]. New York: New York Public Library.

Part Six   Shakespeare's Romances

Unit 1 What Is Romance?

章节概述

　　莎士比亚的戏剧创作生涯通常被分为三个阶段。第一个阶段恰逢伊丽莎白统治的兴盛时期，受时代氛围影响，莎士比亚主要创作喜剧和历史剧，且剧情多有戏谑，生动有趣。第二个阶段莎士比亚主要创作悲剧，这一阶段是其戏剧创作的辉煌时期。此时的莎士比亚一改之前明快的风格，在剧中塑造了一系列的悲剧英雄及人文主义理想人物，虽然描写的是年代久远或异国他乡的故事，但都深刻地反映了当时英国的社会现实，戏剧作品充满了阴郁和悲怆。第三个阶段莎士比亚主要创作传奇剧。这一时期的莎士比亚恢复了对人文主义的信念，阅尽人世沧桑之后看待社会现实也更加平和、包容。因此，传奇剧大多以悔悟、宽恕与和解为主题，剧情富于传奇浪漫色彩，文风绮丽。"传奇剧"（romance）或 "晚期戏剧"（last plays）的概念是由 19 世纪晚期的莎学家道登（Edward Dowden）首次提出的，他认为《辛白林》（*Cymbeline*）、《冬天的故事》（*The Winter's Tale*）和《暴风雨》（*The Tempest*）"这三部剧自成一组"，合称为"传奇剧"。① 这个说法②在道登首次使用后大为流行，是诸多学者在描述莎士比亚晚期戏剧时使用最为频繁的术语。后来，道登又将《配力克里斯》（*Pericles, Prince of Tyre*）增加进来。这四部剧在体裁、主题和风格上自成一派，与这一时期之前的喜剧、悲剧和历史剧都存在明显差异。的确，在莎士比亚的整个创作生涯中，就戏剧风格而言，要数几部后期悲剧与晚期传奇剧之间的变化最为显著。

关于传奇剧的起源众说不一。有学者认为传奇剧中的故事源自古希腊散文传奇文学，属于文艺复兴时期被重新发现的古典世界。然而，其情节又与中世纪奇幻背景下的宫廷爱情故事极其相似。也有学者认为这种浪漫传奇剧是王朝更替时期剧作家们为了迎合群体审美而精心制作的一种新型戏剧，让悲剧故事拥有一个喜剧的结局，"这些伊丽莎白时代戏剧的故事'是要变得奇异而美妙的'；它们被设计成'浪漫传奇剧，部分目的是为了满足喜欢浪漫的观众对传奇的喜好'"③。目前虽然无法明确定义，但莎学家们通常认为晚期创作的传奇剧有别于之前的作品，有着相似的戏剧主题、情节元素以及语言风格，"反映莎士比亚此时在世界观、创作手法上的创新"④。这些作品往往包含一系列常见的情节要素：宫廷爱情、田园牧歌、魔法神谕、精灵音乐、悲剧冲突和圆满结局。道登之后的莎学专家认为传奇剧具有以下特征："1. 成剧晚于莎士比亚成熟期的悲剧；2. 悲剧元素充分，喜剧结尾；3. 情节围绕悔过、宽恕和修好展开，结尾处年轻一代谈婚论嫁，离散亲友久别重逢；4. 有神明或超自然力量干预事态发展；5. 故事时间跨度大，地点至少

---

① Dowden, Edward. *Shakspere: A Critical Study of His Mind and Art*. 3rd ed. New York: Harper & Brothers Publishers, 1903, p. 338.

② 第一个将莎士比亚晚期作品称为 "romance" 的人是道登，但第一个以 "romantic" 这个词描述莎剧的人则是浪漫主义诗人柯勒律治，他将《暴风雨》定性为一部 "romantic drama"，不过这里的 "romantic" 也许译作 "浪漫主义" 而非 "传奇" 更为恰当。

③ 布兰德·马修斯：《剧作家莎士比亚》，罗文敏、魏红华译，北京：人民出版社，2021年，第273页。

④ 陈星：《莎士比亚传奇剧中的历史书写》，南京：南京大学出版社，2021年，第26页。

横跨两国，多隔海。"① 在莎士比亚的传奇剧中，戏剧冲突主要体现在
人文主义理想与社会现实之间，故事情节由意外、巧合、魔法等外力因
素推动，经历从秩序到混乱的过程并最终回归秩序，充满了由宽恕与和
解带来的祥和，也反映了莎士比亚归隐之前平和超脱的心境。

Selected Reading

Shakspere's Last Plays②

Edward Dowden③

In the history of every artist and of every man there are periods of quickened
existence, when spiritual discovery is made without an effort, and attainment
becomes easy and almost involuntary. One does not seek for truth, but rather
is sought for by truth, and found; one does not construct beautiful
imaginings, but beauty itself haunts and startles and waylays. These periods
may be arrived at through prolonged moral conflict and victory, or through
some sudden revelation of joy, or through supreme anguish and
renouncement. Such epochs of spiritual discovery lie behind the art of the
artist, it may be immediately, or it may be remotely, and out of these it
springs. Among many art-products some single work will perhaps give to a

---

① 陈星：《莎士比亚传奇剧中的历史书写》，南京：南京大学出版社，2021年，第24-25页。
有不少评论家认为莎士比亚创作的传奇剧违反了"三一律"，如《冬天的故事》时间跨度
长达16年之久，而三一律规定剧本只能表现一个故事主题，它必须在一天之内发生在一个
地方。

② Selected from *Shakspere: A Critical Study of His Mind and Art* (3rd ed.) published by Harper &
Brothers Publishers, 1903, pp. 336-382. Shakspere 同 Shakespeare，指莎士比亚。在原作中道
登采用了 "Shakspere" 这种拼写方式，而第一对开本采用的是 "Shakespeare"，这也是目
前较为常见的莎士比亚署名，故选文中统一采用 "Shakespeare"。

③ Edward Dowden, an Irish critic, poet and biographer, whose first book *Shakspere: A Critical
Study of His Mind and Art*, published in 1875 and revised in 1881, was the leading example of the
biographical criticism popular in English-speaking world near the end of the nineteenth century
and made him well-known as a critic.

unique experience its highest, its absolute expression; and this, whether produced at the moment or ten years afterwards, properly belongs to that crisis of which it is the outcome. Lyrical writers usually utter themselves nearly at the moment when they are smitten with the sharp stroke of joy or of pain. Dramatic writers, for the purity and fidelity of whose work a certain aloofness from their individuality is needed, utter themselves more often not on the moment, but after an interval, during which self-possession and self-mastery have been attained.

Now, although we are not in all cases able to say confidently this play of Shakespeare preceded that, the order of his writings has been sufficiently determined to enable us to trace with confidence the succession of Shakespeare's epochs of spiritual alteration and development. Whether *Macbeth* preceded *Othello*, or *Othello Macbeth*, need not greatly concern us; the question is one chiefly of literary curiosity; we do not understand Shakespeare much the better when the question has been settled than we did while the answer remained doubtful. Both plays belong, and they belong in an equal degree, to one and the same period in the history of Shakespeare's mind and art, to which period we can unquestionably assign its place. In the present chapter *Timon of Athens* is placed near *The Tempest*, although it is possible that a play, or two or three plays, in the precise chronological order, may lie between them. They are placed near one another because in *Timon of Athens* Shakespeare's mood of indignation with the world attains its highest, its ideal expression, while in *The Tempest* we find the ideal expression of the temper of mind which succeeded his mood of indignation—the pathetic yet august serenity of Shakespeare's final period. For the purposes of such a study as this we may look upon *The Tempest* as Shakespeare's latest play. Perhaps it actually was such; perhaps *A Winter's Tale* or *Cymbeline*, or both, may have followed it in point of time. It does not matter greatly, for the purposes of the present study, which preceded and which succeeded. These three plays, as we shall see, form a little group by themselves, but it is *The Tempest* which gives its most perfect expression to the spirit that breathes through these three plays which bring to an end the dramatic career of Shakespeare; and therefore for us it is Shakespeare's latest plays...[1]

......

The plays belonging to Shakespeare's final period of authorship, which I shall consider, are three: *Cymbeline*, *The Winter's Tale*, and *The Tempest*. The position in which they were placed in the first folio (whether it was the result of design or accident) is remarkable. The volume opens with *The Tempest*; it closes with *Cymbeline*. *The Winter's Tale* is the last of the comedies, which all lie between this play and *The Tempest*. The circumstance may have been a piece of accident; but if so, it was a lucky accident, which suggests that our first and our last impression of Shakespeare shall be that of Shakespeare in his period of large, serene wisdom, and that in the light of the clear and solemn vision of his closing years all his writings shall be read. Characteristics of versification and style, and the enlarged place given to scenic spectacle, indicate that these plays were produced much about the same time. But the ties of deepest kinship between them are spiritual. There is a certain romantic element in each.[2] They receive contributions from every portion of Shakespeare's genius, but all are mellowed, refined, made exquisite; they avoid the extremes of broad humor and of tragic intensity; they were written with less of passionate concentration than the plays which immediately precede them, but with more of a spirit of deep or exquisite recreation.

---

[1] Observing those plays created in the last period of Shakespeare's writing career, Dowden believes *The Tempest*, *A Winter's Tale* and *Cymbeline*, which remain as the three complete plays with shared features, represent the final period of Shakespeare's authorship, considering *Pericles*, *Two Noble Kinsmen*, and *Henry* Ⅷ are Shakespearian fragments. However, Dowden added *Pericles* into this little group in his later writings.

[2] The same remark applies to Shakespeare's part of *Pericles*, which belongs to this period.

There are moments when Shakespeare was not wholly absorbed in his work as artist at this period; it is as if he were thinking of his own life, or of the fields and streams of Stratford, and still wrote on; it is as if the ties which bound him to his art were not severing with thrills of strong emotion, but were quietly growing slack...

......

Yet it is not to be wondered at that Shakespeare now should feel delivered from the strong urge of imagination and feeling, and should write in a more pleasurable, more leisurely, and not so great a manner. The period of the tragedies was ended. In the tragedies Shakespeare had made his inquisition into the mystery of evil. He had studied those injuries of man to man which are irreparable. He had seen the innocent suffering with the guilty. Death came and removed the criminal and his victim from human sight, and we were left with solemn awe upon our hearts in presence of the insoluble problems of life.... At the same time that Shakespeare had shown the tragic mystery of human life, he had fortified the heart by showing that to suffer is not the supreme evil with man, and that loyalty and innocence, and self-sacrifice and pure redeeming ardor, exist, and cannot be defeated. Now, in his last period of authorship, Shakespeare remained grave—how could it be otherwise?—but his severity was tempered and purified. He had less need of the crude doctrine of Stoicism, because the tonic of such wisdom as exists in Stoicism had been taken up and absorbed into his blood.

Shakespeare still thought of the graver trials and tests which life applies to human character, of the wrongs which man inflicts on man; but his present temper demanded not a tragic issue—it rather demanded an issue into joy or peace. The dissonance must be resolved into a harmony, clear and rapturous, or solemn and profound. And, accordingly, in each of these plays, *The Winter's Tale*, *Cymbeline*, *The Tempest*, while grievous errors of the heart are shown to us, and wrongs of man to man as cruel as those of the great tragedies, at the end there is a resolution of the dissonance, a reconciliation. This is the word which interprets Shakespeare's latest plays—reconciliation, "word over all, beautiful as the sky." It is not, as in the earlier comedies— *The Two Gentlemen of Verona, Much Ado about Nothing, As You Like It*, and others—a mere denouement. The resolution of the discords in these latest plays is not a mere stage necessity, or a necessity of composition, resorted to by the dramatist to effect an ending of his play, and little interesting his imagination or his heart. Its significance here is ethical and spiritual; it is a moral necessity.

......

The wrong-doers of *The Tempest* are a group of persons of various degrees of criminality, from Prospero's perfidious brother, still active in plotting evil, to Alonzo, whose obligations to the Duke of Milan had been of a public or princely kind. Spiritual powers are in alliance with Prospero; and these, by terror and the awakening of remorse, prepare Alonzo for receiving the balm of Prospero's forgiveness. He looks upon his son as lost, and recognizes in his son's loss the punishment of his own guilt. "The powers delaying, not forgetting," have incensed the sea and shores against the sinful men; nothing can deliver them except "heart-sorrow and a clear life ensuing."... Shakespeare's Ariel, breathing through the elements and the powers of nature, quickens the remorse of the King for a crime of twelve years since:

> "O, it is monstrous, monstrous!
> Methought the billows spoke and told me of it;
> The winds did sing it to me; and the thunder,
> That deep and dreadful organ-pipe, pronounced
> The name of Prosper: it did bass my trespass,
> Therefore my son i' the ooze is bedded, and

I'll seek him deeper than e'er plummet sounded,

And with him there lie mudded."

The enemies of Prospero are now completely in his power. How shall he deal with them? They had perfidiously taken advantage of his unworldly and unpractical habits of life; they had thrust him away from his dukedom; they had exposed him, with his three-years-old daughter, in a rotten boat, to the mercy of the waves. Shall he not now avenge himself without remorse? What is Prospero's decision?

"Though with their high wrongs I am struck to the quick,

Yet with my nobler reason 'gainst my fury

Do I take part; the rarer action is

In virtue than in vengeance; they being penitent,

The sole drift of my purpose doth extend

Not a frown further."

......

...Prospero's forgiveness is solemn, judicial, and has in it something abstract and impersonal. He cannot wrong his own higher nature, he cannot wrong the nobler reason, by cherishing so unworthy a passion as the desire of vengeance. Sebastian and Antonio, from whose conscience no remorse has been elicited, are met by no comfortable pardon. They have received their lesson of failure and of pain, and may possibly be convinced of the good sense and prudence of honorable dealing, even if they cannot perceive its moral obligation. Alonzo, who is repentant, is solemnly pardoned. The forgiveness of Prospero is an embodiment of impartial wisdom and loving justice.

... In the latest plays of Shakespeare the sympathetic reader can discern

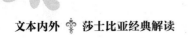

unmistakably a certain abandonment of the common joy of the world, a certain remoteness from the usual pleasures and sadnesses of life, and, at the same time, all the more, this tender bending over those who are, like children, still absorbed in their individual joys and sorrows.

Over the beauty of youth and the love of youth there is shed, in these plays of Shakespeare's final period, a clear yet tender luminousness not elsewhere to be perceived in his writings. In his earlier plays, Shakespeare writes concerning young men and maidens—their loves, their mirth, their griefs—as one who is among them; who has a lively, personal interest in their concerns; who can make merry with them, treat them familiarly, and, if need be, can mock them into good sense. There is nothing in these early plays wonderful, strangely beautiful, pathetic, about youth and its joys and sorrows. In the histories and tragedies, as was to be expected, more massive, broader, or more profound objects of interest engage the poet's imagination. But in these latest plays, the beautiful pathetic light is always present. There are the sufferers, aged, experienced, tried—Queen Katharine, Prospero, Hermione. And over against these there are the children, absorbed in their happy and exquisite egoism—Perdita and Miranda, Florizel and Ferdinand, and the boys of old Belarius.

The same means to secure ideality for these figures, so young and beautiful, is in each case (instinctively, perhaps, rather than deliberately) resorted to. There are lost children—princes, or a princess, removed from the court and its conventional surroundings into some scene of rare, natural beauty. There are the lost princes—Arviragus and Guiderius—among the mountains of Wales, drinking the free air and offering their salutations to the risen sun. There is Perdita, the shepherdess-princess, "queen of curds and cream," sharing, with old and young, her flowers, lovelier and more undying than those that Proserpina let fall from Dis's wagon. There is Miranda (whose very name is significant of wonder), made up of beauty and love and womanly pity, neither courtly nor rustic, with the breeding of an island of enchantment, where Prospero is her tutor and protector, and Caliban her servant, and the Prince of Naples her lover. In each of these plays we can see Shakespeare, as it were, tenderly bending over the joys and sorrows of youth. We recognize this rather through the total characterization, and through a feeling and a presence, than through definite incident or statement. But some of this feeling escapes in the disinterested joy and admiration of old Belarius when he gazes at the princely youths, and in Camillo's loyalty to Florizel and Perdita; while it obtains more distinct expression in such a word as that which Prospero utters when from a distance he watches with pleasure Miranda's zeal to relieve Ferdinand from his task of log-bearing: "Poor worm, thou art infected."

It is not chiefly because Prospero is a great enchanter, now about to break his magic staff, to drown his book deeper than ever plummet sounded, to dismiss his airy spirits, and to return to the practical service of his Dukedom, that we identify Prospero in some measure with Shakespeare himself. It is rather because the temper of Prospero, the grave harmony of his character, his self-mastery, his calm validity of will, his sensitiveness to wrong, his unfaltering justice, and, with these, a certain abandonment, a remoteness from the common joys and sorrows of the world, are characteristic of Shakespeare as discovered to us in all his latest plays. Prospero is an harmonious and fully developed *will*. In the earlier play of fairy enchantments, *A Midsummer-Night's Dream*, the "human mortals" wander to and fro in a maze of error, misled by the mischievous frolic of Puck, the jester and clown of Fairy-land. But here the spirits of the elements, and Caliban, the gross genius of brute matter—needful for the service of life—are brought under

subjection to the human will of Prospero.[①]

What is more, Prospero has entered into complete possession of himself. Shakespeare has shown us his quick sense of injury, his intellectual impatience, his occasional moment of keen irritability, in order that we may be more deeply aware of his abiding strength and self-possession, and that we may perceive how these have been grafted upon a temperament not impassive or unexcitable. And Prospero has reached not only the higher levels of moral attainment; he has also reached an altitude of thought from which he can survey the whole of human life, and see how small and yet how great it is. His heart is sensitive; he is profoundly touched by the joy of the children with whom, in the egoism of their love, he passes for a thing of secondary interest; he is deeply moved by the perfidy of his brother. His brain is readily set a-work, and can with difficulty be checked from eager and excessive energizing; he is subject to the access of sudden and agitating thought. But Prospero masters his own sensitiveness, emotional and intellectual:

> "We are such stuff
> As dreams are made on, and our little life
> Is rounded with a sleep. Sir, I am vex'd;
> Bear with my weakness; my old brain is troubled:
> Be not disturb'd with my infirmity;
> If you be pleased, retire into my cell
> And there repose; a turn or two I'll walk,
> To still my beating mind."

"Such stuff as dreams are made on." Nevertheless, in this little life, in this

---

① This point of contrast between *The Tempest* and *A Midsummer-Night's Dream* is noticed by Mézières, "Shakespeare, ses Œuvres et ses Critiques," pp. 441, 442.

dream, Prospero will maintain his dream rights and fulfil his dream duties. In the dream, he, a Duke, will accomplish Duke's work. Having idealized everything, Shakespeare left everything real...

......

Shakespeare's work, however, will indeed, not allow itself to be lightly treated. The prolonged study of any great interpreter of human life is a discipline. Our loyalty to Shakespeare must not lead us to assert that the discipline of Shakespeare will be suitable to every nature. He will deal rudely with heart and will and intellect, and lay hold of them in unexpected ways, and fashion his disciple, it may be, in a manner which at first is painful and almost terrible. There are persons who, all through their lives, attain their highest strength only by virtue of the presence of certain metaphysical entities which rule their lives; and in the lives of almost all men there is a metaphysical period when they need such supposed entities more than the real presences of those personal and social forces which surround them. For such persons, and during such a period, the discipline of Shakespeare will be unsuitable. He will seem precisely the reverse of what he actually is: he will seem careless about great facts and ideas; limited, restrictive, deficient in enthusiasms and imagination. To one who finds the highest poetry in Shelley, Shakespeare will always remain a kind of prose. Shakespeare is the poet concrete things and real. True, but are not these informed with passion and with thought? A time not seldom comes when a man, abandoning abstractions and metaphysical entities, turns to actual life of the world, and to the real men and women who surround him, for the sources of emotion and thought and action—a time when he strives to come into communion with the Unseen, not immediately, but through the revelation of the Seen. And then he finds the strength and sustenance with which Shakespeare has enriched the world.

" 'The true question to ask,' says the Librarian of Congress, in a paper read before the Social Science Convention at New York, October, 1869— 'The true question to ask respecting a book is, *Has it helped any human soul?*' This is the hint, statement, not only of the great Literatus, his book, but of every great artist. It may be that all works of art are to be first tried by their art-qualities, their image-forming talent, and their dramatic, pictorial, plot-constructing, euphonious, and other talents. Then, whenever claiming to be first-class works, they are to be strictly and sternly tried by their foundation in, and radiation (in the highest sense, and always indirectly) of, the ethic principles, and eligibility to free, arouse, dilate."[1]

What shall be said of Shakespeare's radiation, through art, of the ultimate truths of conscience and of conduct? What shall be said of his power of freeing, arousing, dilating? Something may be gathered out of the foregoing chapters in answer to these questions. But the answers remain insufficient. There is an admirable sentence by Emerson: "A good reader can in a sort nestle into Plato's brain, and think from thence; but not into Shakespeare's. We are still out of doors."

We are still out of doors; and, for the present, let us cheerfully remain in the large, good space. Let us not attenuate Shakespeare to a theory. He is careful that we shall not thus lose our true reward: "The secrets of nature have not more gift in taciturnity."[2] Shakespeare does not supply us with a doctrine, with an interpretation, with a revelation. What he brings to us is this—to each one, courage and energy and strength to dedicate himself and his work to that, whatever it be, which life has revealed to him as best and highest and most real.

---

[1] Whitman, "Democratic Vistas," p. 67.

[2] *Troilus and Cressida*, act iv., sc. 2.

Activities

1. Shakespeare and Today

Direction: After reading the essay above, think about the following questions:

1)Why does Edward Dowden put *The Tempest, The Winter's Tale, Cymbeline* and *Pericles* into the group of romances but exclude *Henry* Ⅷ and *Two Noble Kinsmen*? How do Shakespeare's romances differ from other plays?

2) As Emerson said, "A good reader can in a sort nestle into Plato's brain, and think from thence; but not into Shakespeare's. We are still out of doors." How do you understand Emerson's words? In what ways can we better understand Shakespeare's last plays?

2. Shakespeare and China

Direction: Shakespeare's romances were created in the golden age of Renaissance and rich humanistic thoughts were embodied in these plays. the While in ancient China, we also valued human nature and adopted a people-oriented concept. But Shakespeare's humanistic thought is quite different from that advocated by the ancient Chinese. The former affirms the legitimacy of people's instinctive desire or primitive desire to a large extent, while the latter mainly emphasizes the morality and virtue which regulate human behaviors and social order, based on the idea of benevolence（仁）. Are there any other differences? Are there some similarities? Please create a graphic organizer to disclose the differences and similarities between Shakespeare's humanistic thought and that of ancient Chinese?

3. Shakespeare and Beyond

Direction: Work within groups to research on the following topic.

Shakespeare was in touch with and formed by the literary traditions

(medieval and Renaissance) of non-English-speaking lands. His age also witnessed the Great Discovery of the world. All this suggests that Shakespeare's work should be recognized as part of world literature rather than part of English literature. In what ways might Shakespeare's plays be illuminated by the non-Western literary forms?

Further Reading

BLOOM H, 1998. Shakespeare: the invention of the human [M]. New York: Penguin Publishing Group.

DOWDEN E, 1903. Shakspere: a critical study of his mind and art [M]. 3rd ed. New York: Harper & Brothers Publishers.

HUGO V, 2021. William Shakespeare [M]. BAILLOT A, trans. Shenyang: Liaoning People's Publishing House.

WELLS S, 2000. The Cambridge companion to Shakespeare studies [M]. Shanghai: Shanghai Foreign Language Education Press.

格里尔，2015.读懂莎士比亚 [M].毛亮，译.北京：外语教学与研究出版社.

杨林贵，乔雪瑛，2020.世界莎士比亚研究选编 [M].北京:商务印书馆.

Unit 2 The Tempest

章节概述

　　《暴风雨》是莎士比亚退居斯特拉特福（Stratford）之前独著的最后一部剧作，大约写于1611—1612年，虽成剧于莎士比亚写作生涯晚期，却被置于第一对开本之首。该剧主要讲述米兰公爵普洛斯彼罗被他野心勃勃的弟弟安东尼奥篡位后，流落到荒岛上所发生的一系列魔幻、离奇的故事。忠诚的老枢密大臣贡柴罗在船上为普洛斯彼罗和他的女儿米兰达准备了淡水和食物，还为普洛斯彼罗装上了他喜爱的书籍，因此普洛斯彼罗和米兰达才得以幸免于难，来到这座无人的荒岛。此后，普洛斯彼罗凭借自己的魔幻法术（arts of magic）统治了以爱丽儿为首的精灵，驯化了半人半妖的凯列班。12年后，普洛斯彼罗得知曾经的敌人即将乘船经过小岛，便用魔法掀起了一场猛烈的风暴使船只遇难，船上人员被迫来到岛上。曾经帮助安东尼奥攫取王位的那不勒斯国王阿隆佐苦苦寻找着走失的王子腓迪南。与此同时，酗酒的司膳官斯丹法诺和弄臣特林鸠罗在岛上遇到了凯列班，饮酒后的凯列班高估了二人的"法力"并说服他们密谋杀害普洛斯彼罗以便统治小岛。另一边，腓迪南在爱丽儿的指引下遇见了米兰达，两人立刻坠入爱河。普洛斯彼罗布置了繁重的任务来考验腓迪南，结果令人非常满意，于是他为这对年轻人举行了订婚礼（假面舞）。当剧情达到高潮时，普洛斯彼罗与敌人对峙，阿隆佐和安东尼奥对自己的恶行表示忏悔，普洛斯彼罗宽恕了他们并与众人重返公国。

　　《暴风雨》的剧本原型不知来自何处，但目前学界较为认同的剧情来源是威廉·斯特雷奇（William Strachey）于1610年所著的《托马斯·盖茨爵士船难获救真实报导》（*A True Reportory of the Wreck and Redemption of Sir Thomas Gates, Knight*）。剧中关于海难的描写或许还取材于西尔韦斯特·乔丹（Sylvester Jourdain）的《百慕大发现记》（*A Discovery of the Bermudas*,1610）。腓迪南与米兰达的爱情故事与《罗密欧与朱丽叶》（*Romeo and Juliet*）中的浪漫情节相似。还有一些素材很可能来源于口口相传的民间故事。

《暴风雨》是一部充满魔幻、传奇、浪漫与诗意的剧作，是莎士比亚晚期最具独创性的剧作之一。它将人文主义理想与丑恶的现实对立，将诗意的人文艺术与奇异的魔幻世界融为一体。剧中既批判了邪恶的篡权阴谋，又讽刺了文明对非文明的教化，通过普洛斯彼罗和米兰达的形象，肯定了知识、理性与智慧的力量，弘扬人的价值，赞美"人类是多么美丽"①，宣扬了宽恕与和解的思想，描绘出一幅既有浪漫爱情，又有自由人性的人文主义理想画卷。

莎士比亚的戏剧中充满了矛盾冲突的观念，但它们绝不是简单的二元对立。他"喜爱制造对立，再把他的黑与白淡化成复杂道德里的灰色区块"②。在《暴风雨》中，普洛斯彼罗沉浸于学习，专注于自己的研究，把公国事务都交给弟弟安东尼奥打理，从而给了安东尼奥篡夺爵位的可乘之机。对魔幻法术的钻研使他忽略了现实世界，对知识与艺术的追求使他失去了权力，并促成暴政。然而，在岛上他凭借超自然的力量为自己导演了一出戏，并让篡位的弟弟安东尼奥悔悟。可以看出莎士比亚是反对篡权的，只是在他看来，被篡权者似乎也难辞其咎。在治国理政与知识理想之间存在着一个复杂的灰色区块。在剧中，普洛斯彼罗称自己的法术为"白色魔法"（active magic），和女巫西考拉克斯（凯列班母亲）的黑色魔法不同。西考拉克斯由于不满众精灵的不服从，将爱丽儿等精灵囚禁在一树干中；她虽已死，然而她的力量却通过凯列班继

---

① 莎士比亚：《莎士比亚全集》（第八卷），朱生豪译，北京：人民文学出版社，2014年，第74页。原文是"How beauteous mankind is"。

② 莎士比亚：《暴风雨：英汉对照》，彭镜禧译，辜正坤汉译主编，北京：外语教学与研究出版社，2016年，第3页。

续存在。普洛斯彼罗释放了精灵并与爱丽儿约定只要他完成普洛斯彼罗交代的任务便给他自由。普洛斯彼罗对凯列班的奴役与教化既带有歧视又充满殖民主义色彩，正如凯列班所说："我当初是我自己的王，如今成了你唯一的臣民……你教我语言，我得到的好处是，知道怎样诅咒。"①普洛斯彼罗宽恕敌人，收回公国后，是带着凯列班一起返回米兰还是将凯列班留在岛上继续做他自己的王，我们不得而知。然而，普洛斯彼罗对爱丽儿的统治与情感以及他对凯列班的同情与教化也可理解为黑白之间的灰色区块。值得注意的是，在西方的神话故事里有三种获得超自然力量的方式：一是从父母那继承而来，二是通过交易获得，三是通过后天学习所得。普洛斯彼罗则是通过学习研究书籍获得了此种力量。象征着知识、智慧和力量的普洛斯彼罗依靠这种超自然力量让有罪之人遭受惩罚并忏悔，凭借魔幻音乐促成了一场政治联姻，让世界又恢复了秩序与和谐。此时的普洛斯彼罗有能力惩罚并报复曾经的敌人，却选择了宽恕与和解，并在最后放弃了自己多年潜心钻研的成果。他将魔法书、魔法杖和魔法袍都沉入大海，只剩下自己微弱的人的力量。此后的普洛斯彼罗将靠什么统治自己的臣民？不是统治者对被统治者的绝对权力，也不是人文主义理想世界的知识与智慧，或许正是这黑与白淡化成的复杂道德里的灰色区块。暴风雨之后的"美丽新世界"（brand new world）里，"难能可贵的举动是善行而不是复仇"②，人文主义理想世界里，最重要的是人性的自由而不是知识与权力。

---

① 莎士比亚：《暴风雨：英汉对照》，彭镜禧译，辜正坤汉译主编，北京：外语教学与研究出版社，2016年，第28-29页。原文是 "For I am all the subjects that you have, which first was mine own king...You taught me language, and my profit on't is, I know how to curse."。
② 莎士比亚：《暴风雨：英汉对照》，彭镜禧译，辜正坤汉译主编，北京：外语教学与研究出版社，2016年，第85页。原文是 "the rarer action is in virtue than in vengeance"。

Selected Reading

Act I, ii

Enter Ferdinand, and Ariel, invisible, playing and singing

ARIEL [*Song*] Come unto these yellow sands,

And then take hands:

Curtsied when you have, and kissed

The wild waves whist:

Foot it featly here and there,

And, sweet sprites, bear

The burden.

[**SPIRITS** *Within, sing the*] (*burden, dispersedly*)

Hark, hark! Bow-wow!

The watch-dogs bark: bow-wow.

ARIEL Hark, hark! I hear

The strain of strutting chanticleer

Cry, cock-a-diddle-dow.

FERDINAND Where should this music be?

I'th'air or th'earth?

It sounds no more: and sure it waits upon

Some god o'th'island. Sitting on a bank,

Weeping again the king my father's wreck,

This music crept by me upon the waters,

Allaying both their fury and my passion

With its sweet air: thence I have followed it—

Or it hath drawn me rather—but 'tis gone.

No, it begins again.

> Foot it featly: dance skillfully 曼妙舞步, 柔舞翩翩

> burden: n. chorus, refrain 指副歌

> strain: 相当于 song, 指鸡叫声

> chanticleer: n. rooster 公鸡, 雄鸡

> the: for the

> passion: n. acute grief 伤痛, 哀伤

ARIEL [*Song*] Full fathom five thy father lies,

Of his bones are coral made:

> fathom five: five fathoms (thirty feet) deep 5英寻（等于30英尺）

Those are pearls that were his eyes:

Nothing of him that doth fade,

But doth suffer a sea-change

Into something rich and strange.

Sea-nymphs hourly ring his knell:

[**SPIRITS** *Within, sing the*](*burden*)Ding-dong.

ARIEL Hark!Now I hear them: ding-dong, bell.

FERDINAND The ditty does remember my

drowned father.

> ditty: n. song, lyrics 小调

> does remember: recalls, commemorates 悼念

This is no mortal business, nor no sound

That the earth owes. I hear it now above me.

> owes: owns 拥有

> fringèd curtains: eyelids 眼皮

PROSPERO The fringèd curtains of thine eye

advance

And say what thou see'st yond.

> advance: open 打开

> yond: adv. yonder, over there 在那边

MIRANDA What is't? A spirit?

Lord, how it looks about! Believe me, sir,

It carries a brave form. But 'tis a spirit.

> brave:adj.handsome,noble,splendid 英俊，高贵

PROSPERO No, wench: it eats, and sleeps,

and hath such senses

As we have, such. This gallant which thou see'st

Was in the wreck: and, but he's something stained

With grief—that's beauty's canker—thou mightst

call him

> gallant: fashionable, handsome young man指腓迪南

> but: except that

> something: somewhat

A goodly person: he hath lost his fellows

And strays about to find 'em.

> goodly: adj. handsome, fine （古英语）英俊，漂亮

MIRANDA I might call him

A thing divine, for nothing natural

I ever saw so noble.

259

PROSPERO [*Aside*] It goes on, I see,

As my soul prompts it.—[*To Ariel*] Spirit, fine

spirit: I'll free thee

Within two days for this.

FERDINAND Most sure, the goddess

On whom these airs attend! Vouchsafe my prayer

May know if you remain upon this island,

And that you will some good instruction give

How I may bear me here: my prime request,

Which I do last pronounce, is—O you wonder!—

If you be maid or no?

MIRANDA No wonder, sir,

But certainly a maid.

FERDINAND My language? Heavens!

I am the best of them that speak this speech,

Were I but where 'tis spoken.

PROSPERO How? The best?

What wert thou if the King of Naples heard thee?

FERDINAND A single thing, as I am now, that

wonders

To hear thee speak of Naples. He does hear me:

And that he does, I weep. Myself am Naples,

Who with mine eyes, never since at ebb, beheld

The king my father wrecked.

MIRANDA Alack, for mercy!

FERDINAND Yes, faith, and all his lords, the

Duke of Milan

And his brave son being twain.

PROSPERO [*Aside*] The Duke of Milan

And his more braver daughter could control thee

prompts: v. directs, urges, wills 促使，导致

airs: Ariel's songs

Vouchsafe: v. grant (that) 同意，准予

remain: v. live 居住

bear me: behave 行为表现

wonder: plays on the Latin root of Miranda's name ('mirandus', i.e. 'wonderful')

maid: n. a virgin, unmarried 少女，未婚年轻女子

best: highest in rank (a king, assuming his father is drowned)

where: 指 Naples

single thing: solitary, a bachelor, one and the same person (as the King of Naples)

He does hear me: as I am now king and hear my own grief

ebb: n. low tide (i.e. without tears) 退潮，状况不佳

Antonio's son is never mentioned again; perhaps Shakespeare forgot or cut the part, neglecting this reference

twain: 相当于 separated

control: v. challenge, govern 质疑，反驳

If now 'twere fit to do't. At the first sight

They have changed eyes. —[*To Ariel*] Delicate Ariel,

> changed eyes: gazed at one another, exchanged loving looks

I'll set thee free for this. —[*To Ferdinand*] A word, good sir,

I fear you have done yourself some wrong: a word.

> done yourself some wrong: spoken falsely in your claim to be king

MIRANDA Why speaks my father so ungently? This

> ungently: adv. harshly, discourteously 粗鲁地，粗暴地

Is the third man that e'er I saw: the first

That e'er I sighed for. Pity move my father

To be inclined my way.

FERDINAND O, if a virgin,

And your affection not gone forth, I'll make you

The Queen of Naples.

译文1（辜正坤版）

<table>
<tr><td>

第一幕第二场

腓迪南上；爱丽儿隐形上，边弹边唱

爱丽儿 （歌）快来这黄沙滩上唷，

手儿牵着手。

屈个膝，亲一亲，

浪涛就平静。

曼妙舞步到处跳，

可爱的精灵啊，你们要

唱副歌。

〔**众精灵** 幕内，唱〕（副歌，

</td><td>

Act I, ii

Enter Ferdinand, and Ariel, invisible, playing and singing

ARIEL [*Song*] Come unto these yellow sands,

And then take hands:

Curtsied when you have, and kissed

The wild waves whist:

Foot it featly here and there,

And, sweet sprites, bear

The burden.

[**SPIRITS** *Within, sing the*] (*burden,*

</td></tr>
</table>

散乱地）

听啊，听！汪喔！

看门狗在叫：汪喔。

爱丽儿 听啊，听！我听到

趾高气扬的雄鸡叫，

高唱咯咯啼哆哆。

腓迪南 这音乐在哪儿？在天上，在地下？

这会儿停了。一定是唱给岛上什么神明的。我坐在岸边，

还在哀哭我父王遇难，

这音乐从水上飘过来，

甜美乐音平息了怒涛

和我的伤痛。我一路跟着——

也许是它引领我——可是停了。

不，又开始了。

爱丽儿 ［唱］令尊躺在五㖊处，

骸骨已然成珊瑚；

珍珠乃是他双目。

全身骨肉虽朽腐，

一经大海精细雕，

成为珍贵稀世宝。

海仙敲钟常纪念，

［**众精灵** 幕内，唱］（副歌）

---

dispersedly）

Hark, hark! Bow-wow!

The watch-dogs bark: bow-wow.

ARIEL Hark, hark! I hear

The strain of strutting chanticleer

Cry, cock-a-diddle-dow.

FERDINAND Where should this music be? I'th'air or th'earth?

It sounds no more: and sure it waits upon

Some god o'th'island. Sitting on a bank,

Weeping again the king my father's wreck,

This music crept by me upon the waters,

Allaying both their fury and my passion

With its sweet air: thence I have followed it—

Or it hath drawn me rather—but 'tis gone.

No, it begins again.

ARIEL ［Song］ Full fathom five thy father lies,

Of his bones are coral made:

Those are pearls that were his eyes:

Nothing of him that doth fade,

But doth suffer a sea-change

Into something rich and strange.

Sea-nymphs hourly ring his knell:

［**SPIRITS** Within, sing the］（burden）

叮咚。

爱丽儿 听啊，听：叮咚声连连。

腓迪南 这小调的确在悼念淹死的家父。

这不是凡俗事物；世上也没有这种声音。此刻就在我头上。

普洛斯彼罗 打开你的眼帘，告诉我你看到那边有什么。

米兰达 那是什么啊？是个精灵吗？

天哪，它在东张西望！大人，我真觉得

它长得好英俊。但它是个精灵。

普洛斯彼罗 不对，丫头。它也吃也睡，也有跟咱们

一样的感觉，一样的。你看的这位帅哥

遭了船难。若不是他因为哀伤而略有

愁容——哀伤会破坏美貌——你可以说他

长得挺好的。他失去了伙伴，到处找他们呢。

米兰达 我要称他为

仙品，因为我见过的人

Ding-dong.

ARIEL Hark! Now I hear them: ding-dong, bell.

FERDINAND The ditty does remember my drowned father.

This is no mortal business, nor no sound

That the earth owes. I hear it now above me.

PROSPERO The fringèd curtains of thine eye advance

And say what thou see'st yond.

MIRANDA What is't? A spirit?

Lord, how it looks about! Believe me, sir,

It carries a brave form. But 'tis a spirit.

PROSPERO No, wench: it eats, and sleeps, and hath such senses

As we have, such. This gallant which thou see'st

Was in the wreck: and, but he's something stained

With grief—that's beauty's canker—thou mightst call him

A goodly person: he hath lost his fellows

And strays about to find 'em.

MIRANDA I might call him

A thing divine, for nothing natural

从没这么高贵的。

普洛斯彼罗 ［旁白］有苗头了，我看，

正中我的下怀。[对爱丽儿]——精灵啊，好精灵，

因你办了这件事，我两天之内就释放你。

腓迪南 一定是了，这是那些歌声

侍候的女神！请准许我的祈祷，

告诉我您是否住在这岛上，

可否给我一些好指点，

让我知道在这里该当如何。最后，

也最重要的，是——啊，惊为天人的您！——

您是个少女不是？

米兰达 没什么可惊的，先生，但确实是少女。

腓迪南 讲我的语言？天哪！讲这语言的人里，我最高贵，如果是在讲这语言的地方。

普洛斯彼罗 怎么说？最高贵？这要让那不勒斯国王听到，你成了什么？

腓迪南 孤家寡人，像现在这样；听你说起

I ever saw so noble.

PROSPERO [*Aside*] It goes on, I see,
As my soul prompts it. — [*To Ariel*]
Spirit, fine spirit: I'll free thee
Within two days for this.

FERDINAND Most sure, the goddess
On whom these airs attend! Vouchsafe
my prayer
May know if you remain upon this
island,
And that you will some good instruc-
tion give
How I may bear me here: my prime
request,
Which I do last pronounce, is—O you
wonder!—
If you be maid or no?

MIRANDA No wonder, sir,
But certainly a maid.

FERDINAND My language? Heavens!
I am the best of them that speak this
speech,
Were I but where 'tis spoken.

PROSPERO How? The best?
What wert thou if the King of Naples
heard thee?

FERDINAND A single thing, as I am
now, that wonders

那不勒斯国王,我很诧异。他听得见我,

而因此我落泪。我就是那不勒斯的王;

双眼目睹我父王船难,泪水没有停过。

米兰达 哀哉,好可怜!

腓迪南 是啊,真的,还有他的全部大臣;米兰公爵

和他英俊的儿子也失散了。

普洛斯彼罗 〔旁白〕米兰公爵和他更俊的女儿可以质疑你,但现在不合适。他们才一见面就眉来眼去。〔对爱丽儿〕——机灵的爱丽儿,

为此我要释放你。〔对腓迪南〕——过来说句话,少爷,我只怕你搞错了什么。过来说句话。

米兰达 为什么父亲话说得这么凶?这

才是我见过的第三个男人,是第一个

使我思慕的。愿怜悯打动父亲,

跟我同样想法。

腓迪南 啊,您若是闺女,

To hear thee speak of Naples. He does hear me:

And that he does, I weep. Myself am Naples,

Who with mine eyes, never since at ebb, beheld

The king my father wrecked.

MIRANDA Alack, for mercy!

FERDINAND Yes, faith, and all his lords, the Duke of Milan

And his brave son being twain.

PROSPERO [*Aside*] The Duke of Milan

And his more braver daughter could control thee

If now 'twere fit to do't. At the first sight

They have changed eyes. —[*To Ariel*] Delicate Ariel,

I'll set thee free for this. —[*To Ferdinand*] A word, good sir,

I fear you have done yourself some wrong: a word.

MIRANDA Why speaks my father so ungently? This

Is the third man that e'er I saw: the first

That e'er I sighed for. Pity move my father

To be inclined my way.

FERDINAND O, if a virgin,

感情也没有他属，我要让你
成为那不勒斯的王后。

And your affection not gone forth, I'll make you
The Queen of Naples.

译文2（朱生豪版）

Act V, i

EPILOGUE SPOKEN BY PROSPERO

Now my charms are all o'erthrown,

> charms are all o'erthrown: my magic is relinquished (o'erthrown plays on the sense of "usurped")

And what strength I have's mine own,

Which is most faint: now 'tis true,

I must be here confined by you,

> you: 指观众

Or sent to Naples. Let me not,

Since I have my dukedom got

And pardoned the deceiver, dwell

In this bare island by your spell,

But release me from my bands

> bands: bonds 指镣铐或囚禁

With the help of your good hands:

> good hands: in applause 鼓掌

Gentle breath of yours my sails

> gentle breath: kind words 好评

Must fill, or else my project fails,

Which was to please. Now I want

> want: v. lack（古英语）缺乏

Spirits to enforce, art to enchant,

And my ending is despair,

Unless I be relieved by prayer,

Which pierces so, that it assaults

> pierces so, that it assaults: penetrates so deeply that it moves

Mercy itself, and frees all faults.

  As you from crimes would pardoned be,

> indulgence: approval (playing on the Catholic sense of "official release from sin")

  Let your indulgence set me free.

译文 1（辜正坤版）

第五幕第一场
普洛斯彼罗朗读收场白

现在我已毫无法力，
所余力气都属自己，
微弱无比。确确实实，
你可把我囚禁于此，
或是送往那不勒斯。
我既然已饶恕骗子、
收回公国，请别叫我
为君罚咒，荒岛流落；
有请各位鼓掌欢欣，
释放在下免受囚禁。
看官好评，有如和风
助我扬帆，计划成功，
因我一心讨君喜悦。
精灵法术今我两缺，
结局乃是希望失落，
除非祷告使我解脱：
祈祷有效，直达上天，
得神垂怜，免我罪愆。
　诸位但愿得赦过尤，
　就请宽容放我自由。

Act V, i
EPILOGUE SPOKEN BY PROSPERO

Now my charms are all o'erthrown,
And what strength I have's mine own,
Which is most faint: now 'tis true,
I must be here confined by you,
Or sent to Naples. Let me not,
Since I have my dukedom got
And pardoned the deceiver, dwell
In this bare island by your spell,
But release me from my bands
With the help of your good hands:
Gentle breath of yours my sails
Must fill, or else my project fails,
Which was to please. Now I want
Spirits to enforce, art to enchant,
And my ending is despair,
Unless I be relieved by prayer,
Which pierces so, that it assaults
Mercy itself, and frees all faults.
　As you from crimes would pardoned be,
　Let your indulgence set me free.

译文 2（朱生豪版）

Activities

1. Shakespeare and Today

Direction: After reading, work in groups and discuss the following questions:

1) There are scenes of tempest in many of Shakespeare's plays. Why did Shakespeare name this play *The Tempest*? What does the tempest mean to you?

2) In 1932, British writer Aldous Leonard Huxley (1894–1963) published his famous book *Brand New World*, which was made into film in 1998. The title is quoted from Miranda's words in Shakespeare's *The Tempest*. What's the difference between Shakespeare's brand new world and that of Aldous Huxley? How do the two works echo with each other?

2. Shakespeare and China

Direction: Since 1940s many of Shakespeare's plays have been reproduced in the shape of Chinese operas, such as Sichuan opera（川剧）, Yue opera（越剧）, Kunqu opera（昆剧）, Huangmei opera（黄梅戏）, etc. In 2004, Chinese directors Xu Ke（徐克）and Wu Xingguo（吴兴国）reproduced The Tempest *as Beijing opera. Watch the performance or read the play, analyze the similarities of the Shakespearean play and the Chinese opera, and illustrate what makes it possible to reproduce the play in China.*

3. Shakespeare and Beyond

Direction: Work within groups to research on the following topics.

1) As Shakespeare's last solo-authored play, *The Tempest* has come to be regarded as "the summation of the master's art" and has profoundly shaped responses to Shakespearean plays. What do you think is the most important feature which distinguishes *The Tempest* from other plays and makes it "the summation of the master's art"? There is more than one way to interpret

the play and tell about the world, now it's your turn to build your understandings and share your interpretations of this play.

2）At the end of *The Tempest*, Prospero speaks his farewell soliloquy from the theatre floor, standing on the same level as his seated audience. Suddenly he is nothing but an actor asking his public to release him as he released Ariel. The poet from his own inner self comes to us and says "As you from crimes would pardoned be, Let your indulgence set me free." What does Shakespeare imply here? What are embodied in Prospero's soliloquy?

Further Reading

KNIGHT G W, 1953. The Shakespearian tempest［M］. London: Methuen & Co. Ltd.

MATTHEWS B, 1913. Shakspere as a playwright［M］. New York: Charles Scribner's Sons.

SOKOL B J, 2003. A brave new world of knowledge: Shakespeare's *The Tempest* and early modern epistemology［M］. London: Associated University Presses.

辛雅敏，2016. 二十世纪莎评简史［M］.北京：中国社会科学出版社.

张冲，2004. 莎士比亚专题研究［M］.上海：上海外语教育出版社.

Unit 3 The Winter's Tale

章节概述

　　《冬天的故事》是莎士比亚晚期创作的一部引人入胜的传奇剧，大约写于1610—1611年，首次发表于1623年的第一对开本。该剧主要讲述西西里亚国王里昂提斯因嫉妒猜疑酿成悲剧，亲友离散，在经历种种波折后又与家人团圆的浪漫传奇故事。里昂提斯怀疑他的王后赫米温妮与来访的好友波力克希尼斯（波希米亚国王）有私并命大臣卡密罗毒死波力克希尼斯。忠诚的卡密罗知道里昂提斯的猜忌毫无事实依据，于是将此事告诉了波力克希尼斯并与他一同逃离西西里亚。波力克希尼斯的逃离更加激怒了嫉妒暴虐的里昂提斯，于是他将赫米温妮关进监狱等待审判，同时派廷臣前去德尔福斯①祈求神谕。不久，赫米温妮在狱中生下一女婴，但被妒火冲昏了头脑的里昂提斯认为女婴是王后与波力克希尼斯的私生女，于是命令安提哥纳斯将婴孩弃之户外。路过的牧羊人收养了女婴并为她起名潘狄塔②，意为被遗弃的孩子。审判中，里昂提斯不顾神谕执意认为赫米温妮有罪，这时传来小王子迈密勒斯因染风寒去世的消息，赫米温妮听到孩子的死讯后晕倒在地，随后被宣布死亡。16年后潘狄塔出落得貌若天仙，并与波力克希尼斯之子弗罗利泽坠入爱河。但波力克希尼斯反对王子与牧羊女的结合，于是两人便在卡密罗的帮助下逃到了西西里亚。最终，潘狄塔与父亲里昂提斯重逢相认，两个国王重归于好并同意了这桩婚事，得知潘狄塔活着归来的王后也神奇地复活了。该剧以悲剧性的情爱嫉妒所致亲友离散开始，以喜剧性的宽恕和解结束，从死亡到新生，悲喜交加，充满了田园牧歌的和谐与现实世界的矛盾相互交织的传奇色彩。

---

① 德尔福斯（Delphos）：希腊城名，阿波罗神殿所在处，也是古代著名的神谕所在地。
② 潘狄塔：英文是Perdita，意为the lost one。

　　《冬天的故事》主要取材于罗伯特·格林（Robert Greene）1588年创作的传奇故事《潘多斯托：时间制胜》（*Pandosto: The Triumph of Time*）。这是一部很受欢迎的中篇小说，是伊丽莎白时代的畅销作品，其中包含了许多希腊的浪漫元素——田园风光、善良美丽的公主、王室爱情以及自然和超自然的奇迹。然而，原作并没有王后复活的情节。受古罗马诗人奥维德（Publius Ovidius Naso）《变形记》（*Metamorphoses*）中皮格马利翁的雕像获得生命的启发，莎士比亚独创了王后雕像复活的情节。莎士比亚"对原始素材的背离是最能展现其自我风格的……在充满奇幻之事的最后一幕中，莎氏表面上让还魂之术出自宝丽娜之手，实际上是借由这种还魂之术将表演艺术本身的魔力戏剧化了，为的是使作为观众的我们，如台上诸人物一般，唤醒自己的信念"①。

　　正如剧中迈密勒斯所言，"冬天最好讲凄惨的故事"②，《冬天的故事》一开始便是凄惨的。忠贞贤德的王后赫米温妮被暴怒嫉妒的里昂提斯强加不实的罪名，含冤而死，其子染病去世，其女惨遭遗弃而生死未卜。前三幕都充满了对宫廷阴谋的控诉以及对君主独断专横的批判。里昂提斯的嫉妒令人费解，仅仅因为自己劝留好友不成而妻子却劝说成功便怀疑二人之间有暧昧关系似乎难以让人信服。模棱两可、晦涩难懂的语言也道出了他内心的疯癫与崩溃。让里昂提斯心生恨意的或许并不是妻子与另一个男人之间不清不楚的关系，而是自己对男性权力丧失的痛心疾首与对女性权力的焦虑。莎士比亚通过塑造赫米温妮和潘狄塔两位美好的女性角色，赞美女性的美德与智慧，展现了伊丽莎白时代女性地位有所提升的社会现实，也体现出文艺复兴时期的人文主义者对女性的重新定位。"在晚期戏剧中，大多数女性是正义与道德的化身，是救赎与生机的力量来源。"③潘狄塔对理想与爱情的追求使她机缘巧合地来到父亲的宫殿，父女相认，在赫米温妮的雕像面前，她像是一个救赎者，让赫米温妮获得新生，也让悔恨了16年的里昂提斯获得新生。哀怨悲

---

① 莎士比亚：《冬天的故事：英汉对照》，李华英译，辜正坤汉译主编，北京：外语教学与研究出版社，2016年，第4-5页。

② 莎士比亚：《冬天的故事：英汉对照》，李华英译，辜正坤汉译主编，北京：外语教学与研究出版社，2016年，第34页。原文是"A sad tale's best for winter"。

③ 陈星：《莎士比亚传奇剧中的历史书写》，南京：南京大学出版社，2021年，第143页。

痛的赫米温妮虽然脸上布满了皱纹，却依然不减当年的善良与温柔，没有说一句责备的话便原谅了里昂提斯。里昂提斯说道："责骂我吧，亲爱的石像，好让我相信，你就是赫米温妮。或者说，你不骂我，我觉得你才更像，因为她总是那么温柔贤良。"①剧作家莎士比亚一边歌颂女性的美德，一边呼唤宽恕与和解的仁爱精神。剧中的侍女宝丽娜——如同《暴风雨》中的普洛斯彼罗——通过魔术让赫米温妮的雕像复活，既构建了一个和谐美好的奇幻世界，又重塑了人们的信念。毕竟莎士比亚知道一件艺术作品在一个导演式人物的指挥下获得生命在现实世界里是不可能的，然而在音乐与魔法构建的梦幻世界里却是可行的，借由这个梦幻的世界，莎士比亚让观众和读者将现实看得更清楚，也表达了自己对人文主义理想的向往与追求。

Selected Reading

Act Ⅳ, i

Enter Time, the Chorus

TIME I, that please some, try all, both joy and terror

Of good and bad, that makes and unfolds error,

Now take upon me, in the name of Time,

To use my wings. Impute it not a crime

To me or my swift passage, that I slide

O'er sixteen years and leave the growth untried

Of that wide gap, since it is in my power

To o'erthrow law and in one self-born hour

To plant and o'erwhelm custom. Let me pass

The same I am, ere ancient'st order was

try: v. test(proverbial: "time tries all things")检验	
both joy and terror of: bringer of both joy and terror to the	
unfolds: v. reveals 呈现，显现	
wings: Time was traditionally depicted as winged	
growth untried: development un-examined	
self-born: selfsame, self-created（by Time）	
plant and o'erwhelm: create and overrule	
ere... received: since the beginning of time, before the oldest laws and customs were set down and before those of the present day	

---

① 莎士比亚：《冬天的故事：英汉对照》，李华英译，辜正坤汉译主编，北京：外语教学与研究出版社，2016年，第125页。

Or what is now received. I witness to

The times that brought them in, so shall I do

To th'freshest things now reigning and make stale

The glistering of this present, as my tale

Now seems to it. Your patience this allowing,

I turn my glass and give my scene such growing

As you had slept between. Leontes leaving—

Th'effects of his fond jealousies so grieving

That he shuts up himself—imagine me,

Gentle spectators, that I now may be

In fair Bohemia, and remember well,

I mentioned a son o'th'king's, which Florizel

I now name to you, and with speed so pace

To speak of Perdita, now grown in grace

Equal with wond'ring. What of her ensues

I list not prophesy, but let Time's news

Be known when 'tis brought forth. A shepherd's

daughter

And what to her adheres, which follows after,

Is th'argument of Time. Of this allow,

If ever you have spent time worse ere now.

If never, yet that Time himself doth say

He wishes earnestly you never may. *Exit*

them: 指前文中的 law and custom	
stale...present: redundant and past what is now fresh and gleaming	
seems to it: seems old in comparison to the present	
glass: n. hour-glass 时间沙漏	
As: as if	
Leontes... himself: leaving Leontes to the consequences of his foolish jealousies, so distraught he shuts himself away	
king's: Polixenes'	
pace: v. proceed	
Equal with wond'ring: as great as the admiration her grace inspires	
list not prophesy: wish not to foretell	

译文 1（辜正坤版）

第四幕第一场	Act IV, i
致辞者扮时间上	*Enter Time, the Chorus*
时间 我令少数人心欢，却把一切检验，	**TIME** I, that please some, try all, both joy and terror
善善恶恶，有欢乐就会有磨	Of good and bad, that makes and unfolds

难；

我制造过失，亦让过失自个儿
显现；

请为我取名时间，好让我羽翼
舒展。

我总稍纵即逝，但不要为此心
生埋怨，

我匆匆跨过十六年，略去中间
经过不详谈；推翻规律法则，

一小时内把习俗创建又推翻，

这全是我手中权限。我要依然
故我，

来去自在，古往今来的规则

束缚，抛在九霄云外；亲眼

见过往事不堪的古代，亦要

见识当前的流光溢彩，再把

它变得冗长乏味，一切重新洗
牌，

如同我的故事陈旧无奈。

若各位看官耐性允许，

我便翻转时间沙漏，呈现新剧
情，

就当各位睡了一场，刚从睡梦
中苏醒。

话说里昂提斯熊熊的炉火，铸
就了

大错，正闭门思过。诸位看官，

请想象我在美丽的波希米亚，

此时此刻，国王有个儿子，

你们务必要记得，人们唤他

error,

Now take upon me, in the name of
Time,

To use my wings. Impute it not a crime

To me or my swift passage, that I slide

O'er sixteen years and leave the growth
untried

Of that wide gap, since it is in my
power

To o'erthrow law and in one self-born
hour

To plant and o'erwhelm custom. Let me
pass

The same I am, ere ancient'st order was

Or what is now received. I witness to

The times that brought them in, so shall
I do

To th'freshest things now reigning and
make stale

The glistering of this present, as my tale

Now seems to it. Your patience this
allowing,

I turn my glass and give my scene such
growing

As you had slept between. Leontes
leaving—

Th' effects of his fond jealousies so
grieving

That he shuts up himself—imagine me,

Gentle spectators, that I now may be

弗罗利泽。话说潘狄塔，
如今出落得貌若天仙，她随后的
境遇如何，恕我不便明言。待时机
到来，大家自会明白。那个牧人
做了她的父亲，对于她的未来，
时间会向大家一一说明。若先前
更糟之时诸位已度过，还请继续观赏；
如果不曾度过，时间有一言相告，
他诚恳希望诸位不会感到糟糕无聊。

下

In fair Bohemia, and remember well,
I mentioned a son o'th'king's, which Florizel
I now name to you, and with speed so pace
To speak of Perdita, now grown in grace
Equal with wond'ring. What of her en-
sues
I list not prophesy, but let Time's news
Be known when 'tis brought forth. A shepherd's daughter
And what to her adheres, which follows after,
Is th'argument of Time. Of this allow,
If ever you have spent time worse ere now.
If never, yet that Time himself doth say
He wishes earnestly you never may.

Exit

译文 2（朱生豪版）

Act V, iii

Enter Leontes, Polixenes, Florizel, Perdita,
Camillo, Paulina, Lords and Attendants

LEONTES O grave and good Paulina, the great comfort
That I have had of thee!

PAULINA What, sovereign sir,

> What: whatever

I did not well I meant well. All my services

You have paid home. But that you have vouch-

safed,

paid home: rewarded fully 酬谢

vouchsafed: agreed, granted kind-
ly 准许，允许

With your crowned brother and these your con-

tracted

contracted: v. betrothed 订婚

Heirs of your kingdoms, my poor house to visit,

It is a surplus of your grace, which never

My life may last to answer.

which...answer: which for all my
life I shall not be able to repay

LEONTES O Paulina,

We honour you with trouble. But we came

To see the statue of our queen. Your gallery

Have we passed through, not without much

content

In many singularities, but we saw not

That which my daughter came to look upon,

The statue of her mother.

PAULINA As she lived peerless,

So her dead likeness, I do well believe,

Excels whatever yet you looked upon

Or hand of man hath done: therefore I keep it

Lonely, apart. But here it is. Prepare

Lonely: separate(Folio's "Louely"
is conceivably correct, but a
printer's error much more likely）

To see the life as lively mocked as ever

Still sleep mocked death. Behold, and say 'tis

well.

lively mocked: realistically imi-
tated 逼真

well: well done

(*Paulina draws a curtain and reveals Hermione*

standing like a statue)

I like your silence, it the more shows off

Your wonder. But yet speak. First, you, my

liege,

Comes it not something near?

something near: somewhat close
to resembling her 相像

LEONTES Her natural posture!

Chide me, dear stone, that I may say indeed

Thou art Hermione; or rather, thou art she

In thy not chiding, for she was as tender

As infancy and grace. But yet, Paulina,

Hermione was not so much wrinkled, nothing

So agèd as this seems.

POLIXENES O, not by much.

PAULINA So much the more our carver's ex-

cellence.

Which lets go by some sixteen years and makes

her

As she lived now.

> As: as if

LEONTES As now she might have done,

So much to my good comfort, as it is

Now piercing to my soul. O, thus she stood,

Even with such life of majesty, warm life,

As now it coldly stands, when first I wooed her!

I am ashamed. Does not the stone rebuke me

For being more stone than it? O royal piece,

> stone: hard-hearted, dead (from grief) 比石头更无情

There's magic in thy majesty, which has

My evils conjured to remembrance and

From thy admiring daughter took the spirits,

Standing like stone with thee.

> admiring: adj. full of wonder 令人仰慕的

> spirits: n. vital energies 生命力, 灵魂

PERDITA And give me leave,

And do not say 'tis superstition, that

I kneel and then implore her blessing. —

(*Kneels before the statue*) Lady,

Dear queen, that ended when I but began,

Give me that hand of yours to kiss.

PAULINA (*Prevent Perdita from touching*)

O, patience!

The statue is but newly fixed; the colour's not

dry. (*Perdita stands?*)

> fixed: painted

CAMILLO My lord, your sorrow was too sore

laid on,

> sore: painfully, severely 痛苦

Which sixteen winters cannot blow away,

So many summers dry. Scarce any joy

Did ever so long live; no sorrow

But killed itself much sooner.

> So many summers dry: and an equal number of summers cannot dry up

POLIXENES Dear my brother,

Let him that was the cause of this have power

To take off so much grief from you as he

Will piece up in himself.

> cause: 指 Polixenes 是这一系列事件的起因

> piece up in: add to 增加，指将里昂提斯的悲痛分担一部分到自己身上

PAULINA Indeed, my lord,

If I had thought the sight of my poor image

Would thus have wrought you—for the stone is

mine—

I'd not have showed it.

> wrought: moved, affected 感动

LEONTES Do not draw the curtain.

PAULINA No longer shall you gaze on't, lest

your fancy

May think anon it moves.

LEONTES Let be, let be.

Would I were dead, but that methinks already—

What was he that did make it?—See, my lord,

Would you not deem it breathed? And that

those veins

Did verily bear blood?

POLIXENES Masterly done.

The very life seems warm upon her lip.

LEONTES The fixture of her eye has motion

in't,

As we are mocked with art.

PAULINA I'll draw the curtain.

My lord's almost so far transported that

He'll think anon it lives.

LEONTES O, sweet Paulina,

Make me to think so twenty years together!

No settled senses of the world can match

The pleasure of that madness. Let't alone.

PAULINA I am sorry, sir, I have thus far stirred

you, but

I could afflict you farther.

LEONTES Do, Paulina,

For this affliction has a taste as sweet

As any cordial comfort. Still, methinks

There is an air comes from her. What fine chisel

Could ever yet cut breath? Let no man mock me,

For I will kiss her.

PAULINA Good my lord, forbear:

The ruddiness upon her lip is wet.

You'll mar it if you kiss it, stain your own

With oily painting. Shall I draw the curtain?

LEONTES No, not these twenty years.

PERDITA So long could I

Stand by, a looker-on.

PAULINA Either forbear,

Quit presently the chapel, or resolve you

For more amazement. If you can behold it,

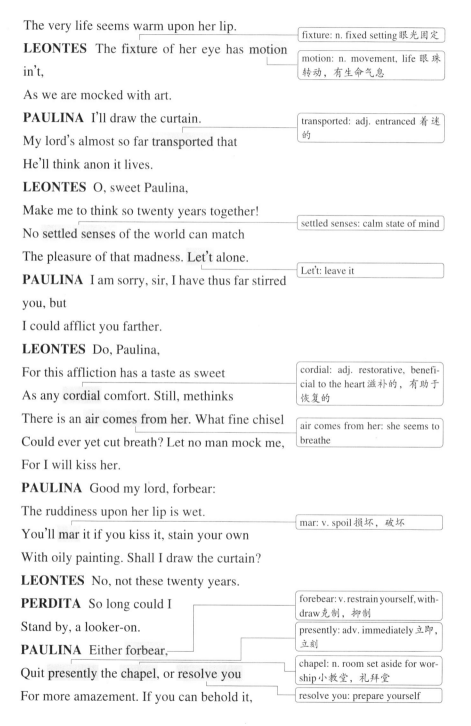

fixture: n. fixed setting 眼光固定

motion: n. movement, life 眼珠转动，有生命气息

transported: adj. entranced 着迷的

settled senses: calm state of mind

Let't: leave it

cordial: adj. restorative, beneficial to the heart 滋补的，有助于恢复的

air comes from her: she seems to breathe

mar: v. spoil 损坏，破坏

forebear: v. restrain yourself, withdraw 克制，抑制

presently: adv. immediately 立即，立刻

chapel: n. room set aside for worship 小教堂，礼拜堂

resolve you: prepare yourself

I'll make the statue move indeed, descend

And take you by the hand. But then you'll think—

Which I protest against—I am assisted

By wicked powers.

wicked powers: witchcraft 巫术，妖术

LEONTES What you can make her do,

I am content to look on. What to speak,

I am content to hear, for 'tis as easy

To make her speak as move.

PAULINA It is required

You do awake your faith. Then all stand still.

On: those that think it is unlawful business

I am about, let them depart.

On: onwards

LEONTES Proceed:

No foot shall stir.

PAULINA (*Music*) Music; awake her: strike!

strike: strike up (sense then shifts to "affect")

(*To Hermione*)

'Tis time: descend: be stone no more: approach:

Strike all that look upon with marvel. Come,

I'll fill your grave up. Stir. Nay, come away.

fill your grave up: bring you back to life

Bequeath to death your numbness, for from him

him: death

Dear life redeems you.—You perceive she stirs.

(*Hermione comes down*)

Start not. Her actions shall be holy as

You hear my spell is lawful. Do not shun her

Until you see her die again, for then

for... double: by shunning her in this new life, you would kill her again

You kill her double. Nay, present your hand:

When she was young you wooed her, now in age

Is she become the suitor?

Must she take your hand?

LEONTES (*Touches her*) O, she's warm!

If this be magic, let it be an art

Lawful as eating.

POLIXENES She embraces him.

CAMILLO She hangs about his neck.

If she pertain to life let her speak too.

> pertain to life: is truly alive

POLIXENES Ay, and make it manifest where

she has lived.

> make it manifest: explain

Or how stol'n from the dead.

PAULINA That she is living,

Were it but told you, should be hooted at

> hooted: v. jeered 嘲笑，揶揄

Like an old tale. But it appears she lives,

Though yet she speak not. Mark a little while. —

Please you to interpose, fair madam. (*To Perdita*)

Kneel

And pray your mother's blessing.—(*To Hermione*)

Turn, good lady,

Our Perdita is found.

HERMIONE You gods, look down

And from your sacred vials pour your graces

Upon my daughter's head! —Tell me, mine own.

Where hast thou been preserved? Where lived?

How found

Thy father's court? For thou shalt hear that I,

Knowing by Paulina that the oracle

Gave hope thou wast in being, have preserved

> in being: alive

Myself to see the issue.

> issue: outcome, child, 指 Paulina

PAULINA There's time enough for that,

Lest they desire upon this push to trouble

Your joys with like relation. Go together,

> they...relation: at this crucial moment others trouble your happiness by relating their own stories

You precious winners all. Your exultation

Partake to every one. I, an old turtle,

Will wing me to some withered bough and there

My mate, that's never to be found again,

Lament till I am lost.

LEONTES O, peace, Paulina!

Thou shouldst a husband take by my consent,

As I by thine a wife. This is a match,

And made between's by vows. Thou hast found

mine—

But how, is to be questioned, for I saw her,

As I thought, dead, and have in vain said many

A prayer upon her grave. I'll not seek far—

For him, I partly know his mind—to find thee

An honorable husband. —Come, Camillo,

And take her by the hand, whose worth and

honesty

Is richly noted and here justified

By us, a pair of kings. —Let's from this place. —

What? Look upon my brother. —(*To Hermione,*

then also Polixenes) Both your pardons,

That e'er I put between your holy looks

My ill suspicion. This your son-in-law,

And son unto the king, whom, heavens directing,

Is troth-plight to your daughter.—Good Paulina,

Lead us from hence, where we may leisurely

Each one demand, and answer to his part

Performed in this wide gap of time since first

We were dissevered. Hastily, lead away.

Exeunt

Partake: v. extend 分享	
turtle: turtle-dove, thought to mate for life 斑鸠，终身忠于配偶的禽鸟	
mate: 指 Antigonus	
lost: adj. dead 死去，失去生命的	
match: n. contract 契约，约定	
between's: between us	
For: as for	
troth-plight: betrothed 订婚	

译文 1（辜正坤版）

第五章第三场

里昂提斯、波力克希尼斯、弗罗利泽、潘狄塔、卡密罗、宝丽娜、众大臣及侍从上

里昂提斯 啊！可敬善良的宝丽娜，

你给我的安慰很大！

宝丽娜 国王陛下，尽管我有很多事

做得不好，但我是尽了心也尽了力。一切微劳您都酬谢了，

但今天蒙您赏脸，同您王兄与已缔结良缘的王位继承人光临寒舍，真是额外的恩典，我将毕生难以回报。

里昂提斯 啊，宝丽娜，我们来给你

添麻烦了。不过，我们是来看王后的雕像。贵室我早已见识过，其间珍品琳琅满目，令人不禁叹赏，可我女儿特意来瞻仰的对象——她母后的雕像，我们也未曾瞻仰。

Act V, iii

Enter Leontes, Polixenes, Florizel, Perdita, Camillo, Paulina, Lords and Attendants

LEONTES O grave and good Paulina, the great comfort

That I have had of thee!

PAULINA What, sovereign sir,

I did not well I meant well. All my services

You have paid home. But that you have vouchsafed,

With your crowned brother and these your contracted

Heirs of your kingdoms, my poor house to visit,

It is a surplus of your grace, which never

My life may last to answer.

LEONTES O Paulina,

We honour you with trouble. But we came

To see the statue of our queen. Your gallery

Have we passed through, not without much content

In many singularities, but we saw not

That which my daughter came to look upon,

宝丽娜 活着时她绝世无双，我深信，

她死后的遗像应胜过你们眼中所见过，或人手所曾制作的一切，

因此我将其单独置放。

在这里，准备好观看一件逼真的雕像，

如此惟妙惟肖，犹如睡梦中的死亡。

看，惊叹这一杰作吧。

（宝丽娜拉开帷幕，亭亭如雕塑的赫米温妮赫然呈现）

我喜欢你们的沉默，沉默更说明你们

很惊讶，不过，还是说说你们的感想。

您先来，陛下，像不像？

里昂提斯 她特有的仪态！责骂我吧，

亲爱的石像，好让我相信，

你就是赫米温妮。或者说，

你不骂我，我觉得你才更像，

因为她总是那么温柔贤良。

可是，宝丽娜，不该有那么多皱纹

出现在她脸上，容颜也不该这般年老苍黄。

波力克希尼斯 是啊，不该有

The statue of her mother.

PAULINA As she lived peerless,

So her dead likeness, I do well believe,

Excels whatever yet you looked upon

Or hand of man hath done: therefore I keep it

Lonely, apart. But here it is. Prepare

To see the life as lively mocked as ever

Still sleep mocked death. Behold, and say 'tis well.

(*Paulina draws a curtain and reveals Hermione standing like a statue*)

I like your silence, it the more shows off

Your wonder. But yet speak. First, you, my liege,

Comes it not something near?

LEONTES Her natural posture!

Chide me, dear stone, that I may say indeed

Thou art Hermione; or rather, thou art she

In thy not chiding, for she was as tender

As infancy and grace. But yet, Paulina,

Hermione was not so much wrinkled, nothing

So agèd as this seems.

POLIXENES O, not by much.

这么老。

宝丽娜 这更体现了雕刻家技艺高超,

他让十六年光阴度过,雕出了她活到现在的模样。

里昂提斯 她本可以给我许多安慰

可现在我的心如刀割般苦痛。

哎!想当初,我向她求婚时,

她也是这样,亭亭玉立,

庄严又温暖,生命里透着勃勃生机;

而如今,冰冷石像映我惭愧内心,

指责我铁石心肠,比石头更无情!

啊!高贵的杰作,你庄严中有魔力,

唤起了我对过去罪恶的回忆,

夺去了你令人仰慕的女儿之魂,

化为石与你并立。

潘狄塔 请准许我,不要误以为是

迷信,我要跪下来求她祝福。——夫人,亲爱的母后,(跪在雕像前)

我刚出生您便香消玉殒,

PAULINA So much the more our carver's excellence.

Which lets go by some sixteen years and makes her

As she lived now.

LEONTES As now she might have done,

So much to my good comfort, as it is

Now piercing to my soul. O, thus she stood,

Even with such life of majesty, warm life,

As now it coldly stands, when first I wooed her!

I am ashamed. Does not the stone rebuke me

For being more stone than it? O royal piece,

There's magic in thy majesty, which has

My evils conjured to remembrance and

From thy admiring daughter took the spirits,

Standing like stone with thee.

PERDITA And give me leave,

And do not say 'tis superstition, that

I kneel and then implore her blessing. —

(*Kneels before the statue*) Lady, Dear queen, that ended when I but began,

Give me that hand of yours to kiss.

请让我吻一吻您的手。

宝丽娜 （不让潘狄塔触碰）啊，等一下！色彩
刚上好，犹未干。
（潘狄塔起身？）

PAULINA (*Prevent Perdita from touching*) O, patience!
The statue is but newly fixed; the colour's not dry. (*Perdita stands?*)

卡密罗 陛下，您的悲伤太过沉重，
十六个寒冬吹不散，
十六个酷夏晒不干。
少有欢乐会持续这样长久，
未有悲伤不很快消散而长停留。

CAMILLO My lord, your sorrow was too sore laid on,
Which sixteen winters cannot blow away,
So many summers dry. Scarce any joy
Did ever so long live; no sorrow
But killed itself much sooner.

波力克希尼斯 亲爱的王兄，
让那个惹起这场惨剧之人，
卸去你的一部分悲痛，
勇敢承担以便补过。

POLIXENES Dear my brother,
Let him that was the cause of this have power
To take off so much grief from you as he
Will piece up in himself.

宝丽娜 真的，陛下，要是我知道，
看见这个可怜雕像，您会
感动心痛——因为石像属
我所有——我就不会给您看。

PAULINA Indeed, my lord,
If I had thought the sight of my poor image
Would thus have wrought you—for the stone is mine—
I'd not have showed it.

里昂提斯 不要拉上帷幕。

LEONTES Do not draw the curtain.

宝丽娜 您不要再凝视注目，以免您
浮想联翩，认为她真的会动。

PAULINA No longer shall you gaze on't, lest your fancy
May think anon it moves.

里昂提斯 别动，别动！难道我也死了，

LEONTES Let be, let be.
Would I were dead, but that methinks

不然我觉得她已经要——
是什么人雕成的？——看，
王弟！你不觉得她呼吸了吗？
而且血管里真有血？

波力克希尼斯　雕得太逼真了！
她唇上
似乎有温暖的生命气息。

里昂提斯　眼光固定的眼睛似
在转动，
好像我们遭了艺术的戏弄。

宝丽娜　我要拉上帷幕，
陛下如此着迷，
会认为她有生命。

里昂提斯　啊，好宝丽娜，让
我这样痴想
二十年吧！世上冷静的头脑要
有
这种疯狂的乐趣，很难。
别拉上。

宝丽娜　陛下，扰乱了您的心，
我很抱歉。
可是我可能会使您更痛苦。

里昂提斯　请吧，宝丽娜。因
为这种
痛苦的味道如同滋补的
抚慰般甘甜。还有，我觉
得她好像在呼气，什么神奇的
凿子可以凿出气息？

already—

What was he that did make it? —See,
my lord,

Would you not deem it breathed? And
that those veins

Did verily bear blood?

POLIXENES Masterly done.

The very life seems warm upon her lip.

LEONTES The fixture of her eye has
motion in't,

As we are mocked with art.

PAULINA I'll draw the curtain.

My lord's almost so far transported that

He'll think anon it lives.

LEONTES O, sweet Paulina,

Make me to think so twenty years together!

No settled senses of the world can match

The pleasure of that madness. Let't alone.

PAULINA I am sorry, sir, I have thus
far stirred you, but

I could afflict you farther.

LEONTES Do, Paulina,

For this affliction has a taste as sweet

As any cordial comfort. Still, methinks

There is an air comes from her. What fine
chisel

Could ever yet cut breath? Let no man

不要嘲笑我，我要吻她。

宝丽娜 好陛下，不可以；她唇上的

红彩未干，若是吻了，会把

它弄坏，油彩还会污了您的嘴。

我可以拉上帷幕吗？

里昂提斯 别，这二十年都别拉上。

潘狄塔 我也要在她旁边，

看上二十年。

宝丽娜 都不行。快快离开这间

礼拜堂，要不然会见到

更多令人惊诧的事。若

你们敢看，我可让石像

真动，甚至走下来，和你们

握手，不过那时你们会以为

我有妖术相助，那我可不承认。

里昂提斯 凡是她做的，我都愿意看；

凡是她讲的，我都愿意听。

倘若能让她动，

让她说话也就不难。

宝丽娜 你们需唤醒信念，

然后静立。丑话说在前：

那些认为我在行妖术的人，

mock me,

For I will kiss her.

PAULINA Good my lord, forbear:

The ruddiness upon her lip is wet.

You'll mar it if you kiss it, stain your own

With oily painting. Shall I draw the curtain?

LEONTES No, not these twenty years.

PERDITA So long could I

Stand by, a looker-on.

PAULINA Either forbear,

Quit presently the chapel, or resolve you

For more amazement. If you can behold it,

I'll make the statue move indeed, descend

And take you by the hand. But then you'll think—

Which I protest against—I am assisted

By wicked powers.

LEONTES What you can make her do,

I am content to look on. What to speak,

I am content to hear, for 'tis as easy

To make her speak as move.

PAULINA It is required

You do awake your faith. Then all stand still.

请出去。

里昂提斯 开始吧，
都不许动。

宝丽娜 （音乐起）音乐，奏起来，唤醒她！（对赫米温妮）是时候了，下来吧，别再做石像了，过来，
让观看的人惊讶。来，我让你复活。
动一动，还要走下来，你从死亡之神
手里赎回了生命，把僵硬麻木交还他。——
你们看，她动了。（赫米温妮走下来）别怕。我已说过
我使的是魔术而非邪术，她的行动
也是圣洁的。不要躲开她，除非你
要见她再次死去；躲开她等于是
第二次要了她的命。不，伸出您的手。
她年轻时，您追求她，如今她老了，
要她主动来牵您的手吗？

里昂提斯 （触摸它）啊，她是温暖的！如果

On: those that think it is unlawful business
I am about, let them depart.

LEONTES Proceed:
No foot shall stir.

PAULINA (*Music*) Music; awake her: strike!
(*To Hermione*)
'Tis time: descend: be stone no more: approach:
Strike all that look upon with marvel. Come,
I'll fill your grave up. Stir. Nay, come away.
Bequeath to death your numbness, for from him
Dear life redeems you. —You perceive she stirs.
(*Hermione comes down*)
Start not. Her actions shall be holy as
You hear my spell is lawful. Do not shun her
Until you see her die again, for then
You kill her double. Nay, present your hand:
When she was young you wooed her, now in age
Is she become the suitor?

LEONTES (*Touches her*) O, she's warm!
If this be magic, let it be an art

这是魔术，就让它成为
和吃饭一样合法的技艺。

波力克希尼斯 她拥抱了他。

卡密罗 她拥着他的脖子。她若
真的复活了，请她说说话。

波力克希尼斯 对，请她讲讲
她一直住在哪里，
或者如何死而复生。

宝丽娜 若我告诉你们她还活着，一定
会被斥为无稽之谈。尽管尚未
开口说话，她是活生生的，这点
很显然。许你们再把她仔细看。——
（对潘狄塔）请过来，公主，跪下求你母后的
祝福吧。（对赫米温妮）——
转过来，夫人，我们的
潘狄塔找到了。

赫米温妮 神啊，请往人间看！请从
圣瓶中泼洒福泽于我女儿！——
告诉我，我的心肝，你在
哪里遇救？住在哪里？以及
如何来到了你父王的宫殿？
从宝丽娜口中，我知道了神谕
内容，说你有希望存活，为了

Lawful as eating.

POLIXENES She embraces him.

CAMILLO She hangs about his neck.
If she pertain to life let her speak too.

POLIXENES Ay, and make it manifest where she has lived.
Or how stol'n from the dead.

PAULINA That she is living,
Were it but told you, should be hooted at
Like an old tale. But it appears she lives,
Though yet she speak not. Mark a little while. —
(*To Perdita*) Please you to interpose, fair madam. Kneel
And pray your mother's blessing.—(*To Hermione*) Turn, good lady,
Our Perdita is found.

HERMIONE You gods, look down
And from your sacred vials pour your graces
Upon my daughter's head! —Tell me, mine own.
Where hast thou been preserved? Where lived? How found
Thy father's court? For thou shalt hear that I,

见你，方才苟且偷生到当前。

宝丽娜 那些心酸事，以后再说，

免得在这个重要时刻，大家
各有故事要讲，害时间骤过，
反使你们兴致萧索。都走吧，
你们个个欢喜，团团圆圆。
我呢，是斑鸠暮年，只有择一
枯枝，哀悼至死，以便去见我
那
滞留阴间永不再回的老伴。

里昂提斯 啊，宝丽娜，不要
悲伤！

你得允许我为你找位情郎，
就像当初我需得你允许，才能
再娶。
这是我们发过誓的约定。你已
助我
找回我的妻，但是如何找回
的，
我还要追问，因为我是亲眼见
她死去，
也曾多次在她墓前徒然哀祭。
无须远求即可为你寻得一如意

Knowing by Paulina that the oracle

Gave hope thou wast in being, have preserved

Myself to see the issue.

PAULINA There's time enough for
that,

Lest they desire upon this push to
trouble

Your joys with like relation. Go together,

You precious winners all. Your exultation

Partake to every one. I, an old turtle,

Will wing me to some withered bough
and there

My mate, that's never to be found again,
Lament till I am lost.

LEONTES O, peace, Paulina!

Thou shouldst a husband take by my
consent,

As I by thine a wife. This is a match,

And made between's by vows. Thou
hast found mine—

But how, is to be questioned, for I saw
her,

As I thought, dead, and have in vain
said many

A prayer upon her grave. I'll not seek
far—

For him, I partly know his mind—to

郎君，

这个人的心意我已猜透几分。——

过来，卡密罗，牵着她的手；

他的品行四海闻名，

这点我们两个国王可以证明。——走吧。——

怎么？看看我的王兄。——我恳求

（对赫米温妮，后对波力克希尼斯与赫米温尼）

你们的宽恕。你二人神情圣洁，

而我却在其间加上了恶毒的猜忌。

他是你的女婿，上天安排这位国王的儿子

与你女儿喜结良缘。——

好宝丽娜，给我们带路，

找个地方我们叙旧畅谈

这许多年来的契阔。

快，给我们带路吧。

　　众人下

find thee

An honorable husband. —Come, Camillo,

And take her by the hand, whose worth and honesty

Is richly noted and here justified

By us, a pair of kings. —Let's from this place. —

What? Look upon my brother. — (*To Hermione, then also Polixenes*) Both your pardons,

That e'er I put between your holy looks

My ill suspicion. This your son-in-law,

And son unto the king, whom, heavens directing,

Is troth-plight to your daughter.—Good Paulina,

Lead us from hence, where we may leisurely

Each one demand, and answer to his part

Performed in this wide gap of time since first

We were dissevered. Hastily, lead away.

Exeunt

译文2（朱生豪版）

Activities

1. Shakespeare and Today

Direction: The Winter's Tale *has become a staple of modern theatrical production, tempting directors and actors alike with its exotic settings, its evocative sense of wonder, and its passionate characters. In 1995, internationally acclaimed director Ingmar Bergman presented a memorable staging of the play at the Brooklyn Academy of Music in New York. Reviewers admire several of Bergman's bold experimental innovations, including imagining the drama as a play-within-a-play set at a nineteenth-century wedding banquet at a Swedish manor house; showcasing Hermione's trial as the pivotal point in the play; and unconventionally interpreting the discovery scene as a somber affair rather than as an occasion for joy and wonder. While commentators do not wholly embrace Bergman's daring conceits, they applaud him for attempting to offer a fresh interpretation of the romance. Critics also praise Gregory Doran's 1999 Royal Shakespeare Company production of* The Winter's Tale *which, they contend, featured lucid direction and a superb ensemble case. In 2001, Nicholas Hytner staged a modern-dress revival of* The Winter's Tale *at London's Royal National Theatre, depicting Sicilia as a monochrome corporate milieu and Bohemia as a communal, woodstock-like environment. While most critics agree that this approach adeptly distinguished the two worlds of the play, they also maintain that the actors' uneven performances failed to imbue the play with its requisite emotional intensity. Work in groups and discuss the following questions:*

1) As Ben Jonson wrote, "He was not of an age, but for all time." Shakespeare's plays have been reproduced by various directors, with freshness and new interpretations. What impact will these multifarious reproductions exert on Shakespeare's plays?

2）In what ways can the modern theatrical production of *The Winter's Tale* help today's audience to understand their world?

2. Shakespeare and China

Direction: In 1921, a young man named Tian Han translated Shakespeare's Hamlet *into Chinese, which is the first Chinese translation of Shakespearean plays. Since then, many of Shakespeare's plays have been translated into Chinese, some prosy, some prosodic. Each one is unique and of great literary and aesthetic value. In this chapter we have selected two different translations of some wonderful scenes in* The Winter's Tale. *Hold a debate in class on the following topic:*

Is translated Shakespeare still Shakespeare?

3. Shakespeare and Beyond

Direction: In 2016, British writer Jeanette Winterson published her new book The Gap of Time, *which is a rewriting of Shakespeare's* The Winter's Tale. *More than 400 years after Shakespeare recomposed Robert Greene's novel in the shape of drama, his work was also recomposed and endowed with vitality and passion in a modern story. How would Jeanette Winterson's novel help today's readers to understand Shakespeare? Can you rewrite the last scene of* The Winter's Tale *to showcase your interpretation of this story?*

Further Reading

ALEXANDER C M S, 2009. The Cambridge companion to Shakespeare's last plays [M]. Cambridge, UK: Cambridge University Press.

HUDSON H N, 1880. Shakespeare's *The Winter's Tale* with introduction, and notes explanatory and critical [M]. Boston: Ginn & Heath.

HUNT M, 1995. *The Winter's Tale*: critical essays [M]. New York: Garland Publishing Inc.

WARREN R, 1990. Staging Shakespeare's last plays [M]. Oxford: Oxford University Press.

华泉坤，洪增流，田朝绪，2007. 莎士比亚新论——新世纪，新莎士比亚 [M]. 上海：上海外语教育出版社.

聂珍钊，杜娟，2020. 莎士比亚与外国文学研究 [M]. 北京：商务印书馆.

Bibliography

ALEXANDER L, 2008. Shakespeare's comedy of love [M]. London: Rutledge.

BARBER C L, 2011. Shakespeare's festive comedy: a study of dramatic form and its relation to social custom [M]. New Jersey: Princeton University.

BELSEY C, 1980. Critical Practice [M]. London: Methuen.

BLOOM H, 1994. The western canon: the books and school of the ages [M]. New York: Harcourt Brace & Company.

BRADLEY A C, 1992. Shakespearean tragedy: lectures on *Hamlet, Othello, King Lear* and *Macbeth* [M]. New York: Macmillan Publishing House.

BRADY F, WIMSATT W K, 1977. Samuel Johnson: selected poetry and prose [M]. Los Angeles: University of California Press.

BRYSON B, 2016. Shakespeare: the world as a stage [M]. London: William Collins.

CALVINO I, 2014. Why read the classics [M]. Boston: Houghton Mifflin Harcourt.

CAMPBELL L B, 2009. Shakespeare's tragic heroes: slaves of passion [M]. London: Cambridge University Press.

CARLYLE T, 1872. On heroes, hero - worship and the heroic in history [M]. London: Chapman and Hall.

CARR E H, 1962. What is history [M]. Michigan: Michingan University Press.

CRAIG L H, 2001. Of philosophers and kings: political philosophy in Shakespeare's Macbeth and King Lear [M]. Toronto: University of Toronto Press.

DOWDEN E, 1903. Shakspere: a critical study of his mind and art [M]. 3rd ed. New York: Harper & Brothers Publishers.

DRMITRIU C, 2011. Shakespeare dictionary of plays and characters[M]. Shanghai: Shanghai Bookstore Publishing House.

EVERETT B, 1989. Young Hamlet: essays on Shakespeare's tragedies [M]. New York: Oxford University Press.

GOETHE J W, 1986. Essays on art and literature [M]. Princeton: Princeton University Press.

GREENBLATT S, 1980. Renaissance self-fashioning: from More to Shakespeare [M]. Chicago: the University of Chicago Press.

GREENBLATT S, COHEN W, HOWARD J E, 2016. The Norton Shakespeare [M]. Third International Student Edition. New York: W. W. Norton & Company, Inc.

JOHANN G H, 2008. Shakespeare [M]. Princeton: Princeton University Press.

KASTAN D S, 1982. Shakespeare and the shapes of time [M]. Basingstoke: Palgrave Macmillan.

KIERNAN P, 1996. Shakespeare's theory of drama [M]. Cambridge: Cambridge University Press.

KINNEY A F, 2001. Lies like truth: Shakespeare, Macbeth, and the cultural moment [M]. Detroit: Wayne State University Press.

LEE J, 2000. Shakespeare's Hamlet and the controversies of self [M]. Oxford: Clarendon Press.

LELAND C G, 1891. The works of Heinrich Heine [M]. London: William Heinemanne.

LEWIS R, 2017. Hamlet and the vision of darkness [M]. Princeton: Princeton University Press.

LIDSTER A, 2022. Publishing the history play in the time of Shakespeare [M]. Cambridge: Cambridge University Press.

MCEACHERN C, 2002. The Cambridge companion to Shakespearean tragedy [M]. London: Cambridge University Press.

MCELROY B, 2017. Shakespeare's mature tragedies [M]. Princeton: Princeton University Press.

MORGAN M, 1777. An essay on the dramatic character of Sir John Falstaff [M].

London: T. Davies.

MORRIS I, 2010. Shakespeare's God: the role of religion in the tragedies [M]. London: Routledge.

NEILL M, 2016. Oxford handbook of Shakespearean tragedy [M]. London: Oxford University Press.

PETZOLD J, 2021. History of the sonnet in England [M]. Berlin: Erich Schmidt Verlag.

RACKIN P, 1991.Stages of history: Shakespeare's English chronicles [M]. London: Routledge.

SADOWSKI P, 2003. Dynamism of character in Shakespeare's mature tragedies [M]. London: Associated University Press.

SHAKESPEARE W, 1593. Venus and Adonis [M]. London: The White Greyhound.

SMITH E, 2004. Shakespeare's tragedies [M]. New York: Blackwell Publishing House.

TAYLOR G, JOHN J, TERRI B, GABRIEL E, 2016. New Oxford Shakespeare: complete works [M]. Oxford: Oxford University Press.

TILLYARD E M W, 1966. Shakespeare's history plays [M]. Harmondsworth: Penguin.

WATT R J C, 2002. Shakespeare's history plays [M]. New York: Routledge.

WELLS S W, 1998. A dictionary of Shakespeare [M]. London: Oxford University Press.

WELLS S, 2017. Shakespeare's tragedies: a very short introduction [M]. London: Oxford University Press.

WILLS G, 1996. Witches and Jesuits: Shakespeare's Macbeth [M]. New York: New York Public Library.

ZAMIR T, 2018. Shakespeare's Hamlet: philosophical perspectives [M]. New York: Oxford University Press.

伯吉斯，2015. 莎士比亚 [M].刘国云，译.桂林：广西师范大学出版社.

陈星，2021. 莎士比亚传奇剧中的历史书写 [M].南京：南京大学出版社.

戴丹妮，2021. 莎士比亚戏剧导读 [M].武汉：武汉大学出版社.

傅光明，2018. 戏梦—莎翁：莎士比亚的喜剧世界 [M].天津：天津人民出版社.

李伟民，2019. 莎士比亚戏剧在中国语境中的接受与流变 [M].北京：中国社会科学出版社.

廖可兑，2001. 西欧戏剧史 [M].北京：中国戏剧出版社.

罗益民，2016. 莎士比亚十四行诗版本批评史 [M].北京：科学出版社.

马修斯，2021. 剧作家莎士比亚 [M].罗文敏，魏红华，译.北京：人民出版社.

聂珍钊，杜娟，2020. 莎士比亚与外国文学研究 [M].北京：商务印书馆.

莎士比亚，1995. 莎士比亚十四行诗全集 [M].曹明伦，译.桂林：漓江出版社.

莎士比亚，2012. 莎士比亚十四行诗：英汉对照 [M].屠岸，译.北京：外语教学与研究出版社.

莎士比亚，2014. 莎士比亚全集 [M].朱生豪，等译.北京：人民文学出版社.

莎士比亚，2015. 哈姆莱特：英汉对照 [M].辜正坤，译.北京：外语教学与研究出版社.

莎士比亚，2015. 亨利四世：英汉对照 [M].张顺赴，译.北京：外语教学与研究出版社.

莎士比亚，2015. 麦克白：英汉对照 [M].辜正坤，译.北京：外语教学与研究出版社.

莎士比亚，2016. 暴风雨：英汉对照 [M].彭镜禧，译.北京：外语教学与研究出版社.

莎士比亚，2016. 第十二夜：英汉对照 [M].王改娣，译.北京：外语教学与研究出版社.

莎士比亚，2016. 冬天的故事：英汉对照 [M].李华英，译.北京：外语教学与研究出版社.

　　莎士比亚，2016.理查三世：英汉对照［M］.孟凡君，译.北京：外语教学与研究出版社.

　　莎士比亚，2016.仲夏夜之梦：英汉对照［M］.邵雪萍，译.北京：外语教学与研究出版社.

　　莎士比亚，2019.莎士比亚十四行诗［M］.梁宗岱，译.北京：人民文学出版社.

　　莎士比亚，2019.仲夏夜之梦［M］.傅光明，译.天津：天津人民出版社.

　　莎士比亚，2021.莎士比亚十四行诗［M］.辜正坤，译.北京：外语教学与研究出版社.

　　王磊，2015.莎士比亚戏剧欣赏［M］.北京：北京大学出版社.

　　王佐良，1991.莎士比亚绪论：兼及中国莎学［M］.重庆：重庆出版社.

　　威尔斯，2019.莎士比亚植物志［M］.王睿，译.北京：人民文学出版社.

　　韦尔斯，2020.莎士比亚悲剧简论［M］.赵国新，译.北京：外语教学与研究出版社.

　　许慎，2018.说文解字［M］.汤可敬，译注.北京：中华书局.

　　亚里士多德，2009.诗学［M］.陈中梅，译注.北京：商务印书馆.

　　杨林贵，乔雪瑛，2020.世界莎士比亚研究选编［M］.北京：商务印书馆.

　　杨周翰，1979.莎士比亚评论汇编［M］.北京：中国社会科学出版社.

　　雨果，1980.雨果论文学［M］.柳鸣九，译.上海：上海译文出版社.

　　张冲，2005.同时代的莎士比亚:语境、互文、多种视域［M］.上海：复旦大学出版社.

　　张薇，2009.莎士比亚精读［M］.上海：上海大学出版社.

图书在版编目（CIP）数据

文本内外：莎士比亚经典解读：英文、汉文 / 张
秦主编 . — 成都：四川大学出版社，2023.11
（明远通识文库）
ISBN 978-7-5690-6457-5

Ⅰ．①文… Ⅱ．①张… Ⅲ．①莎士比亚（
Shakespeare, William 1564-1616）—戏剧文学—文学欣赏
—高等学校—教材—英、汉 Ⅳ．① I561.073

中国国家版本馆 CIP 数据核字（2023）第 221609 号

书　　名：文本内外：莎士比亚经典解读
　　　　　 Wenben Neiwai: Shashibiya Jingdian Jiedu
主　　编：张　秦
丛 书 名：明远通识文库

出 版 人：侯宏虹
总 策 划：张宏辉
丛书策划：侯宏虹　王　军
选题策划：余　芳
责任编辑：余　芳
责任校对：周　洁
装帧设计：黄楚钧
责任印制：王　炜

出版发行：四川大学出版社有限责任公司
　　　　　 地址：成都市一环路南一段 24 号（610065）
　　　　　 电话：（028）85408311（发行部）、85400276（总编室）
　　　　　 电子邮箱：scupress@vip.163.com
　　　　　 网址：https://press.scu.edu.cn
印前制作：成都完美科技有限责任公司
印刷装订：四川省平轩印务有限公司

成品尺寸：165 mm×240 mm
印　　张：19.625
插　　页：4
字　　数：380 千字

扫码获取数字资源

版　　次：2024 年 1 月 第 1 版
印　　次：2024 年 1 月 第 1 次印刷
定　　价：69.00 元

本社图书如有印装质量问题，请联系发行部调换

四川大学出版社
微信公众号